Edith And John

A Story Of Pittsburgh

by

Franklin S. Farquhar

Double 9 BOOKS

Edith And John
A Story Of Pittsburgh
by Franklin S. Farquhar

ISBN: 978-93-71818-80-3

Published by

DOUBLE 9 BOOKS
2/13-B, Ansari Road
Daryaganj, New Delhi – 110002
info@double9books.com
www.double9books.com
Tel. 011-40042856

ABOUT THE AUTHOR

Franklin S. Farquhar was a writer known for his work that focused on social contrasts and urban life. He authored several publications, with his most recognized novel being Edith and John: A Story of Pittsburgh. His writings suggest a deep interest in the industrial transformation of cities and the personal experiences of those living within them. Farquhar's storytelling often highlighted social mobility, class structure, and emotional resilience. His work provides a valuable glimpse into life during a time of significant economic and cultural shifts. He also documented his thoughts and daily activities in personal diaries spanning more than four decades, preserving a record of both his private reflections and broader societal observations. These materials, along with his books and essays, contribute to a fuller picture of his intellectual pursuits. Farquhar's literary voice reflects a thoughtful engagement with the social realities of his era, marking him as a perceptive observer and chronicler of life.

CONTENTS

CHAPTER I
THE WRECKED UMBRELLA

Fog and smoke and grime hung over the city of Pittsburgh: a thickening blanket, soggy in its cumbrous pall. The rain came down like gimlets; the air was savage, miserably embracing; the streets were sodden, muddy, filthy, with dirty streams babbling along the gutters; the lights gleamed ghastly, ghostly, hideously, in radiating through the gloom; water dripped from eave, awning, wire, sign, lamppost—from everything, spattering, trickling, everlastingly dripping, till the whole world seemed to be in an advanced stage of the diabetes. It was a gray, grim, medieval night—a cold, raw, nerve-racking night in November.

The gleaming forges, the ponderous hammers, the monstrous rolls of the mills boomed in the distance, sullenly, ceaselessly, like unto the grumblings of a maddened Tubal Cain irritated beyond endurance. Mill and factory and boat and shop whistles tooted and screeched and howled demoniacally, with little agreement as to rhythm. Trains rumbled, cars rattled, and all manner of conveyances bumped along, over crossings and grades and Y's, through tunnels, under sheds, through yards, beneath buildings, over streets, across bridges; some rapidly, some slowly, some cautiously, some recklessly—all going, coming, hither and yon, with a remorseless energy, and for an inexorable purpose. A medley of bells smote the air with a harshness, a sweetness, a madness, that was startling enough to drive the nervous into a wild panic. The rumble of cart, the thud of horse, the crack of whip, the tread of feet, the sound of voice, was a confused mass of noises added to the greater roaring of the turbulent city of iron and steel.

Tired, wan women, coarsely dressed; proud, haughty women, fashionably attired; strips of boys and girls, shivering and chattering, bedraggled and humped up; horny-handed men, roughly clothed; kid-gloved men, faultlessly groomed: some with bundles, baskets, dinner-buckets, or nothing—all hurrying through the elemental dreariness, bending their way from office, from store, from shop, from mill, from factory to home, to hotel, to palace, to mansion, to hovel, to downy beds, to straw pallets, to bunk, to bench, or doorstep; or to place of nightly service, or to pleasure; to rest and refresh themselves, and await the coming of another day of toil, or leisure.

John Winthrope was a strapping young man but a few months from the country—aged twenty-two. He had quit his pen and ink and account sheets at his high desk in the office of Jarney & Lowman as the clock in the court house tower pealed out six deliberately solemn strokes. He put on his coat and hat, took up a bundle of reading matter selected for its quality from that which daily cumbered the desks and waste-baskets, procured an umbrella from the many that had been left in a rack in one corner, and went out the door, down the elevator, and into the street. As rain was falling, he turned up his pantaloons, turned up his coat collar, raised the umbrella, and joined the throng of hurrying pedestrians, homeward bound.

Home! John had no home in the city. He had left his home behind—the modest, cheaply builded, scantily furnished and illy appointed home of his parents in the mountains—to come to the city to make his fortune.

His home now was a "room"—merely a room among a multiplicity of similar rooms, in between the four angles of plastered walls. His remuneration as the lowest bookkeeper in the line of such functionaries was insufficient to purchase more than the most meager accommodations in a cheap boarding house up Diamond Alley way.

This room in question was in an ancient brick and timber building, that, in its earlier days, was an architectural ornament in its stateliness compared to other business blocks; but by reason of the rapid striding of modern prosperity, it was long ago left in the vast shades that great fortunes had reared into iron and concrete, standing by.

There were only two sides open to the light and air in this low and aged building—one in front and one on top. In between were three tiers of small dark rooms, one tier above the other, resembling very much the little cubes of a concentrated egg case. Two small paned windows looked drearily into them from the street, on each floor, with a smaller time-stained window in each resounding hallway.

The inner rooms were lighted by abbreviated wells dug in from a skylight on the side adjoining the blank walls of a dizzy skyscraper. And cloudy and shadowy and dim and cheerless, indeed, was the light let in on the brightest of days, while on dull days it was nothing more than the semblance of a waning twilight; so that, if used in day time at all, a light were needed to make out and clearly discern any object within.

In one of these dark and inodorous rooms, John Winthrope had his temporary abiding place. There were in it a cheap iron bed, with musty smelling tick, sheet and coverlets; a small oak-grained pine washstand, with such a wavy little mirror hanging over it, that one could not tell, in looking at himself in it, whether he were a Chinaman, a Greaser, or a crooked-faced Irishman toiling in the streets; a small bowl, for washing, and a correspondingly small pitcher, with water in it, sat upon the shaky stand; a cheap chair, a weak imitation of quartered oak, with many marks of usage all over it, stood by a little table, also with many marks of usage on it; a flowered carpet, faded, worn and fretted by the sure hand of wearing time, covered the floor, with here and there ragged spots of bareness to enhance the room's impoverishment.

Leaving the office of Jarney & Lowman on that very disagreeable evening, as mentioned in the beginning of this chapter, John pushed down the foggy thoroughfares, with a rain: which seemed to be coming from a reservoir in the infinite space above: pouring down. The streets were crowded with people, going in various directions, and jostling each other with little regard as to manners. Everybody had, apparently, but one motive, and that was to get somewhere out of the terrors of the elements. Nobody went with any precision as to plan of action, aiming only to reach a near or remote destination.

John pressed along the best he could, with what care that the rain, the umbrellas and the crowd permitted. He drew his shoulders downward, and bent forward, leaning against the driving rain, with his umbrella in front of him. He hugged the buildings closely, stepped rapidly, dodged from right to left of the other pedestrians, who were attempting the same artful measures as himself, to keep out of the rain, if that were possible.

So absorbed was he in his own behalf, that he did not observe a young lady approaching, in line with him, with the same absorbing carefulness as to herself. She had but a moment before stepped from a store, not perceiving that it was raining hard till she was plodding along through it. She was also bending forward slightly, picking her way with dainty but quickly executed steps to get where everybody else was aiming for—home. Like John, she was unobserving as to the actions of the fleeing people about her; and it is difficult to tell just how she expected to keep her feet dry, considering how the water fell, and how it splashed about.

Howsoever, the lady, all of a sudden, came to a stop; two ribs of her umbrella snapped with a loud click, one side flapping down over her shoulders; her hat flew off as if it had been kicked by an athlete, and rolled across the swimming pavement into the gutter. She uttered a little cry of distress, and was in the act of turning around, and repairing to the store whence she came, when she beheld a young man performing an ungraceful act in attempting the recovery of her hat. He was fleeing after it, with upspread umbrella over him, and running and stopping and reaching for the piece of headgear that seemed determined to evade his efforts to secure it. Seeing him thus, in his ludicrous movements, she half smiled, and then decided to await further developments.

Securing the hat, finally, after it had started to float away on the tide of the gutter, John (for that is whom the young man was) returned with it to her, he himself showing some moiling, like the hat, as a result of his gallant endeavors. When he approached her, with it in his hand, she exhibited such an air of respectability and unfeigned independence that John was fairly startled.

"Beg your pardon, lady," he said, handing her the hat, bowing as he did so; "it was an unavoidable accident—or rather the result of my heedlessness. I beg your pardon."

The lady stood a short moment confused, hesitating as to whether she should deign to answer a stranger in the street, any more than to say "thank you," and acknowledge, lady-like, that she was partly in the blame, and ask his pardon also; or accept his blunder in good nature, as he seemed to take it, and go her way. But John's voice was so mild, and his manner so gentlemanly, that she felt as soon as he had spoken that she need have no fear of him.

"Oh, sir," she said, pleasantly, with a laugh; "as much my fault as yours. Thank you."

"May I hold your umbrella while you adjust your hat?" he asked, seeing her dilapidated rain shade, with water streaming off of it on her shoulders, falling about her head.

"If you wish, you may," she replied, shyly. "I fear it is about done for."

"You may have mine," he returned. "May I take yours?"

"You may hold it," she answered, as she began to lower it, having her hat now also in her hand. "My, what a predicament I am in!"

"Pardon me," he said; "but you will be left in the rain, if I take yours and you do not accept mine."

"Why, yes, indeed, I forgot it was raining," she responded, with a laugh that indicated her confusion.

"Give it me," he said, as her umbrella shut up tightly. "Will you accept the protection of mine? The rain is falling hard," he continued, as he took hers; and then reached as far as possible, without going closer, holding his over her, and standing himself in the rain.

"Oh, my, this hat is so soiled and nasty from the street," she said, as she held it before her in the light of a fog enshrouded street lamp.

"If you will give it me a moment, I will make an effort to remove some of the grime," he said, in such a deferential tone that she was moved to reply:

"Indeed, sir, I find now I need your assistance, or perhaps I would be doing a wrong in standing here in the rain with you. I find most men are gentlemen, though, when a lady is in trouble."

"Thank you," he returned. "May I take the hat for a moment?"

She hesitated a second time about accepting his proffered aid, but finally, becoming more convinced of the futility of aiding herself alone, said: "You may."

He then took the hat to clean, and she took the umbrella to hold, and they both stood together, closely, under his rain protector. While he cleaned the hat of its smutage, she watched him with some trepidation as to the propriety of the act.

When she saw him draw forth his pocket handkerchief and begin, with delicate carefulness, to mop the slimy accretions from the rich material, she breathed more easily, and stood as silent noting the performance as the street lamp that gave forth such an haloic light. They were both facing the light, he holding the hat in his left hand, whirling it round and round as he diligently soaked up, with his handkerchief, the water from it. His head was bent forward, with his eyes cast directly upon the object of his attention. She glanced up into his face from time to time, wondering at the strange situation she was in, and seeing how good a face he had. She was very careful that he did not catch her throwing furtive glances at him, fearful that he might think her very bold. John paid no heed to her for the time, so bent was he in attempting to make courteous amends for his awkwardness. But when he had so soiled his handkerchief that it would not absorb any more of the hat's defilement, he raised his eyes to her and said:

"There!"

"Thank you," she returned, taking the hat, and handing him his umbrella. "Will you be so kind as to hold the umbrella while I put on my hat?"

"With your permission," he replied, with condign simplicity. "I am delighted to be of service to you for the grievous work I have done this night," and he took the umbrella again, and held it over her.

After a few minutes of prodding about her head with two long silver pins, with something sparkling like diamonds on one end of each, she said, as she lowered her hands:

"Now, my umbrella, if you please?"

"You may have mine," he answered. "Yours is so desolate looking that you might as well go on your way without one as to attempt to use it again."

"You are kind, indeed," she replied, with reserve, as she was making an effort to hoist her wrecked umbrella, which he had turned over to her, but still standing under his.

She was now facing the lamp that was feebly radiating down upon them, and he could see, plainly enough, that she was pretty. He had divined as much, however, basing his divination upon her beautifully modulated and sweet voice, which he thought could accompany no other than blue eyes, rosy cheeks and cupid lips.

"Will you accept mine?" he asked again, seeing she was having trouble in raising her own to a due and rigid uprightness.

"To whom shall I return it, should I accept it?" she asked.

"Oh, never mind its return," he replied.

"Then I shall not accept it," she insisted.

"If you insist on returning it, then to the office of Jarney & Lowman," he answered.

"Why, what have you to do with that firm?" she asked, with surprise.

"I am one of the bookkeepers in the office of that firm," he answered, hesitatingly, for her tone of surprise was such that he could not guess its meaning.

"Ha, ha, ha!" she laughed. "It seems so ridiculous in me standing here this soggy night, feeling so fearful all the while that I might have fallen into the hands of a ruffian! Ha, ha, ha! I must tell papa as soon as I get home. Such a strange coincidence one never heard of before!"

The pleasant demeanor of the young lady, so suddenly taken on, set John to staring at her, now in a great quandary, now in mingled confusion and hesitancy as to what to say further.

"To whom have I the honor of being so unceremoniously introduced on such an aqueous night?" he asked.

"Why, I am Edith Jarney, daughter of Hiram Jarney," she replied, with so much more confidence in herself that she felt she would not now hesitate to be on friendly terms with this humble worker in her father's office. "And your name?" she was emboldened to ask.

"John Winthrope," he blurted out, a little flustrated over the turn the accidental meeting had taken.

"Mr. Winthrope," she said, extending her hand; "I am very glad to know you, and to know that you are an employe of my father." As he took her gloved hand, she continued, "yes, with your permission, I will accept your umbrella; but it seems so ungracious for me to do so. What will you do without one, and the rain coming down so?"

"I have not far to go," he answered.

He pressed her hand lightly, while she held his firmly and sincerely in her effort to impress upon him how very thankful she was for his kindness.

"It gives me pleasure, indeed, Miss Jarney," he returned, looking steadily at her, "to assist you. I hope I may have the further pleasure of seeing you again, some day; but I can hardly expect that—"

"Why not?" she interrupted.

"—unless it should be by chance," he finished, releasing her hand.

"Mr. Winthrope, really, I have enjoyed our accidental tete-a-tete," she pursued. "When we first ran together, I was somewhat angered, as I had a right to be, at your awkwardness; but when I saw you running for my hat, and when I heard you speak, and when you offered to aid me in my distress, all fear left me. I felt that a gentleman was at hand to mollify the grievous circumstance. Now, you know what I think of you."

"Thank you," he replied, bowing, with considerable condescension, for her praiseworthy remarks.

"I would like to prolong our now quite interesting little episode, were it possible," she said, with more earnestness in her feelings than he could believe; "but this horrid night is already sending the shivers through me, and I am beginning to realize that, should we stand here longer, the rain will have, soaked us through and through."

John gasped at this reassuring confidence and interest in himself. He would have asked her, as a matter of continuing his courtesy, to accompany her to her home, or to some convenient point for her to take a taxicab; but recognizing his station in life was not on a plain with hers, he could not conscientiously attempt to ingratiate himself into her favor, let alone asking the pleasure of her company homeward. He felt it would be exceedingly bold and entirely out of place for him, being as he was poor, to make such a dubious request of her. But still she remained continuing the conversation. And the rain still came pouring down.

"I assure you, Miss Jarney," he did say at last, "I have, since I came to know you, never enjoyed anything so monumentally humorous as this affair; and I would have been greatly disappointed on it, and weightily embarrassed over it, had you not have taken my umbrella, even though I had not learned your name, nor ever expected to see you again."

"That is very clever in you," she replied, with the sweetest little chuckle, being amused at the simplicity of his manner and loftiness of his speech. "The eloquence of your deportment cannot be improved on."

"Thank you, Miss Jarney, for your kind opinion," he answered.

Still Edith Jarney stood, on this cold, gloomy, miserable November evening, talking to this young man from the mountains, who was without money, or fame, or glory, or name, except that which his good parents had bestowed upon him—this young man alone in a big city, with a multitude of others in the struggle for existence, and she so rich.

And still she talked on with this unassuming country youth, emboldened to the act by the strange hand of chance that should bring her to it, and by the novelty of the situation, and by some other unfathomable mystery that caused her to see in him something more than usual, continuing to intimate the while that she was loath to forego further indulgence in their very entertaining meeting; and she so rich, and he so poor. But as all happy events in one's life must have an ending, she at length said, while the rain still kept pouring down:

"Mr. Winthrope, I must express my sincere regret that the time and place are inappropriate for a continuance of our very, very pleasant talk on this highly felicitous event, as it has turned out to be."

Again she extended her hand, and still the rain came beating down as before. He took it, and pressed it more firmly, and she permitted him to hold it as he said:

"The pleasure is not all yours, Miss Jarney, I assure you. Were I—were I equal to the occasion, which I can never hope to be, I might ask the pleasure of accompanying you—part way at least—through this soaking night to your home, or to your nearest friends. But I shall not ask it of you."

"Good bye," she replied, with some disappointment, it appeared to him, as he released her hand.

"Good bye," he returned; and they parted.

She turned, and disappeared, like a spectre, into the depths of the grayish shroud of the melancholy night.

He turned a corner, lost his way in the hurrying crowd, and drew up eventually at a restaurant. After refreshing himself, he returned to the street again, and plodded on, with the broken umbrella over him, through the dampage to his cold and dimly lighted chamber—there to sleep, and dream, perhaps, of a fair young face, miles and miles above his station in life.

And the rain beat down above him with the same homely sound, it seemed, as it did in the past, upon the roof above his chamber in his mountain home.

CHAPTER II
AT THE MANSION ON THE HILL

In Highland avenue, far removed from the crowded thoroughfares, the congested tenements, the cheap homes of the middle class, the rush and roar of industry—out where the wind and sun (when they combine together to have a sky cleaning and an air purification) first lay hold with brush and broom and water to scour away the smokage of the manufactories of wealth—stands a mansion.

It is a dull gray mansion on a hill, with an outlook to the four winds—over every hill and valley, park, suburb, town and community—embracing everything that a prospect could possibly be endowed with. Standing alone in a small private park, studded with oaks, beech and maple trees, and brightened by a sward faultlessly maintained, with gently sloping hillsides, rockeries, aquariums and flower beds, and winding paths and roads and byways, it impresses one not much unlike that of same landed member of nobility when men were masters of men even with less harshness than now.

It does not resemble an ancient castle. It does not resemble a manor house of England. It resembles nothing at all that ever was in the way of abode of men. It resembles more the newer ideas of builders put into stone and mortar and glass—a conglomeration of the old styles blended into one more modern, more pleasing to the eye, more harmonious with the colors of the air, the trees, the fields and all things around—representing the craft and graft and greed of men of this age.

Without, on this November day, it seemed to be forsaken, cold, damp, dull, forbidding, sombre in every delineation of its outline, rearing through the haze of smoke and fog and rain like a stranded Adamaster in a sea of penury, misery and woe, with the lesser lights of affluence beaming dimly in its neighborhood. But within, there were the warmth of the tropics, the effulgence of the Riviera, the glitter of the Orient, the polish of the court of France in the hey-day of its kings, the laughter of youth, the smile of the aged, the cheer of the domestic, and over all the atmosphere of those brought into the world to conquer among men in the science of business.

This is the home of Hiram Jarney of the firm of Jarney & Lowman, makers of iron and steel. Here lived Miss Edith Jarney, the only child.

She was twenty-two, tall, willowy, graceful. She was raised as became a daughter of a man of wealth; but she was not spoiled. She was not a sham, as many such young ladies are. She was not affected. She was level-headed, self-possessed, modest, kind, beautifully unselfish, lovable, very handsome, very noble.

Mrs. Jarney was a buxom woman still, although gray was sprinkled well through her hair. She must have been handsome when young, for yet her cheeks were rosy, with the refining marks of motherhood toning them down to the fading point. She was bouncing in her manner, lofty in her speech, pleasant in her smile, and a little haughty in her bearing, but always cheerful. She had come up from adversity with her husband, climbing the ladder of success side by side with him, adjusting herself to each rung as the dangers of the height increased, till at last she sat, with him, on the top, and scornfully, although not willfully, cast disparaging glances on those below seeking her altitudinous environments.

The husband and father, Hiram Jarney, was a tall, clean-cut business man, proud, vain, nice, neat, with a monumental ambition to accomplish in every purpose he set out to do. And he had accomplished many.

When Edith Jarney took the taxicab for her home, after parting with John Winthrope in the rain, she was in great good humor all the way, and for some hours after arriving at her domicile. Thinking little of the wet condition of her clothing, or her hat, or her shoes, or anything else, she leaned back on the soft, dry cushions of the cab and laughed and laughed, time after time, over the singular episode with that young man. In truth, it raised her sense of risibility to such a degree so often that she had to hold her sides for the pain of laughing.

Nothing in all her short and interesting life appealed to her as so ridiculous, nothing so amusing, nothing so ludicrous, nothing so out of the ordinary, nothing so new, nothing so out of the common run of happenings in her daily ins and outs, as her encounter with this unspoiled youth of the mountains. And the more she thought of it, the more she laughed over her own discomposure, over the cheerful attitude she had assumed toward him, over her apparent boldness, over her clever mastery of a situation made possible only by the cheerless night.

Indeed, so forcibly was she impressed with the affair that she began already, while riding in the cab, to write the incident down in the tablet of her memory as one of the most extraordinary events of her life. And more—the longer she thought of it, the more impressed she was with John Winthrope. His politeness, his bearing, his voice, his face, his size, appealed to her young idea of what constituted proper proportions in a good young man. She gave no thought of him being a poor employe of her father; she gave no thought whether he was possessed with worldly riches; she gave no thought as to whether he had blooded ancestry; or who, or what he was, any more than that he appeared to be above the stuff of the average man with whom she had previously come in contact.

"Ah, he must be a good young man," she said, almost aloud, during one of her oft recurring spells of happiness. "He cannot be so bad," she thought, "when he was so good to me. But still—"

The taxicab was at her home. The door was opened by the chauffeur, who had raised her umbrella, and was standing waiting for her at the door. It took a word from him to rouse her from her meditation.

"Oh, are we home?" she said, as she bounded out. She grasped the umbrella, and ran up the pathway to the big piazza of the mansion.

She was so gleeful that she bolted toward the door, which was not opened soon enough to suit her impetuous haste to get within; and when it was opened, she rushed in, forgetting to lower the umbrella. This action caused the footman to look aghast at the dripping water and her much bedraggled skirts. And not till she had gone to the center of the big reception room, and had left a trail of water behind on the polished floors and turkish rugs, on curtains, chairs and settees, much to their ruination, did she notice her absentmindedness.

"Why, Edith!" exclaimed her mother, with uplifted hands.

"Oh, mamma! mamma!" exclaimed Edith, out of breath, almost.

"What is the matter, Edith?" asked her mother, excitedly, as she came rushing toward her from her cozy corner, where she had been embowered this dreary night, among richly-scented cushions. "One would think it raining in here, Edith, from the way your umbrella is shedding water. Put it down, and explain yourself, Edith!"

"My, oh, my," laughed Edith, for the first time realizing that she was still carrying the umbrella.

"What is it, Edith? What has happened?" continued her mother. "My! Your clothing are so wet! What has happened to that hat?"

"Enough for one night, mamma—enough," returned Edith, now lowering the umbrella, and looking it over searchingly—at the handle, at the material, at the ferrule, at the tassel, at the "J. W." on the silver plated strip that formed a narrow ring around the briar root handle. Then, without answering her mother definitely, she went into the great hall and deposited "J. W.'s" rain shade into a glistening receptacle of pottery with a dragon's head looking viciously at her from one side.

"Mamma! Mamma!" she exclaimed, joyfully, with soiled hat, wet coat and soaked shoes still on.

"What is it, Edith? Do tell me! What has happened?" questioned her mother for the third time, as she stood with her hands clasped before her in expectation of hearing something terrible, and wringing them sometimes to give vent to her wrought up feelings.

"I had a most extraordinary experience this evening, mamma," answered Edith, slowly pulling off her wet gloves that seemed to want to adhere to the flesh. Edith was looking down at her hands, with a very pleasant smile lighting up her face, which she turned into gyratory expressions now and then as she pulled and jerked at the clinging glove fingers.

"Tell me, Edith—tell me quickly, before something happens to me," said her mother, now impatient at Edith's slowness.

"It was such an extraordinary affair, mamma," answered Edith, finally getting off her gloves, and then reaching up to remove her hat, "that I am still all excited about it, mamma—and the old hat is ruined—call the maid to assist me into dry clothing—look at that hat, mamma; it fell into the gutter," and she turned it round and round, just as John had done, looking at it admiringly—not that she admired it for its beauty in its present condition, oh, no; but for something else; and she touched it in several spots with her little bare hands, which she could not forbore doing on any other occasion.

"Edith! Why are you so procrastinating? I cannot tolerate your delay longer! Answer me! What has happened?" demanded the little bouncing mother, with some pretention toward exasperation.

"Oh, mamma," answered Edith, with charming affection, "I will, I will, if you will only give me time. It was such an extraordinary event that I want plenty of breath to proceed with the story. Nothing serious has happened, mamma—but it was unusual."

"Go to your room, Edith, and then return to me with changed clothing, and tell me what it is that excites you so," said her mother, now reconciled and satisfied that her daughter had not met with any serious mishap.

Edith, thereupon, kissed her mother, fondly patted her cheek, and then, when her maid came, tripped lightly to her dressing room.

"Sarah, I never before felt like doing things for myself as I do now," said Edith to her maid, as she sat down to have her shoes removed.

"And would you?" meekly asked the maid, looking up at her mistress.

"Indeed, I would," returned Edith. "I would commence to learn at once were it not for giving offense to my parents."

"And leave me without my lady to wait on and love?" asked the maid, apprehensive of her position. "I could not bear it, dear lady. Why, Miss

Edith, I have been with you since you were a teeny baby, and I love you so that I imagine sometimes you are my own dear child."

"Never mind, Sarah; don't be alarmed," returned Edith. "I will keep you if I do learn to wait on myself. But I was thinking, Sarah, that you cannot always tell what might happen. Every one of we mortals is a possible subject for the poorhouse; and if it should come to anything like that I should want to know how to bear my own burdens."

"Don't tell me, Edith," cried Sarah, now alarmed, "that it has come to that!"

"Oh, no, indeed, Sarah," replied Edith, consolingly. "At least not that I know of anything of the kind as being likely to happen. But that was not it, Sarah—not it—why, what am I saying?—it is something else."

Sarah looked up quickly at Edith. Edith was half serious, half mirthful in the little laugh that followed her words. And she toyed with Sarah's graying hairs.

"Edith, are you keeping any secrets from me?" asked the suspicious Sarah.

"Now, Sarah, do not be cross with me, will you, if I tell you?" asked Edith, with some hesitancy about revealing what had so recently happened to give her such a wonderful new vision of life.

"Never—never, Edith—unless you say," promised Sarah.

"I met the finest young man this evening, Sarah," began Edith, slowly, blushingly, still toying with Sarah's hair, Sarah still being on her knees before her mistress. "There—I have let it out! Now, don't you tell, Sarah. No, of course, you will not?"

"Since you have forbidden any of the young bloods of your own set coming to see you, I am anxious to know just where you got your 'finest young man,'" said Sarah, sarcastically.

"I found him!"

"Is he rich?" asked Sarah.

"Never thought of that!"

"Where did you find him, Edith?"

"Bumped into him in the streets—now, don't scold me, Sarah!"

"Why, Edith!" exclaimed Sarah, rising, and holding up her hands, and opening wide her prudish eyes. Sarah's sense of the proper fitness of things old-maidenishly would not permit her even to meditate on such a horrible deed.

"Do not be unduly alarmed, Sarah," calmly remarked Edith. "It was an accident—oh, such an extraordinary accident, Sarah, and so ridiculous on my part that I still feel the effects of it on my mirthful nature."

"Tell me all about it, my dear Edith?" said Sarah, now buttoning up the back of Edith's dinner gown.

"If you will not tell—promise?"

"You have my promise, Edith; but you wouldn't keep such a secret from your mother, would you?"

"I do not want to, Sarah; but I am afraid, if I tell her, she will scold me."

"Now, what did you do, Edith?" asked Sarah.

"Stood in the rain the longest time talking to the strange young man."

"Why, Edith!" exclaimed Sarah, for the fifth or sixth time.

"No why about it, Sarah. It was an unavoidable accident. I ran into him, he into me. My hat fell off, rolled into the gutter, and my umbrella was rendered limp in one of its poor wings. Now, could I help that, Sarah?"

"Perhaps not."

"Well, he recovered my hat, held his umbrella over me while I put it on again, gave me his umbrella and he took my crippled one."

"Is that all?"

"We talked some."

"Talked? Good gracious!"

"Yes, talked, Sarah—really talked."

"Why, Edith!"

"Now, Sarah, be sensible, and listen. He was so polite, so courteous—"

"They're all that way," interrupted Sarah, a man hater.

"—but him," returned Edith, not meaning it in the same sense that Sarah did. "I was going to say, Sarah, that I could not resist his good face."

"Who is he?" asked Sarah, coldly.

"John Winthrope!"

"What does he do?"

"Works in my father's office!"

"Lordy!" exploded Sarah at this revelation, for really Sarah was the snob instead of Edith. "And you stopped to talk with him in the street?"

"Sarah, you are mean—real mean—cruel, exasperating. Sarah, I will have nothing more to do with you, if you talk that way any more! I will get a new maid, or have none at all—that I will, Sarah! Now, take your choice!"

This from Edith, who was usually so calm, so even tempered, and so reasonable in all matters. But Sarah had aroused her dormant nature by such a reference to class distinction, that Edith, in her liberal way of looking at the world in general, could not reconcile Sarah's views with justice, if each human being concerned was equally endowed morally, physically and mentally.

"I will say no more, Edith," humbly surrendered the prudent Sarah.

Dinner was announced, and Edith descended to the brilliancy of the great dining room, where her parents were awaiting her arrival to be seated with them. Edith was charming in her changed habiliment. Could John but see her now! But John had no password as yet to this rich home.

"Now, Edith, to the story," said Mrs. Jarney, after they had seated themselves around the sumptuously provided table.

"What is that?" asked Mr. Jarney, looking at his wife, and for the first time getting an inkling of Edith's experiences, then turning his eyes questioningly upon Edith.

"Nothing serious, papa," said Edith, noting that he was surprised over the manner in which her mother had put the question.

"Well, then, dear Edith, go on," said her father, in his usually kind tone.

"Promise, papa, that you will not be hard on me?" pressed Edith.

"As long as you have done no wrong, Edith, I promise," he replied.

Then Edith related her tale, down to the minutest detail, even as to how it affected her afterwards—except that she kept the impression that it left upon her heart as her own inviolable secret.

"Edith," said her father, after she had finished, and after he had pondered a few moments over the possible effect on the young man in the office, and after smiling and laughing heartily, "Edith, it certainly is a peculiar coincidence. I am glad to know the party turned out to be our newest addition to the office force, and not a ruffian."

This ended the general conversation about John Winthrope. None of them considered the event in any other light than if she had had a similar encounter with the ash-man—except Edith. But still they did not cease referring to the matter occasionally for some time, for after all they could not help but marvel on it.

Edith was unusually cheerful after she found her parents were not vexed. She sang and played on the piano, read a few pages in a novel, talked, laughed, went up and down the rooms, wondering, wondering what it was that agitated her so and raised her spirits to such a high tension.

Finally, after what appeared to be an age in passing, she became weary, and went to bed, to sleep, and dream, perhaps, of a fair young man, miles and miles below her station in life.

And the rain beat down upon the roof above her with the same homely sound as it beat down upon the roofs above all mankind that night.

CHAPTER III
THE OLD JUNK SHOP

The rusty perspective of a four story building rises in the midst of many similarly nondescript structures, between Wood and Liberty streets, looking out over the cobblestoned wharf skirting the Monongahela river, flowing lazily by.

It was builded in the days when it was a lofty office building: when its three flights of darkened stairs were mounted by leg muscle: in the days when its little windows were barn-doors of undimmed light, and the panes were of minimum size for economy sake: in the days when the steamboat trade was a valuable asset of the river front merchants: in the days when men fought in the merry war of competition, and when life was not so strenuous as it is now: in the days when its name stood prominently among the business blocks in the city directory. But now it has no resemblance to its former self; it makes no impression on the passer-by, unless he be the curious delving into ancient lore; it is silently languishing into the past, waiting for the strong arm of Progress to raze it to the ground for something more imposing in its place.

Here, in the past, were offices on the upper floors devoted to the exclusive use of professional men; while on the ground floor, for years, a merchant held sway with an assortment of merchandise that equaled in variety, if not in quantity, the great department stores of the present.

Where the store was, there is a junk shop now, and it is called The Die. In it may be found, collected together in an heterogeneous mass, a miscellaneous lot of rubbish that even the bearish-like proprietor himself wonders, sometimes, where it all comes from, and whither it all goes. Here may be found the worn out and cast off articles of rivermen: boatmen, wharfmen, raftsmen, and every other class of men who ply their trade in, on, and about the water. Here may be found an indeterminable assortment of wearing apparel, for all ages of men, women and children, in all conditions of wear and tear, from a riverman's oiled coat, with greasy spots upon it and burned holes in many places in it, to a worn out pair of infantine shoes. Here may be found a hecatomb of articles of the household, of the store, of the office, of the hotel, of the church, of the school, of the cemetery, of the railway yards, of the building of justice, of jail, of penitentiary—from every place, almost—all telling a tale of grandeur, of poverty, of happiness, of misery; of pride, of modesty, of virtue; of honor, of dishonor; of sickness, pain and death.

The keeper of this shop, at this period in this narrative, was Peter Dieman—a red-jowled, pig-eyed, sharp-nosed, dirty-mouthed, frowsy-headed, big-bellied American, whose ancestry may be determined by his name. A glance into his gloomy place was enough to convince the most unobserving that he was specially adapted to his established trade of buying and selling all manner of second-hand goods, ranging in value from a penny to the enormous sum of one great American Eagle; and seldom, if ever, did anything go above the latter figure, when he was the purchaser; but when he was the seller—that was different.

In the rear of the darksome room, on the ground floor, there was a little cubby-hole built around a little window that opened on the rear street. The window was so begrimed with dust and cobwebs that it was necessary, even on the brightest days, to keep a sixteen candle power incandescent globe going continually to furnish sufficient light for the proprietor to see himself, and enable him to scribble down his accounts, what few he kept in books. In this gruesome little office Peter sat, from early morning to late night, smoking his foul smelling pipe, receiving his cash from sales, and also receiving the people who did not call on strictly commercial affairs; and betimes he peered through a smoky glass-covered square hole that perforated one side of the thin partition that circled him about, into the store, watching, with squinting eyes, Eli Jerey, his clerk, dealing out the junk to the poor purchasers.

Peter Dieman was a fiend incarnate, after money. He was avaricious to the core. He was relentlessly pressing in the collection of overdue bills, and heartlessly "jewing" in the purchase of the worn-out, worm-eaten, moth-ravaged articles that he gathered up, in his rounds, from the unfortunates, the n'er-do-wells, the hopeless mortals who had to sacrifice their goods and chattels to make ends meet; or who, peradventure, were glad to dispose of any cumbersome article of their more prosperous days. Further, besides being a close dealer, he was a shaver of notes, a conscienceless dealer without regard whatever for the principles of justice, or the duties of a citizen, or the honor of the brethren of his tribe of men. And still further, he was so selfishly constituted that no barterer could ever equal him in his surprisingly pronounced talents for cheating, filching and over-charging. Without education, and alone, on his own initiative, and through his own painstaking, persistent, persevering efforts he arose from nothing to, what would be considered by many, a state of enviable affluence for his station in the ranks of the commercial men of the city.

He could neither read nor write when he started out for himself on the road of life; but by dint of much endeavor he learned to write by rote, like a blind man, and talk by imitation, like a parrot. For many years he was his own buyer, his own seller, his own bookkeeper, his own handy man and henchman. But when he had accumulated a world of experience, a great quantity of junk, a large sum of money, and the desire to be an expert ward heeler, he hired Eli Jerey, as a boy of ten, to be his helper.

Now, Eli was a lad with no more ambition than a toad. Being obsessed with that slavish passion one finds in so many of his class to serve a master for a mere competance that would meet his daily expenses, he went about his business with such translucent simplicity and dutiful obedience to his master's will that he worked from six in the morning till seven in the evening with such a zeal that Peter could make no complaint whatever to his energy in keeping shop, while he in turn kept office and watched through the little square hole aforesaid.

This place became known as The Die early in the career of Peter—a corruption of the name of Dieman, and perhaps a revealer of his principles.

One day, in September, while the fog and smoke hung darkly over the river and everything, a short heavyset man, very plainly dressed, but with an inquisitorial air in his bearing, sauntered into the shop, and looked about as carelessly and indolently as if he were a sojourner come to view, with a curious eye, the accumulation of things as if on display in a museum. The stranger walked about, with his hands in his pockets, through the narrow aisles between ropes, chains, furniture, pictures, old shoes, hats, clothing, saws, hammers, hatchets, and a thousand and one other things piled up, hanging about, swinging here, or perching there. He was so mysterious in his movements that Eli, upon concluding a simple deal with a louting riverman, came timidly up to him in such a condescending manner that the stranger was struck with amusing amazement at the deferential halo that seemed to pervade the shrimp-like head of the clerk.

"Anything?" asked Eli, approaching.

"Well, I don't know," answered the stranger, his eyes roving about the room. "I just came in to see if you had anything I wanted." Still gazing abstractedly into a far corner where lay deeper piles of junk, he went on, "I guess, though, from the looks of things, I might get anything I want here, from a gimlet to a gibet."

Eli stared doubtfully at the man, wondering at his utter lack of concentration on the object sought. In the meantime, Peter was not off his guard at his peephole. He was standing, looking out, rubbing his hands and squinting, in an effort to make out the identity of the man.

"Nothing in iron? Nothing in ropes? Nothing in old clothes? Nothing in furniture?" asked Eli.

"Don't know just yet," answered the stranger, now with his eyes cast down upon the docile but ever guardful Eli.

"What then?" asked Eli, still pursuing his questioning, and still indecisive as to how to approach this uncommunicative customer.

"I am just looking," answered the stranger, vacantly. "Oh, well—just to see if I can see anything of benefit that I might carry off."

Then off he went, mozying through the congested aisles, with that vacuous stare about him that is assumed, usually, by a Jehue in a vaudeville show. Eli followed him, very closely, watching very sharply, being suspicious all the time that he might pick up a stray pin and carry it off without just compensation to his close-fisted master. The stranger strayed on, in and out, in and out, among the junkage, till he came at last to the cubby-hole, eyed through at that moment by old Peter.

Arriving at the entrance of Peter's sanctuary, the stranger stopped, looked about him listlessly, and took hold of the latch of the door, pressed his thumb slowly upon it, opened it, and walked within, without invitation, or concern as to who might be the occupant therein—bear or man.

"Good morning," said Peter, eyeing him suspiciously. "What do you want?"

"Well, sir," answered the stranger, "I just stepped in a moment to see if you could supply me with a kit of tools."

"This is my office, sir; my office," said Peter, cross as a she-bear. "Why didn't you ask my clerk, sir; my clerk?"—now rubbing his hands briskly and leering at the stranger. "He will supply your wants, maybe, sir, if he has what you want."

"I always deal with the proprietor of an establishment," remarked the stranger, seating himself. "No harm in that, I reckon, sir?"

"None," returned Peter, with a growl. "None, sir."

"Then, do you have a kit of burglar tools?" asked the stranger, with a suavity of an oily-tongued vender of patent medicine.

Peter looked him over again more critically, eyed him more suspiciously, growled out an unintelligible word or two, and sat down himself in a corner, but in such a position that he still could keep one eye on his loophole of observance.

"No, sir!" deliberately groaned out Peter, "I never carry such articles by choice."

"Then by chance, perhaps?" questioned the stranger.

"Nor by chance, if I can help it," screeched the crusty Peter. "I am an honest dealer in my wares."

"I presume so," returned the stranger, with his eyes roaming about the four bare walls of the cubby-hole, as if he were unwinding his thoughts preparatory to a plunge into the secrets of something hidden within his breast.

"You doubt my word, sir?" said Peter, on his dignity.

"Your veracity, I presume," calmly remarked the stranger, "is equal to the rest of men in business."

"It is, sir," answered Peter, foaming.

"Well, if you have not got what I want, I must leave your place without it," said the stranger, with a nonchalance that caused Peter to squint one of his little eyes up like a question mark.

"I am a fair dealer in all things, I am, sir," retorted Peter, "and I don't like for strangers coming about here and eyeing as if I was in league with criminals, or any other such disreputables."

"That's all right, stranger," replied the stranger, with mollifying effectiveness. "This being a junk shop, I took it to be no more than natural to find here such tools as I have indicated."

Peter rubbed his dirty hands together for a moment, gave an avaricious curl to his under lip, squinted his porcine eyes, and asked:

"What do you propose doing with them tools?"

Then he suddenly turned his head, with a grin of malice on his countenance, and looked through his peephole at Eli, whom he saw at that moment parlying with a forlorn creature of the feminine gender. After gazing thereat for a moment, he turned to the stranger to receive an answer to his question.

"Nothing, any more than that I want them," answered the stranger, carelessly.

"That is not a satisfactory answer," said Peter, again turning to his peephole, from which place he could not now unrivet his eyes.

"That's my only answer," replied the stranger. "Your name is Peter Dieman, is it not?"

Peter quickly unriveted his eyes, and looked up with astonishment at the peculiar tone in the stranger's voice, and the sharp look in his steel-gray eyes.

"It is my name," growled Peter.

"I knew it was—judging by the sign over the door," said the stranger.

"Then why in the devil do you ask such a foolish question, if you knew it?" said Peter, ferociously.

"Because, I wanted to make sure," said the stranger. "Say, Mr. Dieman," he now asked, "do you know Ford & Ford, who are after the contract for repaving 444th street with wood blocks?"

"I do."

"Do you know Councilman Biff?"

"I do."

"You know all the other councilmen?"

"I do."

"Very well. Do you know the chief clerk?"

"I do."

"How many can you buy?"

Peter eyed him again, growled again, again peeped out of his place of espial at Eli and the forlorn creature still parlying, rubbed his hands, ran his greasy fingers through his thin setting of hair, coughed, sneezed, looked out the peephole, screwed his mouth to one side, hem-hawed, then snorted:

"Who do you represent?"

"Ford & Ford. Here is my passport to you," replied the stranger, handing Peter a typewritten sheet of paper signed by a member of that firm.

"Why, in the devil, didn't you make yourself known in the beginning?"

"Oh, I just wanted to lead you up to the question."

"What do they want?"

"They want the contract."

"Have they got the money?"

"They have."

"It will cost you—"

"We have the necessary amount."

"—Fifty thousand to get it—money first."

"When do you want the money?"

"Tomorrow at eleven o'clock."

The stranger arose, went out into the smoke and fog, and disappeared somewhere into the infolding channels of great business undertakings of this wonderfully prosperous city of steel and iron, where even the hearts of men are as the material that the great blast furnaces spew out, day and night, for seven days in the week, week in and week out.

CHAPTER IV
IN HELL'S HALF ACRE

The forlorn individual whom Peter Dieman saw through his spyhole, during his soul stirring conversation with the stranger, was Kate Barton, the wife of Billy Barton, the waterman, and the ragged but chunky young woman with her was her daughter, Star Barton.

They had come into Peter's place to redeem, if possible, or to take away as a gift of charity, if lucky, a few battered and broken kitchen utensils that Billy Barton had sold during one of his thirsty spells while staggering through a vaporless period of inebriacy.

Kate Barton's outlook on life was hopeless. She came into the world as poor as the proverbial church mouse, and seemed doomed to go out of it even poorer. She married Billy Barton, a shiftless young man, with an inherent predilection for hankering after the flowing bowl, and ere she had passed a score of years of wedded life twelve innocent starvelings had opened their eyes to her as their mother to gravitate for themselves around the "old block."

The poor woman! She was a meek victim of the direst kind of circumstances that could possibly surround a human being. She was one of those submissive and inept mortals that blindly plod the road of domesticity without a spark of the beautiful to light up the narrow channel of unrequitted effort. When she married Billy Barton, she went about it with that fatality of purpose as is usual with her class, and bore her burdens with the equanimity of a horse hitched to a loaded cart on the uphill pull, without a thought for anything beyond her daily tribulations, save that vague idea that the good Lord would take care of her in the after while. She had no ambition further than the difficult task of caring for her home with its limited accommodations and plethoric adornment of young life. The unworthy addition of an imbibing husband, on whom she looked as an inalienable part of her existence, did in no sense tend her thoughts to any less love for him than if he had been a more renowned character among men. Poor, helpless woman!

When Peter Dieman saw her that day through his place of outlook, he saw a woman as lean as a bean pole, as tall as a rail splitter, as cadaverous as a ghost, with a hook nose, deeply sunken gray eyes, a complexion that was a cross between yellow and black, brown stringy hair and toothless mouth. Her dress was of faded black alpaca, her shoes coarse and well worn, with a dirty yellow shawl hooded over her head and hanging with frayed edges over her shoulders.

After the stranger had left him, Peter stood a few moments, blinkingly observing her. He then stepped out of his office into the less dingy shop. He lumbered up to where she stood having an altercation with Eli Jerey.

"Well, Mrs. Barton," he said, rubbing his hands as if very cold, and grinning like a cheshire cat; "can't you and Eli come to terms? What is the trouble?"

"Eli Jerey says I cannot redeem my goods without I pay a profit for your trouble," she answered.

"Can't have what?" he quizzed.

"Them things that Bill sold you to get drink money with," she replied.

"What things?" asked Peter.

"Them dishes of mine—them tin pans—them knives—them forks—them spoons—he carried off," she whimperingly returned.

"I paid him the cash for them—the cold cash, Mrs. Barton," said Peter, with a stony smile.

"You did, no doubt, or else he wouldn't've been drunk last night," she replied.

"I never ask any questions where the things I buy come from—I give all anything is worth; no more, no less, and never ask where the money goes when it leaves my hands—I expect to sell them for a profit, or else what am I in business for?" thus screeched the junkman.

"Oh, Mr. Dieman!" wailed the poor creature. "I have nothing left to cook with or eat on. He's taken the last dish in the house. My children have been eating off the bare boards—and eating their vituals raw."

"That's not my outlook, Mrs. Barton," retorted Peter, rubbing his hands now more vigorously than ever, as if he had a fresh chill, or had just come in out of a cold blast of weather.

"I thought you might return them to me," said Mrs. Barton, appealingly.

"Thought nothing," he answered, with a croak. "Give me my price and you can take them."

"I have only fifty cents," said the forlorn woman, "and I need that to buy something to eat."

"I have nothing to give you, Mrs. Barton," he snorted, turning his back to her, and rubbing his hands as if in meditation, and batting his small eyes, as if he were winking at his little god—Mammom.

Feeling that it was hopeless to plead with him for the articles, and wanting to save her fifty cents, Mrs. Barton turned slowly, pulled the yellow shawl closer over her head and shoulders, and started to leave the junk shop. Eli stood by agape, without a sign of sympathy for her, or an emotion of any kind, any more than if he had been a fence post. Mrs. Barton bowed her head as she walked away, and her daughter, Star, after casting a disdainful look at Eli, followed. Eli stood still looking after them. Peter stood still rubbing his hands and batting his eyes, as if he were preparing to offer up devotion to his deity. Then of a sudden he turned, and roared:

"Come back, Mrs. Barton!"

Mrs. Barton stopped as suddenly as Peter had cried out, faced about, and looked blankly at the object who gave the command.

"Come back!" roared Peter again.

The poor woman, having no reason to be independent about the matter, went hesitatingly toward him. When she came up to the blinking idol of greed, she stood waiting for him to speak further.

"Take your old things, and tell Bill the next time he comes into my place of business I'll tear him to pieces," he cried. "I've had enough of him already. He's nothing but an old sot, unworthy of a woman like you," now with commiseration in his sordid heart for her, and only condemnation for her weak husband. "Take them, and go, and tell him that I'll get even with him sometime."

"Thank you; thank you," said Mrs. Barton, with a gleam of merciful gratitude in her eyes for this philanthropic pig.

"Eli," said Peter, without returning a "welcome" to Mrs. Barton, as he turned to that dutiful menial, "give the woman her trumphery and let her begone."

Then rubbing his hands more furiously, and squinting his eyes more swiftly and gritting his teeth more viciously at the turn this action of benefaction gave his conscience, he waddled to his black office, where he resumed his smoking, and took to calculating to a certainty as to how he could recover from some one else the small pittance he was out by this disreputable transaction, as he termed it, on the part of Billy Barton, the waterman.

Eli Jerey at once proceeded to obey his superior, for that was his only aim at that period in his life. Into a gunny sack he piled the chipped and broken dishes, the battered pans, the rusty iron forks and knives, and tin spoons, composing the entire culinary outfit of Kate Barton.

With the sack thus loaded, Mrs. Barton swung it once in front of her, and with a quick jerk whirled it over her right shoulder, bent under it as if it were of great weight, said good bye to Eli, and strode out, with Star following. They crossed the street and went down the glacis of the cobblestoned wharf. Following the water's edge, they passed among the miscellaneous collection of freight piled high on every hand. Over taut ropes, holding boats, barges and rivermen's houses, they stepped, catching their toes now and then, and almost falling; proceeding ever on, through all kinds of heaps and piles of freightage; ever on, among the men moving about performing their duties silently. Ever on, Kate Barton led the way, a tireless, fearless, forbidding being, who created no more comment among the habitues of this district than if she were nowhere to be seen; till, at last, she, like one with the joy of success bound up in a spiritless heart, arrived where a dog-boat lay tethered to a ring-bolt in the stone abutment of the Point bridge.

Into the boat she tumbled her bundle, with no thought as to the result such an act might have upon the dishes, ordered Star to climb in and take a seat in the rear, untied the rope, and jumped in herself as she gave the boat a shove into the stream. Taking up the oars she bent to them with the energy of a man, and pulled through the puffing, snorting, wheezing, churning craft for the farther shore—where house boats lay moored; where shanties hugged dangerously close to the water line; where decrepit buildings stood in all stages of deformity; where every inch of ground on the narrow space between the margin of the river and the verticle cliff behind was utilized to its utmost with everything imaginable, from the detritus of the hill to a pretentious manufacturing plant of equivocal worth in its baleful aspect. The hill above was straight up and down, almost, rock ribbed and bleak, a barrier to the pleasant places above and beyond; and at its base a railway system held indisputable sway; while betwixt it and the river were the straggling homes of men, with a few stunted and wheezy domesticated animals and fowls roaming about them.

Once upon a time this place bore the evil name of Hell's Half Acre.

To a low-browed, unpainted, unadorned, uninviting three-roomed shack Mrs. Barton took her way, with the bundle of precious household articles on her back, with Star following. They passed along narrow, winding alleys, with frightful looking fences bulging out, or leaning in; past foul mud holes; past filthy doorsteps, where brawling children, like her own, screamed at her, or taunted her, or spoke friendly to her; through sticky mire, over rickety board walks, over stepping stones at watery places, and on, over everything and through everything that had a squalid and sickly hue she went—with Star following—and with one unswerving gait, or changed expression of her leathery face, to the door of her own abode.

The door squeaked with the pain of lassitude as she shoved it open. She entered the kitchen—Star following. Dropping the sack on a dilapidated chair, she began lifting the contents therefrom, as the children gathered around, in all stages of filthiness, to see the operation. A toddling three-year-old grasped a spoon, as soon as he saw it come forth, and resorted to the ashes in the grate as material by which to test its usefulness. Another child took up a knife and began hacking at a table leg; another took up a cup and ran out to procure some water; while another took up a small battered tin pail to fetch in a little coal to replenish the dying fire.

The children ranged in age from one to nineteen, the eldest—Michael—being away earning money for his own keep, so that she had a short dozen mouths to fill for the nonce.

After completing the task of unburdening the sack, Mrs. Barton delivered the youngest child unto Star to tend while she set about to cook a meal. Her bill of fare was meager and simple, withal. It consisted wholly of fried potatoes, dough-bread hurryingly mixed, and coffee. After the fare was spread upon the table, ten greedy youngsters and their mother sat down to dine, while Star stood off, waiting to take potluck with the leavings. Unselfish child, as she was, she deferred always first to the appeasement of the hunger of the others. The savory provender lay heaped in a lusterless dish in the center of the table, and the coffee stood hot in a tin pot on a corner of the stove, while the bread was broken into fragments, as per age of child and capacity, and laid by each place. As plates and cups and saucers, knives and forks, were not sufficient to go around, the younger children fought and scratched and pulled as to whose turn should come "next" in being served. Some being ferociously hungry, and impatient over delays, dipped into the platter with their hands, clapping the contents to their mouths, like monkeys, and ate their bread with such an eager determination to get filled up that they almost choked. Some drank the coffee out of the pot, and spluttered and cried and slobbered with such wild frenzy that they were called she-wolves by their mother sitting by eating sparingly but as contentedly and as heartily as if her young hopefuls were angels instead of brats.

"Where's your pap?" asked the mother, directing her question to any, or all, of them, so indifferently was the question pronounced.

"Went to the city," answered the eldest.

"Naw he didn't," said the ten-year-old, after taking a swallow of the faintly discolored water called coffee.

"When did he go?" again questioned the mother, after the lapse of a few minutes.

"Soon after you left," answered the fourteen-year-old, indifferent as to where he went, "and took his overcoat with him."

"To sell it, too, s'pose," said the mother unconcernedly.

"Yep," replied the ten-year-old; "said he'd bring me a pair of shoes."

"I see you gettin' a pair of shoes from him, Liz," retorted the mother, without the least concern whether the child had any or no, as she rolled the fried potatoes and dough-bread between her gums.

Thus the mother and the children talked about "pap," the father, who had that day wandered out of his beaten course, the one that he had learned to travel in so regularly for twenty years or more. This course lay between his squalid home and the tempting saloons that lined the streets of old Birmingham farther up the river way. Billy Barton was a man with an unconquerable appetite for strong drink as might be judged from what has been said heretofore. All his unvarying life before this memorable day he had but one thought, but one ambition, but one predominating idea, and that was to get drink—either by buying, begging, stealing, or trading for it. But when his wife left him this morning, with the parting word that she would fetch home the things that he had sold the day before, he, too, left shortly after her departure, taking with him an old rusty overcoat.

As he departed from his door, with his flock of half-starved children standing in it watching him leave, he went with a new resolution in his mind, a new determination formed, a new purpose in view. This was that he would go away and find work—away from his old environments, away from his drunken associates. With this new resolve burning feebly in his irresolute breast, he struck a course for the mills in the Soho district.

That night he did not return; nor the next day; nor the next night; nor the following day. Mrs. Barton and the family thought little of his failure to return in the space of time, for they had been used to his absence on a spree for almost a whole week at a stretch. But when a week had gone by, and when ten days had gone by, and two weeks had finally passed, they began to feel uneasy at his prolonged absence. When a third week had passed and he did not put in an appearance in the hilarious condition they anticipated to behold him wheeling down upon them, the mother thought it time to make some concerted attempt to ascertain the cause of his disappearance.

She took the matter very calmly, consoling herself with the reflection that her spouse was safe somewhere, or otherwise she would have heard about him through the police department, or through the gossips of her disreputable neighborhood. Little by little she began to inquire cursorily among the neighbors, then among the keepers of the saloons, then of the policeman of the district. She got no tidings of him. A month passed; no news. Another month passed; no news. He was gone.

So Kate Barton, with her twelve children, was left alone to fight against starvation, or go to the poor house, or have her family broken up, and scattered among the charitable, who are very often among the worst as saviors of the outcasts.

Alone, alone! What if we, who live in gilded halls, had to take her place! Ah, we would call on a merciful God to deliver us! For there are things in this life, mind you, my good keepers of the loaves and fishes, that are even worse than death—worse than death.

Alas, too often, men of piety are prone to shun their christian duty. Millions of beings, such as she, vegetate from the cradle to the grave and never see the ministering hand of the followers of that Christ who taught that it is more blessed to give than to receive. Millions go up and down the obscure pathways of this world, within the sacred sound of the clanking bells of religion, and never receive the helping meed that was promised them. Millions live like the rioting motes invisible in the air about us as if all the philanthrophy of Christendom were set aside for the chosen few. The successful gloat over and glory in their achievements, and extend a cursory hand to those below as if they were fulfilling the ten commandments as a great finale of their extravaganza. But, do they do any good? There are many Kate Bartons all around us, the natural among the unnatural, who deserve more compassion from those preachers of the Good Will than they ever receive. It is not believed by all that only the chosen few shall answer the call. It is not believed by all that the doctrine of the Christ should prevail one day in the week and be sunk in oblivion for the other six. No, not by all.

But Kate Barton's day shall come, some day; and those who shun her now will assert their cringing hypocracy when she has been lifted up, and not lifted by their hands.

Charity is not what the Kate Bartons want—it is the meed of opportunity.

CHAPTER V
STAR BARTON SEEKS A NEW HOME

Star Barton? She was the one scintillating light that shone out of the milky way of the Barton family. She was a sport of the family tree—a lily nourished in a quagmire. And how a wondering world marvels at such unaccountable things of nature!

Through eighteen weary summers and eighteen dreary winters she went, before seeing a light above the dim horizon of her impoverished world. Through babyhood she crawled in frightful filth, as if it were a part of her wretched existence, seeing nothing beyond the bare walls and bare floors of her cramped up playgrounds; through childhood she toddled, with the same dismal conditions abetting her expanding innocence; through the period of adolescence she walked without a thought of what the outside world contained, except as she intuitively gathered such knowledge as the thick curtain of ignorance slowly rose before her; till now she had come to the springtime of womanhood, full of its snares and pitfalls for such as she. Then, like the bursting of the sun through a rent-way in the clouds on a rainy day, she, for the first time, saw the beckoning star that should lead her on—on—on—to a life of rectitude, or—dissoluteness.

Star Barton was the second child of Kate Barton, and early in her teening years gave some promise of her future. When only ten she began to be a drudge, doing all the things that her delicate hands could, with exertion, be laid to. She was the patient "little mother" to all the new babies as they yearly floated out of Paradise to this place of desolation. She was the scrub-woman, the washer-woman, the charwoman, the cook, the chamber maid, ever cheerful in her efforts to perform her tasks. Illy clad, scantily fed, roundly abused by her father, continually scolded by her mother, and never praised by either parent, she mutely submitted, like a black slave, to all the torments of blighting servitude that could be heaped upon her. Thus, for eighteen long years, Star Barton was subjected to all the demoralizing influences of drunkenness and poverty; and how she came out of it unblighted any one may wonder at. And now, at this age, she stood looking out the narrow window of her vantage point, seeing the promise of a brighter life.

Then why was she a freak of nature from the family tree? Because she had a round face, pink cheeks, two even rows of white teeth, two mild blue eyes underneath dark eyebrows, a sharp, shrewd, straight nose, and dark hair; and because she was of average height, well formed, muscular and courageous; and still, because nature had provided her, as it provides the offspring of the weak, sometimes, with all the qualities and graces that were necessary to combat the deteriorating effects of a life of toil.

As suddenly as she had seen the new light mount the horizon of her life, as suddenly did she long for better ways, a better home, a better life. This longing came to her the very time her father disappeared. She sought work, and found it, still as a drudge, in a lodging house up in Birmingham. The small pittance that she earned she took home every Saturday night, and gave it to her mother as a helping mite towards banishing the horde of wolves that constantly prowled about her door. This small sum was not sufficient to maintain a successful contest with those beasts of starvation that gnawed their way, like famished whelps, into the growing bodies of the ten starvelings of Kate Barton. But, notwithstanding, Star never failed in her willingness to turn her last penny for their sustenance. An older brother had been her assistant in this trial, and he kept it up with a good will till about the hour the father had deserted them; but he, losing heart, after acquiring new habits and forming ill-savored acquaintances, so far forgot his duty to his mother that he also deserted her in her time of greatest need. He went away as suddenly as her father—they knew not where. And Star was ever faithful, ever trustworthy, ever to be relied upon by her hapless mother.

One day, after ten hours of the severest toil, Star came home, with the little bundle of her personal effects under her arm. It was on that memorable day in November when the heavens seemed to have bursted their flood gates and let out a deluge to come down in gimlets to pierce the fog and smoke with its weird pattering. Without cloak, or coat, or protection of any kind, Star waded through the sodden streets, arriving at the door of her home as wet as a drowning rat. Entering, she deposited her bundle on the only table in the house, and took up a position close to a cast iron stove that was about as cheerless in its warmth as the evening itself. She was so thoroughly soaked that every lineament of her form could be seen through the thin garment that clung to her body as closely as paper on a wall.

"Mother," said Star, as that lean creature came indolently into the room, "I have quit my job."

"You have?" answered the mother, about as carelessly as if she were talking gossip over the back fence.

"Yes, mother, I have quit."

"Very well, I've lots to do here; I reckon you can keep busy," said the mother, as if the future had been provided with all the necessaries of life.

Star left her mother suckling a child by the stove, and proceeded to her dark and shabbily furnished room for a change of clothing. Presently she returned looking less distressful. Then she bathed her face in a water bucket that stood on a box by a besmoked window, following with the combing of her long dark hair. After which, she rolled her hair into a knot at the back of her head, looked into a crooked mirror, dampened her fingers on her tongue and touched her eyebrows, then set to work to cook the evening meal for the brats caterwauling around like so many wild-cats.

Kate Barton gave no concern about Star's future. She asked no questions as to why she quit her work as scrub-woman at the lodging house. She said nothing that would leave the least impression as to what she thought about providing for the family. Deplorable mortal!

"Mother," said Star, after awhile, "I am going away tomorrow to look for a new place."

"It makes no difference, Star," was the response of the mother. "I can use you here."

"How will we live, if I don't work, mother?"

"As we have always lived, s'pose."

"And that has been poorly, mother."

"Yes."

"Don't you want me to go away, mother?"

"It makes no difference, s'pose," answered the mother. "I've put up with it this long, s'pose I can put up with it the rest of my days."

"Mother," said Star, whose love for her mother was of the undemonstrative kind, the kind born of instinct, and is taken for granted among the very poor; "mother, I am going to the East End tomorrow to look for a job as a domestic in a rich man's home."

"Yes," replied the mother.

"A woman came to me today and told me to go to a certain house, in the East End, where I could get work at six dollars a week, and board thrown in."

"Yes, Star," returned the mother, now showing a little more interest in the conversation than she had shown in any thing before—unless it was, perhaps, her drunken husband.

"Mother?"

"Yes, Star."

"That is twenty-four dollars a month; that will keep me in clothing, and plenty for the children to eat."

"Yes, Star," said the mother, as she rose from her chair, with the suckling still hanging to her breast, and walked across the floor, for no purpose whatever, other than that perhaps the performance might dissolve her cold brooding into a semblance of interest in her material welfare. Then she sat down again and rocked to and fro with the rockerless chair, as a jolting dose of soothing syrup for the pain that had suddenly twisted the child's mouth into a howling breadth.

"And mother," continued Star, "the woman gave me the address of a rich family that wants a maid for a young lady, or a cook, or something else, I forget which."

"Yes, Star."

"And she said I could get the job if I go at once."

"Yes, Star," responded the mother between the infinitisimal intervals of the noise of the thumping chair and the yelling child.

"And mother, she said they live in a grand house as big as all our forty shanties here put together."

"Yes," said the mother.

"And she said it was lit up by electric lights, and had steam heat, and furniture as grand as any place, mother—as grand as any king's palace, mother. I am going tomorrow, mother."

"Yes," returned the mother, as she turned the yelling child over her knee and gave it two or three smacks, causing it to become so red in the face that its phiz shone more brightly than the lambent rays that filtered through the smoky chimney of the kerosene lamp sitting on the table.

"And she said, mother," still pursued Star, as she went about among the battered pans and rattled the cracked and broken dishes she was displaying on the family board, the while stirring the frying potatoes in the sheet-iron skillet, and watching the coffee pot that it did not boil away all the aroma, "that the young lady who wants a maid is so very handsome and so fine that I cannot sleep till I get there."

"Yes," croaked the mother, a little irritated, it appeared, by all these revelations that Star was unfolding before her; for nothing disturbed her so, it seemed, as the mention of such hifalutin things, although she herself, in all her lowliness, never disparaged, by word, anybody who had more than she, being a woman absolutely contented with her lot.

"May I go?" asked Star, who always felt it a matter of filial respect to defer to her parents' beck and call.

"Yes," dolefully replied the mother, as she rocked the squalling brat on the rockerless chair with greater vigor than had been her practice.

That night Star Barton went to bed with more stirring imaginings in her untrained head than she had ever presumed upon before in all her dreary life. For a long time she lay awake seeing of the new vista that so suddenly opened before her disreputable habitat; dreaming of another place, so widely dissevered from hers, that it was like the enchanted land she once read about in a book that some roving spirit had conveyed to her haunts; dreaming of the wonders she had oftentimes conjured up to placate her plagued thoughts that hung like burning tapers of despair in her abiding place of want; dreaming, yea dreaming, for the first time in her whole unvaried life, of the things that are beautiful, grand and regal. Then she went to sleep to dream some more:—of the fantasies of an idle brain, of the children of her unconscious world, of the evil spirits that had ever been a part of her uneventful being, of the spirits that come to checkmate us in our mad rush, causing us to turn aside to ponder over their real meaning.

But none of the visions of the sleeping hours was as promising as the fancies of her wakeful time. For when she awoke in the morning, the lustre that had pervaded her dreaming had waned, and she faltered over making the new and uncertain step. Oh what a bad little imp it is that seems to possess those of us, at times, who, when a new undertaking is to be entered upon, hesitate, procrastinate, pause and deliberate, till the time of opportunity is over!

Star was, on this morning, in such a state of uncertainty, probably very much on account of the continuation of the nasty weather, that it was near the noon hour before she could resolve finally to spend ten cents for the fare to take the journey she had so set her head on the previous day. She donned her best blue gingham dress; coiled her hair up into a knot on top of her head; tied a faded black ribbon in it; adjusted an odd looking round black straw hat, with some faded flowers breaking its sombre monotony, to her head; looked into the crazy little mirror that reflected her not much unlike some distorted beast with a white face; threw a grayish cape over her shoulders, and went out into the rain.

After a period of time that was very slow in passing, and after much fluttering of her virtuous heart, and considerable indecision whether to go on or to return to the place she knew so well, she arrived at the Highland avenue address given her the day before by the unknown, but friendly disposed, woman who met her at her last place of bondage. When she reached the great iron gate that opened into the spacious yard of the mansion on the hill, she again hesitated, and walked back and forth on the pavement so many times that the keeper of the gate, with suspicion cast upon her, came out to inquire the meaning of her actions.

"I have come—I have come—" faltered Star, feeling like fleeing from him in that moment of her bewilderment over the bigness of the outside world, "—to look for a place. They gave me this number," handing the keeper a card.

The keeper, who was an oldish man, and perhaps had a daughter of his own, took the card, looked it over, looked at her, then looked at it; then looked at her. He saw that she had a beautiful face, was innocent and unbeguiling.

"This is the place, miss," he answered, kindly. "This is the way in," and he opened the large gate, and passed her in.

Star went up the smooth asphaltum walk with considerable trepidation, heeding nothing about her, and seeing only the big house at the end. The most serious thing that she did was to go directly to the big front door, with its shining knocker that looked to her like the face of a bull in brass with a pendulous ring in its nose. She was in such a flurry that she could not have believed her own tongue, had she spoken then and there. She had never, in all her dreaming, imagined such things. Her head was in a whirl, and more than once she was on the point of turning back to her forlorn mother, where she felt she would be equal to her surroundings.

However, summoning up all the courage and fortitude that she possessed, she at last tapped timidly at the door. No answer. She touched her red knuckles on one of the polished panels. No answer. Then, merely as a matter of curiosity, caught hold of the ring in the bull's nose, pulled on it, and let it drop back into place, which was immediately followed by a dull brassy ring. Suddenly the door swung wide open, appearing to her as the door of a factory building, in its immensity.

A tall, pompous gentleman—dressed like the men she had seen in a book on colonial characters, only this one had short hair and scragly sideburns—loomed up before her, like the Giant did to Jack, perhaps. His sudden appearance caused her to involuntarily start and draw back, with a greater desire than ever to flee; but in a moment he spoke, hoarsely:

"Go to the rear door!"

Whereupon, he closed the door. The way into such gilded piles of luxury, for such as Star Barton in her present condition, is not by the front entrance. No graven lintel was ever raised to pass such as Star thereunder. Away, away, like a rat to its hole, steal into the less prominent openings leading to the apartments of the flunkies!

Star was dazed by this action; but not knowing that it was any more than a big apartment house for the rich, she judged she had gone to the wrong door. So she, with a still fluttering heart, proceeded in the direction indicated. Before she had found the proper place, she had tried a number of the openings in the grim, gray walls, receiving the same reception at all of them as at the first. "Go to the rear," "go to the rear," was repeated so often to her that she began to feel dizzy from its repetition, and drowsy and faint over the possibility of failure.

Then she came to a door where a cook answered her knock. He wore a white, brimless cap, and a big white apron covered up the rotundity of his front clear up to his chin and almost to his feet. He was large and fat and filled up almost the entire space of the opened door. He was red-faced and genial, and had a merry twinkle in his blue eyes. He reminded Star of a big German butcher whom she knew in the marts of Birmingham.

"Well!" he exclaimed, seeing the visitor to his quarters was a lady.

"I came to see if you want a cook," said Star, now feeling more composed since some one deigned to talk with her.

"A cook!" he exclaimed, grinning.

"A cook, yes, sir," she answered.

"We employ none but men cooks here, lady," he replied, and was about to close the door.

"Surely, I have made a mistake," thought Star, in this moment of her rebuff, as she took it. Her heart was failing her. She felt disconsolate. She was about to turn and flee—back to her own elements, back to her own humble surroundings; to all the shortcomings of her home, to her stupid mother, to her unfortunate brothers and sisters, to her wretched existence again, and there take up her burdens as she before had borne them.

The fat cook noticed the pallor that had come over Star's face, as the consequence of his remark, and instead of closing the door in her face, as he intended, he opened it wider, and said:

"You must be in the wrong place, Miss."

"No sir; I am not," she answered. "This is the address that was given me, where a cook was wanted—or I might be mistaken—it might be a maid is wanted for a young lady."

"Very doubtful," said the cook, scratching his head.

"None wanted?" she asked.

"To get a place here you must have recommendations," he answered.

"I have never worked away from home," she replied, "except for a few months. I have never been a maid to a lady. But—but—I want to learn."

"Wait," said the cook, quickly, as if he had thought of something that had been commended to his keeping and it had slipped his memory, as he retreated, and closed the door.

In a few minutes the cook returned, with a smile on his round face that made him look like the full moon, and bade Star to walk within. Star walked within, dazed, trembling and mortally afraid of the line of domestics, before whom it appeared she was passing in review. She was conducted into the presence of a bouncing little lady, dressed like a princess, with gold on her wrists, in her ears, on her breast, around her neck—a charmingly spry little lady, with a dignified nose, a pretty smile, and an air of geniality about her that might not be expected in the mistress of such a household. The little lady looked Star over, scrutinized her from head to foot. Every inch of the plumpy girl she seemed to weigh in the fine scale of her discrimination. She was neither pleased, nor displeased, so far as Star could see. She took her in as if she read the whole story of her life without the aid of a palmist's text book, or geanalogical dictionary from which to take her cue.

"So you want to be my daughter's maid?" asked Mrs. Jarney, for that is whom the lady was, the mother of Edith.

"I had thought I would like to learn," replied Star, who was already feeling at home in the presence of this fine lady.

"Have you had experience?"

"None; but I can learn."

"How old are you?"

"Eighteen, past."

"You are large for your age."

"But I have worked hard—that has made me strong."

"You will need a little fixing up—what's your name?"

"Miss Barton."

"I kn—I mean your given name?"

"Star."

"Have Edith come down," said Mrs. Jarney to her maid; and she told Star to be seated.

Edith came down in a few moments. She was so radiant that Star fairly held her breath. Edith advanced and presented her hand to Star, saying:

"What is your name?"

"Star Barton."

"I kn—that is a fine name," replied Edith, holding Star's hand, and for the first time she began to feel that there was some mystery about her coming here, or else why this kindly greeting? "Mama," she said, still holding Star's hand and turning to her mother, "I shall like her, I know. I shall take her to my room and have her redressed. Will you come with me? Yes, of course."

Edith, who had been very light hearted all that day, wheeled gracefully, lifted her skirts, and went up the stairs so lightly that she was like a bird of Paradise, so fairily did she trip along. Star Barton, in her poverty-stricken clothing, followed in such a delirium of amazement that she felt as if she were treading the clouds into Heaven itself.

And thus into a new Heaven she went, with as little formality surrounding her going—once she was let into the mansion by the ever guardful servants—as is seldom found in this world of inequality.

CHAPTER VI
THE TRANSFORMATION OF STAR BARTON

To Star Barton, it was like going into a fairyland. Edith was the fairy, Star the lowly nymph. Edith was the sparkling diamond that gave it its setting, Star was the rough jewel come to be recast.

The rich, velvety, orange-colored rug, with pale pink flowers blooming like butterfly eyes peeping at her, was as soft as snow to the rough maiden's touch; only it gave back, instead of a chill, an enthralling sensation like the sound of a distant harp that beats upon a wayfarer's ears. The creamy, snow-fringed curtains evolved themselves into miniature cascades of dazzling frost, to her eyes; and gave back, instead of a shiver, a lulling peace to her disturbed imagination. The gilded furniture, the beautifully crocheted lavender cushions, the paintings, the photos of friends, the pink tint of the walls, the shining chandeliers, with sparkling globes and translucent shades, gave back, instead of a frown, a smile.

Edith was, on this occasion, the advent of Star Barton into her life, an animated piece of pinkness, which gave the room its vitality. To Star's eyes, unused to such things, she was an angel without the wings. Her gossimer gown of pink, her gold, her diamonds, her fine face, all appealed to the poor girl of such lowliness to such an ecstatic degree that she was astonished beyond belief.

It was all so entrancing, so enrapturing, so overpowering to her theretofore undemonstrative spirit that she sat down and burst into tears. This was the outward sign of her joy over her disenthrallment. Poor simple maiden! To be brought from a hovel to this place of glory, so suddenly, was even more than her strong nature could endure. The transition was too sudden. The climax to the fanciful things she had conjured up in the short time she had put into such imaginings was too real. No pathway had ever been struck out by her with such beautiful borderings as this. No, no; not in her limited sphere. Simple, uneducated, modest, as she was, with a pure soul and a heart that beat for better things, she gave way when the door of chance was thrown open for her, at last, and poured out her joy in the agony of tears.

Edith, who had been so radiantly happy, and who had formulated such great plans for this girl, ceased in her joyous behavior when she saw Star sink into a chair and put her soiled handkerchief to her eyes. Edith at once divined the cause of Star's weeping, and knelt down by her side in commiseration. She took both of Star's rough hands between hers, so soft and delicate, and cried herself in the fullness of her heart.

"Do not weep, dear girl; it grieves me so," she said, looking up into the blue eyes of her poor benighted sister.

"Dear, kind lady, I cannot help it," returned Star, in an effort to stop her tears.

"Come, come, my dear girl, you must prepare yourself to be my companion," said Edith. "Be brave; that is a good girl. I shall love you."

"Dear lady, I am not fit to be here," said Star, still weeping. "These are all the good clothes I have."

"I have new clothing for you, my dear; come, and make ready to go down to dinner with me," said Edith, rising, and still holding Star's hands.

"Oh, I am so rough, I am afraid I will contaminate this place should I remain," replied Star, hesitatingly.

"No, no; you must not think of such a thing, my dear girl. Cheer up and follow me," said Edith, as Star arose from her chair. Edith kissed her. Star wiped away her tears, and smiled.

Then Edith lead her to her private bath room, which glistened so in its whiteness that Star drew back when she came to the door of it. This was something that Star had never seen before; but she entered, as if it were a place to be shunned, and was seated. Edith knelt down, in all her finery, and unfastened Star's coarse shoes, and removed them, revealing a foot that was as small as Edith's, but reeking with water. Edith then prepared the bath, and gave Star instructions how to use such a modern thing of sanitation—all foreign to Star. Then Edith left to fetch new garments, when Star should give the signal that her ablutions had been performed. In the course of time, Star gave the signal as agreed upon, when Edith opened the door and entered, with both arms piled to her chin with sweet smelling clothing, and a merry smile on her face, and a laughing twinkle in her eyes. Modesty caused Star to conceal herself behind the door, in the attitude of the statue of Venus.

"My dear girl, do not be alarmed at me; I am as harmless as a kitten," said Edith, as she beheld how naturally modest Star impelled herself to be, even in the presence of her own sex.

"It is my nature, dear good lady," replied Star, reaching for something to conceal her person.

"In deference to your modesty, dear, I shall retire, if it is your wish," said Edith, laughing, as she put down her bundle of clothing.

"Just for a moment, if you please, kind lady," said Star.

So Edith sidled out of the room without looking around at her protege, while Star pulled on her unmentionables. After which she called Edith to assist in the furtherance of her dressing in some of the new things she was thereafter to be seen in.

"These must have been made for me," said Star, as one article after another was adjusted to her form, seeing that they all fit so well and so charmingly.

"They were," said Edith, buttoning up the back of Star's dress, an act she had never done before, being as she always had a maid for that performance.

"Made for me?" replied Star, with some surprise.

"Yes, you, my dear girl."

"By whose orders?"

"Mine."

"I don't understand," said Star, still more surprised.

"Didn't you know you were to come here?"

"Why, no; I thought I came by chance!"

"You apparently did."

"I wonder who had that much interest in me?" asked Star, for the first time realizing that she had not been so altogether overlooked as she imagined she had been.

"I had—I have."

"How? Tell me, dear lady."

"It is a long story, dear girl, and I will tell it you some other time. Dinner is about ready. You must go down with me. Put your hair up quickly, so we will not keep them waiting. Oh, let me help twist it round for you! How do you do it? I will learn some day, perhaps. Yes, this way. Now, look in the mirror. Isn't that better? It certainly is. You are charming. Why, I didn't know you were so sweet. Let me kiss you now to bind our companionship henceforward. There!"

This from Edith while she was acting as maid, in her finery, for this poor girl, who but an hour before exhibited all the characteristics of having been pulled from the ruins of Peter Dieman's junk heap. Indeed, such a transformation had Star gone through in that short hour that the fair Edith herself hardly recognized her as the same untidy being who had come to her boudoir for what she knew not.

"It is all so strange, dear lady, that it seems more like a dream," said Star, now with her cheeks aflame from the bathing and the attending excitement of the ordeal through which she had passed.

"Oh, stranger things than what has already happened you may come to pass," replied Edith, as she turned to take the lead down the stairs.

"What about my old clothes?" asked Star.

"I will send the washer-woman after them," answered Edith.

"I shall want to send them home to mother."

"Never mind them," returned Edith; "your mother will be provided for."

"Oh," said Star, mystified.

Star Barton was now a fit subject of envy for any young lady, even with less aspiring thoughts than she. Edith might have been jealous of Star's good looks, had it been her nature; but Edith was not so inclined, in this instance. The fact is, that Edith was so pleased over her handiwork, in rejuvenating this fair damsel, that she bubbled over with happiness. Star was now clothed as became a lady of rank, except that sparkling jewelry was lacking as yet. Star's dress was almost a counterpart of Edith's, and set her off to advantage, in a comparative sense. Her mild blue eyes, pink cheeks, noble white forehead, dark wavy hair, caused the dining room attendants to stare when she came down the great staircase and passed under the brilliant lights into the presence of the mighty man of wealth and his bouncing little wife. Hah, even those two august personages held their breath for a moment when they cast their searching, but kindly, eyes upon her.

"This is Miss Barton, papa," said Edith, as she came up to him with her fair charge and presented her, "and my mamma, whom you have met before."

Both parents received her so graciously that Star was dumfounded, and exceedingly awkward in returning their salutation.

"Miss Barton, I am happy to make your acquaintance," said Mr. Jarney. "I assure you that you are welcome."

Neither Mr. Jarney's pride, nor vanity, nor money, prevented him from taking kindly to this young maiden, for he knew already whom she was, and often longed for the time to help her, although at present he must act with some circumspection toward her for reasons that he did not wish her to know. And Mrs. Jarney, for the same reasons, had to conduct herself accordingly, and meet Star on the basis of a stranger to the name of Jarney.

So keeping her in ignorance of her true relationship to them, they hoped to make a lady of her, and do all that generous hearts could do, under cover of being Edith's companion, to help her to a brighter life.

Star needed some instruction in the art of being a grand lady, which function she never conceived in acting when she humbly presented herself, so recently, at the back door of this mansion. The transposition of her habitat was so expeditiously executed that she saw in it something of the miraculous. In nowise, on so short a notice, could she be expected to conform to the spirit and the letter of the laws of usage in this undiscovered country to which she had been unceremoniously transported. So, recognizing these deficiencies in Star, Edith took it upon herself to be her teacher and took a seat by her side at the table. But Star was not so uncouth that she was wholly deficient in quickness of perception, and constantly kept on guard; noting every move that the others made; noting every move of Edith with sly glances; noting every action of those opposite, so that she should not, if possible to prevent it, make herself ridiculous in her first appearance on the stage of grandeur. Thus, with much carefulness on her part, in this respect at least, she got through the dinner fairly well, considering the great length of time—one hour—they took in mastication, conversation, deglutition. Finally, when it was all over with, she arose, with the rest of them, with a gladsome thanksgiving beating in her breast.

But the worst ordeal yet, for her, was to come. The entire family adjourned to the parlor, where Edith sat down to the piano, and ran her hands across the key-board so rapidly and with such a wild harmonious result that Star almost had the ague. Then Edith sang a song—a lullaby—so appealing in its sentimentality that Star was lost in oblivion for a time. She let her agitated thoughts wander, unrestrained, back to her own haunts—to the misery, want and woe she had left behind; to the crooning mother attempting a similar lullaby; to her dark old face, to her tearless eyes, to her faded cheeks; to her hopeless life, in her sad, dull, stupid, sullen contentment in her wretchedness. Verily, what mortal, with a heart, could withstand the contrasts as were revealed to this tender maiden? No one could. She broke down under it, like the strongest of us break down, sometimes, under the strain of sentiment when dear ones are under the ban of misfortune. The sweet voice of Edith was to her an angelic orison to heaven for a lost soul; and who knows but that the angels then were pleading with the Great Father to send His benediction down upon that other home and save it from further damnation.

Without being the least concerned as to who might take notice, or without any effort to control herself in the company of those grand people, Star let her emotions have full swing, and the tears flowed down her cheeks as freely as they flowed when her father beat her as a child. The dainty handkerchief that she now carried was soon soaked with the lachrymose outburst of her misery. Her eyes became red, her cheeks paled, and her hair, which had not been put up by trained hands, fell down over her shoulders. Despair! despair! despair!

Edith played on, and sang, wholly unconscious of Star's sad moments. But her mother, happening to look Star's way, noticed her despairing plight, and went to her side with a consoling smile and a sympathetic word. When Edith had finished playing, she wheeled about on her seat, with beaming face, to receive the plaudits of her auditors; but a mournful silence greeted her. Her smiling face calmed to a serious tone when she saw her friends standing about Star in all manner of comforting attitudes. Then Edith, grasping the situation at once, glided to her side, and, kneeling down, took Star's two red hands in hers, and cried. Dear Edith, so good of you. Then she assisted Star to rise, placed her arm around her waist, and conducted her up the great white stairs, like a guiding angel going into Heaven with a new soul.

CHAPTER VII
JOHN WINTHROPE PROMOTED

The day following the accidental meeting of Miss Jarney and Mr. Winthrope, under such wretched meteorological circumstances, was spent by the latter in the office of Jarney & Lowman as usual; with this exception, that the young man went about his duties as assistant bookkeeper with more alertness and decisiveness of purpose, at the same time pondering over another chance meeting of the morning.

He arose an hour earlier than had been his wont, sleep having been dispelled by the train of thoughts that the awakening moments had set in motion in his brain. Notwithstanding that the inclement weather held almost at the same steady pace as on the night previous, after dressing himself, he went out, with the broken umbrella over him, into the streets to wander aimlessly about; observing, as he did so, the mad rush of the people; or taking a percursory view of the store windows; or standing in the shelter of a door; or beneath an awning, looking idly at the crowd, ever on the go.

He wended down Fourth avenue to Smithfield, up to Fifth, down to Wood, down to Second; halting now and then, in his sauntering, to gaze in the windows, being interested in nothing in particular any more than to have time go as rapidly as it would go, so that he could get down to the absorbing task of putting down and reckoning up columns of figures in his books. So he wended on in this irresponsible manner till half way up the block on Second avenue, when he was compelled, by a sudden outburst of the elements in pumping down more water than he could contend with in the flabby condition of his umbrella, to take shelter in a doorway that was sunk deeply into a wall of brick, which was grimly garnished by the wear of years.

He had let down the umbrella, and was scanning it, with perhaps some vagrant thoughts as to its former user; of the fine quality of the material, and of the "E. J." engraved on the gold handle; when the door at his back opened noiselessly, and was closed just as noiselessly, and quickly. A young man stepped to his side with a rain shade of his own in his hands. He was of medium height, dressed fairly well in a hand-me-down, and sported a flaming red necktie. His face was neither handsome, nor ugly, but there was in it signs of recent dissipation.

"A beastly morning," he remarked, as he began turning up his collar and buttoning up his coat.

"A very bad morning," answered John, not with the view of striking up a conversation, but simply to be civil to a stranger.

"Couldn't be worse in h—!" said the stranger, as if talking to himself.

"No; I suppose there is not much water falling in that region," said John, looking up at the cork-screws of water twisting their way down, and breaking into pieces on the hard pavement.

"I reckon not," responded the stranger, for the first time turning his dull gray eyes upon John. As John made no further response, the stranger continued: "What are you doing in here? Looking for a place like this, eh?"

"I merely stopped to await a moderation of the rain," answered John, innocently, knowing nothing of the character of the place into which the door led.

"Then you are not looking for a joint like this?" said the stranger, eyeing John.

"What kind of a place is it?" asked John.

"Don't you know?"

"Have not the least idea."

"You must be from the country?"

"Not very long since I came from that indefinite place."

"Come around some evening and ask for Mike Barton, and you'll find out," said the stranger, in a whisper, sizing John up as a likely victim for such an institution.

"I never go to a place unless I know of its character first," returned John.

"Huh, you don't! I pity such greenhorns as you," flippantly retorted the stranger.

"You scamp!" exclaimed John, hotly, and his dark blue eyes snapped with anger, as the insolent chappy cringed beneath him. "Don't leer at me, or I will wipe up the streets with you."

"Now, my dear sir," replied the stranger, seeing his mistaken opinion of the man he had met; "don't get angry; I feel a little blue this morning."

"You should be more courteous, young man, whatever the time, or place, or your state of mind," answered John.

"I'll heed your advice hereafter," said the stranger, with a sarcastic smile. "But take the number and come around sometime, when I'll make amends for this insult, if you choose still to take it as such."

"Oh, never mind about that; but what did you say your name was?"

"Mike Barton. Your name?"

"John Winthrope."

"Do you work?" asked Mike.

"I do."

"Where?"

"At Jarney & Lowman's."

"Jarney & Lowman! Jarney! Jarney! Hah! Well, good morning," saying this rapidly, Mike Barton stepped to the wet pavement, hugged the walls as he went along, and disappeared directly.

John Winthrope then resorted to a cheap restaurant. After eating a hearty breakfast of bacon and eggs and coffee, he, having plenty of time yet to spare, mozied out into the elemental downpour, and sauntered to his office. He arrived there just in time to see the doors flung open to let in an army of clerical men and women for the day. His shoes being damp, he exchanged them for a pair of slippers, a supply of which aided in cumbering up a rubbish room in the building. In selecting a pair, through the scramble with the others, he was unfortunate enough to get a size too small. Thus he was caused no little pain in his big toes during the rest of the day, which detracted his attention a great deal from his work.

It was a busy day in the office of Jarney & Lowman, by reason of the approaching end of the fiscal month; and he was therefore kept busy, sparing not a moment from his accounting for casual conversation with his associates, or for anything for that matter.

In about the middle of the afternoon, while John was very industriously setting down, and adding up, and balancing and counter balancing books in his department, Miram Monroe, a thin, sleek, middle-aged gentleman, with the polish of a Chesterfield about him, came up to him as silently as a mouse steals up to a trap, and tapped him on the shoulder.

Now, Mr. Monroe was the general manager of the office, and went about his duties in such a sly unsentimental manner that no one could ever unravel his motives when he approached an individual of the staff. There was never any change in his expression, nor in the hump of his shoulders, nor in his step, nor in his actions whenever he took upon himself his bestowed privilege of approaching a subordinate, either to inspect his work, or to tell him gently that his services were not wanted longer. He was always the same in handing out his authority. He never laughed. He never smiled. He never winked. He never talked, except in a low voice, and then in an unrhythmic monotone.

So, knowing the peculiar character of this gentleman, John had a severe shock of surprise when he turned at the tap on his shoulder and beheld the light brown eyes of Mr. Monroe shedding their unintelligible lustre on him.

"Mr. Winthrope," said Monroe, so smoothly, so gently, so mildly, so blandly, that John felt a faintness steal all over him, "will you have the kindness to step into the private office of Mr. Jarney?"

Ho! John had never been in that office before. What did it all mean? Was the head of the firm to dismiss him? For what? It was, indeed, a very deep mystery to John.

John obeyed the summons, and followed his conductor through many rooms, with a fear possessing him all the while that he was to be summarily dealt with for some unaccountable transaction with which he had been charged. He was ushered to the inner sanctum of the head of the firm. He saw Hiram Jarney sitting in a deep mahogany chair before a big mahogany roll-top desk that stood in the center of one side of the room. On the floor he saw a green Turkish rug, and on the green-tinted walls he saw, displayed appropriately and proportionately about, steel engravings of Washington, Lincoln, Garfield, McKinley and Roosevelt, the latter being directly above Mr. Jarney's desk, from which high position that bespectacled president and mighty nimrod continually looked down upon him, as if he were the chief's main idol of modern strenuousness.

John halted a moment, on seeing all these things, stepped lightly, with his pinching slippers causing him to wince, into the deep velvet, as if he were treading on a field of the most delicate violets. He took in the room at a glance. He had never seen the head of the firm but once before. This was the first time he had come face to face with the great captain of industry. Although he was uncertain of the wishes of Mr. Jarney to have him in his presence, he did not quail at advancing to be presented; but he trembled unnecessarily over the fear that he might be discharged, and thrown out of a position, for what, as he thought, as the affair of the night before.

"Mr. Jarney, this is Mr. Winthrope," said Monroe, almost in a whisper, and he turned and left the room, going as quickly as a fleeing ghost.

"Glad to meet you, Mr. Winthrope," said Mr. Jarney, rising and presenting a warm hand. Mr. Jarney shook the extended hand of John's with such vigor that John came near losing his tight-fitting slippers and his balance in the pulling force of Mr. Jarney's grip.

"I am glad to know you," returned John, recovering his surprise over Mr. Jarney's graciousness.

"Sit down," said Mr. Jarney, releasing John's hand, and motioning him to a deep mahogany chair by his desk. John sat down.

Without removing his eyes from John, Mr. Jarney drew a box of cigars out of the depths of his desk, and, opening it, extended it toward him.

"Have a smoke?" he said, pleasantly.

"Thank you; I do not smoke," answered John, confusedly.

"Good!" exclaimed Mr. Jarney, as he flapped the lid on the box. As he laid it away he still kept his eyes on his visitor.

John was so uncomfortable in the big chair, and the slippers were pinching him so unmercifully, that he was very miserable. When he leaned backward, he seemed to have fallen to the floor on his back; when he sat up straight, his back pained him; when he leaned forward, he felt awkward.

"Young man," said Mr. Jarney, easily, lighting a cigar, and still keeping his keen eyes on John, "this is an unusual procedure on my part, you will no doubt think."

"I don't know," gasped John.

"Well," continued Mr. Jarney, "I have summoned you here for a quiet chat."

John wondered what this great man could find in him to talk about.

"Yes, I want to talk with you," he continued. "You are a good young man, I understand. How old are you?"

"Twenty-two."

"Hah! twenty-two; the proper age. Where is your home?"

"In the city, at present."

"I mean, where were you raised?"

"In the mountains of Fayette county."

"Hah! just so. Another point in your favor. Now, then, do you have any money?"

"None; only what I earn here."

"How much is that?"

"Fifteen per week."

"Hah! what do you do with your money above your keep?"

"Send it to my parents."

"Hah! another point in your favor. With whom do you associate?"

"Have not been in the city long enough to acquire intimate associates."

"Hah! four good points in your favor. What is the extent of your education?"

"I attended the common schools of my district, then learned bookkeeping and stenography at a business college."

"Hah! five good points in your favor. That is enough. Would you like to be my private secretary?"

John was calm under the ordeal of this examination into his character and habits and ability, answering the questions as deliberately as if he were before a court-witness examiner. But when the last question was put to him he became unduly nervous, as is so often true of young men of sterling worth and latent capabilities. The question came so unexpectedly and from such an unexpected source that he could not, at first, clearly comprehend its meaning; nor could he frame an appropriate answer on such a momentous proposition. While he was ambitious and desirous of rising to an eminence in the world of business that would place him where he thought he deserved, he, at the same time, knew his failings, if any he had worth mentioning.

"Mr. Jarney," said John, finally, after studying for a few moments; "this has been unsought on my part, and is a great surprise. If I deserve such a promotion, so soon after coming into your service, I assure you I am thankful, and shall endeavor to make good."

"I take it, then, that you have accepted?" said Mr. Jarney.

"I have."

"Mr. Winthrope, your duties will be to look after my private affairs. You will have your office in the adjoining room. You are to be under no one's orders but my own. Your salary will be increased to twenty-five per week, and if you prove satisfactory, after a fair trial, which I believe you will, you will be compensated according as I value your services. Be at your desk at ten a. m. tomorrow. Now you may go."

John arose; Mr. Jarney arose. They stood a moment looking at each other. Mr. Jarney then laid his hand upon John's shoulder, and said:

"Mr. Winthrope, I believe you will make good."

"I will be faithful to any trust imposed in me," returned John.

Together they walked across the room. Mr. Jarney opened the door, as he said, "Good bye." John stepped out. The door closed behind him. John stopped a few seconds before that blasted flower, Monroe, who gazed at him without the least intimation of what was going on in his apparently inactive brain. John gazed at Monroe as if he meant to inquire the reason for his unimaginative stare, for he thought he wanted to ask a question. John stood waiting for it to issue forth from his thin lips; but, as none came, he went out through the labyrinth of offices, and to his desk, where he resumed his pen and figuring as if nothing in the world had come up to alter his preconceived routine of existence—except the pinching slippers, which he soon discarded.

At the quitting hour, Monroe, as empty as ever in his stare, came to him and whispered:

"He has told me of your promotion."

"Yes," answered John, without looking up.

"Your desk will be ready at ten."

"Yes, I have been instructed."

"Yes," returned Monroe; and he walked away, with the same mouse-like tread he always assumed among the main office force.

That evening, in his dingy little room, John meditated a long time over this extraordinary turn in his wheel of fate. He could attribute it to no other cause than the incident of the night before. What other reason had Mr. Jarney for selecting him, he thought, for this important post, when there were above him in the office men with more experience, more capabilities, more knowledge of the world of business than he? Could it be, he thought, that Mr. Jarney was repaying him for his gentlemanly actions toward his daughter? Could it be? Mr. Jarney gave no reason for his promotion, nor intimation as to why he favored him above so many others who had been in his service so much the longer time. John never thought that such men as Mr. Jarney give no reason for their actions, except, perhaps, on graver questions.

If it was not for that affair, then what was it? But why should Mr. Jarney favor him for that? He had given Edith Jarney a great amount of compound consideration. He thought of their chance meeting from the viewpoint of one, who, knowing fully his lowly station, could not, by any unheard of reasoning, ever hope to meet her on friendly or intimate terms. He might chance upon her, of course, sometime, somewhere; but that was, while possible, hardly likely—unless it should be in her father's office. But recalling that he had never seen her there, nor ever heard her name spoken in the office no more than if she did not exist, he was still less inclined to a faint hope. Such young ladies were not the topic of confabulating remarks among the employes of such great fathers as hers.

Still, with all his meditating, deliberating, weighing this and balancing that, he could not get her out of his bucolic head. Ah, he thought, he would fill a new position on the morrow! Perhaps she would come to her father's office, sometime; not an improbable thing for Edith to do. Then, in that event, he could only hope to bow to her as she should switch her way in or out past him, with a toss of her dignified head; or a contemptuous look out of her bright blue eyes; or, more like it, to give him a blank stare for his presumptuous ogling.

Would Edith Jarney do this? Dear Edith, it is hoped that John has a wrong impression of you.

So, after thinking on all these things, John could, in nowise, bring himself to believe, or ever to expect that he would receive any recognition from Edith. Therefore, with such extraneous ideas excluded from his thoughts, he concluded that day-dreams were useless; and with all the assumed wisdom that was stored up in his soul, he deliberately cast her aside as beyond his attainment.

CHAPTER VIII
PETER DIEMAN RECEIVES VISITORS

Peter Dieman, since he had reached his present state of affluence and influence, did not condescend to wait on customers. He was now above that menial branch of his trade. He seldom went into his store, as a clerk; but he went occasionally to settle some dispute, of one kind or another, that Eli Jerey was continually involved in with some one of the many people, who, for one reason or another, visited The Die.

Eli, in this period of his trammeled existence, was a combative sort of an individual—not through a natural disposition in that direction, but mainly by force of circumstances. Being a creature who was impelled by any line of action by the urgent necessity of earning his bread and butter, he became a willing tool in the hands of Peter for the furtherance of that man's business, or any other of the transactions with which he might be connected. Eli, therefore, was a good servant more through a sense of duty, than through any reason he would bring to bear in applying himself. He might be classed with one of those trusties who is purblind to any one else's good, save that of his employer. Hence, he loved Peter, not for any attraction that the personality of the man had for him, but simply for the job that he filled.

Peter Dieman had that way about him that causes men of any rank, almost, to bow down to force and power and money. While he was revolting in his general aspect, as a man socially, he was certainly a genius when it came to manipulating the "ropes" that so often lead men and women into combinations against society's welfare. Even in the building up of an established business in the marts of other men, he exhibited a wonderful gift of sagacity in organization, and in a knack of accumulating wealth, so far as his endeavors went in the one particular line that to the world at large he was supposed to follow.

One day Peter was sitting at his place of espial, intently concerned for the time with the one predominating thought as to whether his spider-like clerk, Eli Jerey, could accommodate all the customers he saw in waiting, before any of them could get away without leaving a few shekels behind. As he looked, he rubbed his hands nervously, whimsically, naturally, as was his habit; then he squinted up one of his piggish eyes, and scowled menacingly. The reason for this contorting facial expression and revolutionary exhibition with his hands was that he noted his clerk suddenly throw up his left arm to a guarding position, rear backward, clinch his fists, look daggers out of his cat-like eyes, and then lunge forward, with the force of a battering ram going into execution. He also saw two other long arms whirling through the air like a Dutch wind-wheel in motion, saw a head duck, saw the bodies of two men writhe and squirm, and then saw them fall together on a bundle of dirty coiled-up ropes. Seeing all which, he put down his pipe, put on his black cap, and waddled out with the intensity of the furies spread over the wide expanse of his red and rounded visage.

"Wow!" he roared like an exploding blunderbuss. "What in God Almighty's name be you doing, Eli?"

Eli did not look up to respond to the query. He could not look up had he wanted to. The stranger, with whom Eli was in combat, had him gripped so tightly around the neck with one arm, that Eli could neither hurt his antagonist, nor get hurt himself. All that Eli could do was to breathe heavily, strike out at random with his one free hand, hitting the ropes, the floor, a bench leg, and many other things about him. Meanwhile the stranger seemed to lie contentedly on his back surveying the upper regions of the interior of the junkery.

When Peter came up to the combatants, he stopped, with his hands upon his hips, and his arms akimbo, sized up the situation in an instant, and then seized Eli by the scruff of the neck, and raised him to the floor, with his victim still clinging to him in a very loving-like embrace, and with Eli still beating the air at random with his free hand.

"Loosen yourself, brute!" squealed Peter to the stranger. "Loosen yourself, I say!" he shouted.

But the stranger paid no heed to him. Whereupon, Peter, using his fat hands as an entering wedge, heaved away with mighty force, to left and to right, and the twain came asunder. The stranger now stood back, with tousled head and frightful mien, glaring savagely at Eli; while Eli looked the same in the matter of dishevelment, his scanty face showed little more of the baser passions than would a paving stone.

"You rascals! What's all this about?" demanded Peter, directing his eyes on Eli.

"Nothing," piped Eli.

Then turning to the stranger, who was a young man, Peter said, stentoriously: "Clear out at once!"

The stranger took up his fallen hat, turned malevolently upon Peter, and hissed: "All right, you hog! You will pay dear for such an insult!" He turned toward Eli. "You scoundrel," he shouted, "your master keeps you here to insult people—" but he did not finish the sentence, so wroth was he in his anger.

Peter rubbed his hands so rapidly that it would be a wild guess to say whether he was doing it in jest or in earnest. The stranger proceeded toward the front door.

"Wait!" exclaimed Peter, as the stranger was about to make his exit.

The young man turned about, very deliberately, in his tracks, leered at Peter as if he would again hurl a terrible threat at him, but he said nothing.

"Mike Barton," commanded Peter, for that is whom the young man proved to be, "come to my office."

Whereupon, Peter led the way, and Mike Barton followed him to the little black office. Peter removed his cap, resumed his pipe, and sat down, wheezing like an asthmatic pup, near his place of espionage; and he looked curiously at Mike, who had taken a seat unbidden.

"What was the trouble, Mike?" he asked.

"I simply sought to pass him to get to your office, when he confronted me with the insulting remark, 'No pimps allowed in there—your office—without permission of the boss.'"

"He's a good clerk, Mike; he is; and he serves me well."

"Too well, Mr. Dieman, for your safety."

"Ha, ha! Well, he has my instructions, and you know the password to this office."

"I do, sir; but I resent the insult."

"All right, my boy, it's over with now; Eli is a good one for me, you know."

"I reckon he is," returned Mike.

"Now, what can I do for you?" asked Peter, eyeing Mike with one of his singularly inquisitorial stares, which gave Mike a spell of the fidgets.

"I was sent here by the keeper of our place to know the outlook for a continuance of police protection," he replied without any circumlocution about saying what he had in mind.

"Eh!" Peter ejaculated.

"Yes; we want to know—or they want to know. What's the prospects?"

"Eh?"

"What's the prospects? is my question," said Mike, surlily, put out by the evasiveness of Peter.

"Hey?"

"You have my question."

"I have."

"Then answer me."

"How much more is it worth?"

"You and your gang are getting enough already," retorted Mike.

"Don't get gay, young man; don't get gay," said Peter, raising his furzy eyebrows with surprise. "You people are in business—I'm in business—we're all in business—for money."

"Yes, Peter, yes; all in business—all in business—a nasty thing it is, sir, this grafting business," returned Mike. "But my employers are getting tired of having their legs pulled so often. All the profits already go to your bunch—how can they pay any more?"

"Eh, young man, you are talking a little too gay—a little too gay, for one of your experience; hey?"

"Well, it's the truth," answered Mike.

"What have I to do with that? Yes, I, sir; I? Answer me that question?" asked Peter, with a little more animation than he had previously shown in the conversation.

"A whole d— lot!" exclaimed Mike.

"Don't! don't! don't! boy! Don't cause me to throw you out!" roared Peter, now looking out his peephole.

"I am not a bit afraid of you—no more than I am of that door knob," answered Mike, haughtily.

"Maybe not, Mike; but you fellows must be reasonable," said Peter, less uproariously than before.

"So must you fellows," remarked Mike, placidly, as he indolently shifted one leg over the other and bent forward.

Peter pursued his quest no further for a few moments, being interested in Eli in the outer room. He drummed with his fingers on one arm of the chair, then rubbed his fat hands together. Peter then turned to Mike, as Mike said:

"I want to know, Mr. Dieman, what your gang intends doing?"

"One thousand more per month," was Peter's reply.

"That means two thousand for our house, does it?"

"If I figure right, it does."

"Then, you can go—to—h—!" returned Mike, rising to depart.

"Five hundred will do this time," said Peter, now feeling inclined to be decent in such a deal.

"Go to—" responded Mike, looking back at Peter over his shoulder, as he turned to go out the door.

"Set down, boy, and be respectable," said Peter in a mollifying tone. "Anything new, Mike?"

"Nothing unusual, only I hear that my sister left home today for a finer home in the East End."

"Did sh-e-e?" asked Peter, with a comical leer out of his right eye, which he turned upon Mike, as if the information was of vast importance to him.

"She did," answered Mike.

"Good for her!" said Peter, musingly. "When did you learn this?"

"This afternoon, when I was home for the first time since I got my new job, over three months now," replied Mike, looking down at the floor. "I meant to take her out of that place myself to a finer one, where life is worth while; but she eluded me—if that is the right word, eh."

"Did you intend taking her to the place where you work?" asked Peter.

"I did."

"I have always had such a notion of you in my head," said Peter, squinting at Mike.

"You had? How did you know?" shouted Mike.

"Guessed as much," said Peter, rubbing and looking Mike squarely in the face.

"You old reprobate!" exclaimed Mike, hotly.

"Be careful, boy; be careful. I am no fool," admonished Peter, unruffled as yet, in outward signs. "What other news?"

"I understand my sister's at Hiram Jarney's home," said Mike.

"Yes," responded Peter.

"A strange coincidence," mused Mike. "I met a young man named Winthrope this morning, who works in Jarney's office."

"Good or bad subject?" asked Peter.

"Bad—I judge from his answers."

"That's good," said Peter, rubbing his hands vigorously.

"I don't understand," said Mike.

"You don't?" quizzed Peter, drawling out the words sluringly.

"No, d— if I do!"

"Well, then go about your miserable business and quit bothering me," commanded Peter.

"You haven't answered me yet about police protection," said Mike.

"Oh, go away; they'll not bother you," replied Peter, impatiently, shaking his head as if he were shaking the words out of his mouth.

"Have I your word for it?" demanded Mike.

"That's all I have to say. Go!" snorted the now exasperated Peter, resuming his habitual work of spying.

Mike retreated, like a man who is cornered by a bear in his den, going out at the opportune time. Passing through the store he beheld Eli looking as dumbly as a lamppost at him. Mike skinned his eyes, as it were, lest Eli should pounce upon him again, and complete the operation of a sound threshing. But Mike got safely to the outer door, and was about to go out, when he turned and hurled back at Eli, shaking his fist:

"I'll fix you, you hireling!"

Eli, becoming riled at the threatening taunt, made a rush for Mike, like a terrier after a scampering cat; but Mike soon disappeared around a corner, leaving Eli standing in the door shaking his fist at the vanishing figure, who did not cease running till he got two or three blocks away, so fearful was he of Eli.

As Eli turned to re-enter the shop, he ran counter to a man—a tall, slouchy fellow with a stubby moustache, short hair, red nose, round face, brown eyes, white complexioned—who had entered unobserved, while Eli was sending his sworn enemy threateningly away. The man sallied lazily through the alleys of junk, paying no heed whatever to the ubiquitous clerk, who was dogging his heels at every turn for an opportunity to inquire about his wants. Several times Eli was sure the man was about to stop and make reply to his questions; but in this he was sorely disappointed. For the man proceeded till he came to the door of Peter's cubby-hole, and was in the act of entering it, when, to his astonishment, he found Eli wraithing up before him in the doorway. The man hesitated for an instant, gave Eli a contemptuous smile, then, with a quick sweep of his strong arm, thrust him aside, as if he were only a part of The Die's junk that had got into his way. Eli, of course, was taken off his feet, both figuratively and literally, and went sprawling in a heap in a corner, on a pile of rubbish.

"Come in!" shouted Peter to the man, with no thought as to what harm might have befallen the dutiful Eli, who, on catching his master's voice as meaning an intimate acquaintanceship with the man, gathered himself together, and took up his burdens still feeling unsquelched as a faithful servant.

"Well, Jim," said Peter to the man, when he seated himself, "how's things going these days?"

"Well enough," answered Jim Dalls.

"Ford & Ford got the contract?" said Peter, without a semblance of his gladness over the matter in his own face.

"Yes; they got it; but hell'll be to pay some day for that dirty piece of work," answered Jim Dalls, moodily.

"That's a hard old place to satisfy," remarked Peter.

"Can't be worse than the grafters of this old city," returned Dalls.

"Don't be pessimistic, Jim."

"Don't like to be; but, I say, there'll be a reckoning up some day, I suppose, when the people once wake up, and find out what is going on in this old town."

"Ah, the people; the dear people," answered Peter; "they don't know enough to eat mud pies."

"Why, haven't they been fed on them a long time, eh, Peter? Their stomachs will revolt at the mess sometime, Peter; then, look out!"

"Have no fear, Jim; have no fear; they'll never catch us," replied Peter, with confidence in his secureness behind the throne of graft.

"But, nevertheless, it is rotten business, Peter; rotten business, and I am tired of playing the game," said Dalls.

"Oh, I'm not; I'll play it till I die," returned Peter, with a bravado air.

"You can afford to, Peter; it's been a gold mine to you and your backers. But to me? Look at me! Nothing is all I get—nothing but a pittance."

"You are paid well, Jim," said Peter, severely.

"Paid well; yes; but it takes it all to keep those below me in line."

"Well, what more do you want, Jim?"

"Nothing—I'm quitting the business."

"Ho! you are? You can't quit, Jim; you can't. If you do, what'll become of the ring?" asked Peter, now for the first time bringing his reasoning faculties into play in connection with such a probable event.

"Bust, I suppose," replied Dalls.

"Never!" exclaimed Peter.

"I am going to quit, I tell you, Peter."

"How much do you want to go away from here?" asked Peter, rubbing and squinting.

"Ten thousand," replied Jim Dalls, slowly.

"You are cheap," said Peter. "Come around tomorrow, when I will pay you and furnish a ticket for you to Europe."

"Agreed, Peter! Shake! I always knew you'd be on the square with me. But put it down in writing," returned Dalls, with less gloom pictured in his face than when he entered.

"I never put anything down in writing, Jim; particularly such things as we have been discussing. I consider my word good, Jim," answered Peter, palaveringly.

"I'll take you at your word, then, Peter."

"Very well; you have been a good lieutenant, Jim, and we don't like to lose you. But if you have scruples on the matter, Jim, I want you to leave—get out of the country, and stay out till I call you back. Jim, do you understand?"

"Just so I get the cash, I'll go anywhere, Peter," answered Jim Dalls.

"That will do, then, Jim; come tomorrow at two," said Peter.

"You have a mighty obnoxious clerk out here," said Dalls, rising to go away.

"Oh, he's all right, Jim; you know the password, and didn't give it," replied Peter.

"That's my fault, then," answered Dalls, as he stepped into the shop, there to encounter the angry look of Eli, who was at that moment waiting on a customer, or otherwise there might have been another little affray, on the spot.

Jim Dalls, as he was familiarly known among Peter's henchmen, had been a member of the present political ring since its inception back in the early nineties. He had now but a poor chance of ever rising higher in the ranks than a poorly paid lieutenant; and so what was the use, he argued with himself, of playing third fiddle any longer, if there was any likelihood at all of getting out with a good round sum in cash. So, as a bluff, he preferred to work the "conscientious scruple" scheme to get what he thought was due him for his valiant services in the corporals' guard of the gang; and he went to Peter playing that he wanted to lead a new life, and his bluff worked out better than he ever anticipated.

It was very necessary, in the workings of this mysterious institution, that whenever an officer felt conscience stricken to remove him, with great dispatch, from the scene of operation, so as to keep out the light of investigation when house-cleaning time should come, which it would sometime. Jim Dalls had been bred in the business and knew its entire ramifications in every branch of civic affairs of the city. He had not prospered in it, as some others had, considering the length of his services and the good that he had done, and the care he had taken in fighting for success. He had not been raised to the sublime degree in the ranks of the upper luminaries, where marched the fitted, to which others had been raised, considering the amount of service he had put into the cause. He had not been treated as equitably in the division of the spoils that had come into the coffers of the charmed circle of grafters, as others had been treated, considering the sum of his own earnings he had put into the hands of his own satellites shining around him, as those above him shone around the great center of this gigantic solar system. In consequence, the monster, Disaffection, lurked within his breast, and became a thing for the master minds to watch with care. Yes, watch with care, and hold in check.

Of course, Jim Dalls was no squealer. No—if he got his price. And now, getting his price, he would leave the city. He would leave his country; and go to Europe, and live like an American Captain of Industry lives in that land when his native soil becomes sterile in its bountifulness of pleasure. Yes, he would go to Europe at the behest of his superiors, so that he could not, for a time, tamper with any of their marked cards, and cause a breaking up in their game.

And to Europe he would go, with his trusting wife and family believing that he had earned his lucre honestly; and they proudly looked every one in the face, believing that the world is on the square.

Oh Europe! Europe! If you only knew the private history of many of those Americans you receive with open arms, craft and graft and greed you would see as their only virtues.

But, ho! Let us smile, instead of crying at their follies. For no nation ever yet raised a monument to men representing such principles.

CHAPTER IX
A THANKSGIVING PARTY

In Oakland avenue there stands another mansion. It is a lofty pile of brownish stone, and is luxuriously complete in its every detail. Standing as it does on a prominent hill, it comes in for a great share of excellent praise for its beauty and magnificence, and is classed as a close rival of that other mansion in Highland avenue.

Here lived, when in the effulgence of his power and influence in the complicated machinery of a big city, one Jacob Cobb—a short, squatty, round-faced, blue-eyed, clear-complexioned man of business, so far as anybody knew about his worldly affairs. Here his wife Betty, and daughters, Susanna and Marjorie, entertained the eclat of society according to the à la mode of fashion; and many were the gay parties, balls and dinners that they gave for the select few constituting their circle of acquaintances.

Charming, indeed, were these great affairs, unrivaled in all their appointments in the high-toned residential district in this unequaled city of social madness and financial debauchery. Oh, yes; charming they were, indeed, to those select of the very select who pandered to Mammon in the workaday hours and to Bacchus in the time of refreshment.

Aye, aye; here came the proud, the haughty, the vapid, the insipid; the hilarious strumpets of swelldom, the strutting monstrosities of fashion, the pompous parrots of mimicry; the glib scandal-mongers, the gregarious loiterers over afternoon teas; the straight-laced of the kid-gloved gentry, the snobs, the prudes, the fops; the blase young men, the genteel puppets, the vacuous gentlemen, the bombasts, the old curmudgeons; the doting mothers, the innocent maidens; with now and then a sprinkling of the good, the sage, the savant, as a savory condiment to the mess of social pottage the Cobbs dished out of their pot of ethics.

These events were wonderful achievements in the life of Mrs. Cobb, and Mr. Cobb paid the bills without a murmur or complaint.

Mrs. Cobb was sumptuously independent in the conduct of these affairs. All the glories of the Queen of Henry of Navarre could not equal her glorious accomplishments in the one great and only ambition of her life—shining in society. Mr. Cobb was bumptuously indifferent as to how his wife shone, just so she shone, and that in her shining she did not obfuscate him altogether.

Mrs. Cobb was chunky, like her husband. She was the quintessence of charm. She was the substantive mood of the present tense of the verb to be. She was gay, humorous, and a true leader—in her line of activity. She was near the middle time of life, but she had lost little of her beauty. Her dark brown eyes snapped like sparks of fire, and her cheeks glowed pink when she was enjoying the company around her; when in a different mood, she ever had the fine quality of knowing how to be pleasant when most bored.

Mrs. Cobb's afternoons were of course mild affairs, but still very grand to all those idle ladies who deemed it a distinctive honor to receive an invitation, and a compliment to their refinement to be there. Accomplishment and refinement! O, fudge!

Mrs. Cobb must celebrate Thanksgiving day. She and her husband must offer up their oblation, in their own unhampered fashion, to the gracious Lord who had blessed them with so much to be thankful for. And they did celebrate.

It was to be an unsurpassed dinner at seven, a violation of the rule of etiquette for such state affairs; but as dancing was to follow, the order of formality was modified, so that the exhilarating whirl could thereby be prolonged. She, therefore, sent out the exact number of fifty invitations, equally distributed among ladies and gentlemen. The dinner was served in the great dining room, dazzling with its silver, gold, glass and polished wood, with carnations and roses burdening the air with their mesmeric fragrance.

Promptly at the hour of seven, Mr. Cobb, with Mrs. Cobb on his arm, struck out through the maze of palms and smilax and other greenery, for the feasting board. Arriving at the table, with her husband, she delivered him at the head, and she took a seat on his right hand (all contrary to form, but she was original, if anything), with her favorite bachelor friend, Miram Monroe, on Mr. Cobb's left, as a cold balancing weight to old man Cobb's ebulliting spirits. Next to Mr. Monroe sat Miss Edith Jarney. Jasper Cobb sat opposite Miss Jarney, and by his side was Miss Star Barton; and so on down the long table sat the other sublunaries of the Cleopatra of fashion, the number not stopping till a second long table was filled with similarly handsomely gowned ladies, and gloomily groomed gentlemen, with the Cobb girls sitting among them in peek-a-boo fluffiness.

"Mr. Monroe," said Mrs. Cobb, after having made some trifling remarks to some of the other guests, showing her white teeth with the vivaciousness of a young girl, "you appear not to be enjoying yourself tonight."

"Oh, yes, Mrs. Cobb," he replied, with a board-like stiffness, "I am delighted."

"Mrs. Cobb," interjected her husband, beaming one of his sly winks at her, "you should not tease Mr. Monroe tonight. Just behold the fair young lady he has by his side!"

"Mr. Cobb, you are so jolly tonight," she answered. "Mr. Monroe did not salute me when he arrived this evening, so I am in ill-humor with him."

"Beg your pardon, Mrs. Cobb," said the ghostly Monroe. "The fact is I had no opportunity. Sure, madam, I would not slight you for the world, did you give me the opportunity."

"Mr. Monroe," said Mrs. Cobb, in her best humor, "you must get rid of your rigidity of expression, or I will be compelled to get another man, younger than you, to take your place. I am now almost tempted to put my son in your place; Jasper, you know."

"I will not hear to that, Mrs. Cobb," interrupted Edith. "Why, I shall attempt to enliven Mr. Monroe." Then to that sedate imbecile, she said: "Mr. Monroe, cheer up. See, every gentleman present but you is in the fullness of his grandiose verboseness tonight. Cheer up, and be alive for once!"

Mr. Monroe turned a lethargic smile upon Edith, and whispered, loud enough for his near auditors to hear: "Miss Jarney will do me the pleasure, I am sure, of reaching me the salt."

"Why, with pleasure—salt—salt," said Edith, with a gay and mischievous laugh. "This man—waiter, waiter—wants some salt to salt down his opinion of women's rights."

"Good, good!" applauded Mrs. Cobb. "Now, what are your opinions of women's rights, Mr. Monroe?"

"I am salting them down," he replied, sadly, as he began to spray most liberally his salad, which looked, before he ceased, as if it would be in a brine of thick salineness. "My opinion of women is—aside from my mother—that they are a lot of soap bubbles."

"You bad man," said Mrs. Cobb, lowering her eyebrows; "that is no definition. Women's rights—what is your opinion?"

"They haven't any rights, save what the men choose to give them," he whispered looking at Edith, with as much expression as a monkey.

"You bleak old bachelor," retorted Mrs. Cobb. "Edith will never have you for saying that."

Edith turned a wrathful glance upon Mrs. Cobb, and gave a scornful laugh at the jest. Then she turned to Mr. Monroe, who had ceased in his rapid-fire eating long enough to look at her like a plaster cast might look.

"Miss Edith," said Jasper Cobb, who had been earnestly engaged with Miss Barton, paying her the closest attention with his palavering nonsense, "I am jealous of Mr. Monroe."

"Indeed," returned Edith.

"I am, indeed," he answered, and the impropriety of his remark struck Edith's ear discordantly.

"What a great teaser you are, Jasper," said Mrs. Cobb.

"A chip of the old block," said Mr. Cobb, smiling at his joke, as he took it to be.

"Jasper does not mean a word of it," said Mrs. Cobb, at the same time hoping that he did.

"With due consideration for my friend, Mr. Monroe," said Edith, "I will turn my attention to him."

Then Edith summoned up all her latent substitutes for naturalness, and bore down upon Mr. Monroe with such a load of banter and mirthful sayings that that gentleman eventually smiled, to the surprise of everybody. Then it became alarmingly noticeable that Mr. Monroe was paying close attention to Edith's highly interesting but entirely assumed form of gabbling—so much so, in fact, that it was feared by Mrs. Cobb once that he was on the point of taking Edith in his unloving embrace, and running away with her. But Mrs. Cobb saved him from this duncely possibility by saying:

"Be careful, Mr. Monroe, or you will do something desperate directly!"

Mr. Monroe quickly recovered himself and became a living sphynx again.

"Hah, Miss Edith," said Jasper Cobb, catching the trend of things Edithward, "now, I am jealous."

Miss Edith turned to him, with pretended hautiness, and should liked to have said, "Impudence," but forbore that unlady-like expression in deference to her own good breeding. She was relieved, however, from making any answer to him by Mr. Cobb, who arose at that critical moment and announced, most graciously and grandiloquently, that the table would be cleared of the women and menu to make way for cigars and wine.

All of which orders being carried into execution, as per custom, the waiters proceeded to serve those two refreshing desserts. They sat long over their cigars, and longer over their wine—till the air was an ultramarine blueness, and the men in tipsy joyousness.

Mr. Monroe was very thirsty, it turned out, from the number of glasses that he drained, which had an happy effect upon him. For, with the disappearance of the wine down his esophagus, came a set grin on his face, akin to the smile of a disgruntled ghost. Young Cobb, aside from smoking enormously, imbibed freely, much against his personal appearance and qualifications to enter much farther into the pleasures of the evening. All the other gentlemen, including old man Cobb, entered into the libations with rare partiality—except Mr. Jarney, who, it was seen, refrained from participating in the dispatching of the invigorating liquor, a constitutional habit with him. This trait was looked upon by his now inebriating friends as a high breach of etiquette in not sipping wine after breaking bread at the home of a friend, and was an affront not to be condoned on such an occasion. But Mr. Jarney, while not approving of such bacchanalian practices, as far as he and his family were concerned, looked askance at them, so long as they were confined to others, and he made no protest.

After the free lubrication of their unsettled nerves and muddled heads, the men arose to join the ladies, who in the meantime had dressed for the ball, now to follow.

When all was in readiness and the band had struck up a softly insinuating waltz, Mr. and Mrs. Cobb wheeled out on the floor and glided around the room with the agility of two sixteen-year-olds. Mr. and Mrs. Jarney came after them, stately and graceful in their evolutions. Then came the ghost—Monroe—looking like a piece of burning asbestos, as a result of the wine, with his arm around the waist of Miss Edith. Then came young Cobb, whispering words of foolishness into the ear of Miss Barton, as they went round and round in a delirious whirl—to him. Then came all the other ladies and gentlemen, the latter suffering wondrously in the advanced stage of booziness. No, we will not cast all the shame upon the men in their journey of giddiness, for some of the bewitching woman, ah, and even unbewitching, too, presumed it their blessed privilege to partake of a little of the tonic of joy, as an equalizer to the wabbling motions of their husbands or friends.

Number after number, in this wise, was pulled off, each time the bibbers adding more and more wine as a wash down after each exhausting exhibition. So in consequence, after awhile, man after man began to fall by the wayside, and call feebly upon the good Samaritan: Bromo-seltzer, or bromo-something else: to keep them in condition to continue the mad seance. But the little imp Wine, once he secrets himself in the corpuscles of the blood, is a pretty difficult being to placate in so short a time. Not satisfied was he in laying hold of the faultless gentlemen in spike-tailed coats and immaculate bosoms, sparkling with all the iridescence of the purchasing power of money, but he sought out some of the decolleted dames and gauzyed damsels, and enveloped them in his opiatic arms. Even Mr. and Mrs. Cobb were not spared from his envelopment; for, after the fourth set, they became so maudlin in their hilarity that the sober servants were called upon to lead them out of the ballroom, from which they went, in a great state of regal debility, into the seclusion of their own bedchamber, there to sleep away their Thanksgiving potation.

And it was not long till every corner in the house had a sleeper languishing in the happy shades of somnolence. Mr. Monroe, the astute ghost of quietness, after cavorting for a considerable time like a nanny goat in a field of crimson clover, was among the first to succumb to the silencing influence of the giver of potency, and disappeared, like a settling stone, into a whirlpool of revelry. And young Jasper Cobb, the gay and handsome son of the Thanksgiving father and mother, after cutting capers that would put to ignominious flight a colored gen'man at a cake walk, gave up the contest at last and became numbered among the recumbent forms that rested, like so many babes in the woods, along the walls.

You are not supposed to believe that the Jarneys witnessed all these antics of the merry makers at this party, to which a half column space in the society page of the Sunday newspapers was devoted. No, you are not to believe they remained, retaining all their senses, to witness this pyretic debauch of high society. The truth is, that the Jarneys came as a matter of form in deference to Mr. Cobb, one of the high-ups in business; and they left in deference to their conscience and self-respect. The fact is, that after the second number was rendered, Mr. and Mrs. Jarney, seeing how things were going, and also at the solicitation of Miss Edith, took their ward, Star Barton, and repaired to their home.

"Well, how do you like high society?" asked Edith, when she and Star had reached their boudoir for a short lounging before going to bed.

"If that party is a fair sample, I don't like it," emphatically answered Star. "Why, it is no more respectable, if half as much, with all their fine things and glitter, than some of the hoe-downs in Hell's Half Acre."

"I am very sorry we attended," said Edith.

"I am not," returned Star. "It has been a great lesson to me."

"Would you go again?" asked Edith.

"I shall always be guided by you, dear Edith."

"Then you will have no further opportunity to attend a function of that kind, for that is the last for me," said Edith; "especially with that class of people. Papa and mamma care nothing for such doings; neither do I; but owing to business connections, we are obliged to lend our presence, sometimes. Formality! Star; formality!"

"Is it one of the requirements of business?" asked Star, innocently.

"It is a deplorable truth," answered Edith.

"I am glad, dear Edith, you are not wrapped up, heart and soul, with such people," said Star.

"It is my pleasure to be independent, Star."

"And I shall follow your example, dear Edith," returned Star, with unbounden confidence in her friend.

"Say, Star," said Edith, as she seated herself on an ottoman at the feet of Star, and taking one of Star's hands in hers, "I have a trip planned for you; will you go?"

"If it is your wish, I will," answered Star.

"Star," and Edith looked up into her friend's face, blushing the least bit, "you remember the young man of whom I was telling you about meeting by chance? Yes. He is now my father's private secretary."

"Oh, is he?" asked Star, by rote.

"Yes; and by my request, too. I will take you to my father's office tomorrow, and, if he is there, you shall share his acquaintance with me."

"I shall be glad to meet him—if he is your friend," said Star.

"He is my friend, Star—no, not yet—but I want him to be, Star," and Edith buried her head in Star's lap to hide her tell-tale face. Then raising her head, in a moment, "Will you go? Of course you will."

"If you permit me to talk with him," said Star, teasingly, "I will go."

"Who would think of being jealous of you, my dear Star? Why should I? He is no more—yes, he is—" and Edith buried her face again, while Star stroked her long silken tresses in loving admiration.

"Ho, ho, Edith! I know," said Star, pointing a finger of jest at her, as she raised her face.

"Do you guess my secret, Star?"

"Why, dear girl, I cannot help but know it."

"And you will keep it, Star?"

"To my dying day. Does he know it?"

"Oh, no, no; I have seen him only once. Do you think it right in me, Star?"

"I don't know, Edith. How will you ever make it known to him?"

"Oh, Star! I do not wish to; I do not wish to! He must find it out for himself. I know he is such a fine young man; for my father even praises him."

"He may never know it, Edith," said Star, not yet knowing herself the secrets of love, as old as she was; albeit, she possessed a true sense of the great mystery of life; "and then what?"

"I can only live in hope that he will, some day, see and know. Do you think it wrong in me, Star, to say these things?"

"If it is from your heart, no."

"Let me kiss you, Star? There!"

Love comes to a pure woman veiled in mystery, and departs only when her spirit returns unto God who gave it. Were they all as pure as Edith, the temptations of our modern Edens would be as holy as the waters of Siloam's Pool.

CHAPTER X
JOHN WINTHROPE'S SECOND PROMOTION

John Winthrope had a small cozy room by himself off the main office of Hiram Jarney. It was about the size of a twelve by sixteen rug, and so richly furnished that when he got into it, he felt as if he had been clandestinely concealed in a bandbox lined with rare and costly velvets.

There were a green rugget on the floor, a miniature roll-top desk in one corner, glistening in its polish; a typewriting desk near a wide plate glass window; a cabinet for letter stationery; three leather-seated mahogany chairs, one at each desk, and another for company. The walls were green tinted, and around them John had hung some landscape pictures in chromo, mostly rural scenes; photographs of his parents; one of a mountain girl, his sister; one of a big young man, his brother; and those of two boyhood friends.

Every morning at nine o'clock John came into this palatial private office. First, he perused the morning newspapers, then looked over the bundle of private letters that came to the head of the firm, and assorted them according to the postmark, or the nature he judged of the contents as near as he could make out from outside indications; after which he placed them in a letter tray, got ready his note book, and placed them all together orderly, to be picked up, at the ring of the bell, to be carried to the desk of Mr. Jarney, who arrived at the office, when in the city, every day punctually at ten.

John learned rapidly. A week had not gone by, after he assumed his new post, till he was master of every detail of a secretary's work in such an important place. He was quick in taking down the dictation of Mr. Jarney, who was a rapid talker, a clear enunciator, never lacking for the exact word to lucidly express himself. John was speedy on the typewriter; hence he was but a brief time in conveying, what would appear to the average person, the unintelligible phonetic characters into Englishized words, sentences, paragraphs, and finally completed letters, ready for the chirography of that great man to be attached thereto. Many letters of little importance, such as from the beggars, cranks, politicians, boodlers, or of the routine kind, John was soon authorized to answer himself, to the relief of the chief.

For a whole week John had been at this pleasureable labor, doing it with far greater ease than he had the more arduous task of keeping books; and he did it with such dispatch that Mr. Jarney was surprised at his adeptness, and he favored him with due commendation.

For several days Mr. Jarney was taciturn in the presence of his new secretary. He talked with him purely on matters in hand after the dictating period was over, and then but briefly. Not once for nearly a week did he condescend to converse with him on any other question—except that occasionally he would remark about the continuing "beastly weather," as he invariably termed such climatic conditions.

John went through the daily routine earnestly and methodically, with no thought for anything but that he might make good, and prove himself worthy of his hire; and also thinking very often of his good old parents, his dear little sister and big strong brother on the farm in the hills. He had dismissed Edith Jarney from his mind, as a lost cause goes before the reasoning man. He had not seen her, nor heard of her, since that memorable night. He was not presumptuous enough to imagine that she would contaminate her thoughts about him. For why should he be so imaginative? He had no reason for believing that such a conventional lady, as she appeared to be (basing his opinion of her on her station), would ever think of the affair one moment after she was gone out of his sight, or was ensconced in her own palatial home, where the shadow of such as he was not likely of ever being cast.

Still, in his idle moments, he would revert to the event, and simply wonder what had become of her: whether she had gone to some sunnier clime to bask in the smiles and receive the addresses of richer bloods than his; or whether she was not then leading a gay existence among her class in the gilded halls of her surroundings, where flash and gleam the lads and maidens of her own selected set in the brighter light that luxury provides.

But such musings were on rare occasions, and then only reverted to as a pleasing pastime in his lonesome hours. For, since assuming his new duties, he not only was serving his own master, but was serving himself by reading, studying, and working out the mysteries that surrounded the privacy of Mr. Jarney's business. He did this so that, if the time ever came, he should be fitted to perform further duties in the advancing line. However, no matter how busy he was, there were times when homesickness would steal over him, and he would long for his own people and their humble fireside to soften his distraught feelings, whenever they should assert themselves.

Be these things as they may, two weeks, almost, had passed by since he went into his bandbox office, when Edith Jarney, accompanied by Star Barton, came to see her father.

The time was in the middle of the afternoon. Mr. Jarney was sitting at his desk dictating a third and last batch of letters, and John was sitting by diligently taking notes. Edith opened the office door of her own accord, and she and Star walked within unannounced. Edith was dressed in dark colors in harmony with the weather. She carried a sealskin muff, and had a boa of the same fur around her neck, and the cutest round hat possible sat upon her head. Verily, she looked like a princess out on winter parade as she advanced toward a broad, flat-top table in the center of the room. Star, dressed much in the same fashion, and looking as stately as any lady at court, followed Edith.

Both young ladies sat down at the table to await Mr. Jarney's convenience to greet them. John was sitting with his back to them, and so silent was their tread that he did not hear them enter. His pen flew from left to right on the pages of his note book as Mr. Jarney talked in his low monotonous voice, without inflection to his words, or change in his countenance. Mr. Jarney saw the young ladies enter, but, through a habit of his of never being disturbed when in the throes of grinding out letters, the young ladies' coming did not bother him in the least.

Edith and Star sat quietly, abiding their time to speak. Edith tapped the polished top of the table with her gloved hand. Star sat meditating, with her eyes bent upon the young man. Thus they sat for ten minutes or more, watching master and servant at the fountain head of industrial achievement.

Then, without a word to John, Mr. Jarney arose; and, coming forward, grasped his daughter by the hand and kissed her on the lips. Turning to Star, he accorded her the same fatherly greeting.

John arose as Mr. Jarney arose, and was folding his note book as he was taking a step to make his exit. In that moment, when Mr. Jarney was saluting Edith, he looked toward her. Recognizing the young lady, he hesitated for a second, flushed, faltered, hesitated again, for he had not known they were present. As Mr. Jarney turned to Star to greet her, Miss Edith turned to John. Her face flushed also. She stood a moment, with that light of recognition in her eyes, that gives a peculiarly sensational effect upon the beholder, sometimes. He was uncertain. She was uncertain. He made a step forward to continue toward his office, when Edith smiled, came up to him, and extended her hand.

"Mr. Winthrope, I believe?" she said.

John was in the act of bowing when he saw her extended hand, and foregoing a completion of that act of politeness, he extended his hand to meet Edith's. John looked very grave. He had needs to look grave, if the beating of his heart indicated a particle of his feelings at that moment.

Edith continued smiling as only she could smile. Then John pulled himself together sufficiently in his embarrassment and said:

"Miss Jarney, if I am not mistaken?"

"You are not mistaken, Mr. Winthrope," she said. "I am very glad to meet you again; but under more pleasant circumstances than when we last met."

"The pleasure is not all yours, Miss Jarney," he replied, releasing her hand.

"How are you?" she asked, still smiling.

"Fine, thank you," he answered.

"I want you to meet my dear friend, Miss Barton," she said to him, and then turning to Star: "Miss Barton, my friend, Mr. Winthrope."

Star advanced, and made a low bow in return to that of John's. Mr. Jarney stood off a few steps taking in the formal introductions and salaams of his daughter and her friend with his new secretary, at the same time looking as unbending in his demeanor as a cast iron pillar, from all outward appearances; but really relishing, with a glad heart, the simplicity of his beautiful daughter in her cordiality toward Mr. Winthrope.

"Star—Miss Barton, this is the young man of whom I was speaking." Then, looking at him, with a quizzical air, as if she wanted to be patronizingly humble, said, directing her words at Star: "He is the young man, Star, who rescued my hat and gave me his own umbrella."

"That was a gallant act," said Star, smiling genially upon him. "I have heard nothing but praise of you for the past two weeks."

Edith thereat blushed more crimson than ever before in all her innocent career; and sought to turn the subject by saying: "Oh, Star—it is spitting snow," looking out the window as she said it.

John's face turned a pinky color also, and he began to have qualms of consternation in being detained from a prompt execution of his work at hand.

Star immediately saw she had made a blunder, and tried to make amends by continuing: "I told Miss Edith that I should be happy to meet such a gallant young man, as she says you are."

Edith was now more flushed. She burned with confusion and despair over Star's untimely statement of facts.

"If you ladies will excuse me, I will resume my work," said John, to avoid further complications between Edith's expressive face and Star's expressive words.

"We will excuse you, Mr. Winthrope—business before pleasure, always," said Edith.

"I am glad to meet you—to have met you—and hope to see you again, Miss Barton," said John, bowing to Star; and then, bowing to Edith, he departed.

In the meantime, Mr. Jarney had taken his seat at his desk in a highly flustered state of mind by reason of his daughter's sudden change of countenance over the unintentional reflect assertion of Star's. When John had closed the door of his office behind him, and the two ladies were alone with Mr. Jarney, the latter turned about in his chair, as if in a passion of rage, and said:

"My dear Edith, what is the meaning of your actions?"

"Why, papa, dear," she answered, "it is only my way of showing my appreciation of his former kindness."

"My little chit," he returned, as she put one arm around his neck, "you exhibited more than simple appreciation in your looks, when you greeted Mr. Winthrope."

"Now, do not scold me, dear papa; if you do, I will cry," said Edith, fumbling for a handkerchief somewhere about her garments, with which to stay the flow of tears already glistening in her eyes.

"Ha, ha, Edith," replied her father; "I am not chiding you; I know my little girl would do nothing unbecoming."

"Papa, is it unbecoming to be civil to a young man like him?" she asked.

"Not in the least, my child; he is a fine young man—" and Edith hugged her father more closely—"and—ah, Edith, you make me wonder, sometimes, at your way of looking at other young men of our class."

"None of them is as good as he, I know," she said, with such sincerity, and so pensively, that her father was really disturbed.

"I know he is a good young man; but, Edith, it would be very naughty for you to encourage him," he said advisedly.

"Then, you do not like him, papa? I know you do not. Wish I had never requested you to advance him to this place, then—then—I would not have seen him again."

"Why, Edith, my child! what are you saying? If you persist in your talking that way, it will be necessary for me to dismiss him at once, and have no more of this benefactor business on my hands," replied her father, sternly; at the same time winking at Star, belying the asperity of his voice.

"Now, papa, you do not mean that," she responded, patting him on the head. "I know you too well, you bad dear papa. If I thought you did, it would make me feel very cross toward you. There—now—papa—do not—say—any more." She concluded the last phrase with kisses between the words.

"My dear, we will drop the matter," he said. "I mean to keep him, Edith; for I like him; really I do. Miss Barton what is your opinion?"

"The same as Edith's," she answered.

Edith turned quickly and looked at Star, a mobile stiffness clouding her face, not knowing how to take Star's words.

"Ha, ha, ha," laughed her father; "you are an extraordinary girl, Miss Barton—as extraordinary as Edith."

"Thank you," returned Star, bowing to him. "I have reasons to feel extraordinary since two weeks ago."

Father, daughter and ward whiled away the time for an hour in such kind of interchange of colloquy. Then John returned, with his tray full of letters, and set it down on Mr. Jarney's desk.

"Mr. Winthrope," said Mr. Jarney, looking up, with a deceiving frown, which caused John to have queer sensations go through him at first; "Mr. Winthrope, I am going to—I am tired of signing letters, and shall delegate that power to you. So sit down here at my desk, and put your 'John Hancock' on these, using my name, of course, instead of your own. You may do this while Miss Barton and I take a little turn down the street. Edith, I will leave you here to see that Mr. Winthrope does not shirk his work."

John was amazed; Edith was astounded; Star was astonished. Mr. Jarney repaired to the cloak room, from whence he returned in a few minutes wearing a high silk hat and heavy overcoat, and carrying a gold-headed cane.

"Miss Barton, will you accompany me?" he said to Star, after his preparation, taking it for granted that she would not refuse.

When they went out, Edith seated herself in the chair where John sat when he took down her father's dictations. John sat in her father's chair at the desk, looking so near overwhelmed at the turn of things, since morning, that he felt like sinking through the floor, or going straight up to the ceiling and out through the roof to some other country. As Mr. Jarney and Miss Barton went out the door, John turned and looked at Edith. He blushed; she blushed.

"This is certainly an unusual situation," said John.

"It more equals our encounter that night," she replied.

"But under pleasanter circumstances," he returned.

"If we had that old umbrella of mine, how realistic we might make it," she said, giving a little laugh, and sinking back into the depths of the cushioned chair, folding her gloved hands as though perfectly at ease, although showing some timidity of expression in her conversation.

"I have it yet," he said, as he took up a pen loaded with ink, as if it were his intention to commence signing the letters but looking at Edith shyly.

"Yet?" she raised her eyebrows.

"I put it away among my other keepsakes," he answered, turning now as if he really did intend to execute his "John Hancock" on the letters.

"What for?" asked Edith, tapping a finger on the arm of her chair.

"Oh, as a hobby; I always try to keep something to remember any unusual happening in my life," said he, forgetting to sign the name of "Hiram Jarney."

"Do you know what I did with yours?" she asked, folding her arms.

"Consigned it to the garbage heap, I suppose," he replied, letting the ink fall off his pen to the spoilment of a letter.

"You are not a good guesser," she replied, her blue eyes sparkling. "It came near going there—but I have 'J. W.' as an ornament in my boudoir."

"I imagine it would be out of harmony with the rest of the decorations," he said, dropping more ink, and still neglecting to sign the name.

"It harmonizes with my sentiments on certain matters," she said.

"For instance?" He looked at her.

"Class distinction."

"What does mine signify?" attempting to sign, but only getting down the capital H.

"You," she looked to the floor.

"And yours?" Now interested.

"Me." Still looking down.

"Then, we should exchange them," he said wonderingly.

"That would not be to my liking," as she looked up.

"Not?" he asked, turning from his paper and pen.

"No," she said, demurly.

"Ah, Miss Jarney," he said, with despair indicated in his voice, "I have presumed, at times, to wish to be better acquainted with you, since that night; but I have thought it useless."

"Mr. Winthrope, nothing would give me more happiness than to be on good terms with you."

"But I see no possibility of that, except—I believe we ought to be on good terms—that is, friends."

"So do I."

"May I hope—no, I must not—may I hope to see you here again, sometime?" he asked seriously.

"I used to come here often."

"I never saw you here before."

"No—I did not like the last secretary."

"Then you will come again?"

"I anticipate that I shall."

"Then we may become better acquainted?" dropping his pen.

"If you wish it, Mr. Winthrope," she answered, looking at her hands lying on the arms of the chair, then up to John, who was taking up his pen again to reach for a new dip of ink.

At that moment the door opened and Mr. Jarney and Miss Barton entered. He carried his hat and cane in one hand, and arrived at his desk in time to see John completing the signing of his name to the first letter of the pile before him.

"Mr. Winthrope," he said, "you have been remiss in your duties. Edith, I am afraid you would make a poor overseer in this office."

John, thereupon, fell to work with a will to expedite the signing of the letters that had been so woefully neglected during his entertaining tete-a-tete with Edith.

Edith and Miss Barton prepared to take their departure. Both were standing before Mr. Jarney in low conversation, when John turned around, as a new thought came to him, and said, to Miss Barton:

"Miss Barton, do you have a brother?"

"I have several brothers, Mr. Winthrope," she replied; "but one of them disappeared months ago."

"What was his given name?"

"Michael."

"Meeting you today. Miss Barton, reminds me that I met a young man about two weeks ago who gave the name of Mike Barton."

Then John related to her the incident of meeting her brother, and of the words that had passed between them, without making it clear to the young ladies, however, that the nature of the business that he followed was of the most questionable.

"Poor brother! that must be Michael," said Star, when John had concluded his story. "Wish I could see him; I know I could prevail on him going home."

"Would you help us find him?" asked Edith, directing her question to John.

"It would give me pleasure to aid you," replied John.

"How interesting a company we three can make in this undertaking," cried Edith, with enthusiasm. "Papa, will you permit me to join them?"

"If Mr. Winthrope is your guide, you may," he answered, now interested himself.

"When shall we begin our search?" asked Edith, eagerly looking at John, and beaming one of her sweetest smiles on him.

"Whenever Mr. Jarney gives me leave of absence—or, better, I can do it before or after hours. How will that do?"

"Capital!" cried Edith. "Papa, that will be fine. You can trust me with Mr. Winthrope?"

"Oh, of course," he answered.

"Good, papa, dear!" she exclaimed. "Now, Star—Miss Barton, we will go home. When shall we begin?"

"When I notify you," replied John, rising to bid the ladies good day.

The two young ladies departed. To John, it was like the going of two sunbeams that had crossed his lonely pathway, to shine for a moment, then disappear, with the promise of returning on a fairer day to come.

CHAPTER XI
THE AUTOMOBILE ACCIDENT

Mike Barton, the rounder, knocked off from his lecherous avocation the afternoon referred to in the previous chapter, as was his custom every day at that time, and wandered aimlessly through the throngs of pedestrians in the main thoroughfares of the city. He was submerged in an elegant overcoat of black that shut him up from head to foot, so that only his feet stuck out below, and his head half protruded above; for the day was in its nastiest mood. A new derby hat sat cocked to one side of his head, and his hair was in imitation of the devotees of the game of football.

With his hands poked deeply into his side coat pockets, he shambled along, smoking a cigarette, that, at times, sent up a cloud, like a halo of fog, around his head. He was careless, unconcerned, and impudently independent in his gait. He pushed his way through the crowds with such an abandon of gentility that the curious stared at him, and gave a shrug of their shoulders, as much as to say, "There goes a bad one." He would stop at times, when a crowd had formed to gaze at some new attraction in a window; then, with a toss of his head, would push on, maybe shouldering a meek little woman out of the way; or sidling up to an unsophisticated girl with a licentious stare, or a suggestive smile; or he would drop into a saloon, or billiard hall, or tobacco stand to see his fellow touts; and then go on, ever aimless in his peregrinations.

After lighting a fresh cigarette, he took up a position on the steps at the main entrance to the Park building; looking into the faces of the passers-by, or doing nothing but kill time; when his attention was arrested by a tall, sleek gentleman in a plug hat and heavy overcoat, and who was slinging a gold-headed cane, crossing Smithfleld street, with a lady on his arm.

"By the Gods!" he exclaimed, so loudly that those standing by gazed at him in wonderment. The cause of his exclamation was the lady and gentleman in question, crossing the street.

The tall gentleman was talking animatedly, and the lady was smiling and laughing in return, as if what he said gave her great merriment. As they passed the corner, going down Fifth, Mike stepped to the pavement, and followed. He kept a few paces in the rear, but always in sight of the swiftly moving pair.

The plug hat loomed above the heads of other people, and the lady was conspicuous by her elegant costume. As they walked on, he followed, ever in view of the high hat. They turned up Wood, he followed. They crossed Wood and went down Sixth street, he followed. They came to Liberty and went down Sixth avenue, he followed. They went out on the Federal street bridge, he followed. They stopped at the center span, he stopped. They looked down the river, he took up a position behind an iron girder of the bridge, and peeped around at them.

The wind was blowing briskly, skudding snow-like clouds across the sky, and white caps danced upon the river. Smoke from factory chimney, or train, or boat, lay in horizontal rolls of grayish blackness, like tubular pillars floating in the air on the breast of the wind. They looked down the Alleghany, facing the pelting breezes—through the maze of craft; through the uplifted arms of many bridges, rearing themselves like spider-lines criss-crossing the vista of the river; through the distance over black buildings, sheds and shanties, and everything, they looked, over and above to the bald bluffs of Washington Heights, where clung the homes of the middle class, like crows' nests in aerie oaks. Then down beneath that hill of rock, staggering under its weight of poverty, they looked—she seeing, as if in a vision, the depressing hovels of the very poor; and a tear came to her eyes. But Mr. Jarney did not see those tears. He was intent only in passing away a short space of time with Star, as a gratifying diversion in his daily course of life.

The wind brushed by her skirts with great vehemence, and blew her hair about her face in straggling strands of plaits. She placed one elbow upon the iron railing, and rested her chin in her hand, and looked down at the dancing water. Her mild blue eyes were still moistened, and she wondered how deep and cold the water below her was, and what there was beneath its surface. Her lips were blue from the chaffing wind, her teeth chattered from the chill, and her cheeks paled before the scurrying blasts.

"I wonder if there is life down there in that dirty yellow water," she said, meditatively.

"There used to be many fish in there, at least there was when I was a boy," he answered, leaning over the railing and looking downward; "but the defilement of the water by the mills and mines has killed every bit of life, almost."

"Nothing escapes the hand of men, it seems, in their search for wealth," she mused.

"Nothing—you have been crying," he said, turning his eyes upon her.

"No; it is the wind," she answered.

"Ah, the wind; it is raw today," he returned. "Let us turn our backs and go to the other side of the bridge."

They crossed the bridge; and looked northward—through the interminable spans of other bridges; through the blue fog and smoke that rose in the distance like vapor from smouldering pits of peat, suffering their eyes to wander over the serrated house-tops that filled Alleghany City as a checker-board filled with "men." He directed her attention, by his raised and extended cane, to some prominent objects that stood out bolder in the landscape than any of the rest.

And of all their movements, Mike Barton was a stealthy observer from his place of espionage. He recognized his sister when first he set eyes on her. He was inclined to approach her as she stood with Mr. Jarney on the bridge, and make himself known, and take the consequences of the possible result of meeting such a gentleman under such dubious circumstances. But the longer he stood observing them in their quiet contemplation of the scene, the more disinclined he was in attempting to carry out his scheme.

Mike Barton knew very well where his sister had gone when she left home. He knew the home that she lived in; but in his vaccillation he could not formulate a plan that he could operate tending to its fulfillment, in reaching her. Therefore, he concluded to wait his time to meet her alone. This was the first time that he had seen her since she had entered upon her new life, or in months for that matter. Ah, my dastardly brother, with all your vile thoughts and debased notions, thy chaste sister is beyond your unholy machinations! He was not deterred, however, by pity, or brotherly love, or homely feelings from pursuing his purpose.

After the panorama had been viewed from the bridge to Star's complete satisfaction and joy, Mr. Jarney, after taking out his watch to note the time of day, turned, with Star on his arm, and began retracing his steps. Mike followed doggedly, surreptitiously, going into stores, into hotel lobbies—out again into the streets, always at a safe distance, that his actions would not be noticed by those being followed.

Finally, the trail and the quarry ended at the entrance of the Frick building. Here Mike took up his post, after Mr. Jarney and Miss Barton had gone within. There he stood buried deeply in his collar, still smoking the delectable cigarette (to him), with as much energy and enjoyment as when he started out on his perambulatory quest for fresh air. The air being chilly, Mike crouched in a corner beneath the big arch of the doors to keep the chills from going up and down and through and through his snakish frame.

An enclosed auto, complete in all its appointments, stood closely hugging the curbstone, the chauffeur having taken refuge from the rawness in a nearby lounging place, where a little warmth was obtainable while he waited for his charges to be taken homeward.

Shortly, after Mike had taken up his position as a sentry might on more important and graver business, the great doors by him suddenly bursted open, and the two young ladies hurried out. They approached the auto together. Edith opened the door of the cab, and let Star within, she following. After being seated, they leaned back on the soft cushions of the enclosed conveyance to wait the coming of the chauffeur to take them at a giddy speed to the mansion on the hill.

Mike, from his sentry corner, watched their every movement. Twice, or thrice, he was tempted to approach them, and make himself known; but he was restrained by an inward impulse that told him, even in his vapid sense of reasoning, that he would be committing an egregious mistake, should he do so at that time and place.

The chauffeur did not come. The ladies sat quietly, happy, oblivious of their surroundings, quietly talking; with now and then a little laugh from each other as a climax to their joyous spirits. Still the chauffeur did not return; and still the ladies sat on, paying no heed as to whether the chauffeur was at his post, or off somewhere in China.

Suddenly the machine puffed, snorted, and sent up a fog of acrid fumes. Then a lever clicked over a rachet, then another; and the auto began puffing regularly, and moved slowly out into the street. It creeped and crawled among the wagons and carts and horses to Smithfield street. Up that crowded thoroughfare it went, weaving its way certainly, cautiously, deliberately, determinedly, till it was out of the congested district; and out where the streets were freer from the impedimenta of human contrivances. As the distance increased, the speed of the machine increased, accordingly; and they were directly whizzing onward at a lively whirring, gathering speed continually as the course lengthened into the thinly traversed streets.

Onward they flew—over crossings, past wagons in a flash; past street cars, autos, vehicles of all kinds and without number; past block after block, dingy and austre, shooting by like moving picture scenes; up hill and down, over smooth asphaltum, jolting over cobbles, over rubbish, over everything imaginable; fleeing, fleeing, with policemen shouting at the driver to cease his mad race, and noting down the number for haling him into court.

But on, ever on, they went, with silent tread, but wild whirring of the thing that gave it life; and still on, with a swerve and a turn, and a humming; past naked trees, tall gangling poles, beautiful residences, sere lawns, barns, stables, fences, open fields and now wooded places, they traveled, with meteoric speed; up steep hills, down; up, across, over—ever on, at the same hair-raising flight, throwing mud and water and gravel with a furious splashing.

At first, Edith and her companion supposed they were bounding homeward at the usual rate of progress in that direction when riding in the Jarney auto. But when Edith beheld new scenes—new objects, new places on the way, and finally a countryside in its wintery dress, she became necessarily alarmed; and she was still more alarmed when she saw that darkness was hovering over the land, and they not yet home. Star, being composed and guided mostly by Edith's actions, was not bothering herself, but when she saw Edith exhibiting intense anxiety, she, too, became alarmed.

Whereupon, Edith attempted to attract the attention of the chauffeur to the strangeness of the places they were passing; but he paid no more heed to her calling than if she were not inside; and he went on, ever faster, if possible. Edith opened the side door of the auto once, and put her head without, but owing to the swaying of the machine under the prodigiousness of its hurrying, she momentarily closed it again, fearing an accident.

In the flight, Edith and Star paid no attention to the identity of the man at the steering wheel, believing that he was their old faithful one, who had gone quite crazy, or had met with hail companions, and had imbibed too freely.

"Oh, oh, Star!" cried Edith; "if we do not stop that man there will be a terrible accident soon," and she tapped on the plate glass window in front of her.

"He must be crazy," suggested Star.

"Poor man, if I could only get at him, I would soon check the machine," said Edith as the car turned a corner, throwing her into the arms of Star, who caught her, in her fright, and pressed her to her breast. Edith was in a very agitated state of mind, for their situation, seemed to her, to be of the most precarious kind.

Star had already clasped Edith in her arms, but she wanted to hold her closer, if possible, to whisper consoling words. And as she was about to say a word of comfort, there was a sudden stoppage of the machine. They were thrown forward, and it turned on its side, buckling up like a crushed egg shell. All that Star remembered was a terrific crash, a grinding noise, and the breaking of glass—then darkness.

Edith rose up from the middle of the road, stunned, dazed, bewildered. She stood a moment beholding the wreckage; then, quickly surveying the scene, rushed to the ruined cab, from which she had been flung, and seized Star by the arm, and lifted her up and dragged her out. Star was unconscious. Edith administered a little dirty water, taken from a puddle in the road, to her face; and she soon recovered.

"Are you hurt?" asked Edith, kneeling by her side, as she lay by the roadside.

"Not much," she replied. "Only had my wits knocked out a little; I am all right now. Are you hurt?"

"Not much," answered Edith, as she brushed back the hair that had fallen over Star's face. Then Star arose.

"Where are we?" she asked.

"We seem to be in the country," replied Edith. "I see a house across the field aways. We must have help, Star, at once. I do not see the chauffeur; he must have disappeared."

Edith now released Star, seeing that she was not hurt, and began to brush her clothing to remove some of the be-spatterment that came as a result of her dropping so miraculously in the mire of the highway.

"The chauffeur may be under the car," said Star.

"Why, I do not see him; it is strange," said Edith, as she walked about the car, and looked beneath it. "Let us search the weeds by the fence."

Carrying out the suggestion, the two young ladies, now fully recovered, but much excited still, began to tramp among the dead herbage by the fence. Edith plunged in among the weeds and thistles and briars, with as much courage as she would have shown in hunting for some piece of finery in her boudoir, having no regard for the dispoilment of her fine clothes any more than if they were of linsey-woolsey. Star climbed the fence and was treading down the reedage of the field with an earnestness of purpose that became her character to act her part well in any employment.

"Here he is!" shouted Star, after trampling down a few square feet of bramble to get to a spot, where she thought she saw, while mounting the fence, a man's coat. "He is dead!" The man was lying on his face, and Star stood over him.

"Dead!" cried Edith, climbing the fence, and running toward Star, tearing her dress on the briars in her haste to join her friend.

"Dead!" she repeated, as she took Star by the arm. "Dead! Poor man!"

Both stood looking down upon him, wondering what next to do. Edith stooped down and turned him on his back.

"Oh, Edith! He is my poor brother!" wildly cried Star.

Edith arose, shocked by Star's sudden outburst, wondering what it all meant. Star knelt down by his side, and tenderly took up one of the dead man's hands in hers.

"He is dead! dead! dead! Poor brother!" she said sadly, with her tears falling over him. "We have found him alone, dear Edith, ourselves. God must have sent him on this wild ride to reach the pearly gates before his time. Poor brother! We did not know it was him. It is better that we did not know. Poor brother, he is dead!"

Edith bowed her head and wept in sympathy with the grief-stricken Star.

The hollow face of Michael Barton turned up to them, like a Death's Head, in the twilight. He was dead! And this loving sister never knew of the depravity of her fallen brother. It is probably well. For he must have his reckoning with his God.

CHAPTER XII
JOHN IS CALLED UPON AN EXTRAORDINARY MISSION

John Winthrope was sitting by his inelegant little table, and was reading, by the dim gas light, a new text book on modern business methods, and feeling perfectly contented and extremely happy over his prospects for the future, when there came three distinct and quickly repeated knocks at his door. The knocks were made apparently by a person impatient to gain admission. John dropped his book; ran to the door to ascertain the cause of the alarm, so significantly given, and threw it wide open. A messenger of the telephone company, standing in the hallway, handed him a message, and with it the additional information that he (the messenger) was to await an answer. Nervously John tore open the envelope, took out the contents, and read, with considerable trepidation, the following, dated eight p. m.:

"Come at once to my Highland avenue residence. Hiram Jarney."

Without taking time to think or meditate for a fractional part of a second over the call, John hastily wrote out the following: "Will be on hand as soon as possible," and gave it to the messenger, with the instruction to dispatch it immediately upon arrival at the office.

He then began grooming himself for the journey, so suddenly called upon to undertake. He could not conceive the urgent necessity of the summons, except in the light of his position as a servitor of Hiram Jarney, who, he thought, might have very important matters to look after that night. He pondered confusedly, while dressing, over what the business might be that required attention so promptly, and at that late hour of the day. He had never been called on such a mission before; nor had he been instructed that he would, at any time, be requested to go to Mr. Jarney's home on business.

As he always dressed neatly and looked very tidy while on duty in the office, he deemed it advisable, on such an occasion, to don his best Sunday suit; for he did not know but that some fortuitous event might occur to take him into the presence of the young ladies, who had that day made such an impression on him. So in less than a half hour he was prepared to start, and in fifteen minutes more, so speedily did the taxicab travel with him inside, he was pulling at the ring in the bull's nose at the Jarney front door. He had noticed, on ascending the high front steps leading to the great piazza of the mansion, that people were moving about in the interior as if everybody and everything was in commotion; and this puzzled him. No sooner had he given the alarm, however, than the door flew open, and he saw a brazen man standing like a statue before him. It was evident that he was expected, for the flunkey, after receiving his card, passed him in without ceremony, and without relieving him of his coat or hat.

He now saw, at a glance, that something out of the common had happened. The maids and waiters were rushing about excitedly, and Mr. Jarney was pacing the floor with nervous movements; and the little bouncing lady, all in pink, was ringing her hands and crying. On seeing John, Mr. Jarney rushed up to him, with the tension gone from his nerves, and grasped him by the hand, saying:

"Mr. Winthrope, I am glad you have come—something has happened my daughter and Miss Barton. They have not been seen since leaving the office this afternoon."

John gasped.

"What can I do to aid you, Mr. Jarney?" he asked. "I am glad to be of any service my help will avail."

"I do not know what has occurred to cause them to disappear so mysteriously," answered Mr. Jarney. "We must find them, if possible, this night."

"Have you notified the police?" asked John, believing, like many people, that these hawkashaws of the law readily knew how to solve any kind of a mystery.

"I have already informed the police—miserable service we have—some two hours ago, and no tidings have they found," he replied, as he again took up his nervous walk, leaving Mrs. Jarney to talk with John.

"No clue?" asked John.

"None whatever," said Mr. Jarney, turning again to him.

"It is strange," said John. "Where is the chauffeur?"

"Why, that rascal was off his seat, and a stranger is supposed to have driven the car away," replied Mr. Jarney. "Beg your pardon, Mr. Winthrope, in my distraction I have so far forgotten myself to fail to introduce you to Mrs. Jarney." This formality being then dispensed with, although John had already struck up a conversation with that lady, Mr. Jarney said. "Mr. Winthrope, I have called you here to lead a searching party for their recovery."

"Oh, Mr. Winthrope," wailed the little lady; "I hope you can find them this night."

Just then a maid came rushing in with the information that Mr. Jarney was expressly wanted at the telephone.

"It has been ringing all evening, and to no purpose," said Mr. Jarney, impatiently; "answer it."

The maid retreated; but in a moment she returned again with the further information that a lady was at the other end of the line, and wanted especially to see Mr. Jarney, as the maid put it.

Mr. Jarney begged John to accompany him to the phone room of his residence, and, when the former took down the receiver, he made the following replies to the voice at the other end:

"Hello! This is Mr. Jarney!"

"Yes; this is he."

"Talk louder?"

"Talk louder?"

"I can't hear yet!"

"Who is this?"

"Ed-d-Edith?"

"God bless us!"

"Where are you?"

"At Millvale? Good gracious!"

"What the deuce are you doing there?"

"You were!"

"You did?"

"Ah, she is safe?"

"He is dead! Who is dead?"

"Mike Barton?"

"Killed! Accident!"

"Farmer brought you to Millvale, eh?"

"Coming in on the street cars, did you say?"

"I'll send Mr. Winthrope in a taxicab for you."

"Yes, he is here."

"Yes; he came out to direct a search for you."

"Wouldn't know where to look for you?"

"Never could have found you?"

"You wait there till he arrives."

"Well; I thought you would be glad."

"Do with the body?"

"Leave it there, of course."

"Yes; he will come at once."

"Good bye!"

Putting up the receiver to disconnect the phone, Mr. Jarney called up the main office of the taxicab company, and ordered a cab post haste to his residence. Then turning to John, he said:

"It is very strange; very strange! Miss Barton's brother was killed in an accident with my machine! Very strange, indeed."

John took the answer to the voice at the other end of the phone to mean a peremptory command for him to go; still he thought his services were not now particularly needed to conduct the lost ones home. Mr. Jarney simply wanted him to go and act as their body guard on this momentous night. John would have been glad of the opportunity to thank him for the new trust imposed in him had Mr. Jarney asked him to go; but as he did not make a request for his services, but a command instead, he took it to mean that he was to comply implicitly, as any faithful servant would have complied.

When the taxicab arrived, and after John had been admonished repeatedly as to how to proceed, and loaded down with wraps and robes and other things, he made his exit and went upon his mission.

Arriving at Millvale without incident, but feeling very much concerned as to how he should conduct himself with his charges, he found Edith and Star both laboring under great mental and physical strain, as a consequence of their experiences, with Star at that moment the worse of the two, by reason of the tragic ending of her brother. Both young ladies were bedraggled. Their fine clothes were bespattered with mud and their shoes soaked with water. They trembled from the strain, and shook from the cold. But John could do nothing at that hour to give them relief, except to wrap them up in blankets and bundle them into the cab; which he did with much tenderness and courteous behavior toward each, slighting neither in any little attention that would tend to their immediate comfort. Then, after giving orders for the disposition of the body of Mike Barton, he seated himself within the cab, and they were directly speeding homeward.

On the way, Edith related to John, with many a break in her story, of all that had befallen them since leaving the office that afternoon.

"A very sad ending, indeed, for you, Miss Barton," said John, after Edith had concluded.

Star was not of an emotional nature, consequently she bore up under the ordeal with great fortitude. She felt very sad; naturally, very sad.

"It is a miracle that we both were not killed," said Edith. "The car was left a total wreck by the roadside. It struck a telegraph pole in making a turn, and Star was struck unconscious, while I was thrown to the road. Star's brother was thrown at least forty feet away, so terrific was his driving."

"What impelled him to such a trick, do you suppose?" asked John.

"I cannot fathom his motive," answered Edith. "Nor I," said Star. "Poor boy!"

"Perhaps he was unawares of whom you were," suggested John; "and was out for a lark to give some one a scare."

"Poor boy!" said Star. "I will forgive him."

"Oh—my—I am so dizzy!" suddenly exclaimed Edith. "I do not know whether it is this car or my head that is whirling round so. Oh, o—o!"

She was sliding forward on her seat, and her head was falling to one side. She sighed. "Oh—o—o!" she uttered. Sighed; then was quiet.

In the darkness of the cab John could not discern her movements plainly; but he knew, by her heavy breathing, that something was wrong with her. Star being in a very distressed condition herself, failed to understand or comprehend the suffering signs of Edith; so John, noting all these things, lent his personal attentions to Edith, who was just then in a mortal state of suspended animation.

John was very careful that he did not make himself promiscuous in either one's behalf, except when the most imminent danger was confronting them. By the reflected lights of the streets, as they were whirled along, John caught a glimpse of Edith, and was not slow to see that she was in need of care from some source. He therefore caught her by the arms, just as she was senselessly keeling over, and raised her to a sitting posture. As he lifted her up, her head fell to one side; but in a moment she roused herself and attempted to sit up straight. In another moment she lapsed unconscious, and limply declined into helplessness.

At first, John placed her head on the cushion in the corner of the cab. Seeing this position made her look uncomfortable, he then put an arm around her, and laid her head upon his shoulder. Thus they rode for a brief time. Then he lifted up one of her gloved hands. Finding it wet and cold, with Star's assistance he removed the gloves. After having chafed her hands, and rubbing them together to start up a circulation brisker than appeared to be natural, he drew his own heavy gloves over her quivering fingers. After which Star removed Edith's shoes and stockings, and rubbed her cold damp feet, and wrapped a blanket around them. Shortly her blood resumed a freer circulation, and she roused herself, faintly asking where she was.

"We are on our way to your home," answered John, removing his arm from around her.

He acted voluntarily in this matter, always having the fear upon him that what he might be then doing for her would appear to be impertinent. But she was growing more serious, and in spite of his desire to withdraw his arm from her support, he was compelled to hold her more firmly than before. She was now breathing heavily and her hot breath he could feel in his face as her head lay on his shoulder. She was like a child, and was beginning to mumble, and mutter inarticulate words, disconnected in their sequence, none of which could he form into intelligible sentences—except the two words, "Papa and mamma." Once he thought she was trying to say "Mr. Winthrope"; but he could not exactly tell. This troubled him some now, for his only thoughts toward her were of dutiful respect in this her hour of great trouble.

They arrived home at last, with Edith still in a comatose state, and breathing like one entering into the dreadful sickness of pneumonia. She was hot and feverish. Her hands twitched nervously. She was muttering incoherently, but not ravingly.

When the cab rolled up the driveway to the side entrance of the mansion, John lifted Edith up in his arms, and, bidding Miss Barton to collect their effects together and follow, went into the brilliantly lighted hall. He was about to hand her over to her parents, but, by their direction, he continued, silently, with the father and mother, maids and physician coming after him, to her own room, and there he laid her down upon her bed.

As he released her, he gave one longing look at her pretty white face; and trusted, in his heart of hearts, that her parents would tenderly care for her, and fetch her back to life and health. Then, bidding them a whispered adieu, he departed for his own simple abode, with some lingering regrets that he could not have stayed by her bedside and nursed her through her illness.

CHAPTER XIII
SECRET WORKINGS OF THE SYSTEM

Peter Dieman was happier than usual one morning, if he could ever be called happy by any possibility of reading such a state of feeling in his otherwise perverse and irascible countenance.

Happy! Well, Peter was never more happy in all his born days; but what the extent of that emotion might become in his after life was hard to predict at that time. Whenever he was in good humor, it was his never failing custom to puff at his pipe like a locomotive getting off a dead-center, and to rub his hands with less expenditure of energy, and to squint his eyes with less vigor, and to shut his mouth with less desire to keep it closed. In fact, on such rare occasions, it might be said of him that he was in his subconscious region of retroflection, one peculiarly of his own conception.

The cause of all his good humor was nothing more nor less than the refreshing information, imparted to him the day before by Jim Dalls, i. e., that Jim Dalls had decided to go to Europe. Ever since this enlightening piece of intelligence broke in upon the deepness of Peter's outward density of intellect, that gentleman was in a high fever of unemotional genuflexion. Why, mortal man! Peter sat in his chair all that night offering up his devotion to the Gods that They might be propitiated for Their timely intervention. And betimes eating cheese and crackers, and drinking beer, and surfeiting the air with the delicious fumes of his strong pipe. He was, as it were, riding on the back of Alborak into the Seventh Heaven of satisfaction.

Not only did he offer up devotion to his Deity, but to other people's Deity as well. Oh, ah, he would think often, but never utter; it being merely his manner of getting rid of superfluous enthusiasm. And his oh, ah's extended on through the night, mixed with cheese, crackers, beer and smoke, to the hour of nine o'clock in the forenoon, at which time he suddenly aroused himself to the position of the hands on the dial of the dollar-clock that hung above his desk, where he could always keep his eyes on its horological exactness.

Having noted the time, Eli, after having opened the shop without the least interference with his master's meditations, was summarily summoned into the august presence of Peter through the tintinnabulating medium of a large iron spike applied to a piece of sounding brass suspended by a string from the ceiling on the right hand of his chair. Eli came to attention, with the alertness of an orderly, before Peter, and waited to be commanded.

"Call up 206070-m and tell him to come to my office by 9:45 sharp," said Peter in a less tragic tone than he had been used to in hurling his commands at Eli.

"Yes, sir," said Eli, departing. Directly he returned, stood attention, and said: "He will be here."

"Ha! Good!" cried Peter. "Go to work, you lazy scamp." The last to Eli.

Peter sat still and mused on in the same barbarous manner, with only one change in the program of his devotions, and that was, that since 7:30 o'clock he had kept his face close to the peephole that gave him a view into his store, and upon Eli's performances.

With his sharp little eyes he saw the store, with all its junk and jumble; he saw poor imbecilic Eli skipping about with undying devotion in his heart; but his devotion was to serve his master, and serve him well he did. Verily, he saw everything within the store, almost; at least what he did not see, he knew of, as if his eyes were optical divining rods. And he saw also beyond the confines of the four walls that bound him about during his personifying period of the devil:—He saw his henchmen going here and there, like earth-worms, through the devious passages of the dark and dangerous undermining of the civic welfare; he saw the policemen on their beats, wielding their maces, as if he had as many hands as there were officers, and doing the execution thereof himself; he saw the aldermanic bodies sitting in grave deliberation on important or unimportant questions, knowing well himself what their action might be on anything out of the purely routine order; he saw the fawning sycophants, with their justifiable tale of complaint, being brushed aside by the higher hands; he saw the givers of tribute paying into the coffers of the system the doubloons of unwholesome preferment; he saw special privilege unsatisfied, always; he saw the needy come up with their last dollar out of the depths of their nefarious haunts and lay it at the feet of the King of Graft; he saw the glow-worms of society in a trail of phosphorescent splendor making the welkin ring with the hallelujahs of their perfections; he saw the merchant, the lawyer, the doctor, the craftsman, the civic officer, the banker, the broker, the justice, the bailiff, the warden—all he saw bending to the power of the system in all its ramifying debasement.

Aye, aye, he saw, too, the danger of it all to that system; to himself, to his friends, and to those who sat above him on the high throne erected to the debauchment of popular government, should Jim Dalls not be removed to some other ruler's domains. And Jim must go; and he must remain away; and all those of his present tendencies must go, and they, too, must remain away, if money was all that were needed to that end.

While Peter was reflecting on all these things, there came into view in the store, the short stalky form of a man past middle life. He walked with a business air in his every movement directly into the presence of Eli, to whom he gave the pass, which was 206070-m, and then continued through the alleyways of junk to the black hole in the rear occupied by Peter. Arriving at the door, he stepped inside, took off his hat, and sat down, sniffing with some annoyance at the foul atmosphere.

"Now, what is the game?" he asked Peter.

"I want ten thousand by ten o'clock," replied Peter, without any ceremonious introduction of the question.

"That's mighty short notice, I must say, Peter," replied the man.

"Fifteen minutes is time enough to rob any man or institution," answered Peter.

"The pull on our purse strings is very great at present," said the man.

"Cut the strings," retorted Peter.

"Cut them, you all say; but that won't preserve enough to pay the fiddlers," responded the man.

"Fiddlers be damned," roared Peter; "we must get Jim Dalls out of the country."

"Is he wanting to squeal?" asked the man, with upraised eyebrows.

"He is ready," answered Peter.

"Can't he be staved off by bluff?" asked the man.

"He's best in Europe."

"Is he going there?"

"He's going."

"When?" asked the man, bluntly.

"Get the money, and buy a ticket also."

"Why, Peter, it will take a little more time than you have given to complete the transaction."

"You may have till 10:30 to fix it up."

"I will return at that time with the amount," said the man, reflectively.

The man was rising to pass out, when the tall figure of Jim Dalls entered. The latter halted, and stood a moment gazing at Peter and the man, with a contemptuous smile breaking up his smooth features.

"Well, Jacob Cobb, you here?" he asked, with some asperity in his voice.

"Who else do you see, Jim Dalls, I would like to know, besides we three?" asked Jacob, for that is whom the man proved to be, and who was known to Peter only as 206070-m; and to his henchmen as the same.

"You fellows are not turning a trick on me?" asked Jim Dalls, with suspicion.

"We will be only too glad to get rid of you," answered Peter.

"And see you safely out of the country," joined Cobb.

"I think I should have more money," remarked Jim; "ten thousand won't last long in Europe, where you have to bribe every sonofagun who looks at you; it's worse than Pittsburgh."

"How much more?" asked Peter, in alarm.

"Twenty thousand ought to be sufficient," answered Jim.

"Bring three tickets, Cobb, reading from Pittsburgh to Paris, and twenty thousand," said Peter. "And that's the last sou I'll give you, you cur."

"Don't be too sure, Peter; I may ask for ten thousand more," said Jim, independently.

"You won't get it," barked Peter. "Get the tickets and the money, Cobb."

Jacob Cobb forthwith departed, going direct to a vault in one of the big banking institutions. Procuring the money, he purchased three tickets for Jim Jones and wife and daughter. Returning with the tickets in his pocket, and the money safely lodged in the depths of an immense sack, he hiked it, with expeditious tread, to The Die; and thereat turned the sack, with its valuable contents, over to the lamentable Eli for secret delivery.

In the office. Jacob Cobb confronted Jim Dalls with the three tickets, which that gentleman refused, at first, to accept without the accompanying "dough;" but being informed that that little feature of the transaction would be consummated through the faithful Eli, Jim returned to the store to be further set upon by more mysterious signs of secrecy as to the source of the money.

On entering the store, Jacob threw the sack, with all its preciousness, under a bundle of other similar sacks, and told Eli to offer it for sale to the man in the office, who would, in a moment, be along to make a purchase in that article of usefulness. So when Eli saw Jim Dalls approaching, not then being busy himself, he casually withdrew the sack, and laid it upon a table, and asked him if he did not want to purchase it. Only ten cents, he said, was asked for it. Didn't he want it in his line of business, whatever that might be? Jim caught the cue, of course, and paid the ten cents without protest. After obtaining it, he returned to the office.

"Good bye, Peter; good bye, Jacob," he said, extending his hand. "I'll be off this very day; but, remember, if I should run short in touring Europe, I expect more help from you two."

"You dog!" howled Peter.

"Ah! you may 'you dog' all you want to now; I have you where I want you. I will see that as long as you fellows play the game, I am properly cared for—so long, gentlemen."

With these parting remarks, Jim Dalls took his leave; and in another twenty-four hours had vanished from his beaten tracks in the city that knew him so well. A newspaper announcement said that he had gone to Europe for his health.

Alter Jim Dalls left that day, the implacable Peter turned upon Jacob Cobb and said:

"We must raise the levy."

"It's already reaching the high tide mark," said Jacob.

"We will let her reach it; then we will let her ebb, after this sum is raised," said Peter, rubbing his hands.

"But we may be drowned in the flow before it turns," answered Jacob, with emphasis on the may.

"Let her drown," replied Peter, resolutely.

"We'll go down in the wreck, if we get too reckless," said Jacob, fearfully.

"Who cares?" responded Peter, inexorably.

"I care," said Jacob, with some humility.

"I don't," said the dogmatic Peter.

"But I have daughters and a son," protested Jacob.

"No more than lots of other men," replied the angry Peter, rubbing excitedly.

"But look at the difference?" now pleaded Jacob.

"There isn't any," snapped Peter.

"Do you infer, Peter, that you will play false, too?" asked Jacob, seized with the impression that his fellow grafters would desert him.

"I infer nothing; I act," said Peter, turning to look out his place of espial.

"You think you are safe?" said Jacob.

"I think nothing; I act. If I fail, I fail, and don't cry!" he shouted.

"You are exasperating, Peter; come, now, let's get down to business—what will we raise it on first?" asked Jacob.

"On every resort in town; I'll send word tonight to my entire force to press on the screws," answered Peter.

"Good!" exclaimed Jacob, now in full accord with Peter's views.

"Have you seen Monroe?" asked Peter, now turning to a new subject.

"Had a talk with him yesterday."

"What did he say?"

"Said he was with us still."

"Can he be trusted?"

"Without a doubt."

"Does Jarney know of his connection with us?"

"No."

"Jarney, the goody-goody, must be made to pay for big knocking."

"Monroe has been detailed to work on him," said Jacob.

"And you can trust to Monroe for that?" asked Peter.

"I believe we can; but he is handicapped now by the firing of Jarney's old reliable secretary."

"He's been fired? Who has he now?"

"A young country bumpkin."

"Can't you get him in your ranks?" asked Peter.

"I fear not," replied Jacob, with a shake of the head. "He's been approached, and seems to be as susceptible as a cow."

"Ah, we must get rid of him, some way—get him out of Monroe's way."

"That's what Monroe will attempt to do," said Jacob.

"Can he do it?" asked Peter, squinting.

"If he's slick enough, he can; nobody else can get so near the scene of operation like Monroe."

"How's Jarney's adopted daughter coming on in society?" asked Peter, with a faint attempt at smiling.

"Fine, I hear," answered Jacob, rising in his chair, and turning around with his back to Peter.

"That's a funny piece of business on Jarney's part," said Peter, puffing very hard at his pipe.

"His daughter took a fancy to her, on seeing her one day while slumming on the South Side, and she's trying to make a lady of her," said Jacob, sitting down again, after throwing away the stump of a cigar.

"Can she do it?" asked Peter, with considerable interest.

"She's doing it," responded Jacob, who noticed the change of Peter's interest, which was now of the kindly kind.

"God bless her!" exclaimed Peter, as he turned again to his ever present peephole expression.

"Mike Barton's dead," said Jacob, slowly.

"The devil!" shouted Peter, turning from his peephole.

"Yes; didn't you hear of it?"

"No. How?"

"Automobile accident."

"There are others to take his place," said Peter, grunting like a satisfied pig after eating heartily. "How did it happen?"

"Stole Jarney's auto, with the two young ladies in it; run it like h— to the country, to kidnap them, I suppose; ran into a telegraph pole—busted the machine, and busted his head."

"Poor wretch! I am glad he is gone, for his sister's sake," said Peter, sighing, which he could do sometimes.

"Ah, I see you are very compassionate for the girl all at once," said Jacob, eyeing Peter.

"I have reasons to be," replied Peter, spiritedly. "Were the girls hurt?"

"No; but Edith Jarney is very ill—."

"Very ill! What?" interrupted Peter.

"Brain fever, she's got."

"Ah, she is too good to live," said Peter, looking out his peephole again. Then turning quickly, with his peculiar little eyes turned up sidewise at Jacob, he said: "Say, Jacob, we must put our sleuths on the trail of that old drunkard, Billy Barton. He has been gone a long time, and not a single word from him."

"What do you want with the sot?" asked Jacob, mystified. "He's no good."

"That's my business—poor Billy," and Peter lapsed into a moody spell, for sometimes he seemed to have a little of the feelings of a natural heart; but this quality in him was as rare as the air on Pike's Peak. "His family must be cared for."

"Jarney's doing that," answered Jacob.

"Is he?" jerked out Peter, wrathfully. "I'll not allow it from him, the interloper!"

"You are getting generous all at once, Peter; I should not begrudge him the privilege."

"Well, then, I don't," replied Peter, after a moment's reflection. "Let him keep them; he owes it to them."

"It is time for me to be at my office, Peter; so good bye," said Jacob, rising to leave.

"Remember Monroe," said Peter.

"Oh, I'll see to that," said Jacob, as he went out.

So are the "ropes" laid, as per the rule of things, to further the ends of the men who neither toil nor spin. Were the dear people less disposed to supine indifference toward their public officials, the government of our country would be as perfect, no doubt, as that of the fabled Utopia.

CHAPTER XIV JOHN WINTHROPE IS SURROUNDED BY PERPLEXITIES

The morbidly silent Monroe went about his duties with the serenity of a cat out on a dark night. The immobility of his starched face left no impression on the beholder of it as to whether he could be successfully punctured with the light of pleasantry. His feline movements from office to office among the clerical force cast an uncanny glamour over them all; and when not in the act of always appearing to be ready to make a spring upon them, as he glided whisperingly through the aisles of desks and high stands, he would be sitting at his own desk, in a corner of his private room, scanning sheet after sheet of reports and balances, and running over leaf after leaf of notations that had been left on his spindle for his especial perusal.

He was a very precise man, very accurate, very painstaking. He was a very obdurate man, very exacting, very positive. He was a very efficient man, very dependable, very obliging. He was a very incomprehensible man, very calculating, very mysterious. And besides, he was by nature very crafty, revengeful and egotistic. None of which traits could be read in his marble-like physiognomy; but they had to be worked out, to see them plainly, by a system of watching, and close scrutiny of his acts. He had risen in the office force from the bottom, and held his present post by right of apparent merit.

No one under him, or above, for that matter, ever dreamed that behind his iron mask lay another man, unscrupulous and unfaithful. No one ever thought of him but that he was honest, upright and beyond reproach. No one ever thought of him being a depraved man, as being licentious, as being impure in thought and actions; because all these things were hidden under his bushel of contrarieties.

At his desk, Mr. Monroe always worked with dispatch in disposing of the matters that daily came before him; and rarely could he be approached, except by the carrier of messages, or by an important personage, and then by announcement—except the head of the firm, who, of course, had free access to his room.

He was sitting, one day, enveloped in a great pile of work, when it was announced that Mr. Winthrope, the secretary, desired an audience with him. The secretary was admitted; but he was not asked to sit down. He stood before him in his own power; and he drew his own conclusions. But he said:

"Mr. Monroe, do you have at hand the balance sheet of last month?"

"I can get it," he answered, automatically.

"Mr. Jarney desires to go over it again," said John.

Mr. Monroe procured the sheet, and stiffly handed it to John, with one of his stony stares. John took the sheet and left him. When he reached the door, going out, he turned and caught the stolid face of Monroe still upon him. Neither said a word. John went out. Mr. Monroe pressed a button. A short, heavy set, square shouldered man, with green eyes, answered the button's call. He was Welty Morne, the head of the bookkeeping department.

"Welty," said Monroe, familiarly, "do you ever see the secretary after work hours?"

"No."

"Do you know where he lives?"

"At The King House, Diamond alley."

"He is never out at night, is he?"

"I have never seen him."

"He never associates with the boys, does he?"

"He seems to be a seclusive chap," said Welty.

"Yes; and very selfish," said Monroe, quietly. "Does he spend any money?"

"Have no way of knowing—except, perhaps, he pays his board and rent."

"Let us call on him tonight, and initiate him; will you?"

"I should like a little outing in this disagreeable weather, and will be happy to join you," replied Welty, with his green eyes beaming in anticipation of a lark.

"Will you call at my place at nine p. m.?"

"I will—whee-e-e!"

Welty Morne retires. The button is pressed again. Bate Yenger, assistant to the head bookkeeper, enters. He sits down, and looks indolent. He is a slim chap, with a fair face and black eyes, which show indications of night-hawking.

"Bate," said the impressionless Monroe, "have you met the new secretary after work hours?"

"Have not."

"Know anything of his habits?"

"Nothing."

"Do you want to go on a lark tonight?"

"Wouldn't mind it."

"Then come to my place at nine p. m."

Bate Yenger disappears. Monroe resumes his work. John returns the balance sheet, and hands it to Monroe. Monroe takes it, and scans it over. He sees some check-marks upon it. He folds it up, and puts it away. John remains a moment, as if he would like to speak to Monroe; but Monroe does not speak. John, then, goes out.

Promptly on the hour of nine p. m., Welty Morne and his boon companion, Bate Yenger, called at the apartments of Mr. Monroe at the St. Charles. That chunk of stiffness they found was ready, and together the three fared forth for a night of rounding.

They called upon John Winthrope in his dingy quarters—a hideous contrast, they thought, to their own bright and luxurious living places. John was surprised, of course, to see them. Would he go out with them? Whither? For sight-seeing.

John looked at his open books and papers on his little table, glanced down at himself, half inclined to accept; but very perplexed about it. He hesitated, and then asked them into his room. They entered, but did not sit down, as there was only one chair, which later was preempted by Welty.

"Why don't you get decent quarters, Mr. Winthrope?" asked Welty, who was a lively and a very talkative fellow.

"Cannot afford it," answered John.

"Oh, bosh! You receive as much, and more, than many of the other young men in our office, and the way they fly one would think they were millionaires' sons," replied Welty.

"I have a mother and father to assist," said John.

"Won't you go tonight; we will pay the way," insisted the persuasive Welty.

John still hesitated. He pondered a moment, and then replied: "No, thank you; I do not care to go."

"Just tonight, Mr. Winthrope; three is a company, and four is a crowd," pursued Welty.

"I thank you very much, Mr. Morne; but really, now, I do not care to go," persisted John.

During this ineffectual conversation, Monroe stood leaning against the door as passive as a tombstone, with Bate Yenger leaning awkwardly against the wall near him, looking as vapid as a snake in winter time. Welty was disconcerted, disappointed, and aggravated. At John's last remark, he tried to hide his displeasure of it beneath a subtle smile that was a cross between sarcasm and disgust. John sat on the edge of his bed in a thoughtless mood, chewing the end of a tooth-pick. All four were silent for an uncomfortable period of time. Then Welty broke the spell.

"So you won't join us?" he asked.

"No; thank you; I do not care to go," answered John.

"Ah, he is not so easy as I thought," said Monroe to himself.

Silence followed. John sat still, masticating his tooth-pick, being little concerned as to how they took his answer. He wanted to be curt to them, by demeanor; and wished they would depart. For reasons of his own, which he considered private, as far as he was concerned, he did not desire their company under any circumstances. Therefore, while he aimed always to be polite to the triumvirate schemers, he would rather show himself to be a boor than to have them about him.

So, disgusted with John's susceptibility to fall into their trap, and displeased at their own lack of tact, the three gentlemen went rattling down the stairs, and out into the street.

"He's a Sunday-schooler, all right," said Welty, as they lined up side by side, with Monroe in between, to go down the avenue.

"Aw, a cheap skate," said Bate.

After Monroe began to realize the abject failure of his scheme, and after the words of the other gentlemen had percolated through his adamantine head, he remarked, in reply to each of the other's opinion, that Winthrope was a sissy, which application, it is readily seen, was not well placed; then he said: "He is an impeccable good-for-nothing. He needs to be shown a thing or two in this old town—but he will learn all right, like the rest of them."

"You are a poor inveigler," said Welty to Monroe, facetiously.

"My time, like that of all dogs, will come yet," said Monroe.

"Well; I would like to know your motive?" asked Welty.

"Oh, I just wanted to get him limbered up a little," answered the astute one.

Thus being vanquished in his purpose, Monroe excused himself, after they had walked a few blocks, and retreated to his rooms, there to enter upon the duties of outlining a more ingenious campaign toward the destruction of John Winthrope's name, and to ruin his chances for continuing in the office of Jarney & Lowman. His first conceived plan was to get John Winthrope out of the way, in the head office. This he could only hope to do by besmirching his character, or cause him to commit some overt act of deportment that would be laid up against him in the eyes of Mr. Jarney.

So, after being rebuffed in his first effort, Monroe concluded to take another tack, and would thereafter become and be John's intimate friend, a good fellow towards him, and a hearty supporter of him before the firm, and thereby get results. These things he thought out pretty clearly, and definitely decided that on the morrow he would bombard the fort from another angle.

So on the morrow, as soon as Mr. Winthrope had arrived, he was surprised to receive a polite little note, via the messenger, to call in the office of Mr. Monroe as early as convenient, and without interference in his official capacity. Ever prompt in complying with such informal invitations (which he took it to be, instead of a command), and having time to spare before the arrival of Mr. Jarney, he repaired at once to the sanctum of Mr. Monroe.

That gentleman, John was also surprised to see, had unbended to such proportions, that, when John approached his desk, he arose, and shook hands with him, an heretofore unheard of performance of cordiality on Mr. Monroe's part.

"I have asked you in, Mr. Winthrope," said Monroe, "to apologize for intruding on you last night. It was only a whim of one of the boys out on a lark, with whom, unfortunately, I fell in with at the untimely hour."

"Oh, that is all right, Mr. Monroe," replied John. "I took no offense at your visit."

"I thought, perhaps, you might have been offended."

"The fact is, I was very busy last night and forgot all about your intrusion after you had gone," said John, smiling affably, but with noticeable indifference in his voice.

"I should like to have your confidence, Mr. Winthrope," said the wily one. "Inasmuch, as we are near to the head of the firm, we should be on better terms."

"Perhaps we should," answered John, still indifferent.

"I shall deem it a pleasure to have you call on me some evening, and accompany me to dinner; or, if you will set the time, I shall call on you."

"You are very kind, Mr. Monroe."

"May I call, or will you call?"

"Neither," replied John, without exhibiting a sign of what he meant.

"Then, I am to understand, you do not court my company?" said the unruffled one.

"No; not that, Mr. Monroe. I am very busy of evenings. Sometime I may accept your invitation; but not for the present," responded John.

"What is it that so engrosses you of evenings, may I inquire?" asked the worming Monroe.

"Yes; you may ask whatever you please—I am taking a post-graduate course in business on my own time," said John.

"To what end?" asked Monroe.

"That I may be better prepared to perform my duties; for that reason I do not care to spare the time to go out."

"Very well, Mr. Winthrope; success to you," said Monroe. "But may I not anticipate your company to dinner before very long?"

"I cannot now decide, Mr. Monroe—not now; but will inform you of my decision at a later date," replied John.

Hearing Mr. Jarney enter his office at this juncture, John said good bye to the cat, and retired. He found Mr. Jarney tuned to a conversational degree that morning that perplexed him. Mr. Jarney dictated a few letters, beginning on them as was his custom, immediately after taking his seat, and looking over some important ones; then he lighted a cigar, and reared back in his chair in pleasant contemplation of the circles that he blew out and sent upwards like escaping halos. John sat regarding him for a few seconds with calm complacency; then, seeing that he did not intend to proceed further, for the present, with the dictation, said that he would retire and transcribe the letters.

"No hurry, Mr. Winthrope; no hurry," said Mr. Jarney, looking searchingly at John. "You are the most unfathomable chap I ever saw, Mr. Winthrope," he continued. "Here a week has gone by and you have not yet made inquiry about my daughter's health."

John was astonished at this statement.

"Mr. Jarney, I should have inquired," he said; "but I felt it out of place for me to be so familiar with your family matters."

"Why so?" he asked, with sharpness.

"I feared you might think me presumptuous," replied John, timidly.

"You presumptuous? I am not snobbish, Mr. Winthrope," he returned.

"Well, I felt that I would be keeping my place, by keeping silent," said John.

"I never mentioned the matter, Mr. Winthrope, because I wanted to see just how long you would be silent," said Mr. Jarney. "And don't you care to know?"

"Why, Mr. Jarney, nothing would give me greater pleasure than to know that Miss Jarney is improving."

"She is not," he said, despondently.

"Is she serious?" asked John.

"Very serious," he replied. Mr. Jarney must have noticed the pallor that stole over John's face at this unwelcome information; but if he did not, he divined John's eagerness to know more of Edith's complaint, and continued: "Yes, Mr. Winthrope, she is very serious. She has brain fever. The escapade of young Barton brought a great blow upon us all; for I have great fears of her recovery."

"Do the doctors give no hope?" asked John, eagerly.

"No hope," was the reply, as Mr. Jarney shook his head, and resuming his old demeanor of being affected by some inward impulses that had pervaded him for the week past.

"I am very sorry, Mr. Jarney, that I did not know of this before now, so that I could have sympathized with you," said John, feelingly.

"I appreciate your modesty, Mr. Winthrope, in not inquiring, and I deplore my disposition in not being more communicative; for I knew all along you were anxious to know, after the kind services you rendered us by bringing her home," said Mr. Jarney, speaking now with considerable emotion.

"I know I should have inquired, Mr. Jarney, and was on the point of doing so several times, but I always felt that you were indifferent as to how I felt about the matter."

"Mr. Winthrope, I must be frank with you, for dear Edith's sake, and tell you all. She—"

"—not expected to recover," interrupted John, bending forward intently.

"No, that is not what I was about to say," he replied, scanning John's face. "While in a delirium, she repeatedly calls for you. Every day and every night she has been doing this, since you brought her home. We would have sent for you to come to see her had we believed your presence would have been of any avail in bringing her to her reason. But, as the doctors said that is true in all such cases, we deferred to their advice. As her father, I do not believe their opinion is of much moment in her present critical condition, so I am going to request you to accompany me to my home this evening for dinner, and incidentally you may see Edith, for what comfort she, or you, may have in such a meeting."

This was certainly startling information to Mr. Winthrope. He had put through many fruitless hours wondering about the outcome of Edith's illness, and suffered some pangs of heart thereby; but little did he dream, or anticipate, that he could, in any manner, be considered by the lady, whose station in life was miles and miles above him. The statement of Mr. Jarney only caused him more regret, for he considered Edith's use of his name, in her delirious hours, the wild fancies of an afflicted brain. And he was perplexed.

"If it is your wish, I shall be glad to go with you, Mr. Jarney," said John, after gaining his composure.

Mr. Jarney noticed the effect of what he said upon the young man, and he could not restrain from saying: "I shall deem it a pleasure; and I know it will be a great favor to Mrs. Jarney if you go."

"I shall go," he said.

"Then we will leave the office early," said Mr. Jarney.

"May I have time to dress?" asked John.

"All the time you require, Mr. Winthrope. You may leave the office at three, and be ready to go at four."

"Thank you; I will be ready," returned John, as he gathered up his note book and papers, and repaired to his office.

CHAPTER XV
WHAT DOES THE HEART SAY?

An auto being in waiting at the curb, and John being ready at the appointed time, he and Mr. Jarney joined each other at the main entrance of the office building; and together were whirled away, in a twinkling, toward the mansion on the hill.

This was the second time that he had been summoned to that palace of a Croesus; for a second time he went, not of his own volition; for a second time he drew near the place, with a strange feeling in his soul; and he wondered if Fate, after all, is not a strange outliner of one's life. The first time, a deep mystery surrounded his sudden summoning, ending with a very romantic sequel; the second time, the cause leading up to his going was as deep a mystery as the first, with no telling what the climax might be. So, with these thoughts alone passing through his head as he rode silently by the side of his superior through the whizzing wind and beating rain and whirling smoke, he was not a little agitated when the chauffeur drew up at the side door, and the master had stepped out, and he was bidden to follow.

He remembered well that entrance on the former occasion, in the night, with its beaming lights and glistening panels of glass and brilliancy of the interior reflecting over him in his amazement. He remembered very well the gliding through the rooms of the family and the attendants, like roving spirits in despair in a fairy bower. He remembered all these things through the eye of the night:—of his sudden departure from the mansion; of his mission through the space of miles, and his quick return, and triumphant end—for the sake of duty. All these things he recalled, as if ruminating on a hazy dream. But when he came the second time, in the gloom of the late afternoon, and seeing the sombreness of the walls, the doors, the porches, the lawn and everything, stripped of the glare of artificial light, he felt that within the house a similar gloom prevailed.

He followed Mr. Jarney, now with a palpitating heart. The valet took his coat and hat and umbrella; and he was escorted to the warmth, the cheer, the beauty, the radiance, the grandeur of the parlor, and was begged to be seated. And he saw that the house was as silent as a morgue; he saw the long faces of the servants, and noted their confidential looks and glances toward him; he saw that the lights were burning dimly, and as they might burn for several days to come; he saw friends of the family glide in like spectres, with inquiring faces, and whisper, and saw them depart as silently; he saw the piano was closed, and the music piled up. He saw Mrs. Jarney coming down the great white stairway, darkly clothed, with tear-stained eyes and tired movements. He felt the oppressive dread that was over all. And he trembled.

Mrs. Jarney approached him, with Mr. Jarney at her side, he having met her at the foot of the stairs. John arose as she put out her hand, and when he shook it, he noticed that she was excessively perturbed.

"I am very happy to see you, Mr. Winthrope," she said, with some effort. "I wish to thank you for your services in behalf of my daughter on that dreadful evening."

"You have my sincere sympathy, Mrs. Jarney," responded John. "May I inquire if Miss Jarney is improving?"

"No improvement, Mr. Winthrope, that we can see," she replied.

"Is it so that Mr. Winthrope can see her?" asked Mr. Jarney of his wife.

"He may go now, if he does not feel it too great a favor to us," replied Mrs. Jarney, wiping away her tears.

"I assure you, Mrs. Jarney," said John, "that I do not hold such a matter in the light of favor; but as a matter of the gravest importance to you both."

"Mr. Winthrope," said Mrs. Jarney, placing her hand upon his arm, "there are trials in this life, to a mother, which no man can understand; and this is one of them. We have asked you to come here because we believe in you, because we know and feel that you are good. Do not think that we are not under obligations to you, and that my dear Edith will not be thankful to you, if she recovers. We know and you know that your coming is by reason of unusual circumstances; and as her mother, I do not want you to think, Mr. Winthrope, that my emotions have gone beyond my reason. She has called your name so many times that I could not bear to hear it longer without you coming here. I fancied, at first, that it was, as the doctors have said, only the fancy of an afflicted brain; but I believe it is more than that. I beg your pardon, Mr. Winthrope, if I have spoken too plainly. Now, if you are ready we will proceed to her room."

John was proud himself, though poor. He was proud of his good name; proud of his old father and mother, and his own dear sister and brother in the mountains; he was proud that others held him in high esteem; proud of their friendly consideration, of the confidence in which they held him, and of their frankness. When Mr. Jarney first broached the subject of his going to see his daughter, he took it as a question of duty, albeit he was not altogether dum to its influence on his heart; and when Mrs. Jarney spoke to him, with even more freedom than her husband, he could not resist the effect any longer.

He therefore went up the stairs in a state of mind that was a mixture between despair and hope. He was preceded by the parents of Edith. They passed through a hall bewildering to John in its elegance, he following, and at length came to the door of a bed room. Mrs. Jarney opened it, and they silently filed within, like going into the chamber of the dead, so softly did they move.

At one side of a bed sat a nurse, on the other sat Star Barton, faithful in her bleeding heart. On the bed lay the fevered form of Edith in snowy whiteness. To the beholders she was like a transporting angel, only the flush of life was in her cheeks—the flush of her affliction. Her white hands lay twitching over the coverlets. Her face was upturned, her blue eyes staring, her lips mumbling indistinct words. She was apparently dead to all things mortal. No wonder Star was in tears; no wonder the parents felt a dread shudder pass through them; no wonder the nurse had a solemn face; for the spirit of this pure young woman seemed to be passing, passing.

John was not unmoved by the scene, for even his brave strong heart sent forth a sigh. The parents stood by the bedside looking down upon their unconscious child in her struggle. After a few moments Mr. Jarney turned to John, and whispered:

"We will leave you alone with her and her friend, Miss Barton."

Then they went out, and the nurse went out. John spoke a word of recognition to Star, and drew a chair up to the bed and sat down, looking meditatively at Edith.

"Has she been unconscious since the night I brought her here?" asked John.

"Almost all the time," answered Star. "Sometimes she is rational—then she calls for you."

"If she should become rational while I am here, and should see me, do you think my being here would have any beneficial effect upon her?" asked John.

"That is the opinion of her parents," replied Star.

"You appear to be pretty well worn out by your vigil, Miss Barton," said John, turning to her, sitting close by his side.

"I have been in this room ever since she took ill, or since you brought her here," answered Star.

"Haven't you taken any rest?" asked John, dubious about her statement.

"I lie down on the couch there sometimes," pointing to one in the room; "but I cannot sleep."

"I fear the trial will be too much for you, Miss Barton."

"Oh, it is no trial for me to sit here, where I can see her dear face all the time," responded Star, and then she burst into tears, and John could hardly restrain his own from flowing, through his deep sympathy for her in her simple faith.

Just then Edith turned her face toward them, and gazed wildly about with her pretty blue eyes rolling in their sockets. Then she threw one hand over the side of the bed. John lifted it up tenderly, and laid it back in place, and then it was that he became aware of how feverish she was. Edith mumbled something.

"She is making an effort to speak your name," said Star, who was now used to her strange fancyings, and could interpret almost any unintelligible word she spoke. Then bending over Edith, she said: "He is here, dear Edith."

Edith looked up at Star, with what appeared to be a faint smile. Star took one hand, and held it, patting it lovingly. "Here he is, dear Edith; don't you see him?" she said, as Edith now uttered the name distinctly.

Edith paid no heed to Star, but rolled her head and muttered John's name. Then she became calmer, and lay still; arousing herself after a few minutes, and repeating the name again.

"He is here, Edith, by your bedside; can't you see?" said Star, bending over her. "Come closer, Mr. Winthrope, that she might see you."

John thereat moved nearer to the bed, and leaned over her.

"Here is Mr. Winthrope, Edith," said Star, as she placed a hand upon her hot forehead.

Edith turned her head, and sighed. Her eyes ceased their starey look. She became calmer; sighed again. Then, without assistance, she raised herself up, and her long hair fell over her shoulders. In her illness now, John thought she was prettier than before when he saw her in her best of health. As she arose, Star caught her by the shoulders, and made an attempt to lay her down on her pillow again; but Edith shook her off, with her fever-strength supreme in her. She then crossed her hands before her, bent her head forward; then threw it backward, and gazed across the room to the farther wall, like one staring into the infinitude of time in its blankness.

John sat watching her, moved to piteous supplication for this fair young lady in her distress of mind.

"Star," said Edith, turning upon Miss Barton, in a strange clear voice, "have you seen Mr. Winthrope?"

"Here he is, dear Edith," replied Star, stroking her hair. "Here by your bed; don't you see him?"

"That is not Mr. Winthrope," she answered, in the same strange tone.

"No, no, dear Edith; he is here—Mr. Winthrope look into her face?" said Star, turning to John, whose head was bowed under the weight of the impression that this girl's ravings made on him. John obeyed Star's request, and looked Edith in the face. Edith then put out a hand, and touched that of his; then fell back, burying her head in her soft pillow, with her hands over her face.

"She knows you," whispered Star.

"Shall I retire?" asked John, believing that the crisis had been reached.

"Oh, not yet," answered Star. Then leaning over Edith again, said: "Edith, do you want to see Mr. Winthrope again before he goes?"

Edith reached out a hand toward him, turned her head, and let her eyes move slowly in his direction. Then she laid her hand upon his. He picked it up, and she permitted him to hold it.

"Mr. Winthrope?" she said.

"I am he," he replied.

She smiled, and her eyes became less roving. "I am better," she whispered.

"Edith, I knew you would be better as soon as he came," said Star, kissing her. "Are you not glad, Mr. Winthrope?" asked Star of him.

"Very, very," he responded. He touched his lips to her fevered hand; and how it thrilled him.

"Now, you may retire, if you wish," said Star.

"Will you come again?" said Edith, in a very low voice; "often; often?"

"If I am permitted," replied John, releasing her hand, and rising.

"You have my permission," whispered Edith, feebly attempting to smile. "Oh, I am so weak, I am afraid it will be such a long time before I can leave this bed." Turning to Star, she said: "Have mamma keep him for dinner, if it is near that time—or breakfast, or lunch."

"He will remain," answered Star.

"You will come in before you go—you will come again, Mr. Winthrope?" asked Edith, faintly.

"By your father's permission," he answered, smiling down upon her.

"He will permit you," said Edith.

"Good bye," said John, taking Edith's hand again.

"Good bye; don't fail to come in again before you go?" said Edith.

"I shall come," he said, kissing her lily hand; after which he lay it down with the greatest reluctance.

Then he left her, with a world of thrilling emotions consuming him. Seeing no one in the hallway, he proceeded alone down the stairs to the parlor, there to be met by the gloomy countenances of Edith's loving parents, who were at that moment in such a distracted state of mind that they almost collapsed over wrong expectations over this singular meeting of their daughter with John Winthrope. Both rose as they saw John approaching, and sighed.

"How is she?" both asked together.

"Better," was John's response.

Mr. Jarney took John by the hand, and said: "How greatly relieved I am." Mrs. Jarney did not wait for further information; but ran up the stairs, and went headlong into her daughter's room.

"Oh, my child! my child!" she cried in the excess of her joy, seeing the token of rationality in Edith's face. She fell on the bed by Edith's side, almost in a faint, throwing her arms about her. Edith was not in condition to withstand such a stormy outburst of motherly affection. Star, understanding the bad effect such extreme commotion might have upon her charge, persuaded Mrs. Jarney to be calm, and all would be well.

"Did you know him, Edith?" asked her mother, still mentally agitated.

"Yes, mamma," replied Edith, so low she could hardly be heard.

"Was it he that effected a cure, Edith?"

"Oh, mamma, I am not well yet," said Edith; "and it may be a long time before I get out of this."

"Was it he, Edith, that brought about the crisis?" persisted the mother.

"It might have been, mamma," said Edith.

"Edith, are you keeping a secret from me?" pursued her mother.

"Dear mamma, I cannot bear up, if you keep on," whispered Edith, growing restless.

"Mrs. Jarney, it would be best not to disturb her any more; she needs sleep," said Star, advisedly.

Mrs. Jarney, realizing her mistaken enthusiasm, quieted down, and slipped out of the room, and bustled down the stairs in an uncontrollable plight of flusteration. She rushed up to Mr. Winthrope, and was almost in the act of embracing that young gentleman, who had earned his way unconsciously into her faver to such proportions that the good lady could not keep away from him all evening. In verity, Mrs. Jarney was so dignifiedly considerate that she would have, under the spur of the stimulent of joy, given her consent right then to John becoming a permanent member of her household (had he thought of asking that privilege of her) had it not have been that a little bit of money-pride overbalanced her gratitude. And, in truth, too, Mr. Jarney might have fallen under the same magic that John had also cast over him, had it not have been that his pride was a little greater than he could consistently overcome. But this did not prevent Mr. Jarney from showering upon John encomiums of all kinds for the rest of his stay in the house that evening.

John, being prodigiously sensitive on the matter of the propriety of a thing done, was with difficulty persuaded in his own mind that Edith's wish was any more than a good woman's gratefulness. Although he made a great effort that evening to keep down the blazing fires of the one great human passion, he could not extinguish them altogether, for the more he thought of the cause that led up to his coming there, the fiercer the coals blazed within him: till his soul was almost afire.

Dinner was eaten in great state, the first of the kind for John; but he, being an adaptable young man, was equal to anything that confronted him. And while dining, he did not fail to notice the changed spirits of all the inmates of the house, from the head of it down to the waiter; for the later were profuse in showing him deference, in their looks and actions; he did not fail to notice the change in the lights that gave back a much more cheerful caress, where before they were feebly lifeless; he did not fail to notice the change in the countenances of the friends of the family, who came in with a deadening look, and went out with a smile; he did not fail to notice all these things; nor could he help but feel that he was the one person who might have brought it about. In consequence, he passed through the evening in the ascending mood of rapturous delight; but, though, always with a fear—a fear bound up in one corner of his heart—that he was only being rewarded for his services as the servant of this great man of money, the father of Edith. But John, do not despair; there are worse people in this world, who are rich, than the Jarneys.

John kept his promise, and called to see Edith just before he was ready to leave the mansion. She was sleeping when he was let into the darkened room; and when he looked down upon her, in her purity, dreaming, perhaps of him, he felt the power of love that was bearing him down. Were everything made of sweet toned bells, and they were every one ringing, no greater would be the alarum than that which at that moment knelled through him. The fear of death coming to her, the fear of her loss should she come back to life, the fear of those who brought her into the world, the fear of Fate, the fear of Chance, struck him dumb. Would her death be worse than life? he thought; would her life be worse than death? Sleeping calmly, peacefully, without a murmur from her lips; breathing lightly, evenly, without a break in the respiration; resting now as if the angels had brought a cure from out the skies—John felt the holy thrall which controlled him.

He knelt down by the bed, and took her white hand in his, and tears of his mercy wet her limp fingers; and he prayed.

Then, rising, with his heart too full to speak, he turned to the door to leave. Miss Barton, seeing his agitation, came up to speak to him, with her eyes also filled with tears.

"Wait till she awakes," she said.

"I cannot," he replied.

"She expects to see you before you go."

"Tell her—" and he was gone.

CHAPTER XVI
BILLY BARTON'S FLIGHT

When Billy Barton left his home and family, he went without a clue to his destination; and he left no word behind of his going.

The world to him had been a series of degenerating allurements ever since he could remember anything; and Evil Repute was the sum of his reward. He was brought up amid the scenes of the river's traffic as a wharf man, or roustabout; and was called the waterman, by reason of an ineradicable habit he had of invariably falling into the stream when intoxicated. This predilection of Billy's might have cured such a failing in any other man; but the more often Billy fell into the river the less inclined he was to accept the water cure. The frequency of these periodic immersions grew to such dimensions that his qualifications as a wharfman became nil, and he thereby lost his right to a permanancy among the gang, causing him, one day early in his years, to be placed on the reserve list to take his chances for obtaining work as an extra.

Billy was like many another man of his class: he had no inclination to reach a higher level, or lacked the ability to go higher; and by these well developed attributes, in him, he found it pretty hard picking among the dispensers of jobs. It appears that he was continually in ill-luck, when it came to making assignments for the long line of men in waiting. Sometimes he would put in a day or so of work, with a disposition to be light-hearted over his luck; but it very often happened that when he was wanted, he was under the influence of drink; or had just recovered himself from a baptism in the river; and so he was many times overlooked. This vicarious situation did not tend to better his condition. It only made him worse. What between his few spells of work, and his numerous spells of sprees, he had a petty sum left on which to keep his growing family.

Billy Barton was a very clever man in his sober moments; but so seldom was he ever in that state of good behavior, that his cleverness was overlooked even by his most intimates. What is hereof meant by this use of the word clever, is that it was applied to him in the vernacular sense, and not in its strict usage. So when in that state of temporary sanity, he was ever ready with a rough wit of the hang-dog style—the wit of the waterfront, of the grog shop, of the slums, of the rough-and-ready characters of his calling;

and this he carried to his home, very often to his sorrow. He used to tell the "boys" that he had an "old woman" who could give any one spades in cards in her fetching ways toward general cussedness. But Billy would condone all that poor woman's incapacities, whenever he would get drunk, and, with a great display of imaginary wealth, which he said he would fall heir to some day, impress upon her impressionable mind the beauties of their future.

Thus by such tactics, he, for a number of years, kept her hopefully on the high wave of anticipation and expectation. This trait of Billy's was one of his redeeming qualities, if he ever had any other; so much so that ere he had reached his present age of discretion, he began really to believe that he was as rich as the man in the mansion on the hill; which mansion he always kept a weather's eye out for, no difference how much smoke or fog clouded his sense of perception.

But Kate Barton, long ago, began to realize that his tantalizing predictions and promises were merely vaporings. So, when things with her became inordinately unbearable, she began to attempt a reformation of him by the process of her voluableless tongue. At first she scolded him gently; then firmly, then remorselessly; tongue-lashed him; berated him from Soho to McKee's Rocks; and, finally, seeing that this method was without effect, adopted the corporal punishment plan. But by no such inducements, however, could she prevail upon him to reform, and act the true part of a husband and father. Thus, being in an environment that would, without a doubt, corrupt old Satan himself, Billy went from bad to worse, and from worse to the finite degree of dissipation. Resorting to the saloons as a solace for his sorrows, he there found out, when too late, that as long as he had a penny he could secure the required consolation that he craved. Ultimately, reaching an end in this direction, he became obsessed with the desire to flee. And flee he did.

Any one standing, at any point, on the south side of the Smithfield street bridge, on the day of his departure, might have seen the bent form of a once well built, square-shouldered, red-faced, blue-eyed man, wearing a slouch hat, check shirt, blue overalls, faded coat, and brogans on his feet, and a rusty overcoat on his arm, aimlessly walking across it, going northward. Had he been followed, the observer would have seen him turn up Second avenue, with the same shambling gait, and with his nose directed toward the devious ways of Soho.

They would have seen him wind in and out among the alley ways and bypaths between the mills and factories and shops, have heard him ask for work, and have heard the answer, "Don't want you." They would have seen him come out into the street, stop, hesitate; go on, with the same determination in his bleary eyes. They would have seen him continuing, with an inquiry here and there; they would have seen him brushed aside, and go on. They would have seen him treading the ties of the Baltimore & Ohio, through the interminable region of noise—of belching furnaces, of rattling factories, of shouting men, of screeching engines, mile after mile. They would have seen him stop at a poor man's house—one almost like his own—and heard him ask for food and bed, and would have seen him receive it, sometimes. They would have seen him stop, and rest, and meditate; have seen him sneered at, chased by policemen, stoned by boys, hooted by ruffians, scolded by women; have seen him rejected, dejected, despondent, and in despair—a weary wayfarer, an outcast, discarded by his family, condemned by his fellow man—a human wreck, with not a hand outstretched to him to lend him the aid and encouragement that he needed in that hour—except, perhaps, the hand of the Almighty, in retribution.

And more; they would have seen Billy Barton go through the suburbs of Glenwood, Hazelwood, Rankin; through the boroughs of Braddock, of Homestead, of Duquesne, and on to McKeesport, meeting always with the same inglorious reception—day after day, week after week, asking, begging, starving. They would have seen him sleeping in deserted buildings, in fields, in box cars; by the roadsides, on the hillsides, in the woods; everywhere where man was not, save some stragglers of his own ilk. They would have seen him eventually entering saloons in the slum quarters; have seen him set upon, beaten, kicked and thrown into the streets, a poor worthless cuss, too vile, even now, for any of his former cronies to recognize, had they chanced across him. They would, as a climax to his wanderings, have seen him dragged into a town's nasty, filthy, foul, venom-infested jail, there to await the merciful order of a just and honest judge, who might, peradventure, take compassion on him; and, as a finality, have seen him sentenced to penal servitude as a vagrant.

Holy of Holies! praise be to God! cry the keepers of the loaves and fishes! But for the goodness of a pure young woman, his children might have starved. And say that the male-man is a generous creature!

In the little black office of The Die, Peter sat humped up, like a drooling ape, scanning the interior of his junk shop through his peephole. He saw the cringing Eli, like a witless ass, having another set-to with a short stalky fellow because he did not give the password. He saw Eli floored, and thumped in the ribs by the man's foot. Whereat Peter gathered up his courage and went out to ascertain the wherefor of the disturbance.

"Hah, Welty Morne," whispered Peter, seeing who the man was; "come in;" and he waddled rearward, leaving the defeated servant to readjust himself as to how he may.

"Set down," said he to Welty, after falling down himself like a bloated lobster, and taking up his pipe, and espionage. "What? What now?" he asked.

"We have heard at last from Billy Barton," said Welty.

"Where'd you get that information? The wretch!" roared Peter, sardonically.

"From Monroe."

"And Monroe?"

"From Cobb."

"And Cobb?"

"From the warden."

"The wretch!" shouted Peter. "Let him die there! What's his time?"

"Six months."

"Good! We'll make it six more."

"Am I to return that information?" asked Welty.

"Yes," snapped Peter. "What else from Monroe?"

"He has failed to rope in Winthrope."

"What next?"

"His new scheme is to put him as treasurer of the company."

"Good! Go to it, tell him. How's the girl?"

"Jarney took the young man to his home to see her, and she is recovering."

Peter frowned at this, that is at that part of the information relating to taking Winthrope to the Jarney home. He rubbed his hands, pulled at his pipe vigorously, almost spat on Welty in an effort to reach a saw-dust box used as a receptacle for his expectorations.

"She's a mighty fine girl," said Peter. "What does Monroe draw from that incident?"

"That Winthrope has inclinations toward her."

"And her father?" asked Peter.

"He permits it."

"Why don't young Cobb push his suit?" asked Peter.

"Oh, she would never have anything to do with him."

"Why doesn't he get Winthrope out of the way!" exclaimed Peter.

"He is laying the ropes to ensnare him," said Welty, showing his teeth like a grinning dog, and flashing his green eyes.

"What else?" asked Peter, ceasing to rub his hands, and looking up at Welty with some anxiety.

"There's going to be a strike on all the papers," replied Welty.

"Oh, that's all fixed up," said Peter, with consuming pride (judging from the speed he rubbed his hands). "The police have instructions to arrest every dog of them so soon as they step out of their jobs. What else?"

"An extra levy has been made on the red-lighters," replied Welty.

"Good!" exploded Peter. "Tell Monroe to watch out for flurries among them."

"They will all come through."

"Hah, I thought Jacob would bring them to time," whispered Peter. "How's he coming with his new company?"

"He'll have a million to float in a week."

"Why didn't he make it ten?" asked Peter.

"He's afraid the people are getting weary with so much stock already on the market."

"The coal combine went," said Peter, smiling.

"But that was the project of the other gang," said Welty.

"Well, I got my tribute, as well as Jacob, for our little assistance," he answered, with more fierce rubbing.

"Ah, they will all pay—that is, the big ones."

"Some of the little ones, too, eh?" said Peter.

"Where do I come in, Peter?" suddenly asked Welty. This question caused Peter to look up quickly, with a leer.

"You're not showing the white feather?" asked Peter.

"No, no; but I need some money."

"How much?"

"A thousand."

"I will have Jacob see you," returned Peter.

Then Welty departed. He found Eli where he had left him, unconscious, with some customers standing about waiting for the young man to take his own good time about rising. The customers had come into the store, and when they saw Eli lying on the floor, remarked among themselves that he was taking an afternoon's nap. When one of them sought to arouse him, they became alarmed as to what might have happened, for Eli would not rouse himself. So they were standing about him in contemplation when Welty came out of Peter's office. Welty glanced at Eli obliquely, as if deigning to stoop so low as to lend aid to his victim, brushed past the onlookers, and made his exit by the front door.

Peter, seeing that something was wrong, strutted out in a fluster, with his belly about a foot ahead of him. He had not observed from his peephole that Eli had not resumed his duties while Welty was in his office, so great was his interest in that visitor. But finding Eli in his predicament, Peter called on one of his customers to assist in his resurrection. Eli, thereupon, was lifted to his feet, but he was so near the limberness of a rope it was impossible to cause him to assume the perpendicularity of a standing man. Then that old remedy—water—was applied, with no effect. Eli looked like a faded piece of blue calico, so deathly was his face.

They called a doctor; with no results. They called an ambulance, and conveyed him to a hospital. They called in the police to make an investigation; with no results. Peter knew nothing. It was a strange affair. The customers, of course, knew nothing; nobody could get head nor tail of what had happened Eli. It was a deep mystery—to the police department.

Peter employed a new clerk, temporarily, and resumed his pipe and peephole. Welty resumed his duties in the office of Jarney & Lowman. In the meantime Eli Jerey's life hung in the balance; and the world of business still moved on; for he was only a poor clerk.

CHAPTER XVII
GOOD BYE! GOOD BYE! GOOD BYE!

As a metaphysician, John Winthrope could not present his bill of services, in the nonprofessional sense, for his visit to the Jarneys. This was the calamitous burden that bore so heavily upon him as he left the mansion on the hill that night, and kept his head in a whirl all the way to the city, and to his room, and to his bed, and even late into the night, till exhausting time relieved him near the breaking of another day.

It was the first time that the real tempest of passion had broken in upon his sea of life; it was the first time that Cupid, with his implements of war, came to offer battle on his serene and peaceful field of budding bachelorhood. It was the very first time for him, so amourously passive was he toward the whiles of the little meddler into one's heart affairs. It is so with many people, men and women; but when the storm once breaks in upon their unimpressionable souls it is like a hurricane let loose, and is unrestrainable.

He now saw a new light in the heavens, even through the smoke of Pittsburgh; a new evening star appeared in his firmament, and whirled through the universe of his night to meet him in the dawn; a new moon arose, and burst into full reflection of shadowy mysticism; a new sun circled the arch of his cold earth, and made the plants of joy come into leafage. Ah, there were no seasons to him now—it was light by day, light by night—and he was seeing everywhere through his visual horoscope—except—always except—as to a solution of the great problem that confronted him.

The next morning after John's visit to see Miss Edith, Mr. Jarney arrived at the office a half hour before his time. He was so different to what he had been on the previous few days that John instinctively felt his exuberance of pleasantry throughout the entire day. Instead of taking up his dictation, as had been his wont, Mr. Jarney paced the floor in his proud and haughty way of doing such things. He spoke to John, on entering, in his calm, formal explicitness, as had been his custom, when John entered to take his seat by his master's desk. John sat waiting for Mr. Jarney to open his letters and proceed; but he did not touch a letter, at first. He said nothing for some time, but walked the floor, pondering, as if wrestling with conflicting thoughts. After awhile he broke the spell.

"Young man," he said, as he stopped in his walk in front of John, with his hands deep in his pockets, and his keen eyes sparkling, "I do not know what to make of you."

"Am I such a conundrum as all that?" asked John, as he met his master's eyes, with his own as sharp as those cast upon him.

"In truth, you are," returned Mr. Jarney. "You are the biggest puzzle I have ever had to work out."

"Mr. Jarney, you place me in a very awkward position," answered John. "I am not certain yet as to what you mean by your allusions."

"My dear boy—" he started to say, then checked himself, thinking his manner too familiar, and went on: "Mr. Winthrope, you are master of your own destiny. You can make it what you will. You can be a leader of affairs, or you can be nothing."

"I only hope for an opportunity, Mr. Jarney, to claim the honor of the first," responded John.

"That is not what I mean, Mr. Winthrope; it is—well, it is—that you can do it."

"I am certainly at a greater loss to understand you, Mr. Jarney," said John smiling, but still believing that he understood. "Nevertheless, I appreciate what you say, and will always regard your views with much favor."

"Let me tell you, Mr. Winthrope," he pursued; "that business life is a terror to the average man. It has so many ups and downs that I have often wondered how so many succeed through all its uncertainties. I started out as poor as you, and maybe poorer, and have arrived where I am, with many a pain to accompany me. And still they call me successful. Had I to start again, I would pursue a different calling—science, literature, art, or music. These are the things that are a compensation to one's peace of mind. But most people believe it is money. I do not. I did once; but I have passed that period of putting money above everything else. Some will say, no doubt, that it is my view now, since I have got the money. Truly, had I not a cent, I would be of the same opinion. It was my opinion before I accumulated it, and I still cling to that hobby. Still I must continue on acquiring it. Making money is an endless chain proposition. Once you get into its entanglements, you cannot let go—you cannot resist its wonderful influence. Why, I should like to be free from its thralldom; I should like to be as you are, without the worry and the bother that money entails; I would like to exchange places with you, were it possible. But that can never happen, I suppose, so long as I have my present connections. I have often thought that I would like to tear myself away from its engrossments, to be free to go at will; to enjoy life with my wife and daughter in some way that would be to our liking—some way that is different from our present existence. I do not say that I will take up such a life; I may. I did not mean to make this lecture to you, Mr. Winthrope; but as I have made it. I will stand by it."

"Still I am in as deep a mystery as ever, Mr. Jarney," said John frankly, and more familiarly than he had ever spoken to him before.

"If I were a young man like you, and had my money, I would go to my home—assuming that your home is mine—and there live peacefully the rest of my days," he replied.

"Would you suggest that I do it, in my present poverty?" asked John.

"No; I am just supposing," he returned.

"I cannot suppose anything, Mr. Jarney; I am not in a supposing position."

"That is right, Mr. Winthrope, don't suppose anything; always believe it, and then go ahead," he said.

"That is what I have attempted to do; but believing a thing and obtaining it are two entirely different matters."

"Yes; you are right."

He then strode across the room, and returned.

"I am shocked at your manner of conduct," he said, looking down upon John. "You have not yet asked about my daughter's health?"

"I fully intended to, Mr. Jarney, at the first opportunity of breaking in on our line of conversation," said John.

"I am very happy to report she is growing better every hour," said Mr. Jarney, turning on his heel and walking across the room again, and returning, with a freshly lighted cigar in his mouth.

"I wish her well," replied John, and then he halted in what he intended to say further—halted for a moment only, when he asked: "Mr. Jarney, with your permission, I should like to see Miss Jarney, once in awhile during her illness. May I have the wish granted?"

"I have no objection—while she is ill," he answered, with that singular proviso attached.

Then he sat down, and took up his work. At noon he asked John to lunch with him. John accepted, and lunched. At four p. m. he asked John to accompany him home for dinner. John accepted, and went.

The combination of circumstances surrounding John's intimacies with the Jarney family was very indefinable to him, at first. But, as the days passed, he was slowly and assuredly convinced that his services as employe of that man of wealth were not of the sordid kind alone. Mr. Jarney's condescending manner, his straight-forwardness, his implicit faith in him, his good will toward him, his extinguishment of form, all showed to him that he was not so unapproachable as might be believed by any young man of the qualities of John Winthrope.

Possessed with an unquenchable desire to do that which is right, honest, honorable, or justifiable, John pursued a course that ever kept him in good favor. He did not do this with any preconceived plan, or scheme, to accomplish a purpose, but it was through an inherent prepossession of his makeup. Through the days he labored with great assiduity to get results; through the evenings he studied with great concentration on his subjects—always busy, always ready to answer a call, or a summons. All these traits in him, Mr. Jarney was not slow in perceiving, and he gave encouragement, as he would, like any other man of his mould, to any one who showed the same relative adaptation and faithfulness. Mr. Jarney looked upon John as having many parts worth cultivating. As he had, for a long time, been gleaning in the field of young manhood for such a reaping, he now considered, since he acquired John, that he had harvested a good sheaf of wheat when he garnered him; and he purposed, if all continued straight in him, to flail out his true worth, if the throwing out of opportunity would be effectually grasped. But while he had these views concerning such material for his purpose, he, at no time, thought that his daughter would, in any manner, enter into the proposition. He would not have thought of compromising his views on business with his paternal ideas; nor would he ever have condoned himself, or his wife, should either have entertained an iota of a notion that it were necessary to bring her name into such mercenary transactions.

By reason of the extraordinary events, however, that had come to pass, anent his daughter, he was perforce compelled to extenuate any qualifying conducements that might connect her with whomsoever claimed the privilege of being his second, as John was, in business. His amiableness toward John during the past few days might be interpreted in one particularity by the reader; which is, that he was encouraging that young man to press his suit for his daughter's hand; but this is farther from the thought than that he would give her away to any young profligate who might ask the favor of him. He was, withal, a true father, in its supremest meaning. He loved his daughter. He granted her every reasonable wish. He even went so far as to make unrelenting enemies among the Four Hundred, of which he was considered a worthy member, by discanting and discouraging their form of pleasures for the young men and women, and looking with disfavor upon the youths who paid his daughter the least attention. One of his most unpardonable offenses, in this connection, was his unsparing resentment toward Jasper Cobb's persistency in wanting to pay court to Edith, with matrimonial intent. The Cobbs could not, naturally, forgive him for such treatment of their young hopeful, who was just then strewing his pathway with the wildest kind of oats. And, as if fortune never failed him, Edith and her mother, coincided with him. This attitude of theirs, therefore, gave him the greatest kind of pleasure, and enhanced his inclination to stop at nothing that would satisfy their claims to his patronage.

The foregoing statement is made to show what manner of man he was with his family; but not to excuse him for the manner of man he was with his business associates. So, in showing favors toward his secretary, he acted from a double possibility, i. e.: one to have a trustworthy employe in a very important position; the other to curry favor with a very lovable daughter, who had an independence that might run wild on a clear trackage of his own building.

He had asked John to lunch with him that day mostly to be generous. He had asked him to his home again mostly for the good that his going might do for his afflicted child, in her hallucination. Nothing more. He did these things in such a cheerful way, and in such an unusual manner, that John was confounded. And he did it without reckoning the consequences, as many fathers act in the excitable moments of their infinite love for their offspring.

Entering the mansion on the hill, on this, his third visit, John had a very different feeling than before. The interval since he had been there had been spent in musing and meditating, with the consequent result of him being hopelessly smitten. No gilded hall of magic palace, no form of cast or idol of fetich, no conventional rule of wealth or arm of power, no scornful threat of irate father or scolding mother, no nothing could desist him in his conquest, if Edith were willing. If not, then he would forgive her, and—perhaps, perhaps—

Edith was sleeping when John was ushered into her room. Star, ever hopeful, ever faithful, sat by her bedside. Seeing John, Star arose and advanced to meet him, whispering, as she took his hand: "She is better—growing better every hour; but very slowly. She now sleeps."

"Then I shall retire till she awakes," said John.

"No; remain; she will awake soon," said Star.

No sound came from the sleeper, so peaceful was her rest, and so low her breathing. Her hands lay exposed above the spotless covers, with no nervous tremors in them. The flush of fever of the day before was gone. Her eyes were closed, and her lips were tightly shut. Her hair lay in ringlets over her temples. Was she dead? thought John; or was it the peace of a tired soul in rest that hung upon her? He trembled with great fear. Those dear blue eyes were closed to the light of day; those rosy cheeks had faded; the smile was gone. There was nothing to convince him that she lived.

Emboldened by the great anxiety that overwhelmed him, he drew up a chair and sat down by her bed. He picked up one of her hands, and felt her pulse. He found it throbbing, and he was relieved. He sat there silently, inconceivably happy, with his own heart throbbing so loudly that he could hear it beating. Ah, Edith, in her slumbering, might have heard its telepathic beating, too, for she suddenly opened her eyes, and turned them upon John, and smiled, so undisturbing was her awakening. She did not withdraw the hand that John was holding, nor did she seem to give a sign of recognition. But she sighed. Was it a sigh of her malady, or a sigh for him?

"How do you feel this evening, Miss Jarney?" asked John, in a low voice, deep with sympathetic tenderness.

Then, she opened wide her eyes, as if surprised, and withdrew her hand.

"Don't you know me, Miss Jarney?" asked John, with a fearsome thought that she had declined to her former condition.

"Is it you, Mr. Winthrope?" she asked, with her eyes lighting up. "Why, yes; I believed you were the doctor. I am so very weak, Mr. Winthrope, that I can scarcely speak."

"Do you feel better?" he asked.

"A little," she responded, feebly. "How glad it makes me feel to think you have come."

"Perhaps it would be better for me not to come while you are so low," he said.

"I feel better every time you come," she answered.

She involuntarily threw her hand over the side of the bed. He took it up, and held it; and then touched his lips to her small fingers—fingers so small and delicate and white now that they were like chiseled marble, pliable in his. She did not resist, through inability mostly to draw it away, had she been so disposed. She made no pretense to conceal her fondness for him, nor did she attempt to talk with any design to hurry him away, when he suggested that she would better rest in absolute quiet. John saw all this. But he believed that, in her frailty, he should be very prudent in how he acted, and leave nature, and what little he could do himself, to restore her to her former mental and physical health.

"You will remain awhile longer, Mr. Winthrope? I am growing better," she said.

"I hesitate about remaining, Miss Jarney, for fear of disturbing your peace," he answered.

"I rest better after seeing you," she whispered, with a trembling voice, as if she would break into crying.

"Then I am assured that I may come again?" he asked.

"You must come often—very often—every day—will you?"

"If your father continues his permission to that extent?"

"Oh, he will; papa is so good."

Is it an hallucination she is laboring under, thought John; or is it the will of a pure heart, feebly speaking? He was still perplexed; but his hopes were not deserting him.

"Mr. Winthrope," she said, after a silent spell, "will you go with Miss Barton on Sunday to her home, and act for me in what I had planned to do before I took ill?"

"Indeed, I shall be glad to accompany her, and shall do anything you wish," he answered.

"I had planned to do so much for the poor in Miss Barton's district," she continued. "I brought her here to be my companion and my aid—such a good girl she is—but I cannot do anything now, unless you will help. Will you?"

"I will, willingly," he responded, wonderingly.

"When I recover I shall enlist you in my service; we can do so much good for those distressed people."

"Nothing would please me better than to help you in this work." "Then, you and Miss Barton may begin it now; I shall join you when I have recovered."

"That will be a fine combination for charity's sake," he replied, enthusiastically.

"I knew you would enter into the scheme. How good you are!" she said, with a feeble effort to express her gratitude for him in a smile.

"I am afraid you flatter me, Miss Jarney," he answered, still holding her trembling hand.

"Oh, no; papa says you are so good; and I know you are."

"What time Sunday shall we go, Miss Barton?" asked John, turning to that young lady, with increasing enthusiasm over his accumulating duties.

"About ten o'clock, perhaps. You call here at that hour, when the auto will be in waiting for us," answered Star, sitting by him, with as much interest in him as Edith had herself.

"I shall be prompt to the minute," he replied.

John had remained an hour by Edith's bed talking in very confidential terms to those two divine maidens—one of them rich, one of them poor, but both blessed with many heavenly virtues. Edith was growing restless; although through it all John had been careful of what he said, and how he said it, so as not to excite her.

"Are you going?" she asked, seeing him rise. "I am sorry I cannot withstand the strain longer."

"I should go," he answered.

"You will come tomorrow? then I will be better," lifting up her hand to bid him good bye.

He knelt down by the bed, and held her hand in both of his for a moment. How it trembled, and how it thrilled him!

"Good bye," she said.

Oh, he prayed, within his heart, that she might be well in that moment of his own deep affliction, so that the fear that was in him might be expelled, and he knew his fate.

"Good bye," she said.

Going down the stairs he could hear that tremulous little voice saying, "Good bye." All through the dinner he heard it ringing like the distant trembulations of a wind-bell; going out the house he heard it calling after him; all the way to the city he heard it tinkling, tinkling from everything about the fleeting things in the streets, turning all the grime and misery into music. Going to his room it kept trembling, trembling, till that dingy little place was a Paradise. And going into sleep it kept singing—singing "Good bye! Good b-y-e! G-o-o-d—b—y—e!"

CHAPTER XVIII
PETER DIEMAN IS AVENGED

Black and sinister, like The Bastille, rears the bulky rambling building of that famous institution where infractors of the law are compensated for their weaknesses. Amidst verdent hills and by the murky river it sits as a ramparted fortress in a savage land. In sunshine and cloud, in fog and smoke and grime, it stands brooding, ever silent, ever sullen; it is a place of the damned, the wonderment of law-abiding men who hap to pass it by. Beyond the sounds of the teeming river, beyond the noise of forge and hammer, beyond the regular haunts of men, it is like a secluded bee-hive, when the workers are all within. No one hears the hammering, no one hears the sawing, pounding, dinning, breaking, singing, chanting, praying of all of those therein, save the unambitious workers themselves. For it is a penal institution.

Grim-visaged men, with loaded gun, stalk through its ringing halls, while haunting faces peer out from behind steel bars. The tread of many feet is hard, in step, on the hardened floors, as the men file to their places, like trained dogs cringing before their masters; the thump of many hammers is like a dreadful funeral march for the lost; the chant of many a tune is heard, in the time of rest, as the only cheerful note issuing therefrom. And above all is the old familiar human smell.

In one corner of a cell, on a cot, lies a man. He is bleary-eyed, and his face is swollen. His feet are bleeding, and his worn-out shoes lie on the floor. His old blue overalls and check shirt are torn, filthy and ready to fall from him. He rolls his head from side to side, and beats his breast with his knotted hands. The spume of an hectic cough hangs around his mouth, and blood flows out his nostrils. He is Billy Barton—dying—dying—alone! While the hammers ring, and the men chant, and the guards pace to and fro; while the clock is ticking for other men to come and go; while the sun is shining somewhere for the happy, the good and the bad alike, and all life outside is palpitating with a vigorous existence, Billy is going upon his final journey.

He was brought from a nasty jail, where mephitic filth was supreme, to this place where brutal men are supreme in their cruelty. Emaciated, gaunt, and made desperate by reason of the abuse heaped upon his crazed head, he was terrible in his obstinacy of prison rules. He was put to work with ball and chain tied about his ankles, when lying down on a feather bed would have been a severe and painful task to him. He was weak. He could not work, let alone stand. He was faint, sick, heartsore. But no one saw his misery. No one wanted to see it. For why should they? He was only a vagabond, and why should he receive attention?

He was pushed and pounded and thumped and beaten because he could not work. He was fed on bread and water for his failure; he was straight-jacketed, hung up by the wrists, given the water-cure; thrown into the dungeon and flogged. But the brute rises in man, sometimes, when met by a brute, and Billy struck back. This was the beginning of his end; for the deputy, being not yet satisfied in the full exercise of his authority, threw more of his brutishness into display, and laid Billy low with a cudgel that he carried, and dragged him, like a dog, to his cell, and threw him on his cot to die—alone!

An investigation into poor Billy Barton's death by the Honorable Board of Authorities revealed one of the most peculiar and singular cases that ever came to their discriminating notice. Billy died of heart failure, they announced. Of course, every man dies when his heart ceases to beat. Even those good and upright members of the Honorable Board of Authorities will die of that disease some day; and no doubt a tombstone will have all their virtues enscribed upon it. Billy Barton's—will simply be, William Barton, that's all.

Who should claim the body? Had he any friends? they punctiliously inquired. Yes; they found one. A man of worth, too—Peter Dieman, the humble junkman; Billy's old friend, of course, who would provide a decent funeral, and see that the last sad rites were said over his corruptible remains. Yes; Peter Dieman would do all this, being very generous, and a philanthropic man; for who would impinge his motives?

The body was, in the true fiction of such events, conveyed in very solemn state to that hovel on the south side of the Monongahela river, near which and within which all of Billy Barton's living time was spent. All his children were present at the funeral, except that one of ill-repute who had preceded his father upon the long unknown trail. All his former friends were present, with one extra added: Peter Dieman. Another friend was present, in the person of John Winthrope, as the representative of Edith, who sent the only flowers.

Had Billy Barton been resurrected the time he lay in his coffin, supported on two chairs, he would have seen a change in the furnishings of his earthly home; he would have seen paper on the walls, where once were the smutchings of discoloring time; he would have seen a carpet on the floor, pictures on the walls, one of which he would have seen was Madonna and her child; he would have seen many things that were not there when he was its besotted, irresponsible master. Ah, he would have seen his little girls dressed in new frocks, with a simple imitation of pride in their deportment; and his boys he would have seen, although still very rude, in a feeble effort to be vain over their new toggery. He would also have seen his slattern wife in a new dress, with her hair done up, and a new hope masked behind her stoical face. And he would have seen that other one, his daughter Star, whom he maltreated all her sorrowful years, come to offer up to God supplication for his soul; and, if his spirit had not yet departed, he would have heard her weeping in her anguish. As he lay in his shroud he would have felt the warm touch of little hands on his hard face, as the little ones stood about his bier taking a last farewell look at "Pap" before the man in black had covered up his face from their view forever; and he would have seen John, in all the freshness and beauty of young manhood, a consoling support to his only child that shed a tear. Still more, he would have seen that exaggerated piece of humanity, Peter Dieman, in all his implacable hatred for him, sitting in one corner, listening with exhultation to the droning voice of the minister saying the ritual words and singing "Rock of Ages."

Solemnly went the funeral cortege through the crowded thoroughfares bearing him away; and as the people looked with awe on his passing, remembering, perhaps, that they would take the same long ride some day, little did they reck how he lived and how he died.

To Homewood, a pretty decent place, they bore him, and put him beneath the ground, with the skeltering winds singing his funeral dirge. Above his grave Star and John placed a tombstone, with, "Our Father, William Barton; born Friday, December 13, 1861; died Friday, December 13, 1907," as the only legend. No virtues had he to be recorded, like those of the Honorable Board of Authorities. But he was gone—finally gone—out of the turmoil of this world.

Peter Dieman again sat in his little black office in The Die, smoking his scandalous pipe, rubbing his red hands, and squinting his piggish eyes; and giving vent occasionally to devlish outbursts of perfect satisfaction. Nothing consumed his mind so much at present as the reflection over his victory—his victory over Billy Barton, the worthless drunkard.

In his youth Peter went into the contest with Billy for the hand of Kate Jarney, a cousin of Hiram Jarney. Kate, being young and ignorant, selected the most prepossessing face, and took up her lot with that face, and all the horrors that accompanied it. Peter being of a revengeful nature, took up his life alone, a disappointed man, and sought to drown his sorrows in the role of Chief Ward Heeler.

Peter was not such a bad man in his younger days, but remorse over his unrequitted love drove him to diabolical things. Hence his attitude toward all mankind. For twenty years, almost, he was cross, crabbed and oppressive; and the wonder is how he maintained his power in his invidious treatment of his henchmen and his superiors. But this may be explained by his one saving grace of knowing how to string the "ropes" for the system—Graft—without breaking any of them, and screening the arch conspirators; for which he was amply rewarded. For twenty years, almost, he lived like a bear, spending his days in his black shop, and his nights in a shabby room above, like a miser—always with an irreconcilable fury burning beneath his hairy breast. For twenty years, almost, he brooded while he amassed a fortune, which gave him but the one comfort that the "some day" might bring. And his day had come at last.

Thus, as he sat in his office smoking and rubbing, the old light came back to him; and he was not slow to act. Leaving the shop in the care of the new clerk (Eli Jerey being yet indisposed) he went out. Finding a purveyor of "houses for sale," he traveled the circuitous rounds with that individual in search of a satisfying heap of stone and mortar. Selecting one of approved style and with the requisite number of rooms, in the rich men's district of the East End, he purchased. Then, fitting it up with all the dazzle that money could buy, he installed therein the entire Barton family, with one exception, of course; and ere the month was out, so little was his compunction as to propriety, he made the withered love of his youth his wife. And the gods caused him to smile, at last.

So affecting was this piece of news on Eli Jerey's mind that he forthwith began to arouse himself from his convalescing lethargy; and by another fortnight was down at his old post, with the same cadavorous look in his face, and the same slavish notions in his head. Since Peter had left his office: which he did immediately after his marriage: that little black hole stood silent, smokeless, with the accumulated filth of years still clinging to it. The little peephole was there, now with no wolfish eyes behind to peer through it, but still a source of much anxiety to Eli, who, so strong was the force of habit in him, even after he knew his master was gone, looked suspiciously at it ever and anon, as if it itself would turn into green eyes and knock him down by their stare, as those without the secret password had often done before. Otherwise, Eli had peace of soul, since that irritable old curmudgeon had surprised him into getting well.

Being faithful to his trust, he could not do different than he did; and it is well for him. For after Peter had returned from his long-delayed honeymoon, he came to the office only as a visitor. So magnanimous was he now, in his rejuvenated character, that he turned the junk shop and all his business over to Eli, to be managed as he willed. But this change in proprietorship in nowise took from the place the name it had acquired, nor from it the honor of being the repository of all the secrets of the System built up around it, with no apparent connection. So, instead of Peter being in his den, curled up like a stoat, he delegated, after awhile, to Eli the perfunctory duties of receiving and transmitting messages between himself and the henchmen, with Eli ensconced in the black office.

One day after taking up his incumbency therein, Eli received a call from Welty Morne.

"Where is Peter?" asked Welty, as he softly entered the sacred precinct of The Die, unawares to Eli.

Remembering his encounter with that young gentleman, Eli bustled up like a porcupine on the approach of an enemy, forgetting that he was to let by-gone be by-gones, and serve his master in a new role.

"Gone," answered Eli, boldly; "I'm boss here. What will you have?"

"Where's he gone?" asked Welty, a little ruffled.

"He's quit these quarters for good," answered Eli.

"Wonder he wouldn't let a fellow know such things," said Welty.

"I'm his messenger; what can I do for you?"

"You! I hope not to that extent!"

"Yes; me—to that extent," retorted Eli.

"Well;" and Welty studied a few moments; then continued: "Convey to him that Monroe wants to get in communication with him at once."

"I will do it," responded Eli.

Whereat, Eli descended into the darkness of his private phone booth, remained a few minutes, and returned, with the information that Peter would see him that evening at eight o'clock at the "Bartonage," as he called his new residence.

"Very well," said Welty, leaving in a sulky temper.

At the hour of eight p. m., Peter was sitting at his home in all his pomp and grandeur, when the starched smile of Monroe irradially floated in upon his complacency in an hitherto unknown expansiveness.

"You old tout," said Monroe feelingly; "you surprise us all by your new stunt."

When Peter laughed, which he did now sometimes, he was the picture of a crying calf, if the simile is permissible; so when he broke his face into one of his cunning signs of mirth, Monroe could not but help feeling amused himself, and accordingly split his barren face up into waves of noncommittal wrinkles.

"Ho, ho, ha, ha," cried Peter, forgetting now to rub his hands, and instead slapped his fat hand on his fat leg; "you old batches will have to fall in line. Look! and see how glorious it all is, Monroe; and to think that I have missed it all these twenty years! Ho, ho, ha, ha, he, he; you ought to try it, Monroe, and get those crimps out of your face!" Peter laughed at this jolly till tears ran down his cheeks.

"Why, I should think you were happy, Peter, the way you are going on about it," said Monroe, gloomily.

"Yes; try it, Monroe; you can get some one; can't you?" said Peter, with an extra bang on his fat leg as an extra emphasis to his seriousness.

"I've never met my Fate—that is, no Fate that would care to take me," he remarked, with the smile gone.

"How about Jarney's girl?" asked Peter, in a confidential tone.

"That young chap, Winthrope, seems to have the way to her door all to himself," responded the gloomy one.

"Who did you say?"

"Winthrope."

"I told you to get him out of the way."

"Well?"

"Well?"

"He can't be got out so easy," cried Monroe, with asperity. "He's an immovable, unapproachable, indefinable young cuss, who can't be inveigled."

"Have you given it up?"

"Oh, not yet."

"What you leading up to now?" asked Peter.

"To have the boss send him to the New York office."

"Will he send him?"

"He may."

"Say," said Peter, whisperingly, with an idea, "get him in the bribing line, and then let him drop."

"He's beyond that," said the undaunted Monroe. "We are going to send him to New York; give him authority to handle money, and lay our net to catch him. This can be done. We will work it so slick, with Bate Yenger as his assistant, that he can't crawl out; and we'll keep the money for our trouble."

"Good!" said Peter, forgetting himself and rubbing this time. "Go on?"

"That's all."

"Humph;" ejaculated Peter. "You are a genuine dough-god!"

"You bear!" scowled Monroe—that is, he tried to scowl.

"You unplastic scoundrel," shouted Peter, turning on him, "if you don't get him out of the way, and get that girl, I'll get your job away from you!"

"Oh, no more of your jollying," said the putty-faced Monroe; "get down to business. How much do I get out of the swag I get with the girl?"

"Half," replied Peter.

"Well, it's worth trying for," said Monroe.

"Say, by the by, Monroe; I received this today from Europe. Read it," said Peter, handing Monroe a letter, which had the following P. S. at the end: "I have lost fifteen at Monte Carlo; send ten, or I will return at once. (Signed) J. D."

"Does he mean fifteen thousand and ten thousand?" asked Monroe.

"He does."

"What will you do?"

"Send for Jacob Cobb."

"What will he do?"

"Furnish the money, of course."

"Jim Dalls is bleeding you for all the game is worth," said Monroe.

"We can do nothing else till we cease bleeding other people."

"You are plain about it, Peter."

"I am always plain, Monroe."

"Have you seen Cobb lately?" asked Monroe.

"Yesterday."

"How're things coming?"

"They're coming for the present," answered Peter. "Don't you think I need them coming to keep up this establishment when I am fully in the swim?"

"You probably do, Peter. I will run opposition to you when I get what's coming to me."

"Be sure you don't get into the Pen, Monroe," said Peter, looking up sidewise at Monroe, with a strange meaning in his eyes.

"And you?" asked Monroe.

"Oh, they can't get me; too much pull with the—"

Just then a howling brat, in silks and satins, came tearing into the room, riding a brass curtain pole as his "horse." On seeing a stranger, the youngster promptly made a flail out of the said curtain pole, and began to belabor Peter over the head with such effectiveness that Peter caught the child by the seat of his breeches, and hurled him blubbering into a corner.

"I thought you enjoyed your new existence," humorously remarked the staid Monroe.

"I do," answered the angered Peter, with a "humph."

"Well, if that is an example of what married life is, I don't think I want any of it in mine," said Monroe, with some dejection in the curl of his lips.

"Don't be so easily discouraged, Monroe; I've got ten like that one, on whom I spend my time in reforming."

"Oh, Lordy!" exclaimed the placid Monroe.

"Yes; it is Lordy sometimes, you would think, if you were here when they are all in."

"Why, I'd soon be in an asylum," said Monroe, despairingly.

"Say, Monroe, I've put Eli Jerey in my office," said Peter, changing the subject.

"He deserves promotion, no doubt; can he be trusted?"

"None more so; that's why I put him there. I'll give him the store when we pull off the next big deal."

"Will she go through?" asked Monroe.

"She will."

"How much?"

"One hundred thousand; then I'll quit."

"And we poor devils will have to take the crumbs," said the disheartened Monroe.

"Every one is paid according to his services," said Peter, in reply. "Get Winthrope out of the way, get the girl, and you'll have yours."

Monroe departed, feeling better.

CHAPTER XIX
WHILE THE FATHER WORRIES, MONROE SCHEMES AND CELEBRATES

"Mr. Winthrope," said Mr. Jarney, abstractedly, pacing his office floor, with his hands behind his back, and his head bowed in commiseration, "my daughter is getting no better—no better."

John made no reply, feeling that no reply should be made at that time, while the father was worrying so; for in that same moment he was moved himself beyond the efficacy of a consoling word. The garish light of the burning incandescents, in that late afternoon, was tantalizing and unbearable. The pictures on the wall stared down like taunting ghosts; the green-hued carpet and the reflect glimmer of the polished furniture seemed to reproach them for any sense of alleviation either might feel. The busy sound, the clamor, the roar and rumble of the streets was a hideous nightmare dinning in their ears. The heavy pall of smoke that heaved and rolled over the house-tops, infiltrating in its aqueous touch, was a magnet of melancholy.

Mr. Jarney stood by the window and looked out upon the flat-roofed buildings sitting below. He wondered if all the life therein and thereabout was so torn with dread expectation as his own; or whether any of them thought of life at all; or of the past, or of the present, or of the future. All his years he had had no inflictions, no sorrows, no troubles to set his latent sentimentality into ebullition. He had gone through the mill of business always prospering, always successful, always a leader, without a counteractive element to his iron will. He had gone through his wedded period with a love for his wife, his child and his home, that was unsurpassable, believing that no untoward thing could ever happen to disturb the tranquility of his perfect life. He believed that God had blessed him in this respect alone, to the exclusion of other men. But now the blasting hand of Fate, he felt, was turned upon him; and he had no peace while his child lay ill near unto death.

Back and forth he walked his office floor, in his anguish, fretfully silent, and deeply feeling for every one who might have a similar burden to bear. Coming to a stop by John's chair, he gazed down at his secretary, with a fixedness that caused John to have pity for his master.

"Mr. Winthrope," he said, "if she dies, my grief will be irreconcilable. The doctors say there is no hope."

"No hope?" faltered John.

"No hope," and the father sat down and cried.

Tears of sympathy came into John's eyes. Under the trying situation, he could not control his emotions. The breaking down of that strong man was more than he could stand, and he arose and walked across the room to a window, where he stopped for some time looking out, contending with his own passion. Then he returned to his chair, where he stood in an undecided frame of mind as to what to say.

"Mr. Jarney, you have my full sympathy," he said, about as expressive as he could say it, without unburdening his own heart's secret.

"Mr. Winthrope," he replied, turning to John, "it may seem weak in me giving way so easily; but you do not know, you cannot know what a father suffers in such extremities—no man can know, if he has a heart, unless he goes through it as I have these past few weeks. With all my worldly ambitions, I have willingly permitted my whole being to be infolded by her being, till no other thought so dominated me. She was such a lovable child, so good, so kind, so generous, so unlike any one else I ever saw, that my fatherly soul rebelled at the thought that anything would ever happen to tarnish her name, or that of my own. Of these things I was very careful that they did not come to pass. I have brought her up and educated her, with the one purpose, that she would be my one consolation in my declining years. And I intend, if she lives, that all I have shall be hers; and I know that she will give no cause for me to ever regret, like so many of the daughters of the rich do. I am rich, Mr. Winthrope, very rich; but I will give all I have, if that would save her for me, and would face the world anew without a dollar. Oh, you do not know—nobody can know what my anguish is!"

"Mr. Jarney, I realize what it might be," said John.

"I had hopes that when she came out of the trance the first time the crisis had passed," he went on. "She did improve for a few days; but suddenly she took a relapse and began to weaken, and weaken day by day, and now I fear for the worst. She is of my own flesh and blood—oh, God, I cannot bear it—yes—I must bear it. But in bearing it, what have I as a compensation? Money is nothing; home is nothing; life is nothing, without some one like her depending on you. A child might be ever so bad, but still a parent's love goes out to it, in all its misfortunes and shortcomings. But to have a child like her is not given to every man, and the parent of such a child should be doubly blessed. I know that I am selfish in these views. I know that other parents will differ with me in what I say as to my child being the best; but no one can say that I am wrong did they but know her. I do not know what I shall do, if she is taken from me—I do not know. I am already losing interest in things."

"Mr. Jarney," said John, after he had ceased, "I hope the doctors' conclusions are wrong, and that your expectations will not come to pass. I believe that she will recover; I have believed it all through her trial; but I may be mistaken."

"I hope you are not mistaken, Mr. Winthrope," he replied. "I hope I am. I have never hoped before that I might be mistaken, and I hope I shall not be disappointed this time."

Mr. Jarney then took up his accumulation of letters, that had not been attended to for three days, and began dictating answers. He was so overcome by anxiety, dread and fear, that he had great difficulty in composing himself sufficiently to go through them all. Some he answered with a line, where a whole page would have been necessary before. Many he did not answer at all, being indifferent as to what became of them. He was nervous, agitated, and careless. After he had finished, although not very satisfactorily to John, who had been used to his methodical handling of his correspondence, and after John began to prepare to depart, he turned to him and said:

"Mr. Winthrope, I am thinking of promoting you; would you like to go to New York?"

"I should not care to leave you, Mr. Jarney, so agreeable have my connections been in this office; but if you desire me to make a change, and if I am capable, I shall go wherever I am sent," said John.

"An assistant treasurer is wanted for the New York office; how would you like that?"

"Well, Mr. Jarney, this comes as a greater surprise than when you gave me this position; but, however, I shall accept, if it is the wish of my superiors."

"They want a man immediately for the place; but—I do not want to see you go away yet, though I want to see you get the place. You are capable, and deserving of it."

"I would rather remain here; but if I am to go higher, I suppose I should go at once to wherever I am to go."

"Another thing, Mr. Winthrope; you should not go while my daughter continues ill. Or—or—No, you shall remain here till she recovers. Some one else can fill the place till that time comes. It may seem strange for me to say so, her recovery may depend upon you remaining. It is only an hallucination of her mind, I know; but if her seeing you will do any good, I shall not forget it."

"Do you believe it is an hallucination?" asked John.

"Can be nothing else," he replied, gravely and reflectively. "You were the last one whom she saw and talked with while in her rational mind. The doctors say this is invariably true in all such cases—the impression of that person is indelibly left on the mind of the one afflicted, and remains there till recovery."

"But Miss Barton was there also," returned John, in disputation of his theory.

"That is true; but Miss Barton is with her all the time," he replied, as an argumentative fact.

"It may be," said John, in a deeper quandary than ever. "Then I am to remain here?"

"Yes—till her recovery, or—Be ready to go home with me an hour later today—five o'clock," said Mr. Jarney, as John left him.

In the meantime, while the confidential conversation was going on between master and secretary, Miram Monroe sat in his office scheming against his employer, against the secretary, and against the sick young woman, whose knowledge of things worldly was now a blank. It is always true of men of limited ability that they aim far above the possible. Monroe, with his microscopic smile this day stretched almost into a cynical grin, so satisfied was he with his genius, was perusing page after page of complicated figures. He was doing this mechanically, though, or otherwise he could not have O K'd them, being as he was in such a ruminating turn, with his mind set on other things so much dearer to his undefiling heart. Who was possessed with his special inborn faculty, qualifying him for his employment? Who had such a special disposition to accomplish what he purposed? Who had such a presiding genius for good or evil over the destiny of other men? Why, Miram Monroe—Mr. Monroe, if you please. He rang a bell. Welty Morne stepped within, and closed the door behind him, meeting his superior with a superior smile to that of the rigid face.

"Welty," said Monroe, with the solemnity of a gray goose, "I have seen the boss of the Board of Directors."

"Well?"

"They have decided, he tells me, to create the office of assistant treasurer in the New York branch."

"No!"

"Yes," without a crow's foot.

"Good, old boy; we must celebrate it tonight," said Welty, in a whisper.

"And the young chap goes."

"No!"

"Yes," without a wrinkle.

"We must celebrate that tomorrow night—When?"

"At once," without a crack.

"Bully! We must celebrate that the next night—Who?"

"You," without a wink.

"No!"

"Yes," without a twinkle.

"Whee! We'll celebrate that the next night—Where?"

"At the Bottomless Pit," with a microscopic smile. "Be at my room at nine p. m."

"With joy, old boy; I'll be with you! Hah, you're no two-spot!" With this Welty expired, almost, over his good feelings that his promotion brought over him.

The bell rang again. In came Bate Yenger, with a crimped smile on his stale face.

"Bate, do you want Welty's place?" asked the marble idol.

"Want it?" exclaimed the idolizing Bate. "Can I get it? or are you buffooning?"

"You have it, Bate," without a twitch.

"When?" asked the anxious Bate.

"Soon," without a quiver.

"Shall we celebrate?" asked Bate.

"We will," with a smack.

"Where?"

"At the Bottomless Pit," with a feathered smile. "Be at my room at nine p. m."

"Bully!" With this Bate also expired—with joy over his air castles.

Accordingly, at nine p. m., the trio met in rooms Nos. 4-11-44 in the St. Charles hotel, a hostelry of good repute where men of disrepute would sometimes get through the cordon of morality that was strung around it. Monroe had a suite of three rooms, as became a man of quality, as he was, with no disparagement of the "quality." These quarters were furnished, of course, in such magnificence that contrast between the riches of the room and the nature of the man was like the temperate and the frigid zones. His bed room was in white enamel, with cream-colored carpet, a frail white iron bed-stead, with dainty white materials on it. Why the combination? It was that he, when he donned his white night gown, imagined he would be in a little heaven of his own, during his nocturnal sojournings into Dreamland—the only heaven he ever would be enabled to approach, perhaps. He had a lounging room fitted up in gray, in which he lounged during his hours of rest, and in which he received his friends. The other room he called the Bottomless Pit—not that it was bottomless, nor that it was a pit, in the strict sense, but that here was where he refreshed himself and entertained. It was done in dark-brown, probably in commemoration of that old jest, "dark-brown taste the morning after."

Welty and Bate had been there before, so they needed no formal reception to cause them to make themselves at home. So repairing to the Pit, a spread was in waiting. The bill-of-fare (ach, god in himmel, it should be menu) was mushrooms on toast, frogs' legs in butter, calves' brains in cracker meal, squabs in stew, oysters in whisky, rolls in brown, butter in squares, sugar in cubes, coffee in percolator, pickles in acetics, cheese in limburger, nuts in hull, desserts in bottle, and cigars in box. All this in honor of Monroe's erudition as a manipulator of things clandestine in his attempt at circumvention of a certain favored young man.

When they sat down at the table, which was just big enough for three to hear each other across with loud talk, with the load of savory things in china, garnished by genuine sterling, upon it, they were all very hungry, and besides very thirsty.

"Gentlemen," said the stiffness, rising, without a break in his metallic visage, the others rising with him, "gentlemen, a toast to the lady; may the good Lord preserve her."

"The lady! the lady!" cried the two Monroe dupes in unison.

"And to Welty and Bate; may they ever prosper in their new jobs," he continued. "Hah, too conscientiously modest to toast yourselves, are you?—take water, you kids." This last remark was made by him when he saw that Welty and Bate hesitated about toasting themselves. However, they toasted.

Thus they toasted, and they gabbled, and they ate, till all the viands had vanished, and nothing was left upon the board but the smeared platters. Then to the bottles they betook themselves with a wild and merry gusto. Monroe pulled the corks, and poured. He drank, and they drank. He smoked, and they smoked, till the air was a blue haze of whirling objects, only to be dispelled by the dark-brown in the morning.

Once, during a fit of eructation, Monroe thought he would surely die, and got ready to make his will.

"Write it out, Welty," he commanded, in a severe maudlin tone; "and write it out so that She shall get it all, with a codicil that you and Bate are to get one-third of what is left, after I am gone. Whoop! Woe me! Woe me!" he wailed, with his face like that of a gargoyle. "Write it out before I die," he said, as he went staggering against a wall, falling over a chair, crushing down a rocker, flailing his hands like bat's wings, as he retched and perambulated through the Pit.

"Give me a pen first, and paper; I can't write (hic) with my fingers like a chink," said the hysterical Welty—hysterical in mirth only over the wild effusions of Monroe.

"I'll write it; I'll write it, if I have to use my toes, if you get me the ink, or tar, or something else that is black—only get it; get it!" weeped the disconsolate Bate, who at that moment had a fearsome feeling that his friend Monroe would die before the act was done, lolling his head the while over the back of his chair, as if that part of his anatomy was too loose ever to be set back to its normality.

At this outburst of Bate, Monroe plunged forward through the door of the Pit to the gray room, and to his secretary, from which he withdrew everything before he found the ink, the pen and the paper. Returning with these articles, Welty wrote the will in such hiroglyphic chirography that a Greely himself could not make it out. But it was writ, and signed, and sealed in due form. Welty in his hilarity did not lose sight of its import, and put it away in a secret pocket, for future use should the occasion ever demand it.

He then shouldered Monroe into his downy bed, in full dress, with "Woe me! Woe me!" escaping in a groan from his unsmiling lips. Then Welty took the inebriated Bate, in the completeness of debauch, and rolled him, shoes and all, into that otherwise spotless couch. Then, before he should completely lose the balance of his own muddled reason, he also tumbled into Monroe's heaven, leaving the dark-brown room to clarify itself of their revelings.

And amid the stillness of the lights, all left burning brightly, they went sailing into the land of ethereal asphyxia, to await the hour of the "dark-brown taste" to bring them back to the time of remorse, and its painful complications.

CHAPTER XX
WHAT THE SPRINGTIME BROUGHT FORTH

Christmas had come and gone; New Years was here, and passing, and Edith still lay upon her bed. Her face was thin and wan and spiritless. Her form had wasted away till she was almost as a skeleton. Her little hands were fleshless and cold, and her eyes were dull. The malady was in her brain yet, refusing to lift its anchorage, although she saw and recognized everybody permitted in her sight.

John came and went every day, in the late afternoons; and every day he came with the same perplexed feelings. The "good byes" rang in his ears, growing weaker and weaker in their timbreling, from morning unto night—following him everywhere, till he was near crazed himself, in his helplessness, for the sweet one that breathed the "good byes" in his ears. He went up and down and in and out the pathways of his small world, and got no comfort in anything, save what consolation there was in his work, which was meagre now in the sadness of his love-making.

As he would sit by the bed holding her hand in his, tears would roll down his cheeks. She would lie so still, so beautifully transcendent in her weakness, looking at him, and speak so low and so trembling that he could scarce make out her words. Oftentimes he would kneel down and pray for her deliverance from the scourge that lay upon her. Sometimes the sun would break through the clouds and smoke, in its setting, and throw its transient rays upon her face, and he would take it as a good omen; but most often the days were dark, and the light was sombre, like his spirits. Sometimes he would sit by the window, while she slept, watching the snow driving by in its purity, and his mind would revert to the sleeper, whose purity was whiter than the snow. Day after day, he would come full of hope, and depart full of fear; for she was growing worse; and all the inmates of that mansion were in despair. Would she die before she waked? they all would question in their looks, looking at her in her sleep. Would she ever reach the crisis again that once before had given joy? or would she linger on, and finally pass away, without a murmur, like a child?

No one could tell—no one could tell! Still she lingered on, bravely refusing to give up her fluttering spirit.

Sometimes she would brighten up, and talk with Star on her only theme—John—and then relapse into comatose. Often she would ask for him, when he was away, as if he were gone forever, and when he would come would only look, with a faint smile of satisfaction in her face. Sometimes she would raise her hand, and lay it on his, as if she wished to express her love, but could not. "I am so weak—so weak," was her constant plaint, as if weary of the fight she was making. Whenever John was ready to depart, she roused herself to the saying of "Good bye, good bye," and then sleep.

O, what are the pains one must endure, in this life, to keep it going!

Through the days and through the weeks this continued, without an indication that there was any chance. Through the weeks and through the months, the Reaper, with his Scythe, sat outside her chamber door—waiting, waiting; and the angels appeared to hover over her—waiting, waiting—to transport her to their own abode, where she seemed more fittingly to belong.

But he, nor they, never entered that chamber door. For the coming of the birds and the budding of the trees was the magic cure. Her eyes opened up, like a startled violet, in the springtime, as if she had slept, like the violet, through the winter season. The wild rose lodged its colors in her cheeks, after playing with the April winds, and the spirit of the new life overwhelmed her. The little skeleton that she had been for months was transformed into a vitalized being. As she once was, she was again, only more lovely, with the effects of a lingering illness still in its subduing tones.

Sitting by the window, when the birds were singing in the park about her home, she was dreaming of the new world that was opened to her view. It was not the singing birds alone, nor the budding trees, nor the greening grass, nor the blooming cowslips or jonquils that she saw outside rejoicing at the turn of the season, that made her heart rejoice; neither was it returning health alone that brought the glint of the diamond in her eyes, the pulsing flush upon her cheeks, the happier smile to her lips, the sweeter tone to her voice. It was—it was—it was that Love that lights the Soul, and causes even smoke and grime to be dancing gems and pearls.

Sitting by the window, she was dreaming of him, who had gone, and who had said he would return—some day—some day. Oh, that some day is what makes the heart so sore, at the parting; for it is an indefinite time of chance, but still a solace to the craving heart. Edith was dreaming of the last words that John had said before he went away, "May I come to see you some day, now that you are getting well." They kept ringing in her ears as a pleading hope, as "good bye, good bye," still was ringing in his. She was thinking of what she had said, as he was going, "You may come, you may come—yes—yes, you may come," as she still was lying on her bed. And now, in this time of her day-dreaming, she hoped that he had not gone. In dreaming back over the oblivious days, she remembered faintly that he came to her somewhere. Was it in this world that she saw him all the time? or had it been in some other that she saw him? or was it a mere illusion, after all? and he had come at last only to say farewell, as a duty. No; she saw him every day through the long silence of her sleep. It was he; it must have been; and did he know, or think, or believe, that she loved him? He must have known it, she kept dreaming, if that were he that she saw every day. And would he return to meet her love in that Some Day. He would, she kept dreaming; he would.

Sitting by the window, on this the first day of her convalescing period, she saw the smoke and fog roll by; she saw the sun warming everything into life, as the time was stirring her into a loving being again. Star was sitting by her side holding one hand in hers, with faith and hope in her own dear heart.

"You are getting well so fast, dear Edith," said Star, patting her delicate hand.

"I feel new all over, dear Star," said Edith, smiling down upon her dearest friend. "Everything is so bright and so charming outside today, it seems it was made just for me in my recovery. How I wish I could go out upon the lawn and pluck the flowers, and listen to the birds, and even sing myself."

"You may go some day, dear Edith; you may go, and I will be the first to go and lead you the way," replied the constant Star.

"Oh, Star! that some day, some day, always keeps ringing in my ears—I hope it will come," said Edith, with a tear of regret coming down her brightening cheek.

"Do not be despondent, dear," said Star, brushing away Edith's tears.

"I am not despondent, dear," said Edith; "I am happy."

"I thought tears were shed in sorrow, Edith," responded Star, in her innocence.

"I have had no sorrow, dear. My life has been one of happiness; and when I am most happy, I shed tears, sometimes," said Edith.

"Oh, Edith, I know," said Star, with a mischievous look.

"Does he know?" asked Edith, putting her arm around the neck of her friend.

"He must know," answered Star, seriously.

"Tell me all about it, Star—all?" said Edith.

"Since you first took ill?" asked Star.

"Everything—I want to know," said Edith.

"My, Edith! he did so many things, that it might make you blush, did I tell you," said Star, laughing.

"Why! what did he do?" asked Edith, with an inkling that she had not been dreaming all the time.

"Do? Why, Edith! the first thing he did, was to put his arm around you in the cab coming home that night," began Star.

"Why, my faithful Star! Did you permit him to do that?" asked Edith, appearing to be repellent in her tone.

"He couldn't help it, dear; you was as limp as a rag, and he had to hold you up. When we got home, he picked you up, and carried you into this very room, and laid you on your bed."

"My! oh, my, Star! he didn't do that, did he?" exclaimed Edith. "How dreadful!"

"It couldn't be helped," replied the sympathetic Star, as her only explanation.

"Now, I am real mad at you, Star, for permitting such a thing. I would have been real mad at him, too—I would not have permitted it, had I been in my senses," said Edith, affecting anger.

"That is the reason he did it, Edith; you couldn't help yourself; you were not in your senses," said the compromising Star.

"Go on, Star," said Edith, seeing that Star was hesitating about telling her more.

"You called for him every day for a week, Edith, till—"

"—I am a little goose, Star; I always knew I was; now I know it. Did he come?"

"He came; and brought you back to your senses, dear."

"I do now remember seeing him somewhere—sometime—I can't think, Star—where it was—what else?" said Edith, growing nervous.

"He came every day, Edith—every day, after that, and sat by your bed for an hour, and held your hand—"

"—now I know I am a goose for allowing such conduct—no, I am not mad, Star. Did he do that?"

"—and he knelt down and prayed for you, every day, almost, Edith."

"God bless him!" said Edith, as the tears came to her eyes.

"—and you talked to him, Edith, sometimes, and always asked him to come again—"

"—I must have been out of my head."

"Don't you remember it, Edith—any of it, at all?"

"I have a faint recollection of something, which I cannot clearly make out—I know—I know, Star. It has possessed me ever since I saw him—I am not provoked at anything he did, Star."

"But, Edith; Edith, listen," said Star, in an admonishing tone; "he came as a matter of duty, believing it was an hallucination of yours."

"He will forgive me, then," returned Edith, with calm resignation, "if I did or said anything unbecoming a lady, who—who—oh, Star, I cannot believe that I did anything wrong, do you? If he never knows, I will keep my secret, and you will help me in my troubled heart, will you not, dear?"

"He loves you, Edith."

"Dear Star," said Edith, as she threw both arms around her friend's neck; "does he? Does he? Are you sure?"

"I am sure, Edith," said Star, kissing Edith. "He told me as much."

"That was not kind in him; he should tell me first," said Edith, pensively.

"But he told me not to tell," replied Star, regretfully; "and he said he never expected to claim your hand—"

"Why? My riches will not be in the way," she said, as she began to cry.

"That is why, Edith," said Star, consolingly. "He said he could not hope to meet you on the same level—"

"Money!" exclaimed Edith.

"Money," replied Star, very low; "he hasn't any."

"That is why I love him, Star; and because he is better than any man I have ever seen, except, perhaps, my father. This is one of the greatest troubles the daughters of the rich have—the finding of a good young man among them; and the good young men who are poor are too self-conscious to seek us."

"But he has asked to come again, Edith," said Star, hopefully.

"Some day—some day," sighed Edith, looking out the window. Then: "I wish I had never seen—no, no; that is not what I mean. Had I never seen him, I would not have this pain, the pain of uncertainty, in my heart. Awhile ago I was very happy; but now I feel like lying down in the bed again, and remaining there till—oh, I wish he would come, and I—no, I could not do that; he must find it out, if he is ever to know. I will get well first, Star, and then we will take up the work, Star, I had planned before I became ill; and work to do some good in the world. I am feeling very weak, Star. This has been too much for me; will you assist me to my bed. Oh, Star, I am sorry—sorry for it all. You do not know, dear Star. You will not know till some good man comes along and strikes a responsive chord in your heart—you will not know, Star, till then. Help me to bed, and let me rest."

Sitting by her bedside, Star heard, for the first time, the story that Edith promised to tell her that day when she first came into Edith's life. After lying down, Edith was more calm, and was still in the mood to continue her confidential talk with Star.

"Star, do you know that you are my cousin?" asked Edith.

"Cousin!" exclaimed Star, as if she did not understand.

"Yes, Star; cousin! Your mother is a first cousin to my father; but I never knew it till about the time I sent for you."

Star leant over and kissed Edith, and drew her face up till their cheeks touched.

"Edith," whispered Star, "you are an angel," and then released her, and assumed a kneeling position, while Edith continued:

"I saw you one day, Star, when I was with my father on a mission of mercy in the poor districts of the South Side. When first I saw you, you were on your knees scrubbing the floor—at that place where you worked. I saw your face, and fell in love with you as soon as I saw you, for I knew that you were good. I told papa that it was a pity for a beautiful girl like you to be doing that kind of drudgery, when he said that we could, perhaps, get you a better place. We asked you your name, if you remember—"

"I remember," said Star.

"—and when you said it was Star Barton, papa gave such a turn to his countenance that I thought it meant something that he had concealed from us at home. So when we came home I asked him what he meant, and he told me then who you were; and he told me who your father and mother were; and how they, when young, ran away from home and were married. I sent my maid, Sarah Devore, to search you out, telling her who you were, and have you come to this place in search of a position as a domestic, for fear that if I told you the truth you would be too proud to work for your rich relations. You came, as you know how, and when I saw you again, I fell in love with you. First, I wanted you to be my maid; but my pride of you was too great to make you anything but my equal in this house. So you see, instead of being my maid, you have been my faithful companion—and nurse. Dear Star, I love you, and if you will always remain with me, I shall be the happiest person on earth."

"Dear Edith," said Star, with tears of gratitude in her eyes, "I knew you were good when first I beheld you; but I never knew that such goodness could be in any kinsman of mine. I never told you of the life I lived; I never told you how we lived at home; I never told you of my father or my mother. For it always gave me grief to think of it. Poor father is dead!"

"Dead!" said Edith.

"Yes; died last December; and my mother has married Peter Dieman, who courted her—"

"Dieman!"

"Yes; the junkman. They live in one of the finest places in the East End. I am sorry, very sorry, that my father died, as he was the only father I shall ever know; but I am glad that my mother has married again. When you get well, I shall take you out to see her, and you can see how she now lives. I never was ashamed of my parents, Edith, never. I did all I could for them, in my simple way, and would do it again, if called upon to do it. After you took ill, I carried out your wish, and, with Mr. Winthrope, went to our home and fitted it out decently for my mother and the children. My mother was always sad and brooded over her troubles, and had no heart for anything. Poor mother! I am glad that she has married again."

Star cried in remembrance of it all; for her heart was good. Even dear Edith could not help but shed a tear. And they sobbed on each other's breast over sorrows that had passed.

Then, brushing away their tears, and laughing over their tender-heartedness, they resumed their talk.

"Edith," said Star, "I must confess that I marveled at your actions. I could not resist you, though. I cannot see how anybody can. It seemed strange to me that any one so good and rich as you should light upon me, and make me your companion. Yes, I marveled at it. Now, I know it is not strange. I love you, dear Edith, and shall never leave you, unless—"

"Unless what?" asked Edith, smiling.

"—he should come to claim you."

"He shall never know from me, dear Star; that would not be womanly—why, yes, you dear, you had to go and tell him. But will he ever see the true light burning—burning for him?"

"He shall, if I ever see him again; or I shall write," said Star, teasingly, still with her eyes red from crying over recollections.

"You must not, Star; I could not forgive you—oh, yes, Star, I would forgive you anything—but not that," said Edith, concealing and revealing her true feelings at the same time. "What do you think papa would say, if he knew my love for him?" asked Edith. "Oh, I dread the time he hears of it! And my mamma? but she will be with me, I know, for she has told me that she likes him."

"She suspects something of the kind, Edith," said Star. "She asked you once just after Mr. Winthrope was here the first time; but she did not pursue the question. She believes it now."

"Star, I shall get well; that is my first duty, now that I am this far on toward recovery. I shall get well, Star, and you and I shall go—go—go—"

"Where. Edith?" asked Star, seeing her hesitancy in saying what she wanted to reveal.

"—to do missionary work among the poor."

True love comes but once in life to the pure in heart. Were we all as pure in heart as Edith, mankind's tribulations might be less irksome.

CHAPTER XXI
MONROE AND COBB VISIT PETER DIEMAN'S HOME TOGETHER

Peter Dieman sat in his high-backed leather-cushioned chair smoking a black cigar, surrounded with all the ease and sumptuousness of a successfully domesticated gentleman. As he smoked his favorite weed, the circumambient gray was as a smudge in the midst of a fruiting orange grove. And above it all, he smelled like one who had been soused in aromatic oils.

A pair of satin-embroidered slippers encased his broad flat feet; a red skull-cap, with a maroon tassel on top of it, bore down upon his rufous head of hair; a purple-flowered mandarin-like robe enfolded his pudgy body. The hairsuite appendage that had gone neglected for years, had been unceremoniously removed from his chin; a yellow stubby moustache, closely cropped, hung above his lips like clipped porcupine quills, and a new set of hand-made teeth filled his sprawling mouth. The rubicundity of his face might have been taken as a danger sign on a dark night, with his green-gray eyes lighted up as a companion signal. A masseur had rubbed the scowl of years and the hate of time out of his face, till its rotundity was equaled only by the full moon recovering from a case of the dumps. So, all that were necessary to complete his personification of Old King Cole were the long-stemmed pipe and the serrated crown. While the latter would not have been essential to the enhancement of his kingly appearance, it might have been a fitting part toward the completion of his princely makeup.

Thus he sat and thus he looked in his spectacular pomp of power—a sub-king of the grafters—since he went into the soul-quieting business of matrimony. Thus he sat and thus he looked, when Miram Monroe, the genteel ghost, was let into his presence. Thus he sat and thus he looked, when Jacob Cobb, the ring-master, was ushered in—one following the other.

Would the visitors smoke? asked His Majesty. Yes, the visitors would smoke, as a favor to this potentate. And they smoked, and they smoked till they filled the air so full of toxic fumes that the fair king was almost obscured by the baleful haze.

"Before we get down to business, gentlemen," said Peter, in all his suavity of new refinement, as he slapped his fat right leg with his heavy right hand, and scratched his head behind the ear with his left, "I must escort you through my palace. I've got a place—" waving now his right hand above his head in indication of the building that enclosed him—"good as any man's; and I want you two old friends to see it before we get down to business. Pleasure first, gentlemen, you know; pleasure first, to me, now."

"I'll be glorified to see it," said the ghost.

"I'll be sanctified to see it," said the ring-master.

Peter arose with kingly mien, shaking the rheumatism out of his joints and the gout out of his toes, and then swelling out his breast to a boa constrictor size after swallowing a goat, wheezing like a horse with the heaves. He led the way, with his robe dragging on the carpet, to circumnavigate the building, the ghost and the ring-master following, respectively, with the sanctimonious bearing of laymen following a high-priest.

"The kiddies are out this evening attending a party, and I have all this great house to myself—" waving his right hand around like a preacher of the Word. "We will go up the stairs first."

Up the stairs Peter went, the ghost next after him, looking ahead and considering fearfully what he would feel like should the king lose his balance, in mounting the steps, which he seemed likely to do constantly as he elevated himself lift after lift, so clumsily did Peter climb; and the circus-master took his time, a safe distance behind, with a sweet air of passivity in his patience over Peter's laughable pomposity.

Peter led the way through brilliant halls and brilliant rooms, without a dark corner in any of them, nor even a blind closet in which to conceal the proverbial family ghost; which shadowy being, however, was not likely to seek a place of concealment in this home, since, as it happens, he had evaded all these pure pleasures of domesticity for so many years; so it would be an hazardous presumption to expect the stalker of family trouble to abide with him.

"Where're you going to keep the family ghost?" asked the real ghost.

"You old batch! Do you think I'd tolerate him round here?" said Peter, with connubial pride. "Cobb has a cinch on them all; eh, Cobb?" with a refreshened squint towards Cobb.

"Don't be so rude, Peter, as to bring me into your argumentations with Monroe here, whose own reputation needs a little stringing up," responded Cobb.

"Never mind your moralizing—show us your house," replied the ghost, without being the least irritated.

When they came to the bath room, they all stepped within; and the visitors were charmed. Peter took on a new halo of beamingness as he saw how delighted his patrons were over this dream of modern bathery, with its shining fixtures and alabastine walls.

"Do you bathe, Peter?" asked the ghost.

"I guess, yes—every morning at eight," answered Peter, with a swell.

"Humph!" responded the ghost; "and you didn't catch cold the first time?" with no attempt to be facetious.

"Alcohol is a great preventative," answered Peter.

"Within, or without?" asked the ghost.

"Without; you mummy," retorted Peter.

"You surprise me, Peter," said Cobb, as he was testing one of the faucets; "the last time I saw you, you looked as if you hadn't touched water in years."

"Once a year then; once a day now; three hundred and sixty-five days in the year," said Peter, grinning.

"I always believed you had some redeeming qualities," said Cobb; "but how does it come you have clean water?" he asked, holding up a glassful between his eyes and the light.

"Private filter," answered the king.

"That's infernal water to turn into the public trough," remarked Cobb. "I mean this, before it was filtered," pointing to the glassful still in his hand.

"It's all they deserve," said the king, snapping his eyes.

"When ought we to work them for a new system?" asked Cobb, emptying the glass. "Pretty decent water, this—when filtered," he observed, washing his hands.

"We'll talk about water systems when we get back to business," answered the king.

"Do you wash your feet in water or alcohol?" asked the ghost.

"Don't get too fresh, Monroe, or I'll loosen up your face with some soap and water," with a hearty chuckle.

"Oh, sometimes I forget, Peter, seeing you heretofore as a bear," as a mollifier to his allusions.

"You're a corrugated donkey, Monroe," said the king, with a louder chuckle than before, rubbing his hands, this time with a towel between them.

"You're a convoluted mule," returned the ghost, tapping the enameled wall with his knuckle, as a clincher to his assertion.

"Here, here! You fellows are getting too personal," said Cobb, stepping forward, as if he expected trouble, so as to be ready as a queller of what he thought might lead to a melee.

"Hah, ha, ha!" roared Peter, strutting out like a gallinaceous cock. "Cobb, you must pay no attention to Monroe's foolishness," as he swept theatrically along the hallway to the stairs; but still presenting the incongruous habits of a waddling duck.

Monroe followed languidly, puckering his mouth into a low whistle, that might have meant more than the blowing out of good humor. With most men, whistling means the venting of a superfluity of joy; but with Monroe, it might have meant a cooling drop in his cup of anger. Cobb came lolling after them, in his usual undisturbed forbearance.

Debouching into the parlor, with the stellar lights trailing, the king touched a button; presto! starlight, moonlight, sunlight, all together, in one grand aurora borealis, flashed mute darkness into palpitating day.

"This is my universe," cried the king, throwing up both hands, as if he were beginning the Sermon on the Mount.

"Grand!" whispered the ghost.

"Grand!" said the ring-master.

"Grand" cried back The Moses, The Napoleon, The Wellington, The Washington, The Roosevelt, The Pathfinder, The Man With the Hoe, The Babes in the Woods, The Doves, The Dieman, on the walls.

"Grand!" echoed Mozart, Beethoven, Wagner, Shakespeare, Milton, Poe, Irving, Longfellow, Emerson, standing about in corners and alcoves in their statuary dumbness.

"Grand!" pealed the Giant Grand resting on four legs, like an exhibition slab of mahogany, in a corner.

"Grand!" laughed the settees, the tete-a-tetes, the rockers, the cushions, the chairs, as if they were ready to jump up and slap the visitors on the back and seat them down.

"Grand!" shouted the king. "Well, I should eat a bedbug, if you can surpass it in this old town for dazzle." And everything hung its head in mortification.

"Grand!" they all said, as the king entered the dining room, with its glitter and its glimmer and its splendor and its grandeur. "Here is where I eat," he remarked, after seeing his friends dumfounded and speechless.

Dumfounded? Why, of course!

Speechless? Why, to be sure!

Shucks! Who said the average man isn't a pompous idiot?

"To business, now, gentlemen; to business," said Peter, waving his hand toward his private den, where first he was greeted in his royal robes by the genteel ghost and the ring-master.

"Well?" said Peter, after seating himself in his chair of state, directing his question to Cobb.

"Let Monroe speak," said Cobb.

"Let Cobb speak," said Monroe.

"Gentlemen, my proposition is the proposed new water system," said Cobb, venturing forth. "What about it?"

"Well, what about it?" asked Peter.

"Can we pull it off?" asked Cobb.

"How much is there in it?" asked the generous Peter.

"Couple hundred thousand," said Cobb.

"Pull her off, then," decided Peter.

"How much do I get out of it?" asked Monroe.

"Aren't you working your little stunt for bigger game, Monroe?" asked Peter.

"What new stunt you up to now?" asked Cobb, suspiciously.

"That's a private matter," replied Monroe.

"What is it, Peter?" asked Cobb. Then to Monroe: "Not scheming behind my back, Monroe?"

"No such intention," answered Monroe.

"What is it, Peter?" asked Cobb, feelingly.

"Monroe, I told you to keep no secrets from Cobb," said Peter.

"What is it. Peter?" asked Cobb.

"Shall I tell, Monroe?" said Peter.

"Dogged if I care," said the unimpressionable Monroe.

"He's after Jarney's daughter and her money," said Peter, rubbing his hands on his legs, and pulling hard on a freshly lighted cigar.

"Ho, that's why young Winthrope was sent to the New York office, was it?" said Cobb, carelessly.

"Yes; it looked too serious seeing him going to her home every day," replied Monroe. "While I also went, sometimes, I never got a squint at her."

Cobb became serious at this piece of intelligence. He thought of young Jasper Cobb, his son, as being entitled to a share of the spoils that might be obtained by an alliance with the Jarneys. He thought all plans had been laid for this catch, and all that were needed was to draw in the net and sort the fishes. He thought that, as a matter of course, there could be no failure. He never thought that his son was unfit for a young lady of the graces of Miss Jarney. He never thought children had a right to be heard in making their choice of a life partner. He never thought that Jarney should be consulted. Men of Cobb's stripe never think of the ethical side of a question. They never think of anything but money—how to get it, and how to spend it. They never think of anything, aside from getting money, but of the voluptuous side of life. And this astounding statement of Peter's, relative to Monroe's plotting, came as a cross-complaint to him. Baseless wretch is Mr. Monroe!

"What're your prospects, Monroe?" asked Cobb, leaning his head far back in his chair, and blowing smoke upwards, indolently meditating over something that did not go down very well.

"Good," said Monroe.

"Explain?" said Cobb.

"Oh; why, that's a private matter, Mr. Cobb," said Monroe, looking more uncommunicable than ever.

"I must know," insisted Cobb, fidgeting in his chair, with a fine interrogative smile of assertive power.

"Tell him, Monroe; tell him," said Peter, rubbing his hands, and blowing smoke like a whale spouting water.

"There's nothing tangible yet," said the yielding Monroe.

"Tell it, Monroe!" commanded Peter.

"What is it?" asked Cobb, sarcastically.

"Well; here goes. First, I am working into the good graces of the father first," said he. "When I accomplish that feat, having Winthrope out of my way, I shall press my suit for the young lady's hand. I have been to the Jarney home a great many times for dinner this winter"—he looked as if he wanted to keep the matter a secret—"and I have always found young Winthrope there. He was permitted to see her, as Mr. Jarney explained, as the result of an hallucination caused by an auto accident, and her illness following it. I never got an opportunity to see her. Of course—" he seemed to be unconcerned about her illness, so listlessly did he talk—"it would have been a delicate matter for me to have attempted to have seen her while ill; so I concluded to abide my time. Getting him away was my first scheme. This accomplished, and, she recovering as I am told, I shall take the first opportunity presented to ask her."

During the recital of the above. Monroe acted more like an automatic talking machine, than a human, so inanimate was his facial expression.

"Would she throw herself away on you?" asked Cobb, drawing one eyelid down as an accompaniment to a mental sneer.

"Am I not as worthy as anybody else, especially Winthrope, who is poor, and has no ancestry?" said Monroe, without a rising or falling inflection in his voice.

"Bully, Monroe; well said!" roared Peter, rubbing and smoking. "But you fellows forget that a woman is usually made a party to such little affairs of the heart. I've had experience, gentlemen; experience; and look at this grand house," waving his hand, with a flourish, around the maroon tassel.

"That's true," assented Monroe, without a tremor.

Cobb assented too, as it suited him to assent. Peter assented to his own theory, looking through his own mirror of experience. They all assented, and reassented, acquiesced, agreed, yielded—to this assertion, time after time.

"Still, I have a fighting chance, like all dogs," soliloquized Monroe.

"Ah, you must win," said Peter, not yet discouraged, like Monroe appeared to be; "I never lost hope."

"But what did you get, Peter?" said Monroe, without a glint that would indicate that he meant a jest; "a woman and ten kids!"

"That's all I wanted," replied Peter, grinning. "Why, you old poltroon, I don't pretend to have ancestry; but I do pretend to have money and gratitude."

"Don't get personal, Peter," said the admonitory Monroe.

"Don't, don't get personal," said the pacifying Cobb.

"Oh, no, Cobb; I do not mean to be personal; but how is the money coming from the dives?" answered Peter, rubbing his hands first, then scratching his ear, then pulling an extra pull on his pipe, then spitting, then squinting, then sneezing as if to give three cheers for his observations on the various subjects up for discussion, in all of which he seemed to have the best of the results.

"Fine!" exclaimed Cobb, with his eyes lighting up. "The police are just rolling it into our coffers."

"I need ten thousand more for Jim Dalls," said Peter, looking gloomy, and ceasing to rub his hands.

"It would be cheaper to send a man over there to kill him," answered Cobb.

"Maybe it would; maybe it wouldn't," said Peter; "but he will be back, if he don't get it."

"Well, send it, then," said Cobb, relenting of his grim suggestion as to the best means of disposing of Dalls.

The door bell rang. A servant answered it. Into the house filed ten children, in all stages of wildness, accompanied by the mother. Seeing them rushing in like an invading army of young Turks, the visitors retreated with as little loss to their dignity as they could spare. And Peter was happy again in the bosom of his family—a Prince at home; a King at the office of Graft.

Mrs. Dieman was now the acme of reincarnation. The jaundice of a sorrowed life had been burned out of her face by the new brand of cosmetics, and she now stood before the world a justly deserving woman. But such is the passage of poverty when embellished by a little of the olive oil of good treatment, fairer living, and a chance. Instead of the downcast woman, with a heart laden with lead, as she once was, she was now an upcast personage, with a heart that was a jardiniere of roses, doing her duty, and bearing her old sorrows silently as the mistress of a mansion. Chance was all that were needed. But still she loved Billy Barton, the drunkard. And this is the way of woman, sometimes.

CHAPTER XXII
THE CONSPIRATORS' PLOT IS REVEALED

Hiram Jarney sat in his lounging chair, in evening clothes, reading the daily newspapers, and smoking a Santa Clara cigar. His feet were encased in a pair of patent-leather slippers. A diamond sparkled on his spotless bosom front. His right leg hung comfortably crossed over his left. His clear cut features denoted his strength, and his active blue eyes his power; both combining to produce a wholesome pride of peace. There was not a smutch to mar his impeccability. He was immaculate from the top of his head to the tips of his toes. His closely cropped hair revealed a head that might be taken as a perfect model by a phrenologist to show the parts of a well-balanced man. With a broad high forehead, high arched brows, fine nose, and a pink complexion, his completeness as a man of parts was unequaled.

As he read the news, turning his paper over and over, as he glanced at the head lines, or waded through the matter of some article that interested him most, an almost invisible vapor lazily ascended from his cigar—a man at ease in the bosom of his family.

Thus he sat and thus he looked, when Miram Monroe, the genteel ghost, was ushered in for a chat and to take dinner. When he saw who his visitor was, Mr. Jarney laid down his paper, crossed his left leg over his right, and leaned back in his chair, in such a resigned state of studied equanimity (always his pose in the presence of Monroe) that Monroe felt he must let loose one of his evanescent smiles.

"Have a seat," said Mr. Jarney, in his familiar way of greeting Monroe; "dinner will be ready soon."

"Thank you," said Monroe, as he stiffly bent himself into the capacious depths of an arm chair, sitting near.

Monroe was faultlessly groomed. He wore an evening suit, and had a diamond in a shirt front that looked no more starched than his frosted face.

"My daughter will be down tonight for the first time to take dinner with the family," said Mr. Jarney, in a conversational mood. "She is improving rapidly, Mr. Monroe; rapidly; and you don't know, being a bachelor, how much I am relieved of worry since she began to mend."

"I imagine how one would feel," said the feeling Monroe, now inwardly cogitating over how to approach the subject that brought him there on this occasion.

Having no hint of Mr. Monroe's intentions, Mr. Jarney proceeded:

"Yes; she has improved so rapidly lately that I feel, myself, like coming out of a long illness. My daughter and I are planning a trip, Monroe, just as soon as she is quite able."

"A trip!" said Monroe, without expressing his surprise in his visage.

"We had thought of going to Europe," pursued Mr. Jarney; "but my business affairs are such that I cannot leave here this summer."

"Where then?" asked Monroe, as if it were any of his affair where they went.

"We may go to the mountains for a few months, so that she can recuperate, and later in the summer we may go to Europe," answered Mr. Jarney.

"Mr. Jarney," said the ghost, in a muffled voice, as if he would burst with his secret, and as if his tongue were tied, "Mr. Jarney, what—what—do you—think of me—as a suitor for your—daughter's—hand?" And then he looked as if he were made of translucent glass, or polished marble, or anything that was hard and white and had a polished surface, with sterile spots on top of it.

This was a stunner to the placid Mr. Jarney. The irrepressible Monroe looked stony enough that he might be taken for a real stone god of the Stares, as Mr. Jarney pierced him through with his piercingly keen eyes.

"You don't mean it, Monroe?" he finally said, after looking at him a long time, with a smile of the ridiculous mould.

"I am in earnest, Mr. Jarney—never more in earnest," responded Monroe.

"Have you asked the young lady yet?" asked Mr. Jarney, still unable to believe the man was in earnest.

"Not yet; but I want your opinion first, Mr. Jarney," answered Monroe, fingering his watch fob.

"You are very amusing, Mr. Monroe; very amusing," said Mr. Jarney, facetiously.

"Then you don't look upon me with favor?" asked Monroe.

"Mr. Monroe, I am afraid you lack experience—at least in this respect," said Mr. Jarney.

"I have money—I have ancestry," said the imperturbable Monroe.

"Oh, fudge, Monroe! fudge on your money, and your ancestry!" said Mr. Jarney. "You need a little schooling in the art of love-making," he said, smiling at the audacity of the ghost. "Do you suppose I would put my daughter up to be sold to the highest bidder, and knocked down to any old money bag that should come along? Do you? Do you? Answer me that?"

No answer.

"Do you think, or presume to think," he continued, "that I would allow a child of mine to be bandied about in this mercenary manner? She is my daughter—my only child; she has a mind of her own; she is independent; so when she makes up her mind to that end, I shall consider it. She will first counsel with me before her intended suitor does. Mr. Monroe, it is very unbecoming, ungentlemanly, ungracious in you to come here this evening, and speak as you have spoken, not having seen her in months, or talked with her at all on the subject. I would do well, Mr. Monroe," continued Mr. Jarney, in the same equinimity of temper, "to dismiss you from my house, and from my service; don't you think so?"

"Beg your pardon, Mr. Jarney; beg your pardon, if I have given offense," said the ghost, with frozen affability. "I have given these thoughts considerable consideration, and I thought it only proper and meet in me to ask your opinion—it was only your opinion I asked, Mr. Jarney; so I beg your pardon. May I ask the young lady, then?"

"You may do as you like about that," said Mr. Jarney, knowing, in his kind fatherly heart, the finality of such a procedure.

"Mr. Winthrope has been permitted to see—" pursued Monroe; but Mr. Jarney broke him off by saying: "Don't mention Mr. Winthrope's name in this connection as an excuse for your imbecility."

Mr. Monroe sat through this grilling, unmoved as a donkey might. After cogitating again for a moment, he said: "I thought I was as good as anyone else, when I broached the subject."

"You have lost the point of view, Mr. Monroe; lost it entirely," answered Mr. Jarney. "Lest you fall into brambles, you would better brush yourself up a little on the subject of courting. You will find a book of rules, perhaps in a ten cent store; get one, and brush up a little, Mr. Monroe."

Dinner was announced. Monroe, unabashed and stiffly congruous, descended upon the dining table with such great gravity that he was likely to break in two before his hunger could be appeased. Opposite him sat Edith and Star. Edith, in her pale blue evening gown, was the essence of delicacy. Her face was fulling into health again, though showing the toning wounds of long illness. Her eyes sparkled almost as the diamonds that were set in ring and brooch. Star was like a fresh young sun on a bright summer day. Mrs. Jarney was as bouncing as ever in her sprightliness. Monroe was cold, as marble-like, as statue-like, as ever. The dinner was very formal, very cheerless, very unappetizing to every one, save Monroe, who ate with relish everything set before him.

The cause of all this coldness may be laid to the front door of Mr. Monroe. He had cast a shade of the grouch over them all. Somehow, the mother was calmed by the sense of some pervading evil thing, inexpressibly unaccountable. Somehow, the two young ladies felt the chilly presence of a tentacled fish out of water, that was wholly inexplicable. Somehow, the father (unknown to the rest) could not raise himself out of the coolness, into which the ghost had plunged him.

The two young ladies had greeted Monroe very gracefully and profusely, when they first came down stairs; but they momentarily lapsed into mediocre silence by the all pervading something they could not fathom. The mother started out to be very gleeful over her daughter's recovering health: but instinctively having a premonition of a mysterious caul overhanging her, she slumped into an unbearable quietude. So dinner was eaten with a sort of wingless spirit in them all, proving a discomforting failure in its pleasureableness.

Monroe, in his impenetrability, did not see anything unusual. Had he seen, had he noticed, had he heeded, he would have departed at the most opportune time. But no; he loitered in the parlor, after dinner, and sought to engage Edith in quiet conversation. And he succeeded. Edith was sitting on a settee, with a silk mantle thrown over her shoulders. Star was drumming on the piano, on which she was now taking lessons, the father and mother being out. Monroe sat down by Edith. After foolishly gazing about the room, as if in an indecisive state of mind about how to entertain himself, he said, icily:

"Miss Jarney, may I have the pleasure of calling on you sometimes?"

Edith was startled at this unheard of piece of rashness participated in by the ghost. She trembled through the inward fear she had of this man of unapproachable demeanor. But summoning up what little of her former courage she had left after the blighting effect of her long illness, she replied.

"Oh, Mr. Monroe, I have no objections to your coming here sometimes as a guest of my papa; but as for calling on me, for the purpose you intimate, that is impossible."

"Why do you object to me, Miss Jarney?" he asked, undeterred by repulses that would have sent any self-respecting man into hiding.

"Why, you are as old as Adam himself," replied Edith, feigning to be gay, but still frightened.

Seeing Edith's dainty hand, with a diamond shining on it, he caught it up, as if he would touch his vile lips to it. Edith withdrew her hand quickly, without a word, arose and walked toward the piano, leaving the ghost sitting alone like a confused statue when hit with a snow ball. Thereupon, Monroe came to his senses, and forthwith departed, leaving a cloud of mystification behind, over his actions.

In a huff (inwardly), he sought his companions, and escorted them to the Bottomless Pit, there to celebrate his great victory, as he called it.

"Well, what luck?" asked Welty Morne, as soon as a bottle had been uncorked, and he held a glass of its contents before his admiring eyes.

"Aye, what luck?" chimed in Bate Yenger.

"Bully good luck," said the ghost, like an owl.

"All right with the old man, I suppose?" said Welty, swallowing down his glassful.

"All right—the old duffer," said Monroe, draining his glass.

"How about the girl?" they asked.

"She fell right into my arms, and accepted," responded the ghost, seemingly without the glint of a frown.

"Whew! Quick work, old boy; quick work! When is it to come off?" asked Welty, speaking loudly.

"Sometime in the future," answered Monroe, mysteriously.

"Drink! and the devil have done for the rest!" shouted Welty, and he imbibed another glass as an additional stimulant to his joy.

"Bully good people, boys; bully good people," said Monroe, pulling another cork.

"How soon you going to drop the pole set up to impale Winthrope?" asked Welty, unrestrained now in his enthusiasm, which he gave vent to occasionally, by whistling and humming a doggerel, alternately.

"The dog," growled Monroe, changing his tone. "Not yet, boys; not yet. It goes up as if nothing had happened."

"When will you transfix him?" asked Welty.

"I am going to New York tomorrow to complete plans," said the invincible ghost.

"Up goes the flag of destruction!" shouted Welty, with Bate repeating the words after him, both raising glasses and emptying them.

Thus they talked and thus they drank, till the potent power of wine laid them low in a delirious sense of delirium in Monroe's downy bed.

After Monroe had left the Jarney home, Edith and Star ascended to the former's chamber for that rest which night should bring to the pure in heart.

Divesting themselves of their day clothing, they invested themselves in their night robes, and laid down together, side by side, in the bed where Edith had lain so long as an invalid. When the lights were out and the coverlets were drawn up over them, Edith heaved a sigh, like one does who lies down in exhaustion to find that peace that darkness and a soft bed fetches on. Star fell asleep directly, and lay in that peaceful calm which comes to one in good health and having no intangible fancies in the mind.

But to Edith, repose was as difficult as the quietness sought by the brook in seeking an eddying pool after long racing down a roughened mountain bed. She turned first on one side, and then on the other, dozing many times almost to the slumberous point, where the transport to the land of dreams is imminent; then awakening with a start, as if the nightmare were treading her down to death, only to see the little imaginary beings that the half-closed eyes see in the illusory light-disks that whirl through impenetrable darkness. She tried to recollect some few of the nights through which she had passed, lying here, as if they were transitory dreams, remembering indistinctly how long and dreary some were, with flitting spirits and hurrying beings filling up the surroundings; she tried to recall the forms of hopes and doubts that seemed always to possess her, and wondered how intangible creative mind is in its wandering; she tried to conjure up the scenes of the tall, handsome figure in black that called every day and knelt by her bedside, but all that she could see was the form kneeling there, and never losing sight of the face, as if it were a part of her existence; she tried to recall the last day that he was there, when he said farewell, but all that she could remember was, "May I come, some day—some day;" she tried to recall whether she had said yes, or no, so uncertain was she now in her remembrance. She did, however, recall very distinctly what the unconfiding Star had told her—a secret given by John—and she was happy. And still there lurked before her the white marble face of a man, whom she had repulsed that evening. She saw it, when she closed her eyes, like a menacing statue in every corner of her brain; she saw it, when she opened her eyes, like a statue in every corner of the room, grimly and remorselessly pursuing her. And she shuddered. Finding sleep impossible under the wild riding of her thoughts, she placed a hand on Star's shoulder, and shook her into drowsy wakefulness.

"Star, Star," she whispered. "Are you awake?"

"Yes," said Star, yawning.

"Star, I cannot sleep; will you talk to me?" she asked.

"Yes, deary," responded Star, in a semi-conscious tone.

"Well, talk then; I cannot sleep," pleaded Edith, to arouse her companion from her natural stupor.

"Yes; I will talk, deary; go on," answered Star, not yet being willing to comply with Edith's request.

"Star, are you awake?" asked Edith, shaking the sleeper.

"I am awake," answered Star, rising full upright in bed. "Can't you sleep, Edith? Lie down and count the sheep jumping over the fence."

"Now, do not be cross, Star," said Edith, sighing; "I am very nervous tonight."

"Poor dear; this day has been too much for you," said Star, leaning over and kissing Edith.

"Talk awhile, Star; then maybe I can sleep," said Edith.

"Shall I tell you about the wolf that comes to poor people's doors?" asked Star, jocularly.

"Oh, no; not so hideous a story as that, Star; I am nervous enough now," replied Edith.

"Then about the mouse that moved the mountain?"

"That is a fable, Star; something real!"

"Then about the man as old as Adam, who asked a maid of twenty-two to marry him?"

"He did not ask me, Star. Do you believe he was in earnest?"

"I think he is a sham, Edith," replied Star; "and I think he was in earnest. Now, Edith, if I tell you what was pledged to me in secrecy, will you not tell where it came from? Yes, you will. When I was home today, Mr. Dieman told me that Mr. Monroe is going to New York for the purpose of causing Mr. Winthrope trouble before he should ever get home to see you again. I should have told you this, Edith, before now; but seeing how nervous you were all evening, I thought it well to put it off till tomorrow; or till you get better."

Star ceased, yawned, and became quiet.

"Did he tell you any more?" asked Edith, sitting up herself in bed.

"Yes, Edith; it is too awful for me to tell you tonight."

"I cannot sleep till you finish, Star," said Edith, lying down again, with Star following her actions.

"Mr. Dieman told me of the whole plot, Edith," said Star, talking in a low sleepy voice; "not sparing himself for the part he played in it; for when the plot was conceived Mr. Dieman was unforgiving toward any of my mother's people who had opposed his marriage to her before she ran away with father. But now, that he is going through a period of penitence and reconciliation with his conscience, he was not loath to tell me all."

"What is the plot, Star? Don't keep me waiting; I am impatient to hear it."

"Mr. Winthrope," continued Star, "was sent to the New York office through the conniving of Monroe, to keep him out of your sight. His aim was to make an effort to have you marry him, get your money, and divide the spoils (that is your money) between himself and his fellow conspirators. That failing, he is to ruin Mr. Winthrope's chances by tempting him to steal the company's money, but stealing it himself and laying the blame on Mr. Winthrope, and then flee to Europe."

Edith lay quiet during the recital, breathing lightly.

"That failing, they will cause him to carry certain large sums of money to a certain place; then hold him up and rob him," continued Star. "They have been planning all winter, and are now about ready to bring it to a conclusion. The time set, was to be as soon as possible after you were able to be seen by Monroe. Having seen him this evening, Edith, it must be time for them to strike. We must intercede to save him, Edith, if possible."

"I cannot do anything, in my enfeebled condition; but I shall see papa early in the morning. I shall forestall Monroe, in his madness! Mr. Winthrope shall be saved from those bad men! Star, something seemed to have told me that all was not going well for him. Bless your dear heart!" said Edith, firmly, sternly, but calmer.

Concluding her story, Star soon fell asleep. Edith, after having her fancies put to rout by the serious things that causes a more determined course to mark its way through the brain, also fell asleep; and did not awake till the morning sun, breaking through the smoke, had kissed the damp of slumber from her cheeks.

CHAPTER XXIII
EDITH REVEALS HER SECRET TO HER FATHER AND HE GOES TO NEW YORK

Refreshing sleep, though late in coming, restored Edith's composure. She came down to breakfast temperamentally disposed to enter into negotiations with her father toward the combating of any plot laid by Monroe and his friends to entice John Winthrope into questionable dealings.

Like a wronged woman, through an excess of virtuous actions, she felt it peculiarly incumbent upon herself to frustrate the plotters—not that it would save John alone; but that it would, as well, be consistently in line with her ideas of just dealings between man and man. During the hour which she consumed in making her toilet, she revolved the whole matter, as related to her by Star, over and over in her now becalmed and determined little head; and the more she revolved it, the brighter became the sparkle in her strong blue eyes, and fiercer grew the militant spirit in her nature. The fatigue that had put her into a nervous state the night before had been routed by that blind force that comes upon depression through a quick series of changes attendant upon a wrong done, to be displaced only through wearying fortitude.

Edith, being primarily one of those strong natures that survives by shock of incident, went boldly to her conceived duty, as though it were given her to be ever strong when the crucial moment arrived. She now knew that her father's good nature was being imposed on by that man of unconscienceable principles. Before she fell ill the year before, the actions of Monroe, two or three times, excited her suspicion, and she had then thought of a plan to forestall him; but by reason of the fatal auto ride, her movements were delayed; and as well did it delay the schemers in their dark and dastardly plotting. It seemed a formidable undertaking for one so frail as Edith, just coming out of a spell of mental derangement; not in its simpleness of action was it so big, but in the momentousness of its results on her enervated system. She would brook no importunate pleading of her friend, Star, to stay her in her course, and leaped into it, as if she were a veritable Goliath of strength.

When she arrived in the dining room that morning with re-enforced courage, she greeted her father and mother, both waiting her arrival, with a kiss, and sat down next to them. Several times she was on the point of bringing up the subject, but lest it should disturb her mother, she calmly awaited a more convenient time for the rehearsal she expected to have with him. Breakfast was usually a quiet affair with the Jarneys, so little was thought of the reserve with which each held speech. After breakfast, Edith took her father's arm and guided him to a quiet nook in the drawing room, and seated him in his favorite seat on one side of a long plate-glass window that opened on his private grounds in front of the mansion.

"Papa, I want a word or two with you this morning before you leave," said Edith, drawing a chair up and sitting down by his side.

"This is unusual, Edith; now, what can my little girl want?" he said, endearingly, taking one of her hands. "You are not going to give me a secret, are you?"

"Too true, papa," replied Edith, and Mr. Jarney expected something else just then than what he heard.

"I am not going to lose my little girl, I hope?" he said, patting her hand.

"Not yet, papa; now, you must sit real quiet, and be not so inquisitive, nor so suspecting till you have heard me," she said, fondly.

"Why, Edith, I had suspected some dark and mysterious deed you had committed; but, with your assurance that I am not to lose you yet. I am listening," he replied.

Then she related all that Star had unfolded to her the night previous; and even how Monroe had acted.

"From whom did Star get the information?" he asked, meditatively, after Edith had finished.

"From her step-father, Peter Dieman."

"Humph! Peter Dieman! and he married Kate Jarney at last—to her betterment," he said, in a ruminating mood. "Well, after all, I am satisfied. Had she heeded me, she would not have gone through all these years of misery that her profligate husband brought upon her. Once I offered to assist her; but she was too proud in her lowliness to respond to my proffered aid. It is better, perhaps; it is better. It seems that the scheme of things is wrong, sometimes; but in the end it is righted."

"Now, what is to be done, dear papa?" asked Edith, seeing that he had taken a discursive course in response to her irrefutable facts.

"I shall act at once," said he, gazing out the window, abstractedly, as if he had been wounded by an aspersion cast upon his magnanimity. "Ingrate!

Ingrate! all of them!" he mused, drumming on the arm of the chair with his fingers, deep in study over some plan of action. "Edith, what would you do?" he asked, as he turned his head and looked at her trustfully. "I have trusted him in his department all these years, and he has given such satisfaction that no one mistrusted his motives, or questioned his integrity. I can hardly believe it, Edith. What would you do?"

"Do you leave it to me?" she asked, her eyes sparkling with suppressed fire.

"I do," he answered, half seriously; half in jest.

"Then eliminate him, and his dupes, at once," she answered, with great seriousness.

"It is hard for me to do that of my own volition," he replied. "He is so fortified with friends on the board of directorate that they must all be taken into consideration."

"Will they not see the necessity of his removal, when apprised of the facts?" she asked.

"They may; but he is so strongly entrenched that his removal would be almost disastrous to me."

"How, papa? How?" she asked, now quickly perceiving a new gleam of the entangling meshes of business associates.

"By turning them against me, if the story should turn out to be false," he answered, reflectively. "But I shall lay it before them at once and investigate."

"In the event that you should remove him, would you bring Mr. Winthrope to your office?" asked Edith, and a tiny flush suffused her cheeks.

"No; Mr. Winthrope must remain in New York," unthinking of the effect his answer might have on his daughter.

Edith turned a little pale at this response, and her hand trembled in his.

"Why, Edith, are you so much interested in him that you want him to be ever present?" asked the father, noting the tremor of her hand.

"Oh, no, papa—not that much—yes—what am I saying, papa—I don't know," she replied, excitedly, turning her head at the sound of her mother approaching, which seemed to have been prearranged at that moment; but, of course, was not. Mrs. Jarney left, after seeing the interview was private.

"It appears to me, Edith, that you are acting strangely about this matter," said her father, beginning to be enlightened.

"Papa, I—I—love him," she whispered in his ear, as she put her cheek up to his to hide the blushes in her face, and to conceal his own countenance which she expected to see turn into a frown upon her at this unexpected answer. "Papa, you will forgive me, won't you?—yes, you will. It is my heart, dear papa—I cannot help it—do forgive me?" she went on, with her eyes filled with tears of happiness and weakness and misery over her uncontrollable feelings.

"Let me see your face, Edith?" said her father, making an effort to turn his head, which she held pressed to her own.

"No, no; I won't papa, till you say you will forgive me," she answered, kissing him.

"To keep peace, Edith, I will forgive you; let me see your face?"

"There!" she exclaimed, suddenly releasing him, and standing off, with tear stains marking through her flushes, and her hair tousled by the performance.

"I believe you," he said, beholding her in a state of mixed emotions; "but I am not yet ready to approve of your selection."

Her heart sank at this answer, and she sank to the floor by his side. Throwing one arm over his knee, and her head upon her arm, she burst into a fit of passionate grief that shook her frame.

"My dear Edith," said he, placing his hand on her head, grieved himself by her outburst of new affliction, "you cause me grief. I would not hurt your dear little heart for anything. Now, come, explain to me fully what that heart of yours tells you?"

She arose, half laughing, half crying, almost hysterically discomposed, rubbing her tears away, as she smiled through them rolling down her face.

"I feel ashamed, papa, for being so weak; but I cannot help it," she said, sitting down on his knee, and throwing her head upon his shoulder and one arm around his neck.

"Well! Edith. I am in sympathy with you," said he; "but you gave me a severe shock being so plainly spoken about such an affair of the heart. Does he suspect it of you?"

"I do not think so, papa—but, papa, he told Star that he loved me, and told her not to tell—and, goosey that she is, she told me, and caused me more—because he said he could not expect to ever meet me on the same level; and that is all I have against him—"

"Well! Of all things I ever heard of," said the father. "I had not been inclined to interfere with you, Edith, in such affairs; but I—" he hesitated. "You make your choice, but be careful, child; be careful."

"Don't you think he is good, papa?" she asked.

"Very good—fine—perfect, Edith! I should not disfavor him; but he must love you for your own dear self before I shall ever give my consent."

"He may never find it out, papa," she said, drearily; "and if he does not, I shall never let him know, and shall go through the world alone."

"That is noble in you, Edith," said her father, kissing her. "It is time for me to go," he said, as she released him.

On arriving at his office, Mr. Jarney was informed that Mr. Monroe had quietly taken himself off that morning for New York. He was further informed that Mr. Monroe had been requested to make the trip by certain members of the Board of Directors; and further, that he was entrusted with a large sum of money, in the form of drafts, made payable to the order of the treasurer of the company at the Broadway office. When this news was flashed upon Mr. Jarney, there seemed to penetrate his tractable mind, like a thunderbolt, the concatenating links of a plot, too realistic to be waived aside; which he was prone to do, when Edith gave him her story that morning.

Side by side with the facts concerning Monroe's leave-taking and purpose, he also learned that the genteel ghost had taken with him certain office books and papers, to be used in checking over accounts while auditing the books of the branch office. This was not in accordance with precedence, and proved another corroborative circumstance in the duplicity of the culpable Monroe.

Putting all these correlated facts together, Mr. Jarney, after due deliberation, and after duely weighing them all as incriminating integral parts, and after combining them with the main story of the plot, arrived at the inevitable conclusion that Monroe was up to some deviltry that should be probed to the bottom. He, therefore, called a meeting of the Board of Directors, and put the whole question, in all its phases, before that body. It was almost noon when the board met. They must act without going through the circumlocution of formal discussion and the entanglements of red tape, he told them. Some of the members were for postponing the meeting till the next day, to await a telegram from New York, so great was their faith in Monroe's honor. Monroe, they said, would be in the metropolis on the morrow. The procrastinating members prevailed in their vote on the question, and adjournment was had till the next day.

But Mr. Jarney was not disconcerted, nor did he allow himself to be wholly blocked in his plan of action. So as soon as the board had arrived at the decision to go slow, he took it upon himself, knowing the shrewdness of John Winthrope, to send him a private wire, addressed personally, briefly saying:

"Beware of Monroe; I will be there tomorrow afternoon, if possible."

Dispatching this message, Mr. Jarney returned home, related to Edith what he had discovered as confirmatory evidence against Monroe, got ready, and left on the next train for the seat of trouble.

Edith, from the morning of her conversation with her father to the time she received a wire from him, went through a siege of terrible mental conflicts. She confided in no one, at first, not even Star, the cause of her father's sudden call to New York. She was in a highly nervous fright throughout the hours that seemed never to pass between his going and the receipt of the telegram. Her flights of fancy went to unreasonable complications for the doomed young man in the New York office. She thought she must rescue him at all odds to her health. Had she been in a condition physically able to bear the journey, she would have gone alone, if need be; or with her father, if permitted; but as it was, she remained in her prison like an unwilling subject in a sanitorium. Thus exhibiting an excitable demeanor in her actions, her mother and Star made futile attempts to draw from her the cause of her fervid agitation. Still strung to a high tension of determination, still overcome with an uncommon fear, still anxious and studiously meditating over the eventualities that might come to pass before her father should reach his destination, she wandered about the house in uncontrollable perturbation, sticking tenaciously to her secret.

"Edith," said Star, approaching her in one of her rounds of walking the floor, "come, tell me what is agitating you so today, that I might be of help."

Placing her arm around Star's waist, without a word, she drew Star along in her walk, looking dreamily, and seeing nothing, save what the illusive eye might see in the distance. Star returned the friendly embrace of Edith, and with their arms around each other, the two walked and walked, both silent. Edith silent over what she was pondering on, Star silent over what she feared was an unnatural mental balance.

"Are you ill today, Edith?" asked Star.

"Oh, no, Star; I am feeling very well today," replied Edith.

"But you are so quiet and unresponsive that I can't quite make you out," said Star.

Then leading Star to the window where she sat with her father the day before, Edith asked her to sit down that she might have a word with her.

"Star," she said, seriously, relenting in her purpose to keep her secret longer, "what you told me two nights ago I have discovered to be too true—at least in a circumstantial way," said Edith.

"Why, then, haven't you told me, Edith, so that I could have a fellow-feeling for you?" asked Star.

"Papa requested me to keep it a secret till he returns; which I should do. But, deary, you know I am like you, it is hard to keep a secret," said Edith, still uncertain whether to proceed farther.

"Now, my dear Edith! I never tell anybody any secrets but you, and you tell them to nobody else, and you never tell any to me, so that is as far as yours ever get."

"Star. I must refreshen your memory a little," said Edith, playfully. "I am not scolding you, you know; but just reminding you a little. Now, didn't you tell Mr. Winthrope something?"

"Well, wasn't he entitled to it?" said Star, laughing.

"Then you won't, in this instance, tell anybody?"

"No—o—hope'm'die," returned Star, crossing her breast.

"Papa has gone to New York to intercept Monroe."

"Has he?" said Star, with wide eyes. "Monroe, then, has gone?"

"Went yesterday morning before papa reached his office. Papa learned some things that substantiated what Mr. Dieman told you, and, putting everything together, he became convinced of the truthfulness of the stratagem of that man Monroe to bring Mr. Winthrope into disrepute. Star, had Monroe succeeded in his designs before I had learned the true status of affairs, I should not have believed anything against him; but now that I have been forewarned, I shall never lose faith in his honor and integrity. Star, I told papa of my love for him, which papa did not accept pleasantly at first, thinking I was in fun, or doing it as a lark to tease him; but when he realized I was never more serious, he called him a fine, perfect young man, and was pleased. There, Star, I have told you what has been on my mind since yesterday. Am I a goosey still?"

"You are a little dove, Edith," said Star, sweetly.

"Star, I should like to see Mr. Dieman," said Edith, changing the subject. "Can you have him come here?"

"I may; but it is doubtful."

"I would go to him, if I could."

"He has a young man named Eli Jerey, who transacts business matters for him. He might be summoned. Mr. Dieman places implicit confidence in him. Everything now must be conveyed through him to Mr. Dieman, I am told. I have seen Mr. Jerey; and I can have him called here to see you for whatever you might want to impose upon Mr. Dieman."

"Is Mr. Dieman so exclusive as that?" asked Edith.

"He is, indeed, Edith. Since his marriage to mother, he has set up in great state, and does nothing but look after his family affairs personally, and transacts other affairs by the way of Mr. Jerey."

"You will vouch for his trustworthiness? at least you can promise that much through what Mr. Dieman represents him to be?"

"Oh, yes; whatever Mr. Dieman says can be relied on."

"Then you may have Mr. Jerey call here at eight o'clock this evening, if he can come."

"Shall I call him now?" asked Star, rising to go to the phone to have a talk with that gentleman.

"Yes. Papa must be in New York by this time; I should know soon, by wire, what Monroe has accomplished," said Edith, as Star was leaving her.

CHAPTER XXIV
ELI JEREY IS CALLED INTO REQUISITION

It is wonderful how prosperity transcends every other medium in working a transformation in a poor stick of humanity, who has been chortled, like a shuttle-lock, through the shifting warp of adversity. It is refreshing to observe, sometimes, how often men and women of lowly state can rise, as it were, by their own boot-straps from the great misfortune of having nothing to the ravishing luck of plentitude. It is, indeed, very promising to know that favoring chance does not fall altogether upon the many who are born with silver spoons in their mouths.

It may not have been by his own boot-straps, unaided, that Eli Jerey rose to his plenary rank, or to his financial exhaltation. It may not have been luck alone, or chance, or extended aid, that hoisted him to the skies in the estimation of Peter Dieman; neither could it have been native ability, for his qualifications were of the superficial kind, to the casual observer.

However, whatever the cause might have been, it is one of the certainties of the things that be, that Eli was now in high favor with his former master, and was prospering like a well-conditioned house cat. For Peter was certainly expiating himself for all the cuffs and rebuffs that he had heaped upon that poor lad's head during the period of his vengefulness. Eli was now made plenipotentiary extraordinary of the former junkman, with full rank of major-domo of his private affairs, insofar as they appertained, incidentally, to the junk shop, and the purveying of news of the System between the main totem himself and his sub-lunary lights.

And this elevation of Eli remodeled him as a being. Instead of the stoop-shouldered, thin-faced, frowsy-headed, dirty, unwashed, ill-clad, uncared-for individual that a scanty stipend produces, we now see an erect, sharp-featured, cleanly-shaved, neatly-clad, bright-eyed young man. Although not handsome, his face called for an adulatory responsiveness on the part of those who came in contact with him. Instead of having his hands continually soiled by the labors that he performed in sorting junk and displaying it to customers, it was not uncommon to see him going about the shop gloved in brown kid. Instead of a dark-brown lay-down-collar shirt that always gave him the appearance of a water front workman, he wore boiled linen, decorated with a sparkling stud and flashy necktie. Instead of a greasy coat that hung loosely over his shoulders, he wore a neat business suit. Instead of the sweat-marked slouch hat, that used to loll on one side of his head, he wore a derby. Instead of a chain made of leather, to which was attached a brass watch, he carried a gold ticker fastened to his vest by a delicately-linked chain. Instead of the black, filthy office, in which his master sat for years, and in which he sat for a time after his advancement, he could now be found in a bright, clean place, papered and tinsled and decorated, with a new desk to write at, and a leather-cushioned chair to recline in. Thus he appeared in his new role, when the phone rang one day, as it often did, but now with a different purport than ever before.

"Hello!" responded Eli, taking down the receiver and adjusting it to his ear.

"Yes; this is Mr. Jerey."

"Eli Jerey; yes."

"Yes; Mr. Dieman's office."

"Very busy day; but we're always open for new business."

"A private interview!"

"Can't you come to my office?—I never go out—except ordered by Mr. Dieman."

"Can I come without him knowing it?"

"That depends on the business."

"Well; who wants me?"

"Can't set a time or date till I know."

"What! Mr. Jarney's residence!" ("Well, did you ever!" on the side).

"Miss Jarney!"

"Who's this talking?"

"Star Barton!" ("Well, did you ever!" on the side.)

"Where are you?" now more interested.

"At Mr. Jarney's?" ("Well, what now?" on the side.)

"What time?" ("Bless me!" on the side.)

"Yes; 7 p. m. will do." ("Ha, me!" on the side.)

"I will be there." ("On the dot!" on the side.)

Eli hung up the receiver, stood a moment tickling his right ear with his right forefinger, a habit of his. He was in a confused and perplexed state of mental consternation. Miss Barton! Miss Barton! Peter Dieman's step-daughter! went through his head in a rollicking way. "Hah! Miss Barton! I've heard of her; and Miss Jarney—rich—young—poorty—and wants an interview with me! Humph!" he mused, after sitting down. "Well, I must make myself presentable and go henceforth to meet them in all my dignity; yes, meet my superiors now in all my dignity—hah!"

In due time Eli repaired to his room in the Monongahela House, a very ancient and a very honorable institution of its kind, no other being now suitable to Eli's enlarged notions of refinement. He clothed himself in his best bib and tucker, swatted down his hair so flat that it looked as if it had been laid by a weaver's hand to his swelling head, and powdered his sallow face till it was resplendent with the polish of good looks.

Now, when all was completed he stood before the mirror, like a coquettish maid primping to make a hit, and there saw reflected back a very well appearing young gentleman. He saw all that the art of massaging and ointing and cologning and talcuming and starching and tailoring could mould out of the material at hand. He saw reflected back a youth five feet ten, with hollow eyes, peaked face, broad high forehead, condensed lips, and good teeth, long fingers, all supported by a suit of black, full dress style, with low white vest and patent-leather shoes. He saw also a diamond in his shirt front, white necktie banding a high collar, dark gray gloves, gold-headed cane, and high silk hat.

Before withdrawing from the allurements of the mirror, Eli touched his fingers to his lips, stroked his sandy eyebrows, turned around a time or two, with admiring glances over his shoulder, as he raised or lowered his brows, or opened his mouth to show his teeth to himself; adjusted the plug correctly on his head, drew on his gloves, took his cane in one hand, and receded from his reflected self, with many glancing and furtive farewells at the glass; closing the door at last, regretful that he had so soon to part company with such an admirable picture of budding manhood.

Settling himself inside a glass enclosed auto, he was whizzed through the appalling roar and grime of the city, like the formal gentleman that he was, sitting among the soft and heaving cushions, and looking to the passers-by, in his flight, like the silhouette of a grand bourgeois in contradistinction to the votaries of swelldom. In his present state of perverted obsequiousness, Eli was intensely vain, usually; but now, while in the gentlemanly act of calling upon a lady, so rich that he could not count all her money did he live a thousand years, and at her own request, for an interview, he was ludicrously haughty, and hopelessly ignorant of the rules of deportment surrounding the secluded haunts of the refined and the mighty ones of power and place. Any failings that he had, he did not recognize. His limitations were his blisses. What he did not know, he took as a matter of no consequence. If he saw a thing, it permeated him with unwarped fascination; if he did not see it clearly, he was not troubled. Rising to his present state, was of more importance as to present results, than as to permanency. In truth, he was a queer combination of meritorious attainments now, meaning well, and doing his best to be an efficient collaborator of his famous mentor—Peter Dieman. He was a person of little imagination. Everything was realistic to him. So, in journeying to the Jarneys on this auspicious occasion, he imagined very little about how he should act, or perform, or conduct himself, any more than what would come naturally to him.

When he presented himself to the two young ladies in the drawing room of the mansion on the hill, he shocked them by sitting down with his hat on his head, though they could not help but admire his rich habiliments.

"May I take your hat?" said Edith, approaching him, of course expecting to receive that piece of fine head covering to deposit it where it belonged at such a time.

"No, madam, no; it is just as well where it is," he replied, showing his white teeth through a crooked smile. "I've been used to setting with it on."

He was so unapproachable that Edith was embarrassed before him. Star had remembered him as the former disheartening clerk of her step-father. She had seen him when she had gone to the junk shop with her mother that time for the redemption of her kitchen utensils, and she had not forgotten how cadaverous and impoverished he then looked.

"I presume you remember me?" asked Star, to break the monotonous silence into which the interview had perforce fallen.

"I don't know that I do," said he, showing his fine teeth again, and lifting his eyebrows. "So many people came into the store in those days that I paid little attention to them all."

"Don't you remember the girl who was so poorly clad that was with her mother the day Mr. Dieman gave back the dishes her father had pawned, and against which you protested?" asked Star.

"Are you the gal?" he asked, with brightening face.

"I am the gal," returned Star, laughing.

"Well! how time makes changes in this world," he responded, looking her over carefully, hardly believing that the pretty face of Star's, with pretty gown to match, could possibly be the same. "It beats all; and you are the sister of all of Mr. Dieman's children?"

"Mrs. Dieman's children," she corrected.

"Yes, that's it—I know your sister May," he said, with a smile.

"Do you, really?" said Star.

"I call on him often, and see her, sometimes—she's a dandy," he said.

"A fine girl," corrected Edith.

"Yes; mighty fine," he answered, as he crossed his gloved hands over the head of his cane standing perpendicularly in front of him, and putting his chin down upon them, as if posing as a rejuvenated old man "by the wayside on a mossy stone," looking steadily at them both. "And you are May's sister? Well!"

"I have that honor," replied Star.

"Well! Who would think it? You are so much poortier," he said, quietly and naturally, without intending to be impertinent.

Star blushed at first; but in a moment became vexed, and looked very black at him; that is, as black as she could look, for no matter how she tempered up, not much sign of her resentment was ever evidenced in her face. Edith was astonished at his rudeness, and glanced at Star for an explanation of the bold manner of this young man. Eli, in his transparent innocence, did not feel the effects of their interchange of glances, and was not disturbed. Anticipating that he might precipitate a scene by an unfortunate remark, Edith took up the subject that had caused her to have him present.

"Mr. Jerey," she began, faltering in her speech, "you are Mr. Dieman's agent, I understand?"

"I am," he replied, loftily.

"Do you know Mr. Monroe?"

"I do."

"Do you know Mr. Morne?"

"I do—he's a scamp."

"Do you know Mr. Yenger?"

"I do—he's another scamp."

"Do you know my father?"

"Not personally."

"Do you know Jacob Cobb?"

"I do—he's a—"

"Do you know Jasper Cobb?"

"I do—he's an—"

"Do you know James Dalls?"

"I do—he's a—"

"Well, now; has Mr. Dieman decided to continue keeping company with these people?" asked Edith, warming to her subject.

"For what reason do you ask?" he asked, eyeing her closely, so much so that Edith was discomfitted by his sharp stare.

"It is a matter that concerns me personally, Miss Barton here, and my father," she answered.

"That's not very informing," he replied.

"Do you know Mr. John Winthrope, my father's former secretary?" she asked.

"I never saw him—don't recall that I ever heard of him—yes, believe so—didn't Mr. Dieman speak to me once about him? (asking himself)—yes, believe he did. Well, what of him?"

"Do you know whether Mr. Dieman bears ill-will against him yet?"

"Let me see," said Eli, now in a cogitating tone, still with his chin upon his hands still on top of his cane, but lowering his eyes to the floor; "he never mentioned him but once, and then in connection with—let me see—what?—with your father as secretary, sometime ago—got a phone?" he asked suddenly, now disposed toward being cautiously communicative.

"Yes; do you wish to use it?" asked Edith.

"I would like to before going farther in this talk. Where is it?"

Edith then led the way to the phone room, Eli following, with his hat still on his head, to the disgust even of the servants.

"I wish to be private," he said to Edith and Star, seeing they were inclined to linger near.

"As you wish," they returned, departing and closing the door behind them.

After finishing his phoning, Eli emerged from the room, and strode through the dining room and on through to the drawing room, whistling a ditty, with his plug hat cocked back on his head, swinging his cane round and round, like one out walking for pleasure. He resumed his seat as before, with the ladies as his examiners.

"Well?" said Edith.

"He says he has no ill-will against Mr. Winthrope any more; and requests me to take steps necessary to right any wrong against him. What's your wish?"

"Before I go farther," said Edith, "may I ask you if it is Mr. Dieman's purpose to remain the go-between in the graft system, of which Mr. Cobb is the head?"

"He's making an effort to break from the gang—he's been making the effort ever since he married; but it's hard to let go," said Eli, casting an admiring glance at Star.

"Now, then; as to my wish, Mr. Jerey," said Edith, trying to get his eyes away from Star; "I want you to assist me and my father to break up the ring; in a quiet manner, if possible; if not quietly, then by law."

"What's your object, mainly?" he asked.

"To get such men as Monroe and his dupes and old Mr. Cobb into the toils. These men have not been satisfied in working the graft system for all they are worth, but they have been plotting for months against me and my father. Can I depend on you?"

"You can. But what has Mr. Winthrope to do with it?"

"That is a part of the plot against my father and me."

"Still I can't see—but never mind, I know the other fellers well, and will help you."

"First, get Mr. Dalls back from Europe, and—"

"Say, miss," he broke in, "how did you know all this and these men?"

"Dieman communicated the information to Miss Barton, and she to me."

"Ha!" he ejaculated, and then subsided into a quiet turn for a few moments. "He did, eh?" he proceeded; "then I know he'll approve anything I agree to here. Understand, I only carry information between Mr. Dieman and the lower men."

"I understand," said Edith.

"I will get Mr. Dieman to throw them all overboard soon as I can get my hooks to going," he replied, rising. "Where is Mr. Winthrope?"

"In New York," replied Edith, rising also, and standing awkwardly by waiting for him to move.

"I don't understand where he comes in?" said Eli, as he placed his cane between his arms behind his back, and spraddling out his legs, with his hat cocked back.

"That is another matter," said Edith, attempting to pass it over.

"I am very busy," he said, half-whistling a tune, then drawing his legs together and whirling round on one foot, he directed his eyes upon Star, and remarked: "You are so much poortier than your sister May; and this young lady (turning to Edith) is poortier than all the rest," after which he smiled broadly, showing his good teeth.

It was rather a delicate moment for the young ladies. It was hard to reprove him, when they had solicited his aid in their great undertaking. Star was vexed. Edith was disappointed in him, for she expected that he would show a little more solicitude for her affairs than he showed in his actions and answers to her questions. She drew down her dark brows when he spoke as he did, feeling indignant, and looking at him sharply, said:

"Mr. Jerey, that is very impolite in you."

"Oh, my! beg your pardon!" he said, with an innocent smile. "I am so used to talking to my own sisters when I go home that I really forgot where I was. If you will pardon me, I will go? and not do it any more—but that's my opinion."

As he concluded his apology he simmered down as to smile, looked serious after seeing the ladies were provoked, struck the toe of his patents with his cane, set his hat squarely upon his head, crossed his legs, put his hands in his pockets, with the cane under his right arm, smiled again, resumed a correct form of standing, expecting the while to hear the ladies go on with their scolding. But as they did not say any more, he turned round, and walked out as straightly as a West Pointer on parade, opened the door himself, and let himself out. After closing the door behind him, he stepped to the piazza, and stopped on the edge of it, gawking around like a country lout.

He was nothing of the kind, being absolutely indifferent as to what people thought of him, or as to how he acted, so long as he was not immorally sensitized. He was playing his part in the drama of a great city's life, and playing it excellently; so what did it matter, if the sticklers for formality were shocked.

Going down the long walk through the Jarney grounds, with frosted incandescents throwing fantastic shadows about him, he whistled something that sounded like a hot time in the old town—sometime soon.

CHAPTER XXV
MONROE IS CAUGHT IN A NET OF HIS OWN WEAVING

Ever efficient and ever advancing, though the time since he left his mountain home was short, John Winthrope had pressed onward and upward till he was not only the assistant treasurer in the New York office, but stood high in the favor of the heads of the great firm; and, if he continued on his outlined course, promised to enjoy still further favors and special privileges. His rapid rising, his pecuniary uplift, his progress in favor, his increasing enjoyment of privilege, his continuing prosperity, did in nowise diminish his sense of duty, nor beguile him from that course which he had laid out to follow when he first became obsessed with the idea of making his mark in the world of finance, as seen through the eyes of steel and iron.

During all the months, dreary though they were, that he went through in the city of Pittsburgh, he continued to live, according to his own adopted code, at the cheap lodging house in Diamond alley. The emoluments of his position, handsome though they might be considered for one so young as he, and for one so new in the ranks of the employed, were not any more compensatory than the allotments, as per schedule of bills to be met, demanded. For, after paying for his simple lodging, his small personal requirements, and sequestering a sum for the inevitable rainy day, he sent the balance to his parents to assist them in the liquidation of a debt of purchase on their home in the hills beyond the roar and turmoil of business; to which home he hoped to go sometime, an ever present dream, to spend his leisure days, or to rest when the burdens of life should become too great for his shoulders to carry.

Being steadfast of purpose, and retired in a social way, he had it over other men in his unquenchable ambition to make good—in that, instead of idling away his time in questionable company, as so many such young men do, or loafing about clubs being a good fellow at a high cost, he enlarged his knowledge of the details of business by utilizing his spare moments in courses of suitable studies, in which he exercised his energies and ability to their utmost.

After being transferred to his new post, he did not change his plans, even though his compensation was enhanced to a surprising and very agreeable amount; nor did he deviate one iota from his habits of living. He did one thing, however, which is pardonable and commendable, and that was to dress as became his office with a much more satisfactory and becoming taste. Blessed with good looks, a frank, open countenance, a finished polish, and a natural grace, any personal adornment was befitting to him. In his case, the clothes did not make the man, but the man made the clothes, as is often true in some men and women. By gradual degrees, his cheap shop clothes, as they gave way to the ravages of wear and time, were displaced by stylish modern cuts, tailored and otherwise; but this only happened as wages increased and exigencies demanded.

So he may now be seen at his desk in a neatly fitting business suit of dark serge, with creases in the trousers, and his coat collar always clean of dandruff and falling hair. His shirt fronts were the nattiest, his collars the whitest, his ties the neatest, his shoes the highest polished of anyone in the office. With his dark-brown hair, clear blue eyes, fair skin, smooth face and dark eyebrows, he could well be envied by those less gifted.

Still, with all these characteristics, he was the least reconciled to his lot. In March he was called upon to take his leave for New York. In March he was compelled to take leave of the sick young woman, whom he had visited every day without a break for months by force of the most unusual circumstances that ever came to a young man, or to any man, perhaps. He had become so accustomed to these daily visits to Edith's bedside, and had become so fraught with the most formidable fire of life, that when the final day came round, he seemed to have buried the object before his going, and lived in a perpetual dream thereafter, still perplexed and confounded by a mystery.

Edith was not yet well when he last looked upon her face; but signs of improvement were ever growing brighter. This is what gave him such pain of heart—the thought that he had to leave when the time had come for him to see her in her reason. But still, he thought, perhaps it was for the best. For was she not laboring under an hallucination, a delusion, a wild estrangement of the senses? And, of course, when she came to herself, he would, by virtue of the natural laws of caste, have to go his own way after all, and find solace for his passion in some other person less worthy. It was better, thought he, that he was away—so far away that he should never see her again; and time, the sure healer of all ills, of all regrets, of all sorrows, of all misery, would bind his wounds from the harrowing effects of proud flesh. He could never hope, was his everlasting complaint, to vie with other men in the conquest of her heart. So why fret away his time on such an improbable question? Seeing all these things in this light, and believing in them seriously and honorably, he exerted his best endeavors to cast the burden from his soul. But the burden was too heavily laden to be so easily thrust aside.

He had not heard from her since the last evening he left her home—except on one occasion, when a letter from her father to another member of the firm in the branch office, indirectly referred to her improving condition. This was all—a very slim thread it was upon which to build any hope that she, in her enlightening mind, ever again called for him, which seemed proof sufficient to convince him of his preconceived opinion.

But—why? but—why? he always asked himself, did she make such an impression on him, unless he had struck, in her heart, a responsive chord. No matter how he reasoned, he invariably got back to the premises of his theme, namely, that he could not hope for any recognition on her part so long as their stations in life were miles and miles apart.

He had spent many days on this unsolvable proposition, in all its various phases, and was still weighing it in his mind, even while busily engaged at his desk, when, one day, Miram Monroe was announced, and led into his office with all those outrageous formalities that flunkies about such offices show to their superior beings, who have the brains and money to conduct gigantic industrial corporations. Mr. Winthrope was surprised more than he felt able to express himself; but he good-humoredly extended his hand and saluted him with a cheerful, "How are you? and how are all the people back in old Pittsburgh," meaning, of course, the people only in the main office.

Mr. Monroe was as stoical as ever, but he greeted John with considerable more cordiality than had been his wont. "They are all prospering," he answered, as he glanced around the room.

John watched him closely, in a critical way, having in mind the telegram he had received the day previous from Mr. Jarney that said, "Beware of Monroe." John did not fully understand the meaning of this telegram; but he read its significance in the face of the man standing now before him, which, as he then looked at it, presented a mixture of tragedy, comedy, treachery and sculduggery. He saw these traits now in Monroe, not that his face had presented them to him on any other occasion, but the telegram had revealed to him too forcibly what he could not before comprehend. Why did Mr. Jarney send it, if the coming of Monroe was not for some insidious purpose? he asked himself.

"You do not often come to New York, Mr. Monroe—at least, not to this office," said John, breaking the ice for a plunge into Mr. Monroe's perverseness toward a hateful silence.

"Not often," he answered, extracting some papers from an inside coat pocket. He began deliberately to run over these papers, as if looking for a particular one. Finding one that seemed to meet his searching approval, he drew up a chair to a desk in the middle of the room and sat down, still very deliberately, with his eyes bent upon the paper that he held in his hand.

Concluding that Monroe was not willing to be communicative about his errand, John sat down at his own desk. Scrutinizing Monroe from a side view, he saw it was the same face that was so indefinable to him in his apprenticeship in the head office; the same lengthened visage that then struck him so forcibly as that of a mountebank, clothed in undeserving power; the same white, wrinkleless skin that reminded him perpetually of a true portraiture of a ghost. John sat spell-bound, drawn irrisistably to this peculiarly eccentric man.

Monroe sat pouring over his papers, as if it had been his custom to come there every day and do the same thing, unbelievably composed in his manner. To John, there was a mephistophelean aspect about Monroe, as he sat at the desk, apparently in the throes of some abstruse problem that he could not readily make out. But, however, after awhile Monroe seemed to have reached a solution of what he was delving into, and directly turned and faced John, with his usual inane stare.

"Mr. Winthrope," said he, with no change in the monotonous enunciation of his words, so precise did he give utterance to them, "there seems to be an error in your accounts, which indicates a shortage in this office."

"An error! A shortage!" gasped John, as if he had been stabbed from behind with a dagger.

"Yes;" answered Monroe very slowly, very mouse-like, very aggravatingly, "a shortage—or an error." He straightened up in his chair, after saying this, to see the effect of his assertion in John's countenance.

Recovering his composure in a moment or so, John drew down his eyebrows to a scornful straightness, and glared at his accuser. John was not very often convertable to such an exhibition of temper; but when his name and his honor were brought under reproach, his resentment became visibly uncontrollable.

"Do you mean, Mr. Monroe," said John, looking straight into his gray-green eyes, "that I am short in my accounts with this office?"

"That is my intimation," replied the insinuating Monroe, opening his mouth squarely at the emphasizing of "my". "I have been sent here to have a reckoning with you."

The very bluntness of his statement was so monstrous to John, that he could not, for a short time, comprehend what it meant for him. The very essence of the assertion was too much for his grasp, so horrified was he for the few moments that he sat facing the serene detractor of his character. The very thought of such a crime was so contrary to his nature, that he was almost blind from the sensations of the blow coursing through him.

"Are you in earnest? or are you here to jest with me, Mr. Monroe?" asked John, rousing himself to face the inevitable.

"I am in dead earnest," answered Monroe.

"Then you," responded John, weighing his words, "lie—or some one else—is lying—for—you."

"Don't get agitated and go off half-cocked," said Monroe, in the same icy tone as before. "I'll show to you, in due time, where you have been peculating."

At first, John was on the point of taking physical issue with the challenger of his good name; but remembering the significant telegram from Mr. Jarney, and remembering also that he was at a disadvantage with Monroe over the question of fact, he subdued his passionate feelings, and thought he would parley for time to await the coming of Mr. Jarney before long.

"Some one has been doctoring the books," said John, smoothly, "if there is an apparent defalcation. I know what I have been doing, Mr. Monroe. My cash has balanced each day. My accounts in this office are straight, Mr. Monroe. I am straight, Mr. Monroe. You are crooked. And I will have no more from you till my superiors have been consulted."

"Well, Mr. Winthrope," responded Monroe to John's asseveration, "I am the auditor of the firm for this office, and I am to be consulted first. According to our books you are short. I was, therefore, sent here to have an accounting with you, and if I find that our books are correct and your accounts wrong, I am to have a warrant issued for your arrest. Believe me, Mr. Winthrope, when I say that I find an error which indicates peculating on your part. I do not want to see your name blackened by an exposure that would naturally follow should I take it in my head to proceed against you. I have a free hand to act any way I choose, be that what it may. Now, I can fix this matter up for you so that no word of it will get out, and so that you can leave with money in your pockets, and mine, and no one will be the wiser. I can compromise the matter by you being reasonable. Will you be reasonable and enter into my scheme?"

John was surely astounded at this long speech of Monroe's. He studied a short moment. He did not want to compromise himself with Monroe in any scheme that, if he were guilty, would cover up the crime with which he was charged. If he was found to be responsible for any shortage, he was fully willing to take the consequences which arrest and exposure might entail, rather than attempt to clear himself of the blame, if blamable. But not being guilty, as he had good reason to believe, he held that justice, unless mercilessly blind, would deal fairly with him. Moreover, he would be making a mistake if he did not draw Monroe out, and secure from him his plan of a secret compromise.

"How would you propose compromising the matter, if I am guilty?" he asked.

"By leaguing with you," answered Monroe, artlessly.

"Leaguing with me?" said John, doubtful of his meaning.

"Yes," he answered. "I have a draft here for one hundred thousand, made payable to the treasurer of the New York office. You can get the money yourself by signing it as assistant treasurer. Get it, and we will divide the amount. I will fix the books at the other end so that a discovery cannot be made till we are safely in Europe or South America. Will you do it?"

A new idea came to John, growing on him gradually as Monroe unfolded his nefarious scheme.

"Yes; I will do it," he answered, with alacrity. "Where is the draft?"

Monroe immediately pulled the draft from an inside pocket of his vest. He looked it over, as if he regretted to give it up; then he turned it over to John, with a hesitating hand.

"Get the money," said Monroe, without an intimation that he was pleased, or not pleased, over the readiness with which John seemed to be falling into his trap.

John leisurely put the draft with a number of other drafts he had in his possession belonging to the firm, placed them all together in the firm's bank book, and retreated, without a word, from the enervating personality of Monroe. After depositing the entire sum in the name of the firm, he returned to the office to report to Monroe.

"That is rather a crude piece of business, Mr. Monroe," said John, as he entered the office. Standing with folded arms on the opposite side of him at the flat-top desk, he gave a laugh, and smiled sarcastically, as he said: "Crude! I should say; so crude that it smells of rusted iron!"

Monroe looked up nonplused at the haughty and sneering tone of his inferior; but he showed no irritation.

"Did you get the money?" asked Monroe, blandly.

"I did," answered John, good naturedly.

"Well, divide up," said Monroe, having doubts.

"Oh, I forgot to return with it, Monroe," replied John, as he laughed in his superior's face. "I placed it to the credit of the firm. Believing there was no hurry about dividing up, and thinking tomorrow would do as well as today for that little formality, I changed my mind between here and the bank. The money will keep where it is, Mr. Monroe."

The door of the office opened. The form of Mr. Jarney stood in it for a brief time. Then he closed the door and stood inside the room. He did not advance at once. As Mr. Monroe saw him first, his face took on a yellow pallor. John noticed the change in the coloring of his marbled visage, and turned about. Seeing who the intruder was, he took a few steps across the room, and lively grasped his former master by the hand.

"Glad to see you, Mr. Jarney; very glad," said John.

Mr. Jarney, in turn, greeted John very warmly, and said he was inexpressively happy to see him looking so robust, and hoped that he was still the same unpolluted young man as when he first met him. All of which abashed John so that he blushed.

"Did you get my telegram?" he asked John, yet not turning to greet Monroe, who sat without a tremor at the desk.

"Yes; I have been looking for you all day," replied John. "Here is Mr. Monroe," he said, as he turned and waved his hand toward that brazen piece of trickery.

"Yes; yes; I see Mr. Monroe," said Mr. Jarney, shooting his sharpened glances at him. "I came here to see about some little tricks he is up to. What have you accomplished, Mr. Monroe?"

"Aren't you laboring under a misapprehension, Mr. Jarney?" asked the ghost.

"Oh, not at all, Mr. Monroe," said Mr. Jarney. "I have found you out. I came here to beard you before this young man," rising almost to the angry point in the vehemence of his threat.

"Why, Mr. Jarney," said the lamentable Monroe, "what have I done that you, whom I have always served so faithfully, should hurl aspersions upon my name and cast reflections upon my integrity?"

"Your name and integrity!" said Mr. Jarney, with rising voice. "You haven't either. Where is that draft and those office books? Turn them over immediately to Mr. Winthrope here for safe keeping."

"I have already deposited the draft," interrupted John. "Mr. Monroe proposed to me that we cash it and divide the money. I assented—of course not. He has accused me of being short in my accounts. But he lies—I am not afraid of an investigation, Mr. Monroe."

"Is this true, Mr. Monroe?" asked Mr. Jarney, fiercely, and piercing him through and through with his firmness.

Mr. Monroe cowered before Mr. Jarney's rage, like an abject criminal brought to the confession stage of his stricken conscience, but as blank as ever.

"Is this true, Mr. Monroe?" demanded Mr. Jarney again, still upbraiding him by his fierce tone.

"I am afraid it is," responded Monroe, meekly, with a crestfallen tone, but no change in his countenance.

"I am very sorry for you, Mr. Monroe," said Mr. Jarney, relentingly. "I was infuriated with you a moment ago, and meant to be harsh; but now all that I can say is, that you deserve my pity. Ingratitude is the worst of all mean traits, Mr. Monroe. My advice to you, coupled with my injunction, is that you hasten to the Pittsburgh office, close up your accounts and leave the employment of the firm, taking the other two dupes with you. You may go now. I have no further use for you here."

Mr. Monroe sat dumbly under this withering dressing up; but he was obdurate in his inexpressiveness. Taking Mr. Jarney's cue, he arose, put on his hat, and departed, without a farewell to either one.

That was the last they ever saw of poor Monroe, alive. His body was found next day on a muddy shore, where the sewer rats fight among themselves for a share of the food that the foul sewage spews out with its bile.

CHAPTER XXVI THE CHIEF GRAFTER IS FOREWARNED AND GOES TO EUROPE

Jacob Cobb, the big boss, sat in his easy chair, surrounded by his spendthrift family, with whom he was communing on the glories of that fame which money brings to those who earn not, nor spin.

It was a bright evening in May, with a red sun setting through the upper haze on the horizon, and throwing back through the windows of his mansion a fiery glare, like the gleam of a blast furnace permeating the density of the pall that ever hangs over the valleys skirting the hills to either side. Had he, or they, or any of them, been of a meditative turn, the evening scene might have been likened to the scenes that surround the tempestuous lives of those who toil and dwell where the counterpart of the sun, in this comparison, holds sway throughout the day and night.

But as they were not of a meditative turn, they never saw the black old buildings of the workmen, as grimy as the squat old mills themselves spouting fire from thousands of smoke-stacks, all huddled together in the narrow ways and defiles, like so many barbarous places of habitation, with sooty walls and streaked window panes, and fuming chimney tops, and nowhere scarcely a sign of vegetation to brighten up the dull tones of the desolation. They never saw the grim-visaged, hard-fisted, half-naked men, sweating blood, almost, subjecting the native element of iron to the changing process of the caves of fire, before which they worked and strained their energies to produce the finished product that made it possible for men like Cobb to live in splendor. They never saw the simple homes, the poor homes, the impoverished homes of some of these workmen; or their children in their styles, their plays, their sports, their love-making, their dutifulness to parent, their respect for law, or their shortcomings; nor heard their ambitious cry; nor saw their cheerful endeavors to improve their worldly affairs; nor saw the blight of poverty, nor the curse of rum. They saw nothing, save the rolling smoke from the factory fires which the poor man teased; and, even though it brought them plenty, it gave them long periods of annoyance that they had to endure it. They only saw the setting sun, in that direction, going down into a tarnished sky. But they saw, in the iridescence of their surroundings, the gloat of pomp, the pride of power, the sen-sen of gayety, the joy of lust, the glib of society, the whirl of scandal—the right to graft.

Jacob Cobb was at ease, if ever there was a man in such a heaven of exalted purification, as he sat in his easy chair on this evening. It was the time of his domestic enjoyment, in which no one ever took more delight, the divorce scandal talk to the contrary notwithstanding; and this is one thing to his credit, if he should have credit for anything he has done in this world. Money was his God. Not being competent to amass a fortune, had he applied his talents in genuine business, he, early in life, became a petty politician. Starting as an election board clerk, he ascended the winding stairs of a ward heeler up the many flights till he reached the chief seat in the inner chamber of the Temple of the Bosses, and there he reigned—till he should be dethroned by an aroused public conscience.

He was now in the hey-day of his power, and he ruled with a clenched fist; albeit, at times, he heard temblors below him that might become powerful enough to shake him from his seat. Through a College of Embasies, with Peter Dieman as the dean, he worked the system through the tortuous windings of every channel of business, collecting his tiths as Pharoah collected his charges on his garnerings in the seven years of famine, with about as pitiless a hand. And these tithings were heavy. They poured into the System's exchequer from every source, like the waters that flowed by the city of his birth to form the La Belle Reviere; but, unlike that stream, which flowed to a bigger sea, they stopped at Cobb's gate to enter silently into his dark pool to disappear via an unseen outlet.

Jacob, not being wholly satisfied with what was clandestinely coming his way, connived at other schemes to perpetuate the inflow to his coffers; which was to his shame. The worst of which of his many other designs, was to marry his children to rich men or women, and divide the loot, if money may be christened, in this instance, by that pelfic name. Susanna, the eldest, and Marjorie, the youngest of his two daughters, were already bargained for by two young scions of the rich who had no more reputation to hang to them than discarded touts of the underworld; but their daddies had money, and that counted for much, while innocence had to suffer. But there was Jasper yet, his own young hopeful, past the age of twenty-six, and not yet disposed of. A glimpse into that young man's character has been given in a previous chapter, so here it will suffice to say that he was a profligate of the evilest sort. And Jacob wanted him to capture Edith Jarney! God forbid such a union! Purity joined to degradation in holy wedlock? Not if Edith Jarney knew her mind; for it would be unholy wedlock. Mrs. Cobb was equally as mercenary with her children as their father. She it was that first proposed the horrid scheme. She it was that taught them how to ensnare the victims marked for their bows. She it was that led them to the idol that they were to worship. She it was that schooled them in the ways of snobbery. And they called her a doting mother. And Jacob willingly acquiesced.

Those who teach that man is only a biologic al entity might find in such sons and daughters good subjects for their experimentation, and prove their theory by the aid of the divorce courts.

"Jasper, it is time for you to make some headway with Miss Jarney," said his doting mother, on this evening, as they all sat around their father in his ease.

Jasper, who had been sitting near in a despondently moping manner, suddenly aroused himself to the importunate remark, and looked disconsolate enough to arouse the sympathy of every one bent on reforming young blades; for he had been out the night before, and showed evidences of heavy dissipation.

"Mother, you are always going on at me about Miss Jarney," he retorted. "She's been sick for the past five months or more; I have seen her but once, and then had no chance of seeing her alone."

"Yes, dear Jasper, you must brace up, now, and make of yourself more of a man, if you want to improve on your opportunity of winning such a prize," said Jacob Cobb, with some disparaging sentiments in his tone.

"Father, you too? Give me a chance, and when the opportunity arrives, I shall propose," returned Jasper.

"You should not lose a minute's time," said the mother, with faith. "That man Monroe is out of the way now, and the other young man is too poor for her to take in place of you. See your sisters! Both already engaged, and soon to be married, yet both of them younger than you. You are too slow in pursuit of such happiness. Why, you should have had it settled long ago. Had I had my way about it, it would all have been over with, and you two fixed comfortably in a house of your own, giving swell dinners, balls and parties, eh, Jasper? Edith is a fine girl, and I know she will be a good keeper of a house for you."

"She is going to the mountains soon, mother, I am informed," said he, with design; "and I have half a notion to go up there for awhile to get away from my associates."

"That's the thing! that's the thing!" exclaimed the father, delighted at the prospect of getting the two together at some summer place. "Go it, boy! go it, and push your suit."

"How nice it would be, Jasper," said Susanna, with glee, "for you to get away from the city for a time."

"It would do you worlds of good, brother," assented Marjorie, "to get away from the smoke awhile."

"You know, Jasper, we had planned to go to Paris for the summer and take you along; but we can spare your company this time," said the doting mother, "if it will give you the opportunity to make good."

This inane conversation anent Jasper's future was broken up by a messenger appearing at the door, with a very urgent note from Peter Dieman, requesting Jacob Cobb to come to his mansion without delay. Jacob responded without delay, and was soon sitting by the throne of that spectacular king, who still was wearing his mandarin robe, fez-like cap, and smoking another vile cigar.

"Have you heard the latest, Jacob?" asked Peter, when Jacob was seated comfortably blowing up clouds of white vapor in corresponding rings with Peter's smoke-stack.

"No," answered Jacob, with no uncommon concern.

"Well, be prepared to hear the worst—Jim Dalls is back from Europe, and is going to squeal on us," said Peter, with as little concern as Cobb at first appeared to show.

"No!" exclaimed Jacob, with a cloud on his face that was sufficient almost to obscure the smoke from his cigar.

"It is true," said Peter, still unconcerned. "He was here this evening."

"What brought him back?" said Jacob.

"Run out of funds, he said," said Peter, blowing smoke with much complacency.

"Couldn't you send him any more?" asked Jacob.

"I sent for him," said Peter, now looking at Jacob with an air of supercilious gravity.

"God man! what do you mean? Do you mean to ruin us all?" shouted Jacob, excitedly.

"Be calm, Jacob; be calm, and save your nerves for what is coming," said Peter, gently. "He came by my request, and is to make a confession before the grand jury—at my request, too. So if you want to save your old bacon, pull down your shaky house of graft and hit the trail for Europe; for you will be the first one caught in the net, Jacob."

"Oh, Lord man! What do you mean? This is awful! This is horrid! This is terrible! Exposed by my chief deputy like that! I'll never forgive you, Peter! Never! And when it blows over, I shall return and cook you a dish that you won't relish!" cried Jacob, now in a frenzy of excitement.

"Why, I am safe from harm," said Peter, calmly.

"What did you do it for?" asked Jacob, in great anger.

"To be plain to you, sir, I may state that that's my business," said Peter, cooly.

"Then, we part enemies?" asked Jacob, with a daggerous look.

"We do—if you want to; but, Jacob, you'd better take my humble advice, and go to Europe as quick as you could skin a cat. You know the whole thing will come out anyway when that bank affair is known, which I am assured will be exploded soon, and then the whole shooting match will be busted."

"You had better call on heaven to help you, Peter, when I return—if I go," said Jacob, rising, and leering down upon the king, who sat looking at the floor now, in quiet thought.

"I am not afraid of you, or any one else, Jacob," responded Peter, looking up. "I am a domesticated man now, Jacob, and intend to enjoy the rest of my days right here, in this house, with my wife and ten children."

"You scamp!" hissed Jacob, snarling down upon him, like one dog snarls at another dog with the prize bone.

"Take my advice, Jacob, and go home," said Peter, looking sidewise at Jacob. "You'd better be there packing your grip than standing here calling me hard names. Europe is the safest place for you for the next ten years; so go. I can take care of myself."

"Things have come to a nice pass," said Jacob, "when a man can't enjoy the comforts of a home in this age without every upstart wanting to interfere in his business!"

"It's a nasty business that of yours," said Peter, remorselessly. "I've been tired of it for a long time, and wanted my chance to get out. The chance has come, and I am getting."

"You are an ingrate," replied Jacob, wrathfully. "Being entrenched yourself with safety lines thrown out, so that no one can invade your private affairs, you care nothing for your friends who have divided with you for years. An ingrate! An ingrate, I repeat, Peter! I shall go, and may those vapid detectives who have been here for months trying to make a break in our lines, find you out, and help to punish you."

"Oh, that's all right, Jacob," said the suave Peter. "I know all about their work in this city; but I am beyond their reach. So go, if you don't want to be pinched within a week. Go, I say, to Europe, and maybe you can enjoy life there; and while you are doing it, think of me sometimes, just for old friendship's sake, and take an extra drink on the side for me—that's all. I shall never forget you till my last breath is gone; and I shall never forget the words you have just now said to me, and what impression they have left upon me. Go! Jacob; go! that I may be done with you; that's all." Peter concluded this speech, without either smoking, rubbing or squinting.

"Good night," said Jacob, leaving the king's throne; and the two old cronies in legalized crime (for that is what graft is, nothing more), parted forever.

"Good bye," were the last words that Peter said to him; but Jacob did not hear them, so blind was he in his rage when he stepped out into the cool night air to take up his return to his home again to seek solace in the bosom of his family.

Arriving home, Jacob put his family into a wild uproar when he told them of the result of his visit to Peter Dieman.

"Well, we were going to Europe anyway," said Mrs. Cobb, as a consoling climax to her bewailment. "It is good that I informed our friends of this trip, so they will now be none the wiser. The wedding of the two young ladies can come off in September, as planned. I can return for that, and you can remain in Europe—ill, perhaps. And Jasper need not postpone his expedition into the mountains, you see."

"No, Jasper; you must not fail in that," said Cobb, still unable to give up any of his schemes, so fascinating were they all to him yet, "as I will be compelled to remain for some length of time. If you fail, our fortunes may be somewhat impaired as a result of all this trouble. So don't fail, my boy."

"Oh, I'll win; don't despair, father, for me; I'll win," said Jasper, hopefully, with more interest than ever now in getting a wife with money.

So to Europe Jacob Cobb and his family betook themselves, leaving young Jasper at home, as agreed, to sport awhile with the vixenish little Cupid. Punctilious, as on every other such occasion of the going of such people, the Sunday newspapers, in their society columns, gave a glowing account of the departure of Mr. and Mrs. Cobb and their two daughters for Europe to spend the season (or several seasons it might have been) in Paris; and probably, if not otherwise detained, to Baden-Baden, or to some other noted place, purportedly for the benefit of Mr. Cobb, who (poor man) had been in poor health for months past.

Mercy on us!

CHAPTER XXVII
ELI JEREY AT THE DIEMAN HOME

Dressed as on the great occasion when he visited Miss Jarney, Eli Jerey called at the home of Peter Dieman but a short ten minutes after Jacob Cobb had left in such a bad temper. Peter was in his jolliest frame of mind, and was still having jerks of felicitation over his fine stroke in besting Jacob Cobb, as he looked at it, when Eli floated into his presence like a fluted lamppost with its light extinguished. Eli sat down with his high hat on the top of his untutored head, as his only hat rack, when Peter took up the thread of the subject about where he and Jacob broke it in their slight misunderstanding.

"When I told him to skip out, Eli, he flew the handle to beat all," said Peter. "He threatened, if he ever returned, to cook a dish for me that I would not relish."

"Did he, though?" said Eli, raising his eyes to the level of Peter's. "Now what kind of a dish could he cook for you, do you suppose?"

"I suppose he refers to the street paving proposition," responded Peter.

"Which one? Where the wooden blocks were used?"

"I suppose so."

"Well, Mr. Dieman, we might as well be honest now and say the truth sometimes; but that was a very bad piece of jobbery for all connected with it—even for the wood blocks, as you will see when a year has passed."

"How?"

"In it, the city got its worst job, the contractors worser jobbed, the grafters got jobbed good and plenty, and the wood blocks will be so jobbed that you will not be able to find any in another turn of the sun around the seasons."

"But how will he connect me with it?"

"He can't, Peter; he can't. I can swear that none of the money came to you by the way of our office. It all went through Cobb's hands, and I have the receipts."

"Bully, boy! Bully for you! When I die, I will leave you the old shop and all it holds. You have a slick head, Eli, for such things. Who'd thought Jacob would have given his receipt?"

"I forced it out of him. Told him: no receipt, no money."

"I knew you'd fix it all right when I left it all to you. Why, boy, you don't blame me for having confidence in you?—But Jim Dalls?"

"Oh, he's to keep you out, as agreed, and is to go free on making his confession, and sticking to it at the trial. I tell you, he'll fix a lot of them high-ups and others who've been in the game so long they can't believe but what they're honest and upright citizens."

"Bully! Then all danger for me is over?" asked Peter, chuckling in such a whimsical manner that Eli felt moved himself to get up and hammer him on the back for fear he was choking on his good humor.

"Over," returned Eli, decisively.

"Good! Say Eli, I was only running a bluff on Cobb at first, when I said they couldn't get me—I hear Monroe's dead?"

"Deader'n a fried oyster since he jumped into the Hudson."

"Poor Monroe, I always thought he would hang himself, if given enough rope."

"I am told Mr. Jarney has cleaned out the gang that helped Monroe in his dirty work—that's what becomes of not being faithful to your job, like I've always been, Mr. Dieman," moralized Eli. "Say, did I tell you about seeing May's sister at the Jarneys?"

"No; do tell me about it?"

"Well, I saw her, that's all; and spoke to her, that's all—and my! she's poorty; but I'll stick to May."

"If I let you," said Peter, squinting his eyes, with a funny little twinkle mixed in their movements.

"Why, I came this very night to ask you, Mr. Dieman," said Eli, as an opener to his subject.

"Really, Eli? Impossible!"

"What's impossible?" asked Eli, disheartened at the word "impossible."

"That you came for that purpose," said Peter with a smile.

"I did, sir; indeed, I did, Mr. Dieman," responded Eli, with much feeling.

"Well?" said Peter, with a bearish look.

"May I have her?" blurted out Eli, as he snapped a piece of imaginary lint from his angled knee with the index finger of his right hand.

"Is she willin', Eli?" asked Peter, changing his tone.

"She is," he responded, firmly.

"You've made fine progress, my boy; but you'll have to ask her moth—Kate—" turning his head as he shouted her name for his voice to carry to where that lady sat in the parlor, in the distance, surrounded by her squirming herd of youngsters—"come here!"

Kate came, looking like a queen—in her "rags"—still bearing some of her old sorrows in her lean face, now reduced to a pleasanter tone by the artful hand of plenty.

"This young man wants May; can you spare her?" said Peter, not giving Eli a show at performing that part of his simple playing in courtship. "I'll speak for him, Kate. He's a mighty good boy, and May might do a thousand times worse."

Eli sat like a docile lamb before the altar of matrimonial sacrifice, humbly waiting his fate. Kate looked at him. He looked at Kate. Peter looked at both. All silent. Intense was Eli's emotions—so tense that he was like a pine board in the hot sun ready to warp with the intensity of the heat that perforated the skin on his brow, sending forth scalding globes of perspiration.

"I re—I gu—how did you tell me to say it?" she said, turning to Peter for intelligence on the right word.

"May," answered Peter, rubbing.

"I may—no, that's not it," she said, appealing to him.

"You may!" suggested Peter again.

"You may, Mr. Jerey," she said, finally hitting upon the proper phrase that would express her answer.

She had no more than uttered the word, than Eli leaped to his feet, dropped his cane, and caught Mrs. Dieman in his sweeping arms, and hugged her powerfully. It could not be told whether he exercised a son's indubitable right to kiss her, for the very momentous reason that his plug hat fell off at the critical moment when he appeared to be performing that gracious act. But, in any event, his future mother-in-law grunted from the grateful embracing that she underwent in the clasp of Eli. Finding his prized and fashionable hat had toppled off with imminent danger of being crushed by ruthless feet, he hastily released her, picked up his hat, put it on his head again, with such grandiloquent precipitation that he made things in the room look as if they were going up in a whirlwind.

After catching his breath, he glanced inquiringly toward the parlor. There he saw May sitting in a very deep and richly decorated chair perusing a novel, which she, since her coming out, had been taught was a beautiful source of pastime for young ladies of noble families. But Eli saw not the novel; neither did he see the pencil and tablet on May's lap, with which she had been instructed to provide herself to jot down the things that impressed her most when reading; nor did he see with what beautiful material she was dressed. All that he saw was the plump little face of May, a face that had no equal, to him; and all that she saw was the tall Eli racing toward her, like a galloping giraffe, with love-lit eyes, with grinning teeth, with plug hat on his head. Then—

"May! May! May!"

The world turned upside-down, and he plunged headlong with May in his arms, into the laughing stars that flecked his heaven of delight.

In the sudden onrush, May dropped her novel, dropped her pencil, dropped her note book; and Eli dropped his hat, which the youngest child momentarily toddled to, and took his seat within it as contentedly as if it had been placed there for his especial enjoyment. Eli minded nothing, not even the cloud of children that rose around him like fairies in astonishment at a bogie man come among them.

But the whirlwind that Eli started soon abated, and its wreck and ruin was more noticeable upon May than any one else; for, in his awkwardness, he had loosened her hair, till it fell down around her waist, and mussed her pink messaline till it needed ironing afresh, and caused a burning place on the one cheek which he pressed so closely to the rough twill of his coat collar, that she seemed to be aflame with indignation. She was not indignant, however. Her little pout was only a sign of shame-faced happiness brought about by the astonishing behavior of Eli in the presence of her family; which she declared was shameful familiarity.

"Why, May," said Eli, in support of his actions, "your mother says yes, and your daddy says yes, and I say yes; now, what do you say—I don't care who knows!"

"I don't care what they say, you had no business to do it," she answered, looking black at him, as she was brushing out some of the wrinkle marks in her dress.

"Is it yes, or no, May? Tell me quick, before I go hang myself!" he cried in his anguish.

"I haven't said no, Eli," replied May, as she attempted to put up her hair, and blushing from ear to ear.

"Is it yes, May?" said Eli, with eyes brightening. "I want to know."

May glanced up pensively, with a hairpin between her lips cutting a smile in two.

"Yes," she answered, as the pin fell to the floor, and her hair straggled down again.

"I am happy, May," he replied; "now will you excuse me for my impetuosity?"

May was gathering up her hair again when Eli said this. She turned to him with a smothered laugh, and remarked: "You are all right, Eli; I am happy."

Whereat, both being perfectly agreed as to their feelings and opinions, Eli looked about for his hat, preparatory to taking his departure.

"Well, Lord bless us! Look here, May!" he exclaimed, standing over the youngster, sitting in his hat.

Then, bursting into a loud guffaw, he stooped down, grasped the hat by the side rims, and lifted it up, baby and all, and ventured forth to the throne room. As he lifted the burden up before him, the baby laid hold of his string necktie with one hand and his collar with the other, as a support to his precarious position. In which position Eli, hat, and baby proceeded, Eli singing a foolish ditty, till they arrived at Peter's seat, by the side of whom sat Mrs. Dieman.

Eli stood before them a moment that they might see the load and the oddity of the situation of baby. They laughed; Eli laughed; baby laughed. He swung the hat this way and that, up and down, and bounced him a little. Eli blowed a tune of coo-coo at him, then whistled, and sang snatches of songs, of all of which baby seemed highly appreciative, judging from his looks. Then—the bottom fell out of the hat, and through it, feet foremost, shot the baby like a stone, and fell in a squalling bundle on the floor at Eli's feet.

At the outcry that followed, all the other children came rushing in and circled around the party; and laughed and clapped their hands in great glee at the mishap to the baby and the hat. Eli picked up the crying child, and stroked his hair, and cooed to him. The child placed his little arms around Eli's neck, and sobbed till his grief was gone. And this was the little child that touched his father's hard face with his little hands, saying da-da; but perhaps he will never remember that day.

Procuring a new hat from Peter, one that fit him illy, Eli tore himself away from this man's dominions, encircled by Billy Barton's family, to return some other day for a beautifully appointed wedding with his beautiful May.

The world may laugh and sneer at such as Eli Jerey; but, after all, in such as he may be found the man who will make marriage a heaven to a poor man's daughter, raised as she was in poverty, and lifted by chance to a higher plane of living.

CHAPTER XXVIII
IT IS DECIDED TO SEND EDITH TO THE MOUNTAINS

It was a morning in May. Happy birds sang in the tree tops, and flowers speckled the green grass of the park with their variegated bloom. The sun, the first for days, threw his lustrous light over the smoke begrimed hills; the air, which a brisk wind from the north cleared, was bracing in its freshness, and all creation was breaking into renewed vitality at the touch of advancing spring.

Edith, on the arm of Star, walked down a bypath bordered by nodding Easter lilies, late in blooming, and watched the bounding butterflies and plunging bees and hopping birds, and heard the call of nature in all its thrilling voices.

Life is beautiful and life is sweet, but what is life when the soul is craving for that which cannot be had? The wind may sing to you in its softest notes, the birds may send forth their enchanting rhapsodies, the flowers may emit their most becalming fragrance, but what are they to a spirit unanswered in its callings? The sun may shine ever so brilliantly, the moon may beam in mellowing brightness, the stars may twinkle in their deepest mysteries, but what are they when love is crying out, with no responsive cry? Deep, deep, unanswerable is the mystery. Edith asked the flowers, the birds, the bees; she felt the soothing wind, heard the sweetening notes, and caught the lulling scents, but they all gave back the answer—mystery! mystery!

They walked the paths together, Edith and Star, arm in arm; they sat in the cooling nooks, and whisperingly conversed; they let the wind play with their locks, like playful fairies; they saw, they heard, they sang, they laughed. But still, to Edith, there was that mystery ever hanging over her—a blot to everything that should entrance her—a dim, dark, cold, benumbing longing that paints frightful pictures from a palpitating heart that gets no response to its secret throbs. Weary, worn out, lagging, spiritless, because of her long illness and worry over late happenings among her father's unfaithful employes, Edith got no comfort now out of her home, or its surroundings. Pale still, and nervous, her spirits ever flagged, even under the promptings of her dear friend Star, who had been resorting to all her charms and graces to give pleasure to the sick young lady that she might be diverted from her moody spells. Edith was bright at times, and laughed and chatted like a child under Star's cheerful influence; but more often she was melancholy, and seemed never to be reaching that time when the shadow of her malady would fall off. Music had no charms for her, nor books, nor young company. Life was lifeless to her. The mansion was a dreary castle. Her days were spent in wishing for night, and nights in wishing for morning. All her mother's endearments, all her father's love, all of Star's sweet companionship, were alike to her—unconsoling. The mother was in despair, the father grief stricken, but Star, of all of them, had hope.

"Edith," said Star, this day, while standing by the pond watching the leaping fountain and playful golden fish, and noting how quiet Edith was. "I wrote to Mr. Winthrope yesterday."

"Oh, Star," said Edith, with a deprecating frown, "I hope you have not gone and forgotten yourself to such an extent that you have written first?"

"Forgot myself, Edith? Why, bless your heart, no; he wrote me first," replied Star, with a merry laugh.

"Wrote first?" asked Edith, in surprise.

"Yes; he just did write first; and I told him that he was real mean in not writing sooner," said Star.

"What did he say?" asked Edith, gazing vacantly into the water.

"About all he said was asking about your health. It is mean in him, I repeat, that he said no more. He said, though, that when your father was in New York, he told him you were fast improving."

"What was your answer, Star?"

"Oh, goodness! I wrote six pages, about everything, almost, and informed him that—"

"Now, Star; you didn't write anything that would be indiscreet, did you?"

"Why, deary, no, of course not; I only told him that you—"

"Star, don't tell me that you have violated my confidence?"

"I will not say what I wrote, Edith, if your are not more attentive. I said that—"

"Star! Star!" said Edith, with tears glistening in her eyes; "do not tell me that you have broken your pledge; if you do, I shall never—no—go on; what did you tell him?"

"That you—that you are getting better very slowly, and that your father will take you to the mountains for the summer. I told him everything else, Edith, but that which you forbade me telling."

"You are very prudent, Star. Will he write again, do you suppose?"

"I wound up my letter with a P. S.: 'Don't forget to write!'"

"You bad girl! I suppose he will be coming to see you sometime?"

"Wish he would," said Star, hopefully, with a teasing expression in her face.

"Really, Star?"

"Yes; I do—I'd turn him over to you," she responded, with a laugh.

"You are a tease, now! If he comes, it must be of his own free will."

"You are not looking well, Edith; we had better go in the house," said Star, seeing the pallor of weakness coming over her face.

"Assist me in," responded Edith, willingly submitting to Star's admonition. As they were nearing the steps leading up to the great piazza, Edith remarked that she would go to the mountains next day, if able, with her father, and, of course, Star was to be her companion.

"I was never out of the city," replied Star, "and I am wondering what mountains look like. Can you tell me?"

"Oh, they are only big hills."

"Do people live there?"

"Yes. Many people live in them. He came from up there somewhere."

"From the mountains?"

"Yes; from the mountains."

"Then, we may see his home," said Star, suggestively.

"We may; but the mountains are very large, Star—miles long and miles wide, with dense woods everywhere and with but few roads through them, and homes of farmers scattered about."

"Oo-oo!" exclaimed Star. "We would not want to go far into them; we might get lost. Do people live there?"

"Yes. There are bears there, Star, and deer and owls; and many birds live in the gloomy depths of the forests."

"My!" exclaimed Star, alarmed. "I would not want to go out after night. Where will we live when we go up there?"

"In a big hotel on top of the mountains."

"How fine! I can hardly wait till I see it all!"

"Our trunks should be packed today, Star, for a two months' stay. Father says I will be benefitted when I get out of the smoke of this city."

"Is your father going with us?"

"Oh, yes; but for a short stay only. He will visit us once a week thereafter."

"Won't that be fine, Edith; and we will get to see the mountaineers, and maybe his home," said Star, with all that fullness of anticipation that comes to one emancipated from a round of daily worry and abject commonplaceness, as they reached the top of the flight of steps, up which Star had been assisting Edith.

Edith looked up into the face of Star with a smile, showing neither hope nor doubt, but full of that wearying pain that leaves a sore upon the heart.

"It will be very pleasant, no doubt, Star," returned Edith; "but I am so weak that I am afraid I cannot enjoy anything. How kind and good you are to me," and Edith glanced up with tears; "you take so much pains in comforting me, and wishing for my welfare. I would be lost, dear Star, if it were not for you—lost—utterly lost," and the poor nerve-wrecked, distracted little Edith fell into Star's arms through utter exhaustion.

Edith was carried to her room, and restoratives were administered. The contemplated journey was therefore postponed for a week to await her recuperation. The weeks passed, and Edith was still no better. Nobody saw her condition. Nobody quite understood what it was. They were all blind.

Lying on her bed one day, when the sun was shining, and the fragrance of the flowers and the songs of the birds came in the open window as a caressing wave of sympathy, Edith was roused from her unpleasant meditations by her father, who came in to see her. Sitting down by her bed, the father took up one hand of his child and petted it, with his eyes full of the tears of his abiding grief.

"Edith, dear," he said, with his voice full of emotion, "do you think you can now withstand the trip to the mountains?"

"I think I will be just as well off here, papa," she answered, faintly and indifferently.

"If you are able, we will go at once, dear," said the father, noticing how low her spirits were, and wishing to do anything that would tend to revive them. "I believe a change of air and scenes will do you good. Do you think you can make the trip?"

"I will try, papa—any place; any place—it makes no difference, papa. I am so weak all the time, papa, that I am—"

"Don't; don't, Edith, my dear child," he said, with anguish in his kind heart, and parental remorse on his conscience. "You would not have been in this state, pet, had you not become so wrought up over that Monroe affair, I know; and I am to blame for being so blind, so blind—so—"

The father laid his head in his hands on the bed, and wept; and as he wept, Edith laid her hand upon his head, and smoothed down his ruffled hair. "Dear, papa," she said, "dear papa, don't cry for me; I will get better."

"Edith," said her father, raising his head, "I have sent for Mr. Winthrope to return to my office to become my chief assistant. I expect him here today, Edith. Shall I have him out for dinner?"

Edith gave a nervous start, and for the first time in days her little heart beat faster, and a color mounted to her pallid cheeks.

"Do as you like, papa; I shall be glad to see him, if he comes to my room," answered Edith. "When did you say you would take me to the mountains?"

"Tomorrow, if you are well enough."

"I will go, papa."

That evening John came, and ate dinner with the family. Instinctively he felt the great veil of sorrow, of fear, of dread, of worry, of sadness that brooded over the household. Strong, healthy, handsome, mannerly, John seemed to have brought a new ray of sunshine with him that was absent there before. His pleasing conversation, his cheerful smile, his hearty laugh, his quick wit in repartee flooded every department of the mansion—even into the cook's chamber, where was sung that evening love-songs of youth long suppressed by the weighty forebodings of the coming of the White Horse and his rider.

"Mr. Winthrope," said the bouncing Mrs. Jarney, now less demonstrative of her spirits by her long siege of fretting, "it seems so natural to have you here. I told Mr. Jarney just the other day that I wished you could come out occasionally to see us, for you were always such pleasant company."

"I don't know whether to take that as a compliment or a pretty piece of flattery, Mrs. Jarney," responded John. "I am sure, however you mean it, I shall not be negligent in expressing my thanks to you."

"Compliment, Mr. Winthrope; compliment," returned Mrs. Jarney, with a sweet deference towards accenting the word compliment. "I never indulge in flattery with people whom I like—leastwise, I do not care to with you."

"I feel grateful to you, Mrs. Jarney, and to Mr. Jarney also, for your kindnesses in my behalf, and friendly consideration of my welfare. The only manner in which I can express myself, is that you have my sincerest thanks for your good deeds and kind words," was the way he thanked them.

Mrs. Jarney never lost an opportunity to say a good word for John to her friends, or to himself. Sometimes he was touched to a modest degree of bashfulness in her presence by her assertive way of praising him. On this evening he was more severely tested than ever before by reason of her motherly familiarity. When he arrived, she was so over-joyed at seeing him, that she was almost in the act of throwing her arms around his neck, and weeping, perhaps, as the mother did on the return of her prodigal son. She, no doubt, would have committed this informal act of gladness, had it not been that to have accomplished it, she would had to have stood on a chair, John being so much the taller. But as it was, she took both his hands in hers in welcoming him, and shook them with such energy that John was disconcerted for a brief time. Mr. Jarney was just as profuse in his greeting, but more restrainful in his actions than his wife. Why all this joyfulness, this gladsomeness, this unusual cordiality, on their part, John never stopped to consider in any other form of reason than duty and gratitude.

"You will want to see Edith before you go?" said Star, after the diners had risen from the table, and as she was walking with him to the drawing room.

"Of course," replied John, "if she is in condition to see a stranger. I should not want to leave without seeing her."

"She knows you are here, and is expecting you. Will you go up now?" asked Star.

"If it is her pleasure, and your wish, I shall go with you," replied John.

Together Star and John repaired to Edith's room, Star entering first and John following. Edith lay in her night clothes, with the covers drawn up well around her throat, her two white hands reposing on the white spread. She had expected him for the last two hours, and began to be weary over the long waiting. So when the door opened and Star entered, she turned her head in time to catch him coming in the door; then as quickly turned it away, in an attempt to stop the fluttering of her heart. When he approached her bedside, she extended to him a hand, which he took, as he sat down on a chair by her side.

"Mr. Winthrope," she said, very low, "I am glad to see you."

John saw that her mind was with her now, and he should act accordingly. The appalling look of illness was in her face yet, the appealing smile of hope was in her eyes. He was overcome again. Oh, for that hour of health for her, when the raptures of a true soul answers to the responsive note!

"You look so much better, Miss Jarney," said John, the moment of his recovery over her glad greeting, "than when I saw you last."

"Do I; really, Mr. Winthrope?" she asked, with her eyes illuminating.

"Surely, you are better; I can hope so anyway."

"I was better for some time after you left in March; but lately I have been gradually growing worse, till now I am in bed again, as you see."

"I plainly see," he said jocularly; "but, if you would get out of here and into the country somewhere, and get the fresh air and open doors, I am sure you would improve rapidly?"

"Do you think so?" she asked, withdrawing her hand and folding them both together, as she turned on her side, facing him.

"Why, nothing would be better," he answered.

"I am going away tomorrow," she said decisively.

"Tomorrow! So soon, and you in bed yet?" he exclaimed.

"My papa insists that I shall have a change of environment at once."

"Can you go? Where will they take you?"

"To the mountains—up somewhere where you live."

"That should make a very enjoyable journey for you, and you should be benefitted," he said, cheerfully. "I am going home in June, and I shall hope to find you improved in health by that time. May I anticipate the pleasure of calling to inquire about your health, Miss Jarney?"

"The pleasure will be mine as well as yours, Mr. Winthrope."

"Then I may call some day?"

"You may, if—" and Edith offered up the daintiest little smile to meet his glowing looks—"if you will take me and Star to see your mountain home."

"Oh, I shall be glad to do that. I have got the nicest little sister and the finest big brother you ever saw, and my mother will cook you such a rare dinner that I know you will recover soon after eating of it."

"My! I can scarcely wait the time, Mr. Winthrope. I can already taste that dinner. When will you be there?"

"The first week in June."

"How delightful! I know I shall recover my health, once I get there. How impatient I am already! Star, is everything packed?"

"Almost, Edith," answered Star.

"We will not want many fine clothes, Star; I am going out to rough it for awhile. Is it rough up there, Mr. Winthrope?"

"Very—in some places," he answered.

"And you will be up in June?" she asked, now feeling enthusiastic.

"That is my plan, now," he replied, uncertainly.

"You will not let anything interfere, for I want to see your sister, and I know Star will want to see your brother," she said, with a weak smile toward Star, who blushed very red at the idea of meeting John's brother.

Edith was by this time worked up to a high state of excitement over the prospect of the new life she was to lead. John, discerning the bad effect it had on her, and fearing further complications should he remain, rose to depart. She raised her hand to bid him good bye. He took it, touched his lips to her fingers, looked down upon her, and said, "Good bye."

"Good bye," she said, "till we meet in the mountains. Good bye!"

And John was gone.

The same wild emotions whirled through his soul, as in those other times, when he was so fraught with the uncertainty of her demeanor during her night of illusions, as he left the mansion on the hill. The same musical good bye, he heard echoing from the buzz of the automobile that wheeled him to the city. The same he heard following him, pursuing him, pervading him and everything—in the crowds of the streets, under the lights, in the hotel corridor, in the lobby, in his room; and, finally, the last he heard singing him to peaceful sleep. But he heard it now played on a different harp from that which lulled him into sleep many times before.

CHAPTER XXIX
EDITH RECOVERS AND YOUNG COBB PAYS HIS RESPECTS

It was another morning in May. The sun was climbing over the wooded hills to the east; the wind was pulsing through the leafing trees; the wild flowers were blooming by the roadside and in the dusky dells; the butterfly, bee and bird were in their delights of mating, and all creation was swinging in the swing of renewed vitality at the touch of speeding spring.

Edith, with the ever confiding Star by her side, sat wrapped in a summer cloak on the eastern end of the sweeping reach of the veranda of the Summit House, which sits, with much pretentious rambling, where the old National way winds up from the east and twists up from the west in its macadamed smoothness in crossing the mountain divide.

Life is beautiful and life is sweet; but what is life without that which the pure heart craves? The wind may sing to you in dulcing notes; the birds may send forth their most ravishing rhapsodies; the flowers may spray you with their cologne of incense; but what are they to the spirit in which the call is answered? The sun may shine, the moon may beam, the stars may twinkle; but what are they compared to the responsive cry of the soul's affinity. Deep, deep, unanswerable is the mystery.

Edith asked the sun, the moon, the stars; the wind, the trees, the birds, the flowers, and everything; she felt the soothing wind, heard the singing birds, caught the lulling scents; but they all gave back the answer: mystery! mystery! It is all a mystery, that bright, beaming, radiating longing that paints the beautiful pictures from a palping heart that has received an echo from its secret throbs.

As the sun climbed up his way, the wind lowered its beating pulses, and a shimmer of warmth spread over the hills and woods and fields and deep valleys. Life came up out of the east; and out of the depths of the hotel. Farmers would pass in their rattling rigs; woodmen roll by in their lumbering wagons; autos puff up the hills with their loads of pleasure seekers, stop awhile, unload, and spin on again. Late risers sauntered out on the veranda—ladies and gentlemen of leisure, and children—in idling costumes, and tramp off time, as a bracer for the morning feast. Noises came out of the interior, like a modified din from chambers of revelry. Bells, on straying sheep, or browsing cattle, tinkled in the distance. Axes rang somewhere in the silent forests; sounds of many kind broke out from everywhere; and the world was full astir.

It was wonderful to Edith, this new life, with its healing balm of fresh air, bright sun, green vegetation, pleasant sounds—all undimmed, untarnished, uncontaminated by smoke and fog and grime of her native city. It was wonderful, to Edith, to see the bright faces of the mountain people, coming and going on their daily trips to Uniontown; it was wonderful to see how light-hearted, how gay, how spirited were those of the leisure class who spent their nights at this health-giving resort, and their days in the towns below.

It was all wonderful, indeed. It was wonderful how fast she recovered her strength; how quickly the fires of health returned to her cheeks; how speedily her drooping spirits mounted to that pinnacle where the flagging soul ceases to repine. But was it all the bracing air, the burning sun, the happy birds, the blooming flowers, that effected her cure, as if by the magic touch of that enchantress, Isis? Mystery!

Among those who arrived that morning from the nether lands was Jasper Cobb. He came in due formality of traveling as was his wont. He had his valet, who had his hat boxes and suit cases and trunks. He had his cane, his pipe and his et cetera. He was surprised, of course, but delighted, naturally, to see Edith and Star sitting on the wide veranda, as he jauntily floated up to them after disposing of his valet and other personal things.

"Well, well! if this isn't a surprise to shock your grandmother and throw your granddaddy into hysterics!" he exclaimed, coming up to them, making a bow that almost threw them into the titters, over its profound ridiculousness. "Why, when did you come here?" he asked, as if he had not known beforehand.

"We have been here for two weeks," answered Edith, respectfully, although she abhorred him.

"You certainly look better, Miss Jarney; you, too, Miss Barton," he said, with a protracted smile of the wheedling variety. "This rarefied atmosphere, away from the Pittsburgh smoke, appears to agree with you two, charmingly."

"It does very well; very well," said Edith, disinclined to be friendly.

"I hope we may see each other often, Miss Jarney—and Miss Barton," he continued, insinuatingly. "If you two have not dined I should deem it a favor to have your company."

"Thank you; we have already dined," responded Edith.

"If you will excuse me, then, I will perform that necessary duty myself," he returned. After a sweeping bow and another wheedling smile that he might as well have kept to himself, he left them.

"I do hope we will not be bored to death by that young man," said Edith.

"What will we do, Edith?" asked Star. "If we remain here and he remains here, it will be rather awkward to get rid of him."

"Oh, we will show him what respect we can without losing our own self-respect," said Edith. "I wonder what brought him here?"

"Pursuing you, I suppose, Edith."

"He will have his trouble for naught, Star," replied Edith, with a toss of her head.

"I should think he would know enough to comprehend a few hints," said Star.

"Some people don't, you know, Star," said Edith, rising and drawing the mantle closer about her shoulders. "Let us go for a walk down the mountain road, so we will not be bothered with him, at least for awhile."

But Jasper was not to be so easily shook by such a furtive departure on the part of Edith and Star; for that young man, immediately after finishing his breakfast, and ascertaining from the keeper of the grounds the direction in which they had gone, lighted his pipe, gloved his hands, and, armed with his cane, went after them at a pace that would do well for a Weston in his hikes. He found them after a short walk down the hill aways, sitting in the shade of a spreading chestnut tree. The young ladies saw him coming, but they could not retreat, nor flee in any direction, so had to make the most of him, for a time. He, being a very brisk and bold young man, with a dandified swagger in his bearing and a distorted vainness about his personality, approached Edith and Star with such a rush of enthusiasm that they had cause to be exasperated at his manners.

"Hah, playing hide and seek with each other, are you?" he said, with an overbearing sweetness and an impertinent geniality.

"Not at all; just resting after our walk down the hill preparatory for the returning climb," answered Edith, with an effort to be a little disdainful; but if he noticed this in her, it was more than anybody else could see, for it was quite contrary to her nature to be disrespectful, except when brought to extremities, no matter how hard she tried, even toward the worst of fists. "Finding it getting warm," she continued, "we sat down here to rest before returning."

"Aren't you going any farther? Which way?" he asked.

“Up the hill,” she answered his implied questions.

“Then I may accompany you on the return?” he asked.

Edith glanced at Star, Star at Edith, for an answer; but neither answered for a moment. Then Edith, seeing the predicament they would be in of either saying yes, or offering a rebuke, said: “We came out for a quiet walk together, Mr. Cobb, and thought we would find rest down here, and be away from the people up there—” pointing toward the hotel; “but if you are going up the hill, we will see who can go the faster.”

“Banter me for a race, do you?” he said, ingratiatingly.

“Oh, not necessarily,” returned Edith, with a laugh.

“All right, then a walk it shall be,” he said airily, not a whit disposed toward being piqued at the young ladies’ desire to have done with him.

Edith and Star started off together at a lively step on the upgrade tramp, Jasper keeping by their side, with even step, in a palavering mood. His talk was simply airy nothings, commonplace enough in its most brilliant stages, and foolish enough for the most twadling and appreciative loiterer of swelldom. He had a sort of rude wit about him that might be very interesting and enjoyable to a crowd of sports, but to Edith and Star he was a driveling idiot.

The walk progressed at such a rate that very soon Edith, in her desire to keep in advance of him, began to lag, and her breath was coming too fast and furious for her benefit; but Star, who yet showed no signs of fatigue, had taken Edith by the arm to urge her along the best she could. Edith’s face was excessively red from the great exertion, and sweat stood out on her forehead like morning dew on the crimson clover bloom.

“Whew!” exclaimed Edith, at last, puffing and blowing, and heaving her breast in harmony with her rapid respiration, and saying between breaths, “that is—a little—too—much.”

“You are blowing like a porpoise,” said Jasper, as he stopped and was contemplating her from head to foot, using his cane for a rest, on which he leaned. “Shall I fetch an auto for you?”

“No; I can make it up the hill; but I must take it slower,” she answered, holding her hand over her heart.

“If you will permit me, I will assist you,” he said.

“Oh, never mind me, I will get there, eventually.”

“Come on, then,” he said, with coarseness, as he laid hold of her arm to urge her forward; and thus between the two they got her up the hill.

Simultaneously with their rounding the hill from the east, there rounded the same hill from the west a double team of farm horses hitched to a cumbersome wagon. On a flat board seat, across the bed in front, sat a young man about twenty years of age, and a lass of about sixteen blooming summers in her face. The horses moved at a slow and lazy pace, after having pulled a heavy load up the winding stretch of three mile grade, and stopped at the apex for a "blow" before relieving the pressure on their collars for the downward pull. At the stopping of the team, Edith and Star and Jasper came abreast in their walking, and also stopped for a "blow" before entering the hotel.

This meeting seemed to have been the result of prearrangement, so natural did the precise moment of stopping appear. The young man in the wagon was a pronounced blonde; but the many seasons that he had spent in the mountains had bronzed his cheeks to a coppery red, and made him a very healthy and rugged youth, withal. He had a regularity of features that could not be gainsayed for their Grecian similarity. His light blue eyes were sharp, steady, penetrating. With a slouch hat on his head, flapping down on both sides, and tending to pokeness at the crown; a check shirt opened in front and turned aside, revealing a deep manly breast, and turned up sleeves exposing muscular arms from the elbows to a set of rough but well shaped hands—he sat like a monument of Strength and Health and Robust Beauty, resting his horses, and indifferent to the astonished gaze of the city bred people standing by. The young lady by his side, in the flower of young maidenhood, was a counterpart of the young man; and they were, without a doubt, from the same family tree. Her pink-lined sun-bonnet of gingham, accentuated by the warming sun, caused her face to glow, as if on fire, and her red calico dress could not have added more demureness to her looks had it been made of the richest silk.

Thus, as they came by chance together, at such a time and at such a place, and under such pleasant circumstances, the three a-foot and the two a-riding cast contradictory glances at each other. Edith thought she saw in the young mountaineer an embossed replica of some one else; and also in the face of the young girl she was sure there was the heavenly-traced picture of another face. Star, with her head thrown back, in contemplative grandeur, looked at them with a stare of uncertain recognition. The young man in the wagon was about to speak, believing them to be friendly disposed vacationists, and would not mind a turn of conversation with him, being as he was of the out of the way places of their humdrum existence; but before he could do so, Edith suddenly plucked Star by the arm, and with her ran toward the hotel entrance, not stopping till she had gained the wide veranda, panting again, and all excited. Reaching the vantage of that viewpoint, and while standing behind a shielding porch column, she peeped from behind it, like one frightened. She beheld the mountaineer, with the little girl, disappear below the hill, and heard the screeching of the rubber blocks of his wagon, and saw the louting Jasper ambling, with a whistling note to keep him step, down the pikeway toward the hotel.

"Star, that was John's brother!" exclaimed Edith, after he had disappeared over the hill, "and that little girl was his sister."

Resuming her composure over the excitement the incident caused, she sat down in one of the lounging chairs, with Star by her looking serious enough herself.

"I believe so, Edith; but why didn't we stop long enough to talk with them?" said Star, apparently disappointed.

"Oh, I wanted to stop to speak—but that would not do, dear Star—would not do at all; but I will have a talk with them when he comes here next week, never mind," cried Edith, with much joyousness in the ring of her voice. "Isn't she such a pretty creature—just like one of those little fairy mountain girls you see sometimes in romantic plays in the theaters, and I know she is more romantic."

"What do you think of him, Edith—the man—her brother—if that is whom he is?" asked Star, blushing for the first time Edith ever saw that intelligible sign in her face.

"If he is not Mr. Winthrope's brother, he is his living stature in bronze," replied Edith; "and now, Star, tell me your opinion?"

"I can't say that I have an opinion, Edith; I am really dumb with amazement. He is such a big fellow—more like a mill-worker, or such—oh, my, Edith; don't ask me for—"

"Well, now, I like that way of speaking about Mr. Winthrope's brother. Maybe it was not him at all, and we have had our little scare for nothing. Oh, goodness! here comes Mr. Cobb again! dear me!" and Edith subsided.

Pursuing the tenor of his prevailing thoughts, Jasper Cobb sought Edith and found her on the eastern end of the veranda. After saluting the two young ladies again quite prodigiously, he asked Edith for a private interview at once. Star, hearing the request, rose and left them, as if she had an errand in her room, before Edith had time to ask her to remain. Star, however, was waiting for such an opportunity to absent herself, knowing what young Cobb's mission was. Having been informed by Edith what her answer would be, she went away satisfied that she would return to find that young man laboring under a severe jolt to his mercenary soul.

Now, when alone, Mr. Cobb drew up a seat and sat near Edith.

"Miss Jarney, we have always been friends—our families?"

"Yes."

"And we have been friends for years, you and I?"

"Yes."

"Would you consider a proposition from me to make that friendship permanent and lasting?"

"Yes."

His heart bounded—a little.

"Well, Miss Jarney—may I call you Edith?—I came here to ask you to marry me?"

"You?" she said, turning on him.

"Yes; me," he answered, dejectedly, for he caught the tone of her voice in no uncertain meaning.

"No," said Edith, firmly, looking at him, with a sort of a commiserated smile for his imbecility. "If you want to be my friend, Mr. Cobb, all right, you may consider me as such; but, as to marrying you, never can I make up my mind to that end."

"Dear Miss Jarney, you don't know the blow that you have struck me—it almost topples me over," he insisted, and Edith came near laughing in his face, so ludicrous was the expression that he had now assumed. "I have always thought you had encouraged me—"

"Oh, never was I guilty of such an offense, Mr. Cobb—never. You are laboring under a misconception, or a delusion, or something else. Encourage you, Mr. Cobb? How ridiculous!"

"Then, you refuse?" he asked, coldly and fiercely.

"I most certainly have my senses with me," she retorted, with a laugh.

"Ah, then, I'll go my old way. I thought I might settle down some day and be a man," he whispered.

"Be a man first, Mr. Cobb, and settle down afterwards, is my advice to you," she responded.

"You are cruel, Miss Jarney—cruel—as cruel as all the other women of the rich, who make monkeys of we men folk," he said, despairingly.

"You must understand, Mr. Cobb, that I am not one 'of all the other women' of the rich, of whom you speak so slightingly," she replied, still keeping a good temper.

"Well, I guess not, Miss Jarney," he said, with a sneer, looking away from her. "I see, Miss Jarney—I am not blind—that you have set your cap for that young man in your father's office."

"You are disrespectful, Mr. Cobb; leave me at once," she replied, with some scorn for the first time exhibiting itself in her bearing. She arose and left him sitting there alone, with his pipe as his only comforting companion. After recovering from this jolt, as Star predicted, he gathered up his belongings, together with his valet, and vanished.

Imagine such a union of hearts! There are plenty of them founded upon the rock of riches. Yes; imagine it! See this young man Cobb, and know his worth! His face was like that of a well bred bull terrier, with a pipe between its lips, and a red cap upon its head. He had a pair of dull-gray pants on his hind legs, and they were turned up, with a pair of yellow shoes sticking out below the turn-ups. Around the middle of his body was a yellow belt fastened by a silver buckle, and above the belt was a silken white shirt, with turn-down collar, and around the collar was a red necktie, in which stuck a scarabee pin. And he called himself a man worthy of Edith.

He had been to Harvard, she to Vassar. She had learned to write a grammatical sentence and spell in the good old Websterian way. She could sing and play on the piano; and converse on the economic questions of the day with the perspicacity of a Stowe. She read the poets down through the catalogue of famous men and women, and the novelists of the class of Dickens and Hawthorne. She knew of the painters, the musicians, the theologians, and could talk intelligently on them all.

Him? He had learned a lot of things. He could flip the Harvard stroke with the ease of a Cook. He could make a touchdown without breaking sixteen ribs of an adversary. He could twirl the pigskin like an artist of the green cloth. He could take the long jump, or the long hike, with the grace of a giraffe. He could dance like a terpsichorian dame. He could drink whiskey, champagne and beer, smoke cigaretts, play cards. He could talk with the profundity of an ass and write with the imbecility of an ox. Yes, indeed, he had all the refinements of a college education—the kind confined to the male gender. The only virtue he had was his prospective inheritance from his father—money.

And he wanted Edith to marry him! Pooh!

CHAPTER XXX
FOR JOHN IS COMING HOME

There is a little frame house sitting, in the shade of maples and oaks, by the roadside to the south aways from Chalk Hill. It is a leaning building, to some extent, in many ways, by reason of its age. A crooked little chimney heaves up on the exterior of one end, by reason of its insecure foundation. Shingles curl, up, as if in dotage, by reason of the sun. Weather boarding warp and twist and turn, grayed by the wash of years, by reason of their antiquity. Windows peep out, with little panes, and rattle in the wind, by reason of their frailty. Wasps and bees, in season, build their mud nests beneath curling shingle and behind twisting board; bats fly out, at eventide, from unseen holes in the gables; and swallows chatter and circle round the chimney top in the twilight of the summer days. An ancient porch, with oaken floor, hangs against the front wall, and the woodbine and morning glory creep and twine and bloom around its slanting columns. A gate swings out at the end of the path leading from the door to the highway. Flowers—the rose, the marigold, the bouncingbetty, the wild pink, the primrose, all as old-fashioned as the people who dwell here—border the pathway. A paled patch of ground stands to one side, as sacred as the Garden of Gethsemane. In the rear a gnarled and aged orchard has but recently shed its snowy burden of bloom, with lingering scents still in the air; and beyond and around, fence-enclosed fields are greening with growing crops, and still beyond are dark forests and open fields and noisy ravines.

Evening is coming on. The sun has gone down over the mountain top. Shadows have disappeared into the gray of fading light. Odors of night are ascending from the cooling earth. The robins are rendering the last stanza of their solemn doxology to the dying day. The whippoorwills send forth their melancholy praises to the approaching darkness through the wooded chancel of their shadowy choir loft. And frogs swell their throats in grave bass tones to the melody of country life at this time of departing day.

A gray-haired farmer, in rough garb, sits on the porch, smoking his pipe, and by his side sits his patient, loving wife. On the top step of the porch sits their young daughter, reading her fate, perhaps, in the evening stars, the while glancing up the road, and listening for the click of horses' feet on the stones. But no sound is heard before night comes on. The mother rises, goes in, and lights the oil lamp, and sets it by a window for the expected visitor to see. For John is coming home.

"They are late in getting here," says the mother, as she descends from the porch, and goes down the path to the gate. She looks up the road through the shadows; then returns, and sits down by her daughter on the steps.

The father relights his pipe, clanks down to the gate, in his heavy boots, looks up the road through its shadows; then returns. "They are late," he says, and resumes his seat.

"I wonder what is keeping them," says the daughter, with an expectant hush in her sweet voice, as she rises, and goes down to the gate. She looks up the road through its shadows; then returns, and sits down.

Listen!

John is coming home.

They hear the clank of horses' hoofs, the rattling wheels, the rhythm of a lively trot; then indistinct voices far in the distance.

John is coming home. The son who went away the year before—the brother—is coming home. The father's boots clank on the porch as he impatiently walks back and forth. The mother rises, and shades her eyes, and peers up the roadway through the shadows. The sister rises, with a dancing heart, and flutters down to the gate, like an angel in the darkness.

For John is coming home. Home! His only place of sweet rememberance.

It is an age, it seems, before the team draws up and John leaps out to catch his sister in his arms.

"Come into the light, Anne, that I may see your face, for I know you are growing so handsome," said John, putting his arm around his sister, and went laughing with her toward the house. Could he have seen those blushes, in the darkness, because of his brotherly praising of her!

"How is mother?" was his greeting to his mother, as he kissed her at the foot of the steps. And, with her clinging to him on one side and Anne on the other, he ascended the steps to the porch.

"Where is father?" asked John, not seeing him in the darkness, standing just ahead of them. "Oh, here he is!" John exclaimed, as he released himself from his mother and sister, and grasped his father's rough hand. "Come into the light and let me see you all," said John, after the formalities of greeting had been performed, to the satisfaction of all around.

The light brought forth a revelation for them all, as light does for everything. The family now saw in John a new being in outward appearance, but still the same loving son and brother. John now saw his father and mother a little older, it appeared, perhaps, from anxiety over his absence, or it may have been their strenuous toil was showing plainer on them. He also saw in his sister, a simple country maiden in the rusticity of young beauty.

"Anne, will you let me kiss you again?" asked John, as he stood in admiration over her by the lamp, holding her hand, after his mother and father had gone to complete the supper that had been almost ready for hours waiting for him.

Anne tip-toed up to her brother, at his request, and put up her sweet lips to his.

"And how has my little sister been all these months?" he asked, patting her on the cheek.

"Very well, John; I hope you have been a good boy," she answered.

"Sister wouldn't expect anything else of me, would she?" he asked, kissing her again.

"Oh, no, indeed, John," she replied, with wide eyes.

"And have you been good?" he asked.

"Very, John," she responded.

"No beaus yet, I hope?" he asked, in his teasing way he always had with her.

"Why, no, John!" and she blushed, not that she had a beau, but through maiden coyness. "You are the only one I've got, John."

Supper was then announced. James, who brought John from town, came in after putting away the horses. And they all sat down in happy reunion once more. For John was home.

"What was the cause of your delay, John?" asked Michael Winthrope, the father.

"Oh, by the way, father, I must tell you about it," answered John, laughing heartily, and looking slyly at James, who was now dressed in his best clothes, and presented as good an appearance as John himself. "I have two lady friends, who—"

"Why, John!" exclaimed the mother, looking over her glasses.

"Wait, mother; will you hear my story?" said John, turning a happy smile upon his mother. "As I was going to say, I have two lady friends stopping at the Summit House. One is the daughter of my employer; the other her cousin. They saw us, as we were coming by, and, of course, we saw them. Knowing them as I do, I could not come on without the formality of greeting them. I introduced James to them, mother; and what do you think?—"

"Now, John, you mustn't be too severe on me," said James, modestly, "for I don't pretend to your polish since you went away."

"Never mind, James; you are a capital fellow, after all—but, mother, James and sister here"—turning to Anne—"saw them the other day, and they are—they think he and sister cannot be beaten as—roving mountaineers—no, they didn't say that sister"—turning to his sister again—"They did say they would come out to see us, if you will drive in for them."

"Law, me, John; we have no place here to entertain such grand people. What do you mean?" asked the mother, holding up her spoon, and shaking it with a remonstrative motion as emphasis to her thoughts.

"Wait, mother; wait, and hear me out, before remonstrating any further," said John, cheerfully. "They wouldn't accept my invitation; but they want sister to drive our old rig in for them, and extend the invitation to spend the day with us. They thought it would be so romantic to go on a lark with little sister"—turning to her again with such a fond look that Anne beamed under his countenance. "Will you go, sister?" he asked.

"Shall I, mother?" asked Anne.

"If John says so. What do you say, James?" asked the mother.

"That is up to John," responded James.

"And father?" asked the mother.

"Whatever John says about it," replied the father.

"Now, everything is up to you, sister," said John. "Are you going?"

"Why, of course, brother," she answered. "When?"

"Tomorrow," replied John.

So it was settled. That night, as John lay down to sleep in his old bed, so pure and white, in a little room up stairs, he heard again, above the screeching insects, the booming frogs, the wailing owls, that old sweet song that carried him into the slumberous land of nowhere—"Good bye! Good bye!"—as on so many nights before.

In the night, when the house was still, a gray-haired man, in night clothes and carrying a lighted lamp, softly stole into John's room. John lay with his face upturned, his eyes closed, and his lips parted in a sleeping smile. The father stood over him a moment, bent down and touched his lips to his son's brow. "He is a good boy yet," he said to himself, and softly stole away.

Anne was singing, as she went about her work, when John awoke in the morning; and life was astir on every hand. The pigs were squealing in their sty; the calves were bawling in their pens; ducks were squawking in their pond; chickens were cackling in the barn yard, and the sun was shining everywhere. John dressed himself and descended the narrow stairway, with tousled head and open shirt front. The mother was milking the cows, James was in the field, and the father was in the barn. Anne was preparing breakfast.

"Now, I may see you in the sunlight, sister," said John, as he sauntered into the old-fashioned kitchen, and stood before her, with folded arms, and half yawning yet from sleep, as she was spreading the cloth upon the table. "I didn't know I had such a dear little sister," he said, as he put his arm about her and kissed her on the lips.

"You are such a fine brother, John, that I am almost in love with you," she returned, as she lovingly left an imprint of a kiss on his cheek; then leaving him to pursue her work.

"Whose love would I want more than yours, Anne?" he asked, in his laughing manner.

"Oh, I don't know, John; maybe you have a girl better than me to love you," she replied.

"I shall never place any one above my dear little sister," he said thoughtfully; "but—for no one can be your equal—except—one."

"Is it one of those, John, whom I am going after this morning?" asked Anne, rattling the skillet on the stove. "One of those whom brother James and I met on the road a short time ago?"

"One of those, Anne—the rich man's only child—but I am too poor for her," he answered, regretfully.

"Is she as good as you, brother—and me?" asked Anne, distributing the plates around the table. She was innocent yet of the ways of the world; but was feeling the first calling of young maidenhood.

"She is very good, Anne; very good; but no better than you," he returned, with the same uncertain cloud of perplexity that overcast him so often before, still pervading him like a wave of blinding light that comes to obscure the vision, at times, by reason of its intensity of purpose.

"She is very fine looking, John—both of them, John. Which one is it you mean?"

"The smaller of the two."

"Oh, the one with the bluest eyes, who took fright at us and ran."

"That is just like Edith, to run."

"I know I could love her, John."

"You are anticipating, sister."

"Why, who couldn't love you, John?" asked Anne, looking up at him, with some doubts as to what he meant.

"That is a sister's opinion, child," said John.

"A sister's opinion of her brother is better than any one else's. Maybe she does love you, John. Did you ever ask her?"

"Maybe she does," said John, going toward the door and looking out over the garden fence and into the fields, and dreamily into the distance; "but she is too rich to accept me, sister," he said, turning about. "How soon will breakfast be ready?"

"As soon as you wash your face," she answered.

John, heeding this hint, went to a basin on a bench in the yard, which forcibly recalled the old days. How refreshing it was to him to soap and souse his face into the cold water! And how inconveniently unpleasant it was, after such soaping and sousing, to rush with blinded eyes, and water trickling down the neck beneath the shirt collar, to the kitchen and fumble, like a blind man, for the towel. But it was home to John.

The rattling wheels and squeaking springs of the old rig could be heard far up the road after Anne, dressed in a clean white frock and wearing a pink sun-bonnet, had left the front gate on her mission, guiding the old farm horses on their sure and steady gait.

Oh, John, John! If there is anything worth while, it is Edith's love, the love that never dies. Blind man, as you are, and too considerate of high state, and too proud of your own, you are the only one to make her sweet soul happy. Bestir yourself, John, and come out of the fog of self-consciousness that has kept you in obscurity so long as to your final intentions. High state and low state are all the same to the Cupid that has engaged you so relentlessly. High caste and low caste do not count for him. Come and see the right, and see the light. She is only mortal, you are only mortal. Money is nothing to her; money is nothing to you. Love is all to her; love is all to you. It is the man and woman, after all, that makes happiness supreme. Come!

John has donned the garb of a mountaineer, which gives him a wild romantic bearing. It is the garb of his former self. This is the one in which Edith, secretly, wished to see him in, sometimes; and she shall have her wish fulfilled. He wears a gray slouch hat; a check shirt, opened in the front and turned up at the sleeves; a pair of blue overalls, with bed-ticken suspenders, and high boots. Typical! He is in his elements now, for his vacation period. He wishes Edith, when she comes, to see him as he once was. It is not vanity; it is pride of home. He wishes her to see life as it really is in a well directed loving home, where toil is the simple reward of living. He wishes her to see what life is to these people of the hills, how they thrive, and how they bear their burdens. He wishes her to see all this in contrast to her own life, and how love and duty can go on perpetually in a humble home, as well as in a mansion.

Work must not cease on the farm, at this season, except in case of sickness or death; visitors must make themselves at home during the work hours, and be entertained only at meal time, or go their way. The wheels of industry must go on there as noisily, ever grinding, as the wheels of industry, ever grinding, in the city. But there are rare occasions, even in both instances, when surcease is had for a spell to meet the call of recreation. And this was one of those rare occasions on the farm. For Edith and Star were coming, and a half holiday was cut out for their especial pleasure. James would cease his ploughing the corn at noon. The father would knock off duty at eleven to help mother get up the feast, and then smoke his pipe thereafter, perhaps, as his company. Thus it was planned.

After Anne had gone, John roamed about the place, speculating on the tender association everything had for him. He went through the house from garret to cellar, and beheld, with warming heart, how dear the old things were, and how different they were to the things in the mansion on the hill. Here was everything still that he knew in his boyhood days, and he saw with a thrill of regret, but not remorse, for it was still his home any time he wished to abide therein. And no one could gainsay him that privilege.

But how would Edith look upon all this, and not be struck by the simple evidence of his lowly origin? Ah, the comparison is too great, he thought, as he went into the garden, where he first learned the secrets of plant life; and then into the orchard, where he first saw the wonderfulness of the fruiting time; and then into the old barn, where was taught him the nature of domesticated animals; and then into the fields, where he had ploughed and sowed and reaped. How different from his life for the past year! How different!

Edith could see nothing of interest in such bucolic surroundings, he thought. She would come, and see, and go, and want to forget him. It is well, he thought, that she sees it now, and of her own coming.

CHAPTER XXXI
IN CONCLUSION

The rattling wheels and squeaking springs could be heard far up the road. Anne was returning with her precious load. The horses trotted down the hill, and came up with a rattle and a bang, and a sudden stop, at the gate, with Edith at the lines, and Anne by her side, and Star in the rear seat alone holding on tightly lest she should be bumped out.

"Wasn't that great!" exclaimed Edith. "I told you I could drive. This is your home?" to Anne.

"This is our home," replied Anne, as she began to climb over the wheel in getting out.

"Isn't it a beautiful place, Star!" said Edith. "Just look at the roses blooming! and all those flowers around the porch! Anne you have such a romantic little home! Well, if here isn't our mountaineer, for a surety!" she exclaimed seeing John coming down the walk. "How do you do, Mr. Winthrope? I see you at last in your true character! How will I ever get over this wheel?"

"If you will be real good, I will help you out—with your permission," said John, as he approached, and offered up both hands for her to fall into, as she liked. "Sister, I will put away the horses," he said to Anne, as he saw she was holding the head of one of the horses to await the unloading. "Remember, this is not an auto," he reminded Edith, as she was cautiously putting out one little foot on the rim of the wheel before her.

"I would not have had so much fun if it had been an auto," returned Edith, looking down into his upturned face, and laughing; "and you have such a fine sister," as she turned her head toward Anne.

"Now, jump," said John, as he caught her beneath the arms, she resting her hands on his shoulders in the momentary act before the plunge. "Down you come—there!—not so difficult after all," he said, as she bounced on her feet on the ground. "Now, Miss Barton, we will see with what grace you can perform the feat."

"You will have to be careful; I am so awkward," said Star, preparing to go through the same acrobatic act.

"Jump, Star!" said Edith, seeing her hesitate.

"Here I go, then!" she said, laughing, as she took the downward dive.

"Oh, my! Miss Barton!" exclaimed John, as she tumbled into his arms, as a big rag doll might. "Are you hurt?" he asked, as he released her from the necessary embracing he had to perform to prevent her from falling to the ground.

"Not hurt, but a little frightened," she answered, flushed from the incident, and brushing out her skirts. "I am all right."

"Now, you ladies go into the house with my sister while I put the horses away. Here, Anne, you take the ladies, and I will take the horses," he said, leaving his guests, and taking up Anne's position in charge of the team.

"May I call you Anne?" asked Edith, as Anne came up to her.

"Yes, Miss Jarney, if you wish; we all use our first names up here," responded Anne, opening the gate.

"You may call me Edith, if you like, and this other lady will be our guiding Star," said Edith, walking with her arm around Anne's shoulders up the walk, her face aflush, her eyes beaming, and seeing everything about, talking continually.

Star was not as talkative; but she was just as seeing as Edith was. She, too, saw something in that home, more than its simplicity, to attract her admiration. Was it the fragrant flowers and hopping birds and cool freshness that she saw? or was it the peace of contentment, indefinably overloading everything? or was it the radical difference in the two homes, ideal though in both, and irresistable in their contradictory elements, that caused her spirits to rise above the normal point of enthusiasm? Or was it something else? Star did not know.

Arriving at the door, arm in arm now, Anne passed straight through the opening, holding on to Edith, and Star followed with considerable wonderment at what she might encounter.

"Take off your hats, ladies," said Anne, withdrawing her arm from Edith's and standing off, with folded hands, looking at her, with gladness all over her face.

"No, you must say Edith and Star," said Edith, seeing how humbly courteous Anne tried to be.

"If you will have it that way; Edith and Star, take off your hats and gloves. Now, I've said it, and I didn't mean to be so rude," said Anne, abashed.

"Anne, I will not love you if you do not call me Edith," said Edith, scolding pleasantly, pulling off her gloves. "I do not like too much formality.

I have had so much of that that it does my heart good to get out where I can be free; and you will let me be free here, Anne, won't you?"

"Oh, yes, Edith," answered Anne; "and Star, too; you may be as free as you please, Edith, for we are such common folk, so long as you don't carry off my brother, John." She said this without the least knowledge of its true meaning; not mentioning her brother James, because she did not think of such things in his connection.

Edith blushed a deep crimson, as well as Star, at this extraordinary remark on this the most extraordinary day that ever came into their virtuous lives. Anne had a faint inkling of what these blushes meant, for she continued: "Now, Miss Edith, since you want to be free with me, I will be just as free with you, and tell you that my brother l—l—likes you."

Edith was not prepared for all this, and she had to turn her head in the most confused state of feelings she ever fell into, all for wanting to be tender and kind and loving toward this mountain girl, who was not yet clearly or fully instructed in the propriety of fine speech. Edith made no reply. She stood a moment, after facing Anne, cogitating on what an appropriate reply should be.

"Anne," she said directly, with a bright smile, "will you let me kiss you?"

Edith held out her hands for Anne to come to her. Anne responded to the ineffable sweetness of Edith to make amends for her offense, which she realized she had committed against the fine lady opening her heart to her.

"I love you, Anne," said Edith, holding the dear little girl to her breast; "I love you; will you be my friend?"

"Why, of course, Edith," replied Anne; then she broke away, and was gone, leaving Edith and Star alone.

They removed their hats and placed them on a table in a corner; and then sat down on a lounge that graced the wall under a window looking out on the porch, both in bewildered confusion and agitation.

"What do you think of his sister, Star?" asked Edith.

"She is a fine young child; no more than sixteen, perhaps," responded Star, "and so lively that I wish I could be here with her all the time."

"I wonder if they will let us take her with us to the city, Star, to be our companion?" said Edith. "We would educate her, and teach her music and everything."

The kitchen door opened, and Anne came in with her mother, who wore a gingham apron as the badge of her position in the household. Anne advanced with her mother and presented her, with much dignity, as she conceived it, to Edith and Star.

"This is my mother, Edith and Star," said Anne, as the two young ladies arose and advanced to the middle of the room.

Edith presented her small white hand and took the coarse hand of Mrs. Winthrope. "I am so glad to know you, Mrs. Winthrope," said Edith, as she kissed the aging woman, whose age was more from toil than years. Star having performed the same act of greeting, including the osculatory part thereof, Mrs. Winthrope held up her hands in an astonished attitude, and said: "Well, well; I declare; and you two are John's friends, are you? I hope you are well."

"We are well; thank you," they both repeated.

"Just make yourselves at home, ladies, with what we have here to entertain you, while I finish the dinner. Be seated by the window where it is cool, for I know you must be warm after the long drive in the sun."

"Thank you, Mrs. Winthrope," they answered; and were seated.

Then the mother and daughter disappeared again; and Anne returned, after a little, with her father, who was in the clothes of a ploughman. Mr. Winthrope was a tall man, a little stooped, with chin whiskers, and gray blue eyes; and, while rough looking, was not boorish. Anne escorted him to the young ladies, who arose at his approach. He greeted them so warmly and effusively that, for some time thereafter, they felt the grip of his vise-like hand on theirs.

"Just make yourselves at home, as you like," he said. "We are farmers, you know, and if you find any pleasure here it is yours. We will be through our work by noon, then mother and me will find time to talk, if you care to be bothered with us at all." Then he left them.

"Are they not very good people," said Edith to Star, after the father had gone out with Anne.

"I like them very much," opined Star; "they are so pleasant."

John came in shortly, and sat down on a split-bottom chair in the middle of the room.

"I hope you ladies are enjoying yourselves," he said, toying with his hat he held in his hands.

"I could not enjoy myself any more if it were my own home," answered Edith. "Why, you have such a delightful home, Mr. Winthrope, and such nice parents, and such a sweet little sister, with whom I have already fallen in love. I am regretting that I have not known them longer."

"That's a beautiful encomium, Miss Jarney, on my native heath; but you know that you and your father and mother have been saying so many nice things about me that I am uncertain whether you mean it or not." John said this while glancing at the floor, picturing intangible things in the woof and warp of the old rag carpet.

"I mean every word of it. Mr. Winthrope," replied Edith, also picturing similar intangible things in the old rag carpet as easily as if she had pictured them out of the delicate flowers in the velvet rug in her boudoir.

Star sat gazing out the window, looking at some intangible shapes that made up the green hills beyond. Their conversation thereafter was not of the progressive kind, nor was it brilliant. Both became secretively reserved, and time was hanging monstrously on their hands. John was dreaming. Edith was dreaming. Both were uncertain as to what to say or how to act, so discomposed were they. But James came in soon to break the spell. He was such a strapping fine fellow, fine in texture, and as good as he was fine.

"I knew very well who you were the day we met you on the road," said Edith, shaking his hand.

"Had I known all this then. I should have bundled you into my wagon and brought you right home," he replied, with considerable liveliness in his speech. "But not knowing you, of course, I could do nothing else but drive on. However, the pleasure of meeting you now, here, is certainly beyond my mean ability to express."

"We might have come," said Edith, with a ringing laugh. "Would it not have been odd, and so romantic, just to have come right along with you?"

"I am sure I would have enjoyed it," he said; "and by this time I would have had you converted into farm hands."

"And wearing calico dresses," said Edith.

"And brogan shoes," said Star, remembering how she used to wear such articles of clothing.

"Yes; it is certain one can't work here and wear silks," responded James. Then looking down at himself, he was reminded that he was still in his rough garb. "If you ladies will excuse me, I will make myself more presentable for appearance at dinner."

He then left them; and when he returned, wearing his best Sunday suit, all brushed and fitting him very well, he was equally as stylish looking as his brother John in his best.

When dinner was announced (dinner is at the noon hour with the mountain people), John lead Edith and James lead Star to the bounteously laden dining table set in the kitchen. It might have been noticed by Edith, had she not been otherwise engaged, that Star was more aflush than ever before, just at this period of her proud behavior. James talked to her very entertainingly during the progress of the long meal, and she was very cordial toward him. She laughed and talked with great glee, being amused at his ready wit and simple manner. But John and Edith were distressingly quiet, for some reason, listening mostly to the conversation of the others. Little Anne, at times, cast side glances at Edith and John, that might have been suggestive of their meaning.

"Would you ladies like to try your hand at fishing?" asked James, who was warming up for any kind of sport that might be introduced for the entertainment of their guests.

"Oh, delighted!" cried Edith. "I never fished in my life."

"Nor I," said Star; "will you teach me how, Mr. Winthrope?" (meaning James.)

"I thought we old people were to entertain you this afternoon," said the father.

"We will return in time for that, father," James said, rising. "John, I'll get the bait; you get the tackle, and we will teach these young ladies how to fish."

"Be careful," admonished the mother; "don't fall into the stream."

"Anne, are you not going?" asked Edith, as she rose with the others.

"I must remain here and help mother; and will await your return," said Anne, as she came around to Edith and put her arm around her.

"You are a dutiful child, Anne," said Edith, kissing Anne thereat.

Edith and Star were both dressed in gray serge skirts, white silk waists and sailor hats. While John and James got ready the ladies prepared themselves for the event of their lives. They were in waiting on the porch when John and James came up, with plenty of bait and tackle in their hands. So off they went immediately: John and Edith together, and James and Star, the father and mother and Anne standing on the porch watching their going.

They struck the mountain stream a mile below the house, and the two ladies fell to the sport with the spirited joy of youth. The pair became separated after awhile, as all such sportsmen and women often do. One pair went up the stream, and one went down, after the elusive fish.

John and Edith came to a pool, after wandering through the bypaths of the forest, far below the other two. Around the pool the trees hung low, and the shades were heavy, and the water was dark and deep. By the pool they sat down on a log, and cast their lines to await the fisherman's luck.

"Isn't this delightful," said Edith, holding her pole with inexperienced hands over the water.

"Fish won't bite, if we talk too loud," said John, critically, but pleasantly, as he sat below her on the log, slanting into the stream.

She became quiet; he became quiet. The water trickled over the miniature falls at the head of the pool in such an isolated tone of ripling that it made wild sweet music for Edith. The trees above them sighed in a low crescendo, and the birds were singing everywhere. The sun rays glinted through the boughs of the trees, and danced upon the water, making a fretted work of moving lights and shadows. Water riders ran back and forth, as if playing with the sunlight let into their darksome place of habitation, and fish jumped up now and then, as if to taunt the patient anglers. And Edith and John sat quietly—waiting, waiting.

Then a fish came along, and caught the bait of Edith's hook; and went tearing away in its struggle for liberty. So sudden was the unlooked for happening that Edith lost her balance, by reason of the gyrations of the fish, which she pluckily attempted to land, and plunged into the water. It came so sudden that John, who was at that moment meditating on the catch he would make, and on how he would boast over the rest of them when he got home, did not notice Edith's danger till it was too late. Without a moment's reflection, however, he dropped his pole and leaped into the pool after her. Edith came up with a scared look, beating the water with her hands, as he went down by her side. He seized her around the waist, and swam for the shore, and when they reached the shore, she laughed, being reminded of another watery occasion; but still permitting him to hold her in his arms.

"I am a pretty sight now," she said, still remaining in his arms on the sloping bank, up which he was assisting her.

"It seems we have an affinity for water, Edith," he said, reaching the top of the slope, still holding her in his arms. "May I call you Edith, now?" he said, clasping her wet form to his.

She laid her dripping head upon his breast, one arm stole around his neck, and she looked up into his face. "Yes," she answered. And he kissed her for the first time on those sweet lips that had so often uttered his name before; but now they said, "John." And still he held her in his arms.

"Edith, will you be my wife, some day?" he asked, looking with the fervor of an impassioned youth into her dear blue eyes, and pushing back the wet hair from her white temples.

"Why, yes; dear John, I love you, as I always have since the first time I met you," she answered, with such an appealing tone for that old responsive note in him that he pressed her closer to his bosom. And the longing in her soul was recompensed in that moment of her eternal bliss.

"You know me, Edith; you know my people now; you know what I am. Are you satisfied?" he asked, still harboring that same old uncertain doubt that always perplexed him so; and still holding her in his arms.

"I know you to be a noble young man, dear John. I know your people now, and I love them. I am satisfied," she whispered. "You are all that I care for, John—all. I love you, I love you," and she kissed him.

"I am satisfied, dear Edith. It was not an hallucination, after all, was it dear?" he answered.

Thus, plighting their troth, they went hand in hand up the shady wood path as happy as two young children over their mishap.

Life is beautiful, and life is sweet; but what would life be to those young people without the love between them?

Coming to the path where they left James and Star, on parting, they found them sitting there, waiting. When Star saw them coming, she instinctively comprehended, and knew that the crisis was over between Edith and John. Star was happy herself over a secret of her own. And together they returned home.

John proudly, on arriving in the old-fashioned sitting room, announced to his parents and sister his intended bride, and told them they could take her now, in her bedraggled condition, for their daughter and sister.

"Now, will you go with me, Anne, to the city?" asked Edith, after she had been costumed in some of Anne's clothing that fit her narrowly. "I will educate you, and have you for my own dear sister," hugging Anne to her breast.

"Some day, Edith; some day," answered Anne, uncertain in her mind. "When will you come after me?"

"When I am your real sister, Anne," replied Edith, stroking Anne's golden hair, and then she looked up at Anne's mother, who could not fully realize what it meant for her future life. "You will let her go, Mrs. Winthrope?"

"I may some day," answered the good old mother.

"I wouldn't want to leave papa and mamma yet, Edith," said Anne, with a happy smile.

"You shall return to see them often; so shall I," said Edith.

"I will go some time, Edith, after you are my sister," answered the coy Anne.

"That will be soon, dear sister," said Edith, folding Anne in her arms and crying with excessive happiness. "You may have two sisters soon, Anne—Star, I am sure, will be your other sister." Star blushed, and therefore told her tale.

The family stood on the porch that evening, and listened to the receding sound of the rattling wheels and squeaking springs of the rig, as John drove away with his precious load. "God bless them," said the good old father; and Anne cried when the last hoof beat came down the shadowy roadway. In silence they sat in darkness till they heard the clanking hoofs returning. The mother went in and lighted the lamp; the father went in, the sister went in, the two brothers went in; and they all knelt down in family worship.

As the curtain of the passing night drew thickly over the mountains, and the lights in the corridor of the Summit House became dim, and their room dark, Edith knelt down by her bed and offered up her prayers to the Good Lord, who had brought her safely through her troubles; and Star, kneeling by her side, said, "Amen."

A few days thereafter, after Edith had written her parents of the happy culmination of her fishing trip, the following message was received by her from them: "Congratulations."

So endeth the story of Edith and John.